Persephone,
Queen of the Dead

Isadora Marie

© 2011 Isadora Marie
All Rights Reserved.

No part of this publication may be reproduced, stored in a retrieval system, or transmitted, in any form or by any means, electronic, mechanical, photocopying, recording, or otherwise, without the written permission of the author.

First published by Dog Ear Publishing
4010 W. 86th Street, Ste H
Indianapolis, IN 46268
www.dogearpublishing.net

dog ear
PUBLISHING

ISBN: 978-145750-725-0

This book is printed on acid-free paper.

This book is a work of Fiction. Places, events, and situations in this book are purely Fictional and any resemblance to actual persons, living or dead, is coincidental.

Printed in the United States of America

To my mother, Barbara, who is with Persephone now.

Also to Hank, Smudge & Edgar.

Special thanks to Mara Cosillo-Starr for her help in editing this manuscript.

I
Persephone

    MY BIRTH NAME is Kore, but modern readers may only know me by the name Persephone; the name my husband gave to me on our wedding day many long centuries ago. You see I am the consort of Hades, the God of the Underworld, known by some as the Queen of the Dead. Throughout the centuries since I took my place within the Underworld, at my husband's side, I have heard many tales of how my uncle, the God Hades, kidnapped me while I was picking flowers with the daughter of Oceanos, the Sea Nymphs, one bright, sunny day; how as I screamed and struggled with all my might, he seized me and dragged me to the world below. These stories relate that once I was concealed within the depths of the Earth, he raped me and forced me to eat the food of the dead, ensuring that I would never be allowed to return to the world of the living. These myths continue with my mother Demeter, the Goddess of Agriculture and Fertility, in a fury destroying lands, crops and livestock; and how the barren lands would not yield any crops for almost an entire year, causing two-thirds of all mortal life on Earth to slowly die, swearing that she would not restore her blessings on the land until I was safely back in her arms. It was my grandmother, Rhea, who was called by the great God Zeus to settle the matter, and it was she who proposed the compromise, hoping to satisfy both of her children, Demeter and Hades. I had no say in this matter, even though it was my Fate that was to be decided.

The compromise was that neither my mother, nor my husband could live with me for the entire year, but each would share me for only a short part of it. After much arguing, mother finally agreed that I would be allowed to live one half the year with her traveling between the earth and Mount Olympus, during which time she would graciously allow crops and livestock to flourish; then for the rest of the year when according to her I am confined to my earth and rock prison within the Underworld, the lands will once again become barren, making this the dark half of the year. Mortals have explained this as a myth only, a story that primitive humans passed down throughout the generations as a way to explain the progression of the seasons. The myths are correct, for before I married Hades and became Queen of the Dead, there was no change of the seasons, all of the earth enjoyed temperate weather and abundant crops year round; winter engulfed the lands only after I took my place at my husband's side.

What follows is the story of my transformation from Kore, the meek daughter of the Earth Goddess Demeter, into Persephone, the Queen of the Underworld. I must stress here that I wasn't an innocent victim of Hades lust; being dragged into the Underworld screaming and fighting as the old myths tell. My greatest transformation hasn't been adapting to being married to Hades, Lord of the Underworld, and spending half of my life deep within the Earth, it was leaving the life of living in my mother's shadow and becoming a Goddess in my own rite, a Goddess who is not only worshiped, but one who instills fear as well. What follows is very different from the patriarchal writings that have been passed down throughout the centuries; it is the story of my life, as only I can tell it.

I was still a young girl, a virgin, when I first glimpse my uncle Hades and instantly I knew I would love only him. It was many, many centuries ago, but I remember it as if it were only yesterday. Early one morning I was alone in the garden on Mount Olympus admiring the Sun as it's first rays gracefully touched the flowers that surrounded father's palace. Alone I sat on the damp grass, my knees pulled into my chest, my head resting there letting thoughts of nothing fill my mind. A gentle breeze blew through my hair as I sat there just enjoying all of Nature. I don't know how long I was sitting there alone before I suddenly was startled back into reality when father, the God Zeus, came into the garden and upon seeing me alone he spoke.

"Kore, your dear mother doesn't have any flowers on her bedside table…" he paused here, making sure that he had my full attention. "I'm sure she would be pleased to awake to the sight of fresh flowers".

I stood up and gave him a slight bow, showing him the respect that he deserved.

He continued,

"I've seen some beautiful flowers growing down on earth, why don't you go pick her some".

I left Mount Olympus as soon as Zeus excused me; I loved going down to earth, and wouldn't pass up the opportunity to spend some time there. Mother, not wanting me to be alone, would make sure that I was always accompanied by many nymphs whenever I traveled to Earth, but this morning was different, there was no one to go with me, and so I came to the city of Attica alone. I saw the meadow covered with the most beautiful, fragrant flowers and I knew that father was right; mother would love to rise to the sight and smell of these flowers. I ran through the field taking in the scent of the flowers and the feel of the damp morning grass on my bare feet before I started filling my basket. It wasn't long before I had already filled the basket half way when I noticed a strange flower, one I had never seen before. The center of the large bloom was dark purple, almost black, which delicately faded to a pale violet as it slowly opened it's lovely face to soak in the morning sun. Within the center of this strange bloom was a light dusting of a silvery substance that glistened as the sun illuminated the dew that had collected there during the night; golden tendrils burst from the center, reaching up to the heavens, while the strong, slightly musty scent filled my senses. I knew that I had to take this flower; mother would be pleased with it, for I had never seen its equal.

As I knelt on the soft, moist grass I stretched my hand out touch one of these flowers and as my fingers caressed the tender bloom I heard a soft thundering that seemed to come from deep within the earth itself. Surprised, I snapped my hand back to my side. I was used to hearing thunder from the skies, since Zeus, the God of the Heavens, is my father. Whenever he would get mad, which was often, thunderbolts would fly causing all of Mount Olympus to shake. I was also used to hearing eruptions coming from the seas, you see my Uncle is Poseidon, the God of the Seas, and he also possessed a quick temper, causing many earthquakes and storms on Earth whenever he was mad. But I wasn't accustomed to hearing sounds coming from so deep within the earth, for my other uncle, Hades, the God of the Underworld, is the only God that dwells within the earth itself, and he seldom made any sound at all.

It was common knowledge that he would rarely leave the Underworld, only coming to Mount Olympus if there was a dire need. Only once, when I was very young, do I remember seeing him. Mother wouldn't allow me to go into the Great Hall and see what all the commotion was about, and after he left she told me he was still sulking about drawing the Underworld as his domain when the three sons of Rhea drew lots to determine who would rule the Sky, Seas, and Underworld. Everyone knew that Zeus was the favorite of my grandmother Rhea, but it was the Goddess Ananke, the personification of the constraining forces of destiny, and not my grandmother who determined Zeus would rule the Heavens, Poseidon the Seas, leaving Hades, the eldest of the three sons, to rule the Underworld. You see mortals are not the only ones who have to answer to the Fates. While humans answer to Clotho, the Goddess who spins the thread of life, allowing their birth; her sister, Lachesis, who chooses their destiny in life; and the Goddess Atropos, who cuts the thread of life and unleashes the God of Death to consume their souls, the Gods answer only to their mother, Ananke. She alone can make or destroy a God or Goddess.

The rumbling grew louder and louder as I felt the earth under my feet began to quiver and shake. All the birds feeding in the grass instantly took flight and I too wanted to fly, but I couldn't move; it was as if my feet had taken root deep within the soil. I watched wide-eyed as the earth beneath my feet started to crack and break causing a small fissure. A strong odor of sulfur seemed to fill my senses and released me from my trance. Finally able to move, and without a moments hesitation, I ran and hid behind a large tree, and thus concealed, I watched as a chasm formed near the place I was standing just a few seconds earlier, and from the midst of the earth two jet black stallions emerged side-by-side, breathing heavy as if it took tremendous energy for them to break free of the ground. I could smell the sweet scent of sweat mingled with the smell of the earth, as the wind blew through their manes.

These stallions, like the beautiful horse Pegasus were winged, but instead of having his soft feathery wings, theirs was only a thin membrane of translucent flesh stretched taught over their bones, such as the wings of bats. Soon two more pairs of these winged stallions, equally as magnificent with glossy black coats appeared from the cavern and I could see they had bright red glowing eyes and fiery breath. Instantly I knew they must be the stallions of my uncle Hades, God of the Underworld, for only he would have stallions such as these. I wanted to run deeper into the forest to get away from these creatures before I was seen, but I was paralyzed with both fear and fascination. Without making a sound, I stood concealed by the tree while I watched as a brilliant ebony chariot swiftly emerged behind the stallions. Riding majestically on this gilded chariot, which was entirely covered with precious jewels; rubies, emeralds, sapphires, and diamonds that twinkled as the bright sun shone down them, was a God I didn't recognize. This must be Hades I thought, for no other God would emerge from the depths of the world below.

At the sight of him my breath stopped, for he wasn't the horrid God I imagined him to be. At first I thought the strange feelings I was experiencing were caused by fear, but no, this wasn't fear. This was a feeling I had never known before. My entire body tingled as my breathing became heavy, and I'm certain that my heart skipped a beat. A quivering shot up my spine filling every cell of my body with a sensation of both pleasure and anticipation. I knew then that Eros, the God of Love, must have been near, for I'm sure that I felt the shaft of his arrow penetrate through my chest and plunge deep into my heart, where its burning flame soon began to melt my soul.

I stood transfixed as I watched the gilded chariot fly by and the cavern from which it emerged slowly began to fill with earth. Within seconds the field looked as if nothing had happened. The chariot stopped for only a brief moment and I was able to get a closer look at the God who had stole my heart. Clad in an elaborately embroidered white himation made from the finest silks, he paused and turned his head to my direction, as if he had noticed something. The robes, which were draped over both the Gods and mortal men at that time in history, with the folds gently gathered at his hips and the excess fabric draped over one shoulder left little to the imagination. Hades' robes fell from his shoulder as he held tightly to the horses' reins leaving most of his upper body exposed showing his white skin and flexing muscles. Sweating, due to the great force he held over the horses, his body glistened with the moister. This vision took my breath away. As you may know from the statues of Greek Gods, their bodies were extremely beautiful, but these statues, made by human hands couldn't compare to the sight of Hades riding his chariot, cracking his whips over the horses heads, urging them to move swiftly on. Even though many centuries have passed, I still remember the sight as Hades turned his face towards me. I held my breath, not wanting him to see me hiding. His dark shoulder length hair, damp with moisture fell in soft curls framing his face. This dark hair, and along with his trimmed beard contrasted sharply with his alabaster skin, I couldn't help but notice the strong facial features he possessed; a square jaw and long slender nose, which drew my gaze up to his eyes. I will never forget his eyes, for when I saw them it was as if I was looking into his heart. His eyes were the brightest green, the green of emeralds; so bright that I was able to determine the color from such a great distance. I stood in awe of the sight of him, wanting him to come to me and take me in his arms. Wanting him to take me away from this place, it didn't matter where he took me, only that I would be with him, with him forever.

After a few moments of scanning the field, satisfied that he was alone, he turned and I watched breathlessly as his chariot thundered into the distance. Once I was sure he was out of sight, I cautiously left the safety of the grove where I was concealed by the trees and tall grass and walked to where he had just emerged from deep within the earth, looking for a way to enter his world, hoping that I would be allowed to wait until his return. I walked around the area looking for a sign that I had not only imagined him; that his chariot really had broken through from the world below right here in this very spot, but there was none. The field looked exactly as it was when I reached for the beautiful flower, only that the flower that called to me was no longer in sight. I knew what I had seen, and without hesitating I rushed back to Mount Olympus, thinking that would be the only logical place Hades could have gone.

When I reached the eastern slop of the mount, I saw the palace glimmering in the distance. I ran up the sloped terraces covered with lush gardens filled with every type of fruit tree know to man, and some that are exclusive to the Gods alone, it is from these sacred trees the sweet nectar Ambrosia, the food of the Gods, is made. Here the grass is permanently green and the leaves never fall from the trees. Birds fill the garden with beautiful sounds as the streams whose sources start near the palace as nothing more than a trickle, flow down the sloping channels bringing life to all the flowers; marigolds, violets, poppies, hyacinths, roses, and lilies that grow there.

Within this garden paradise many mythical beasts dwell. The Centaurs, creatures having heads and torsos of men and from the waist down the bodies of horses, the wisest of them being Chiron, mentored many of the Greek heroes; Griffins, animals who had the body of a lion with wings and foreparts of eagles; the Hippalectryon, a strange creature even to the Gods, they possessed the front of a rooster on the body of a horse, complete with large colorful wings. Pegasus, our most famous winged horse, also lived here; a beautiful red-golden bird about the size and shape of an eagle, whose feathers shinned like the sun, called a Phoenix; and the five immortal golden-horned deer who are sacred to the Goddess Artemis. There are many other creatures that lived safely within these gardens, but throughout the centuries most of them have either been destroyed, or chased far away, but that is another story altogether.

I held my robes up so I wouldn't trip as I ran through the garden, feeling the coolness of the damp earth on my bare feet. I ran past the cottages where the lesser Gods, Goddesses and nymphs dwelled, past the servant quarters and finally past the stables where the beasts that were used by the Gods to pull their chariots were housed. Aphrodite, the Goddess of Love, only used the purest white doves to pull her gilded chariot; Peacocks, her sacred animals were the mounts for Zeus' wife Hera; Apollo favored Swans; and two serpentine dragons drew my mother, Demeter's chariot. All these creatures lived peacefully together, along with the other beasts that the Gods keep as pets. Since I was not yet a Goddess, it was my duty to tend the stables, so I was well acquainted with all these mysterious creatures.

Finally, I reached the marble stairs that lead into the palace. Mortals can't imagine the splendor of the abode of the Olympian Gods. I've often heard mortals describe this palace as being made entirely of crystal. It's charming to imagine a crystal castle, but this is not so. The palace was made of the finest marble, built entirely by hand by the Cyclopes, the gigantic one-eyed Titans who were freed by Zeus during the war between the Titans and the Olympians. In gratitude for their freedom, they bestowed this palace for Zeus on the exact site where the Titans' palace once stood. The largest city on Earth would easily fit within the Great Hall itself, and here all the Olympian Gods and Goddesses and their families lived; all except Hades and Poseidon. Poseidon has his own palace almost as magnificent, deep within the ocean's depths, and Hades, as I stated earlier, lived within the Underworld. I knew little of his palace for Hermes and Zeus were the only Gods to ever have entered this world, and neither of them ever spoke of it.

Out of breath, I swiftly climbed the stairs and passed through the front gate, which was nothing more then clouds watched over by a beautiful Goddess, named Season. When she saw me approaching, she gestured with her left hand in a motion like opening curtains, and instantly the clouds began to part. Hurrying past her without saying a word I was soon within the Great Hall. I was expecting to see all the Gods and Goddess assembled there, for only a very special event would bring Hades to Mount Olympus, but to my surprise I was totally alone. The only sound I heard was my breathing, as I stood there panting, trying to catch my breath.

Mortals can't even begin to imagine the magnificence of the Great Hall, with its center court entirely open to the sky, and lined with two levels of private chambers on each side. Zeus allows neither rain, nor snow to fall from the cloudless firmament, which illuminates the Great Hall during the day. Growing up within this palace you would think I was used to the beauty, but still I become enchanted by the twinkling stars and gentle breeze that flows over the roofless hall at night. The floor is a solid piece of marble and there are caryatids, columns carved in the form of the Gods and Goddesses, lined on both sides of the hall, supporting the upper levels of private rooms. In each of these marble statues' flawless hand is a torch that magically lights at sunset, illuminating the entire hall. Zeus and his wife Hera occupy the entire southern end of the palace, with its spiral staircase leading to their private chambers on the second level: their balcony overlooks the famous Greek city of Athens, while the other Gods and Goddesses dwell within modest chambers throughout the palace.

I share a very large four-room chamber with my mother and my older brother, Iacchus. Some myths say that Iacchus is not my brother, by my son, but this is not true, we are both descended from Zeus and Demeter. Iacchus is older than I; he was conceived on the night that the Olympians finally defeated the Titans. My half sister, and brother, fathered by Poseidon do not dwell within the palace on Mount Olympus, they both live on earth, so I seldom spent time with either of them. I had another brother on my mother's side, named Plutus who was the son of a mortal named Iasion, whom my mother fell in love with while on Earth. Being born of a mortal father, Plutus, unlike us was mortal, therefore he wasn't allowed to live within the royal palace. He lived with his aging father and his stepmother Cybele on earth until death finally greeted him. My mother being an Earth Goddess would visit him often, teaching him how to increase the fertility of the land. On my father's side I have many brothers and sisters, too many to name here. As many of you may know Zeus has had many lovers throughout his life, but these tales I won't relate here.

I knew Hades was here to speak to my father, but why? I ran through the deserted hall, my footsteps echoing as I slammed into each step as I made my way up to my father's private chamber. Once there I found Hermes standing guard, hovering in front of the door. Hermes, being the messenger of Zeus had to be swift, so the God Hephaestus created a pair of beautiful golden sandals with powerful wings attached to the heals as a gift for him. Hermes loved those sandals and could be seen swooping down from great heights with a smile on his face.

"Hermes, I was on Earth and saw Hades emerge from the Underworld. I ran all the way back here to the palace to see him. Is he here"? I asked Hermes still panting.

"He's in there", Hermes said pointing to the closed door. "With Zeus and your mother".

I was shocked to hear that mother was with them. She despised Hades. She tried to pretend that she didn't, but I have heard her speak with Zeus about him with loathing. I always wondered what he had done to her to make her loathe him so, but I dare not ask for fear that I would arouse her anger.

"What's mother doing in there"? I asked, a little surprised.

"Don't know". Replied Hermes, "I was instructed by Hades to tell Zeus of this meeting, and was told that it was not optional".

I attempted to move closer to the door to try hear what they were saying, but all I could make out was mother shouting, followed by the sound of father throwing a few lightening bolts.

"I wouldn't stay here if I were you, your father sounds angry". Hermes said to me with a mischievous smile. Of all the Gods, I think I liked Hermes the best; he was my half-brother, the son of Zeus and a nymph named Maia. He was called by many names such as Messenger of the Immortals, Bringer of Dreams, Thief at the Gates, and Psychompompus, meaning the 'Accompanier of Souls' which was the official title he used when he accompanied the spirits of the dead to the Underworld. He was a Trickster God and loved playing little pranks on the other Gods and Goddess. Even Zeus could be seen laughing at some of his wild pranks.

Before I could respond I was thrown to the ground as the great doors of the chamber flew open and Hades emerged. He smiled as he held out his hand to assist me up when mother, without hesitating pushed him aside and pulled me up to my feet. She grabbed me by the arm and practically dragged me to our rooms. As she pulled me along I kept looking back noticing that Hades was watching.

"What brought Hades here to Mount Olympus, mother"? I asked as we entered our chamber and she finally loosened her grip on me.

She looked slightly pale and changing the subject, saying curtly, "You better dress for dinner, we don't want to be late".

I knew by the tone of her voice I wouldn't get any information. She can be stubborn when she wants to be, as all of the Gods and Goddess can. I hurried to dress and after grabbing my brother's arm we rushed down to the Great Hall. I hoped that Hades would still be there, but was disappointed to find he left immediately after I arrived.

Dinner on Mount Olympus consists of the sweet nectar Ambrosia and grape leaves stuffed with many different cheeses served by the Goddess Hebe, the daughter of Zeus and Hera, and one of my half sisters. Being around the same age as I am, Hebe and I were playmates our entire lives. While my name, Kore, means Maiden, the name Hebe stands for Youth, and Hera determined at her daughter's birth that age would not touch her and named her respectively. Her household duty is to serve the Gods at dinner, and to assist her mother, Hera in harnessing her splendid peacocks to her chariot. Even though it was my duty to tend to the many creatures that bore the God's chariots, Hera wouldn't allow me to touch her sacred birds since I am Zeus' daughter by another Goddess. As I said earlier, Hera only tolerated my brother and I because Zeus forced her to. Being born of an Olympian God and Goddess was to my advantage, some of Zeus' other children born to lesser Goddess's or other immortals were persecuted their entire lives by Hera.

That night at dinner, I sat next to Hermes, hoping to get some information from him. If I were to find out why Hades had come to Mount Olympus, Hermes would be the one to tell. Usually I could convince him into telling me anything, but that evening I got nowhere with my questions. So I tried to ask the others if any of them knew what brought Hades out of the Underworld, but none of the Gods would answer my questions. Mother looked slightly pale and kept trying to change the subject, while Zeus' look warned all to be silent. I knew that for now I should drop it. I was quiet the rest of that night, but for the next couple of weeks I continued trying to pry out from anyone I could why Hades came to visit that day. I dare not ask either father or mother and incur their wrath.

Almost a year passed and even though I didn't see Hades again, I never forget his penetrating green eyes, nor the breathless longing I felt in my heart. I thought about him night and day and with each thought I would feel the same tingling sensation, and my heart ached for his touch. Each day at dawn, while mother was still asleep, I would sneak down to earth where I would wait in the field where I had first seen him hoping that I would once again feel the earth tremble, slowly opening to reveal his emerging chariot. Day after day I sat under the same tree that hid me from his sight so long ago, only to return disappointed to mother. She wondered why I spent so much time on earth when I had all of Mount Olympus to enjoy. I told her that I was visiting the Oceanids, the sea nymphs who lived near the coast of Aechaea. Since they were nymphs and not Gods or Goddess they dwelt on earth with the mortals. When I was young, my mother and I lived with my uncle Poseidon in his palace deep within the Oceans for quite some time and I made friends with many of the nymphs, so she didn't question me.

Finally one day, as I sat in the shade of the tree, half asleep, I heard a noise that startled me. Was I dreaming? The sound was so quiet at first that I wasn't sure if it was just my imagination, but then it became louder and louder until it soon filled the air. It was the same thundering that seemed to come from deep within the earth that I had heard when I first saw Hades, I was sure of it. This time I knew the sound and was determined not to run in fear. I stood my ground as the thundering rumbled and the ground began to shake, sending a quiver of anticipation through my blood. Again the earth slowly spit and from deep within the chasm, the six winged stallions emerged two by two pulling the jeweled chariot, and then… my heart stopped. It was Hades. I was right in his path. Would he run me over? Before I had time to move aside, he used all his strength to pull the chariot to a halt, just inches from me.

"What are you doing here"? He asked me stunned.

I wanted to explain to him how I hid behind the trees so long ago and watched him emerge and go to Mount Olympus, but no words came to my mouth.

He looked down at me and again asked,

"Does your mother know you are down here on earth"?

"Oh yes", I replied, "I told her that I was visiting the Sea Nymphs".

"The Sea Nymphs don't live anywhere near here, they live near the sea. You should know that". He said with a tone that suggested that I might be lying to my mother.

"I know, I had to tell her something. She is so overprotective of me". I said feeling like a child.

"Yes, I know, but you still didn't answer my question. Why are you here on earth"? He again asked.

"I've been coming to this field every day for almost a year". I said, then paused to find the courage to continue. "You see, I was here in the field one day about a year ago, picking flowers for mother and I saw your chariot emerge from the Underworld in the same spot you just came from, and I wanted to see you again".

"Why"? He asked with a look of confusion.

I wanted to tell him that Eros' arrow had pierced my heart and lit my soul on fire with a desire that I couldn't fight, that when I though of him I felt as if my heart was going to stop and a quiver ran from the top of my head to the tips of my toes. I wanted him to know all this but was afraid he would only laugh at me, thinking I was only a silly child. Stepping down from his chariot he took me by the arm. I could feel his strength as he held my trembling hand and we walked toward the grove.

"Where are we going"? I asked, a little nervous.

"I thought we could go sit under the shade of those trees in the distance, and you can tell me about Mount Olympus". He said gently, watching my every move.

I couldn't believe this was really happening. I was with Hades! We were alone and he wanted to talk to me… to me! The trembling in my hands moved through my body as we walked, and when we reached a large tree, I though my legs would give in. He helped me sit down and then to my surprise he sat next to me, his body pressing into my thigh. I felt a flush of heat rise through me.

"How's your mother, Demeter"? He finally asked.

"Fine". I answered shyly.

"You do know that your mother and I don't really get along". He told her even though he was aware that everyone know that Demeter would not even speak to her brother.

"I know". I said, not knowing how to answer this.

I had always wondered what happened between them, why she hated him so, but was too afraid to ask. I knew only too well what happened when one asked a God a personal question. Zeus would use his thunderbolts to pick you up and throw you across the room when angered. The look in his eyes told me he understood my question and I wondered if he did. Many of the Gods and Goddesses possess the ability to read others thoughts to some degree; I flushed with embarrassment at this idea. '*Does he know how I feel about him*', I wondered.

"Your mother's anger towards me isn't the only reason I don't visit Mount Olympus, there are many more". He explained to me, "I do miss my brothers". He said pausing, "I see Poseidon occasionally when I am invited to his palace, but I hardly ever see Zeus".

"I heard Zeus will never set foot into the Underworld again". I said, hoping that Hades would tell me why.

He didn't answer right away, pausing for a moment before saying,

"He entered the Underworld only once a long, long time ago, before I was named as the ruler there. After many adventures, he was finally able to return to the land of the living, but he swore that he would never pass through its gaits again. None of the Gods who live on Mount Olympus, except Hermes, dare enter my world".

"Why don't you come to Mount Olympus since no one will come to your palace"? I asked, hoping that he would enlighten me to the relationship between him and mother.

"When I wish to speak to Zeus I send a message to him through Hermes and if we need to speak face to face we meet on Earth. I would come to Mount Olympus more often, but I just can't stand all the bickering between the Gods and Goddesses". He paused here, then finished his thought, "My home is at least peaceful".

As he said this I thought I noticed his eyes become misty and though how lonely he must be. He looked away for a second.

"Tell me", I finally said, "What brought you out of the Underworld and to my father's palace, no one will tell me anything. They all treat me like a child, speaking in hushed voices whenever I approached".

I could see that he, like the other Gods didn't really want me to know.

II
Persephone

HADES PAUSED FOR a few moments, reflecting on the past before he began to speak to me. "Before you can truly understand what brought me out of the Underworld to your father's palace that day, I must explain to you the circumstances that influenced the Goddess of Fate to name me as the Ruler of the Underworld".

He paused once again and I could see that he had to reach deep down into the pool of his memory to reconstruct the events that must have occurred thousands of years before I was even born, events that decided not only his Fate, but I was soon to find out my Fate as well. After what seemed like an eternity he finally he began his story,

> *"Let me start at the beginning, before the world as you know it was created.*
>
> *At this time in history the Universe was divided into two parts, the Heavens and the Seas, and the Titan Uranus ruled all. Land had not yet been formed, and the sea was lifeless and barren. Life only existed in the Heavens, where your ancestors, the Titans lived for millenniums peacefully under Uranus' rule.*
>
> *All those long years Uranus felt no threat, but then one day as he sat lazily on his thrown, the force of Destiny swiftly came to him and invisible she whispered into his ear,*
>
> *"Uranus, soon all that you possess will be taken from you".*

He opened his eyes to see who dared say such words to him, but only his wife Gaia was in the room.

"My dear, what did you say"? he asked, alarmed that his wife would utter such words to him.

"I said nothing". Was her reply.

The voice came again, and instantly he knew it wasn't his beloved wife.

"Your youngest son will destroy all that you fought for, and then when you are finally beaten down, he will claim your kingdom".

Uranus feared no one, and was determined to outwit Destiny, so in the midst of the sea he created a small speck of land. Once land had been formed, he plunged his hand deep within the newly formed land and there he carved out a void, and within this void he unleashed the countless horrors Destiny filled his dreams with. It was in this dreadful place that he imprisoned all of his children, not taking any chances. The Underworld was thus created, and the Universe no longer consisted of only the Heavens and Seas. Land was formed from his hatred and fear, and this land now separated the Underworld from the Heavens. The Universe now consisted of four realms, the Heavens; Earth, as the new land was to be called; the Seas; and the Underworld.

Uranus had many children with his wife, Gaia, but after the seed of doubt had been planted he refused to lay with her, nor any other. All his children were safely imprisoned, and he would have no other children. After many centuries Gaia longed for another child, so she devised a plan. One day she brought her husband a drink, and kissed him as she gave it to him. He drank it in one great gulp. She brought another, and then another. What Uranus didn't know was that Gaia had placed some herbs that came from the entrance to the Underworld into his wine and soon he was intoxicated. That night she came to him and they made love the entire night. It was not long after that that she discovered that she was expecting another child and fearing that this child would soon be taken away from her and thrown into the Underworld dungeon with his brothers and sisters, she devised a way to conceal her unborn child within her womb until he was fully grown. This child, Cronus, grew within the womb of his mother, Gaia waiting until the day he could enact his revenge on his father Uranus.

After the night of the conception Uranus feared that Destiny had tricked him. He was sure that his wife would bare the child that was destined to destroy him, but as the months passed and nothing happened, his confidence grew. It wasn't long after this that his desires were greater than his fears and he took his wife back to his bed. Many years had passed and during this time Gaia hid her son, but when Uranus wasn't around she would speak to him, preparing him for his destiny.

The time had finally come, Cronus was fully grown, but still concealed within his mother's womb. In a night of passion Uranus came to his wife and made love with her. Cronus seized the moment, knowing that the time had finally come; he must fulfill his destiny. As his father made love to his mother, Cronus castrated him. Once his father's rule was overthrown, he emerged from his mother's womb, covered with his father's blood and grabbed a nearby sword. He held the sword over his head and was about to behead his father, when Gaia spoke,

"My dear son, have pity and spare your father's life".

"But mother, it is destined that I destroy my father and take his kingdom". Cronus replied to his mother.

"No!" She shouted at him, hoping to stop him. "It is destiny that you rule the Universe in his place, but you can do this without killing him".

Cronus spared his father's life, and without a struggle he seized the Universe as his own. Once his kingdom was established he freed his brothers and sisters from their prison deep within the earth. The first few centuries Cronus ruled the Universe peacefully just as his father had done, but this second Golden Age was destined to fail, just as the previous one had. Unlike his father, throughout the centuries the Titan Cronus became a tyrant seeking only power. He didn't hesitate to destroy any who got in his way. The Titans, like the Gods, are immortal and not easily killed; they could only be destroyed by dismembering their bodies and scattering the remains or by cremation. Those who refused to obey Cronus were denied this fate, instead they were imprisoned deep within the same prison that his father sent his brothers and sisters to so many centuries before. This prison became known as the Dungeon of the Damned, Tartarus. Here all forms of tortures and punishments were inflicted on the poor souls for all eternity, those who were trapped there could not even hope for death, knowing that Death would never answer their prayers. There was no escape from Tartarus. Soon all feared Cronus' wrath.

Cronus ruled alone for many more centuries, then one day he decided that he would marry and produce an heir. He chose as his new bride the most beautiful of the Titanides, his sister Rhea. She did not love him; fearing imprisonment in Tartarus, she reluctantly agreed to be his wife. The day of the wedding arrived and all the Titans, Giants and Cyclopes were present, this being the event of the millennium. The ceremony over, it was the second day of the feasting when a loud thundering soon filled the massive hall of the palace and all stopped speaking, silence enveloped everyone as they turned to see where this sound was coming from. To their amazement a small dark shadow started to form in the center of the room. With each heartbeat the shadow pulsated and grew in strength. Within seconds darkness soon filled the entire hall and a purple mist seemed to pour in from the heavens, engulfing all. The guests, ignorant of the cause of this was began leaving the palace in a panic. Above their screams, a disembodied voice that seemed to echo through the hall spoke. All stopped, standing silent as if mesmerized. The voice spoke the following prediction:

> "Cronus, from your union with your sister Rhea you will have six children, and of these six, the youngest born to her will one day rise up against you and destroy you. He will rule in your place, just as you had replaced your father. All will worship him above all other Gods. He will unite your other children, along with your brothers and sisters who you have imprisoned in Tartarus and with their help they will destroy the Titans, and create a new age of peace, a true Golden Age that will last for centuries. Only those who follow him will be spared destruction".

All the guests stood there, silent and watched Cronus, who showed no fear in his eyes. He decided then that he would never let this happen, he wouldn't allow any children born from this marriage to survive. Five years passed and five children were born to Rhea, and all five were swallowed whole by Cronos before she could do anything to stop him. When Rhea conceived for the sixth time, she swore that she wouldn't allow her husband's fear destroy this child, even though she knew that this would be the sixth child, the one the Oracle predicted would destroy his him and rule in his place.

The night of the birth came and as Rhea heard the snores of her sleeping husband she silently crept out of their private chamber and into that of her servant, the nymph Neda. With Neda watching over her she gave birth to a beautiful baby, a son who she named Zeus. She wrapped the infant tightly, and after giving him a kiss on the top of his head, she gave her beloved son to the trusted nymph, begging her to hide him on the earth where she was sure that her husband would never be able to find him. It was only a couple of hours after the birth that Neda left, taking the infant Zeus with her to the island of Crete. Neda knew that she couldn't stay on earth, Cronus would suspect something if she wasn't present to attend to her mistress, Rhea, so she went to two of her sisters, the nymphs Amaltheia and Ida.

"My dear sisters, you must protect this child with your lives".

"Is this the child that's destined to destroy Cronus"? Amaltheia asked quietly, not wanting the Titan to her them conspire against him. "He must be kept safe". Neda begged them. "We'll raise him as our own son". Neda rushed back to her mistress, not wanting to cause alarm.

As Rhea stood there alone, a fear seized her, she was sure that her husband would wake to find her missing. Looking around the room frantically and seeing a stone about the size of her newborn infant she picked it up and wrapped it in swaddling clothes and went back to her chamber. When she entered the chamber, holding what appeared as a newborn child she made a small cough hoping to wake her husband. Cronus, upon hearing the noise opened his eyes and saw what he thought was his sixth child in her arms. He jumped from the bed and quickly snatched the infant from Rhea's arms and without even looking at it he swallowed it whole. This time the tears that rolled down her cheeks were not tears of pain, but tears of joy, for her plan had worked. Cronus thought he had destroyed this child just as he had destroyed the other five. She knew that her son would survive and one day he would return to take his father's thrown and rule the Heavens. The knowledge that her son, Zeus, was safe down on earth allowed Rhea to sleep in peace for the first night since her marriage.

Rhea was finally able to rest peacefully, knowing that soon her son would rise up to destroy his father, but whenever Cronus slept, the Erinyes, the Goddesses of Vengeance and Retribution, came to him in his dreams and whispered to him.

"Your child, the sixth child born from your union with your wife Rhea, still lives. He will soon rise to destroy you".

At first he paid no attention to these dreams, he knew that the child was destroyed, he swallowed the infant on the night of its birth. There was no possibility that his son could harm him. Night after night the Erinyes would whisper these warnings to him, tormenting and haunting him, not even allowing sleep to release him from their taunts. He would wake up from these dreams screaming, and with sweat on his brow he wouldn't be able to fall back asleep. Night after night Cronus would pace in their bed chamber not allowing sleep to come to him for fear of the Erinyes voices.

It was not long before Rhea, noticing that her husband desperately needed sleep, took action. She didn't do this because she felt pity for him, but because the lack of sleep was causing him to abuse any who happened to get in his way. She mixed a sweet honey mead with herbs that she picked from the banks of the Lethe river, one of the rivers that flow into the Underworld, which when mixed properly would induce a dreamless sleep. Cronus took this mead every night before retiring, and with its aid he was once again able to sleep without the nagging of the Erinyes. They no longer were able to torment him during his dreams, but they refused to leave him alone. During the day they continued to torture him, whispering in his ear as he sat on his thrown "Your son still lives". hoping to slowly drive him mad.

Through the years as Zeus grew, Amaltheia told him about how his father destroyed his five brothers and sisters and how his mother saved him, fearing that he would destroy him as well; how Rhea risked her own life, for Cronus knew that it would be this child, the sixth, who was destined to one day take his kingdom, by giving her child to another to raise. Amaltheia explained how on their wedding day the Oracle warned Cronus that his child would destroy him, and how the Erinyes refused to let him sleep in peace, pursuing him relentlessly and almost driving him to madness for his crimes. Zeus' hatred for his father grew as he did, and when he reached manhood he decided that the time had come for him to fulfill his destiny and take revenge on his father. Zeus went to Cronus' palace and confronted his mother.

"Mother, today I have come to free you from the cruel grip of my father and take what is rightfully mine. Cronus will no longer rule the Universe, for tomorrow I will sit on the thrown".

Rhea felt pity for her husband even though she didn't love him, but she knew that there was nothing she could do to stop his death. She came up with plan to distract Zeus, hoping that he wouldn't kill his father, but would devise a way of overthrowing him, just as Cronus had done with his father. She sent her niece, the Titan Metis to Zeus. Metis was not only very beautiful, and Rhea knew that Zeus couldn't pass up the chance to be with a beautiful Goddess, but she was also very intelligent, and she hoped that the two Gods would be able to devise a plan of attack.

Zeus spent several days and nights with his cousin Metis, and even though he was enamored with her, he not once forgot why he had come to his father's house.

Metis instantly fell in love with the young God and wishing to assist him in destroying his father while saving his brothers and sisters, she gave him a drug that would induce Cronus to regurgitate all the children he had swallowed, allowing the young God to fulfill his destiny. Zeus agreed and that night instead of his mother Rhea, he mixed the sweet mead, not only adding the herbs from the Lethe River, but while the potion was simmering over a low flame, he added a second herb, the one that Metis picked from the River of Fire, the fiery river that surrounds Tartartus; he also added one of his mother's tears, along with mandrake root and simmered the potion for several hours. When it was almost ready, he picked up his sword and made a small cut along his wrist, adding a few drops of his own blood, causing a great steam to explode from the mixture as the blood flowed down. Once cooled, Zeus carefully poured the mead into his father's chalice and instructed his mother to give this to Cronus and say nothing of what was added to it.

That night before turning in Rhea walked into her husband's bed chamber with her head lowered, not wanting to make eye contact with her husband, knowing that if he looked into her eyes, she could not hide her dishonesty. She held the poisoned honey mead in her hand and before she could say anything, he took the golden chalice and with one great gulp he drained the cup, not noticing anything was different until he wiped his lips and saw the blood on his finger. Before he could say anything the room began to spin. Faster and faster it spun. He held his hands up to his head hoping this would somehow stop the spinning, but it did no good, the room continued to spin round and round. He couldn't stand straight, he fell against the wall and tried to use this to pull up his weak body. Beads of sweat began to form on his forehead, and soon slid down his face, as his eyes rolled back into his head and his whole body began to first twitch, then convulse in spasms that he couldn't control. He held his stomach as he fell hard to his knees vomiting. First came up the stone that he thought was his sixth son, followed by his other five children all fully grown.

He knew then that he had been deceived and soon his son would come to destroy him. He tried to control his body, to stay awake and fight, but the powerful drug wouldn't allow that. Cronos fell into a deep stupor as Zeus, who was just outside the chamber, stepped in and loosened his robes exposing a scimitar hanging at his side. Rhea with tears running down her cheeks, begged Zeus not to kill her husband.

"Please don't kill him, for he is your father".

"Mother, it is my destiny that I kill my father, was it not predicted by the Oracle on your wedding night"?

Zeus replied as he pulled the scimitar free. Rhea continued to cry as her son beheaded Cronus with a single blow. Blood splattered Zeus' face and covered his white robes as he continued to cut his father's body up into pieces, for this was one of the ways to destroy an immortal. After he was through, he directed his brothers and sisters to each take a piece of the body and disposes of it. Zeus, of course took the head and threw it far into the night sky. I took

Cronus' heart deep into the Underworld, past Cerberus, the three headed hound that guards the entrance, to the River of Forgetfulness where I threw it in, and when his blood mixed with the cold water Thanatos, the God of Death, was born. Poseidon took the penis and disposed it into the seas, where its seeds, once released, began to foam and an eruption filled the seas, creating all mortal life on the planet, for before this only the immortals lived. Your mother, the Goddess Demeter, took his limbs and buried them on the barren earth, and it is from these that trees and grasses began to sprout up. The eldest of the six children, Hestia, took the torso and threw it into the hearth where it was consumed within seconds by the great fire.

The Titanomachia, the war between the Titans and the Olympians had begun with Zeus as head of the Olympian army and Cronus' brother Atlas as the military commander of the remaining Titans. The sky turned a dirty gray color as the Titan Boreas, the North Wind, bellowed and a dark mist slowly rumbled across the sky obscuring the land below. Thunder shook the heaves, as veins of lightening flashed through the dark sky illuminating the Titans as they prepared to shoot their mighty weapons. Not all the Titans fought with their brothers, some immediately took sides with the Olympians remembering the prediction of the Oracle and the terror that Cronus inflicted on all who disobeyed him; Rhea; Cronus' brother Prometheus; the Sea Titan Oceanus, and his children the sea nymphs; the Sun God Helios; and Themis, who ruled over Law and Justice, were only a few of the Titans who were allies of the Olympians while others, who were loyal to their king decided to defend him even in death. Of those who fought against the Olympians were Atlas, Epimetheus, and Menoetius who were Cronus' brothers. Still others remained neutral, since Cronus was dead there was no need to fight, they would wait until the war was over, then side with the victors.

Rhea, wanting to protect Hera sent her to the Titan Oceanus and his wife Tethys in the far west where the sun rests in the evening, for Rhea knew that her youngest daughter was destined to marry Zeus and rule the Heavens at his side. While Hera was away, Metis became Zeus' first lover and wife and it was from this union that the Goddess Athena was born. But Athena was not born in the usual way.

Zeus, feared that if Metis bore a son he would grow to defeat his father, just as he had defeated Cronus, so Zeus decided to not destroyed the child after it was born, but to destroy it before it's first breath. Zeus consumed Metis in a single breath. Nine months later the beautiful Goddess Athena was born from Zeus' head and soon she joined in battle with the other Gods and Goddesses and it was Hera alone of the Olympians who did not fight in the war. Zeus led the army that fought from the sky, Poseidon used his powers to control the winds and waters and I, along with your mother Demeter led the Gods who fought on the land, while our sister Hestia protected the palace grounds.

The war continued with each side holding its ground for thousands of earth years. Each day as the first rays of the Sun emerged from Helios' chariot as his swift horses drew him from the far ends of the world to fill the sky with his golden light, the two great armies would face each other, weapons ready. On the battlefield, the first few rows of the Olympians were entirely covered in a magical armor and shields made from the God Hephaestus, the God of Fire, while those in the back fired arrows soaked in the blood of the Gorgons, the hideous snake haired monsters who could turn mortals to stone with one look alone, for this precious blood not only would destroy the Titans, but if mixed properly it was a remedy used on the wounded Gods during the night allowing them to face their adversaries the following day. Once this poison was within the Titan's bloodstream they began to scream out in pain, the poison was not powerful enough to kill them, since they were immortal, instead their fate was to feel their blood burn for eternity. The Gods within the palace on Mount Olympus could hear their screams over the sounds of the battle. Only a few were lucky and put out of their misery by their companions.

This precious blood, the blood of the Gorgons was the Olympian's only weapon against their ancestors, the Titans, and for thousands of years each side held its ground, until one day the Titans emerged in their flying chariots as Helios' began his daily journey across the sky. As the first rays of the Sun caressed the battlefield the Titans let loose a new weapon causing a terrible blast that hit the six majestic steeds pulling Helios' chariot and instantly their burnt corpses fell from the sky pulling the Sun chariot down with them. The heat from the falling Sun set fire to trees and grasses and caused the seas to boil and would have destroyed the entire universe had not the Wind God, Boreas called all the winds together to let loose all the power of the Universe and with all their might they were able to stop Helios from hitting the earth and prevent the Sun itself from being destroyed.

    The Titans in anger prepared to let loose a second weapon, one even more terrible than the first, a weapon that was capable of destroying the entire universe. When it fired the earth shook and the skies turned blood red as smoke and flame as bright as ten suns lit the sky. The Olympians on the earth fled as fire and brimstone came crashing down on them from the heavens and exploded on impact killing beasts and Gods alike. The screams of the dying couldn't be heard for the entire earth let loose a terrible cry that drowned out all other sound for days. The fires burnt for almost a week straight and when they finally subsided and the damage could be seen, the few Olympians who survived thought that the war was finally lost. The corpses of the fallen Gods were mutilated beyond recognition by the terrible heat of the fires. All life on earth appeared to have been destroyed.

    The Titans, like the Olympian Gods dare not leave the warmth and safety of their palace, for the Earth was alight with fires that came from deep within it's depths. During the first weeks after the initial blast earthquakes, tidal waves, and erupting volcanoes destroyed any life that survived the initial attack. The fires burned for almost an entire year, and once finally quenched, a terrible winter set in, a winter that would last for years. Surrounded by nothing but darkness and cold, those of us who survived, and there were only a few of us left, stayed within the palace that was once our father's, too weak and frightened to dare leave. Even though the Titans were victorious, at least for the moment, they dare not leave their fort either.*

    Hades paused here to reflect on the events that happened so long ago, and even though I had heard many tales of the war between the Olympians and the Titans, I waited in anticipation for what was to happen next. No one on Mount Olympus dared speak of the war in this way. Zeus did not wish to relive those memories, therefore the stories I had heard, while accurate didn't really go into much details. I couldn't understand why he didn't wish to speak of it, but after hearing Hades tell me of what the Olympians endured for so long a time, I could imagine the terror that they all must have felt. I wanted to stop Hades here to ask him about how he felt then, but before I could speak, he continued.

> *"It was during this period that Zeus, tired and beaten decided the risk traveling to the Oracle. He set out on the three day path to the Oracle alone, and when he finally reached it, exhaustion almost overcame him as he stood at an entrance to a cave. Inside Zeus saw an old woman, a woman so old, he thought she couldn't possibility still be alive. "Come" she croaked as she motioned for him to enter. Cautiously he crossed the threshold and as his foot touched the soil within the cave a mist rose from deep within the earth and the Great God Zeus almost lost consciousness as the poisonous vapors began to surround him. He stood still trying to keep his balance, his eyes closed and his breathing heavy when he heard the old woman speaking, her voice barely audible,*
>
>> *The Olympians will defeat the Titans only with the help of the Hekatonkheires and the Cyclopes who are held as prisoners within Tartarus. You must make the long journey deep into the Underworld alone, and continue along the River of Fire until you reach the deepest part. Here you will find the Dungeon of the Damned and while there you must secure those who your father imprisoned as your allies, for only with their help will the Olympians win this war.*
>
> *Upon returning to us, Zeus told what the Oracle had revealed and before we could try to talk him out of making that dangerous trip, he retired to his chamber and began preparations for the journey to the deepest, darkest depths of the Underworld where his father had imprisoned the Hekatonkheires, who were known as the Hundred-handed Giants along with the Cyclopes centuries ago. The other Olympians pleaded with him, to not make go alone, but he wouldn't hear of it, he needed the help of the Giants and the Cyclopes if the Olympians were to finally defeat the Titans,*

and he was determined to go to the Underworld alone. Within hours of his return he left the palace and for six days and six nights we waited praying that he succeed. As the days passed by we could think of nothing anything else but the fear that he was to soon perish within the Underworld and the war would finally be lost.

When I entered the Underworld for the first time, to dispose of my father's head, I took the Acheron River to where it branches and there passed to the left, not daring to go near the river that led to Tartarus, for I had heard that this prison was a horrible dungeon and none who enter its walls are allowed to leave. Zeus took the passage to the right, which led him deeper into the Underworld and he passed many obstacles and faced many monsters that dwelled deep within the earth, until he finally reached his destination. Once there he was able to bargain with the prisoners; for their freedom they would have to pledge allegiance with the Olympians and help them destroy the Titans. The prisoners agreed and as a sign of their pledge they gave the Olympians each a great weapon, weapons that would help destroy the Titans. Zeus was given the magical thunderbolts that Cronus had hidden there in the Underworld, knowing that if one of his sons would possess such a weapon he would be the strongest of the Gods; I was given the Helmet of Invisibility; and Poseidon was given his Trident. With these new weapons, and the help the Cyclopes and Hundred-handed Giants the Olympians were finally able to defeat the Titans. After thousands of years of fighting, within a week after Zeus' return from the Underworld the war was over, and the Olympians emerged victorious.

The Universe now belonged to the Olympians, and after restoring the Sun to it's former brilliance, the God Helios once again emerged with the first dawn of the new age. Zeus, now the true ruler of the Universe, imprisoned all those who fought against him in Tartarus. Once freed, one of the Hundred-Handed Giants, Gyges who agreed to support Zeus and the Olympians left the God's side and returned to fight along with his brothers, the Titans, and after the war he was thrown back into his prison and to this day he remains there. Atlas, Cronus' younger brother and leader of the Titans was sentenced by Zeus to carry the weight of the sky on his shoulders for eternity as his punishment. Zeus, just like his father, imprisoned not only the Titans who fought against him, but any who would not obey his command in the same dungeon that Cronus sent his enemies.

Not long after the destruction of the Titans, Zeus decided that he would split the Universe into three parts, and each of the three sons of Rhea would rule a part. The Heavens would become the abode of the Gods, the Seas would become the birthplace for all life on earth, and the Underworld would be the House of Death. Of course Zeus, Poseidon and myself all wanted the Heavens as our domain, and the bickering started almost immediately. After nine days of fighting, without sleep or food, our mother Rhea decided to take action. Ananke, the personification of unalterable control over the careers of both the mortals and immortals, and who would be the mother of the Moirai, the Goddesses better known as the Fates, the deities who assigned each man's destiny at his birth, was called to decide which God will rule the three parts of the Universe. We agreed that all would follow her decision.

The beautiful Goddess entered into the hall wearing a long white silk gown embroidered with gold threads, with her long blonde hair flowing down in soft waves to her waist. All eyes were on her as she slowly walked towards us, carrying a silver pitcher in her left hand and in her right she held the cards of destiny.

She spoke in a soft voice:

"The cards I hold are destiny cards, they will tell me where each God will rule. But, I must warn you; all must follow the path directed by the cards. Any who do not, death will surely take you".

All were silent.

She continued,

"I have in my right hand a pitcher filled with water from the river Styx. All must swear an oath by this water, that they will abide the decision of these cards. Any oath sworn on this water and broken will cause instant death for all who taste it. I ask that all present partake a sip from this pitcher as your pledge to me and to each other".

She then passed the pitcher to Zeus, who slowly lifted it to his lips and drank. Zeus passed it to Poseidon who also drank. I was next. The water was bitterly cold, but I could feel the heat of it as it flowed through my mouth, down my throat and into my stomach. I coughed slightly, before passing the pitcher to Hera who also slowly drank from it before passing it to Demeter and finally Hestia. After all the Gods and Goddesses drank from this sacred water, Ananke slowly walked to Zeus and pulled a card from the deck she was holding.

The Emperor.

"I have pulled the Emperor card for you Zeus. You have proved yourself as a great leader in the war with the Titans". Ananke said, " I give to you the Heavens to rule, seated upon your golden throne. All Gods and mortals will both worship and fear you above all the other Gods and Goddesses".

As she said this Zeus smiled, he started boasting about the beautiful palace he would build, where all the Gods and Goddesses would live together for eternity.

Ananke held up a hand to Zeus, telling him to wait. She walked up to Poseidon and pulled another card from her deck. This time the card was the King of Cups.

"Cups represent the element of water. Poseidon's skills in controlling the winds and waters during the terrible war was a great asset, therefore, I name Poseidon as not only the King of the Waters of the World, but with his Trident he will also be the Earth Shaker. He will be feared by mortals as the God of the Seas, who not only controls the world's waters, but also the wind and thus the weather".

Poseidon smiled as his fate was told to him.

Ananke walked up to me, and this time she pulled not one card but two cards. The first was Death.

"The Underworld has been chosen for you Hades, for only you have the strength to control Death, and you alone have the endurance to withstand living in this dreadful place for eternity. You will not be Death itself, for that is reserved for the God Thanatos, who was born from the blood of Cronus as it mixed with the rivers of the Underworld. You will be the Lord of those who have died, and all mortals will fear you".

My heart felt as if it was destroyed. I was to become the God of the Underworld. I thought about being surrounded by nothing but death and decay, how no mortal would dare speak my name for fear that my cold bony hand would snatch their last breath. I thought to myself ' How could I bear this loneliness throughout the centuries', and as if she heard me, Ananke answered loud enough for all to hear,

"You will not be alone for eternity. For I have pulled two cards for your future. The second card is the High Priestess", she said as she held the card up for all to see.

"This card states that you will not rule the Underworld alone, for a Goddess born from the union of the Earth and the Heavens will one day sit at your side to rule with you. You alone of all the Olympians will have a marriage that is built on love and trust'.

"Who is this goddess"? I asked

"She will be born from the elements of the Earth and the Air. Her mother will be the Earth Goddess Demeter, and her father will be the God Zeus". She answered.

At this Hera, who was not yet married to Zeus gave him a look of disgust. It was a well-known fact that Zeus would often visit the other Goddesses, and Hera like all the other Goddesses wanted him all for herself.

"My daughter won't live her life with the shades of Death". Demeter shouted.

Zeus held out his hand to his sister quieting her.

"Demeter, we've all drank from the waters of the river Styx, we gave our oath that Ananke would have the final decision. The cards have told us our destiny. If our daughter is to become the Queen of the Underworld, so be it".

Demeter started to say something, but Ananke stopped her, saying,

"The High Priestess sits between two pillars, one white and one dark. She will be pulled in two directions, she will be destined to split her life. When I look closely at this card, it shows the High Priestess sitting on a throne, resting her feet on the moon, telling me she will only be truly happy when she is with her husband in the Underworld".

Demeter started to object, but Ananke only said,

"All have sworn to abide my word, it has been decided". As she said this, she slowly turned and left the room.

Hades had finished his story, and for a few moments we sat there in silence, neither of us knowing what to say next. Finally Hades broke the silence.

"For the next couple of centuries I lived in the Underworld, surrounded by nothing but death waiting patiently for my bride to relieve my loneliness. When you were born I wanted to present your mother with a gift, an offering, but she refused me to enter Mount Olympus for fear that I would enchant you and you would return to the Underworld with me. Since your birth I have only been invited to your father's palace once when Demeter was visiting Earth. You were a very young girl at the time, I don't think you would even remember. You mother is determined that you will not marry me, keeping you close to her side. I'm surprised that she allowed you to come down to earth, knowing that I'm so near. But I see, not only was my fate decided that night so long ago, but your fate as well. Now that you have heard my story, I hope that you will understand what I'm about to tell you".

Hades paused here, took my hand and looked me in the eyes before starting to explain why he met with Zeus that fated day a year ago.

"I came to Mount Olympus last year to discuss with your father Zeus the arrangements for our marriage, but your mother overheard him speaking to Hermes about my arrival and decided to meet me as I entered the gates. As soon as she saw me she started screaming at me to leave the palace at once, that I wasn't welcome there. Zeus quickly brought us to his private chambers, not wanting the other Gods and Goddesses to hear our discussion. Demeter forbade me to take her daughter as my wife. Zeus tried to explain to her, that as the King of the Underworld I was more than a suitable match for any Goddess, but she wouldn't listen to anything he tried to say. I left in a fury without making any arrangements, but I was determined that I would meet with Zeus again. Even though I don't come to Mount Olympus and Zeus will never enter my palace within the Underworld, we do communicate to each other through Hermes, and yesterday Hermes came to me telling me that Zeus arranged to meet me today on the island of Crete to discuss the plans for not only my future, but yours as well. Your mother doesn't know anything about this meeting, if she did she would do anything in her power to stop it".

As he told me this I couldn't believe what I was hearing. For the last year I have fantasized about being Hades lover, and today I was sitting with him under a tree on this beautiful day and he was telling me that I was destined to be his bride.

He looked at me and said,

"I hope you aren't too disappointed to find out that you are destined to marry me, the Lord of the Underworld".

I replied, "My mother was right when she said she didn't want you on Mount Olympus for fear that you would enchant me. You have enchanted me, and now my heart belong to you alone".

Hades smiled and said,

"Will you accompany me to the island Crete to meet with your father, he'll be pleased that you have agreed to be my wife".

Hades stood up, and held out a hand to help me up. We walked quietly to his chariot where he lifted me effortlessly into a seat next to his. I held out a hand to help him up, and he kissed it softly before pulling himself up next to me. Hades took the reins in his hands and within seconds we were off to meet my father to discuss our marriage.

III
Persephone

THE SIX BLACK stallions assisted by their bat-like wings ran swiftly over the land without even pausing when they reached the northern shores of the Greek city Attica. I had seen my uncle Poseidon's horses move gracefully over the water many times and thought that his alone possessed this ability, for he was the God of the Seas; but Hades' horses were just as grand as their hoofs seemed to float effortlessly over the white foam of the waves. It was this foam that supported the weight of the six stallions and gilded chariot, and with each beat of their leathery wings I could see the waters below them stir only slightly as we seemed to skim over the sea. I could feel the cool mist of the salt water on my face as we headed swiftly toward the Island of Crete, and it cooled me, for I was feeling a little warm sitting next to Hades. He held my hand and gazing at me he smiled. We were silent as we rode over the sea, reaching the island of Crete sooner than I would have like to, since I feared that father would order me to return to Mount Olympus when he saw me with his brother.

Did he, like my mother want to prevent me from marrying the Lord of the Underworld? I heard many tales of father's voyage deep into the Underworld during the war between the Olympians and the Titans as Hades had told me, but he, nor any of the other Gods would say what difficulties he endured during his short stay there. As far as I know Zeus had told no one the horrors he faced there, only that he swore never to set foot in that dreadful place again. I wondered if over the span of the many generations did he regret his decision to honor the Goddess *Ananke*'s judgment of my fate, after all he is the strongest of all the Gods, would he now let me, his daughter, marry Hades, the Lord of the Underworld and spend eternity living within his dreaded domain.

When finally we reached Crete I saw father standing alone on shore, waiting patiently for his brother. When the chariot stopped and Hades assisted me down, I noticed that Zeus looked surprised. His eyes were on me as the two brothers embraced each other tenderly before Zeus asked about my presence.

"Kore, my daughter, what brings you here"? He asked, giving no show of warmth in his voice.

I didn't answer at first, not knowing what to say.

"How is it that you have come with Hades, when I have summoned him alone"? Zeus demanded of me, with a tone of voice that I knew all too well, one that told me to speak the truth or face the consequences. I didn't dare lie to father, he could read other's thoughts and would know instantly if I did, but I was afraid to answer. Fear of Zeus sending me back home filled my head, but then I remembered what Hades told me just a few hours ago, that he was meeting with father to make our marriage arrangements. I hoped that if I told him that I indeed wanted to marry Hades, that I had fallen in love with him, he would have no choice but to agree to the marriage. Then it would be easy for him to convince mother. None of the other Gods or Goddesses ever dare go against his wishes, and lived to tell about it.

"Kore, tell me why you have come here with Hades"? Zeus asked again, with a little more anger in his voice this time.

"Father forgive me", I began, "I was down on earth a year ago picking flowers for mother, when I felt the ground beneath my feet quiver and then shake as if the earth would burst open. I ran and hid behind some trees within the grove as the earth where I was standing a few seconds before was split open, and to my amazement, I saw a great glided chariot being pulled up from the Underworld by six magnificent winged horses. When I saw the rider of that chariot, I felt Eros' poison fill my body and instantly I fell in love. Since then, I've waited in that same grove hoping that I would see the Lord of the Underworld once again, only to be disappointed day after day.

This morning started out the same and soon I fell asleep, only to be woke by the sound of my uncle's chariot once again being born from the earth".

Hades interrupted, "Zeus, I am sorry I am so late, but once your daughter told me of this, I thought it was necessary for me to explain to her how on the day we three brothers were given our kingdoms, I was promised that I would one day wed the only daughter of Zeus and Demeter, and how on that day she saw me leaving the Underworld, I was on my way to Mount Olympus to meet with you to discuss the marriage arrangements".

Father, being the stern judge that he always was, held up a hand to his older brother, quieting him before turning to me,

"Do you object to this marriage, Kore"?

"Father, I want nothing more than to wed Hades. When I saw him so long ago I knew that I felt Eros' arrow pierce my chest and penetrate deep into my heart. I have longed for this, for this is truly my destiny". I answered.

"Sit down child!" Zeus barked at me, "While I speak with Hades about this matter alone".

The two of them walked away from me, talking in hushed voices so that no matter how hard I strained, I couldn't hear what they were saying. I cannot explain to you the anxiety I felt just then. My father would decide my fate! I wanted to scream at him, to tell him that it was my decision, not his, whom I give my heart to and marry, but I couldn't. I have seen too many times what happened to others when they crossed father, I wasn't the only Goddess who feared Zeus' wrath.

When my brother and I were growing up Zeus was not around much, his wife, Hera, wouldn't allow him to be near his children from other Goddesses. She didn't acknowledge any of his other children, whether born from Goddess, Nymph or mortal, and there were many of these children. The lucky ones, like my brother and I, she would simply ignore, but others she would torture for their entire life. Hercules was one of the unlucky ones; she was the cause of all of his misfortunes, and it wasn't until after his death, that she finally allowed his soul release. She only tolerated my brother and I because mother was one of the original Olympians, and a powerful Goddess, more powerful then Hera herself. The only time my brother and I would see our father, except of course during the evening meals in the Great Hall, when he would ignore all the children present, including the children born to his wife, was when we disobeyed our mother. After enduring a number of punishments from him, I learned to obey his word without questions. After that, all mother had to do was threaten us saying *'Do I need to inform you father about this'* and we would instantly obey her.

As I stood there waiting, I decided that I was no longer going to live my life according to what mother or father wanted. I was tired of being Demeter and Zeus' daughter. I wanted to be a Goddess myself; I wanted to be Hades wife and rule the Underworld at his side, I wanted to be the Queen of the Dead. I'm sure that it's hard for some who read this to understand my feelings. The Goddesses of Destiny no longer exist within the modern era as they had in the past, therefore humans now have some freedom to choose their own destiny, to choose whom they wish to marry, but when I was growing up not only were humans forced to live by the rules of the Fates, the Gods and Goddesses were also bound by these universal laws. The bride's parents arranged almost all marriages and my marriage would be no different, being decided centuries before I was even born, and nothing I said or did would be able change it.

But then I though, if the story Hades told me was indeed the truth, then the six children of Rhea all swore by the Oath of the river Styx that they would abide by the Goddess Ananke's decision. It was she alone who decided that I would marry Hades, but mother on hearing this swore that she would not let this happen. Would mother risk death to prevent this marriage from taking place? I thought that if I could speak to her and tell her how I felt, that I loved Hades and was willing to give myself to him, to live within his palace deep in the Underworld, that she would agree to this wedding. I think not, no matter what I said to her, she is very stubborn when she doesn't get her way, as are all of the Gods and Goddesses. I had made up my mind, I wasn't going to just sit by and allow father, nor mother decide whom I was to marry. If Zeus objected I was going to stand firm and tell him, not ask him that he blesses this union, and even if he refuses, I would still find a way to marry Hades.

After what seemed like an eternity, the two brothers came back to where I waited and Zeus was first to speak.

"I've decided that I will bless this marriage under one condition".

Zeus paused here and my heart stopped beating for a second, he would allow me to marry Hades, but then my excitement turned to fear, I wondered what his condition could be.

He then continued,

"Don't look so frightened", he said with a slight smile before continuing, "I'll agree to this marriage only after you spend one year and one day on earth, during which time Hades will court you. After the allotted time, you alone will make the decision whether or not you will marry Hades. But..." he paused here once again, making sure that he had my full attention,

"...before you decide though, you must be certain that your love for him endures. If it doesn't, then you'll be free to return with me to Mount Olympus, but if your love lasts, you will spend the rest of your life in the Underworld as Queen of the Dead. I want you to understand, that once the decision is made, there'll be no coming back".

I nodded that I understood.

I would spend one year and one day on earth with Hades and then I could marry him, but then I thought of mother. How was I going to stay here on earth for a year without mother finding out and taking me back to Mount Olympus like a little child?

Zeus knowing my fears, spoke to me,

"I'll tell my dear sister, Demeter, that you're visiting your cousins the Sea Nymphs, the Nereids. I understand that you have been telling her this little lie for the last year". Zeus said as he raised one eyebrow.

He continued, "I'll tell her that it was I who wanted you to live with them so they can teach you the ways of both the sea and the earth, for you being the daughter of the Goddess of Fertility will soon be assisting her in her duties here on earth".

"But where on Earth will I stay, I know no mortals who would allow me to stay with them, father"?

I asked, for I knew that whoever allows me to stay with them would anger my mother, and I didn't know of any mortals brave enough to show the Goddess of Fertility dishonor, not only that, if anything would go wrong than they would also face both Zeus and Hades' wrath.

"I'll speak to Minos, the king of Crete, he's one of my sons and is a just ruler. He'll watch over you for this year while you live within the walls of the royal palace on Knossos". Before I could reply, he continued, "While you are here on Earth, I expect you to obey the king as you would me". Zeus answered. I nodded, and he continued,

"I want you to know that I'll be watching you closely from Mount Olympus".

With this he left Hades and I alone while he went to speak to his son, the king. Hades took my hand and looked into my eyes before speaking,

"We have one year until I can hold you in my arms and love you as my wife". He placed his hand on my chin and lifted my face to meet his and kissed me on the forehead.

"It'll be torment for me to be so near you and not be able to express my love". I replied.

"I've endured centuries waiting for you, one year won't matter to me, especially since you'll be so close".

I wanted to be alone with him longer, I had so much to tell him but Zeus returned after only a short time followed by an elderly man who I knew must have been the King and a beautiful young woman, who I assumed was his wife.

"Minos, may I introduce my daughter Kore to you". Zeus began saying, pausing only a second before the introductions were made.

"Kore, this is Minos, King of Crete and his wife, Queen Pasiphae".

As he was saying this to me, the king bowed as low as his aged body would allow, and the queen curtsied.

Minos was the son of Zeus and a nymph named Europa, making him my half brother. I had heard the stories of how Zeus fell in love with the young nymph and when she refused to acknowledge his advances he changed himself into a great bull and came to the shore where she and her companions would play for months until one day the nymph finally overcame her fear and mounted this magnificent animal. Immediately Zeus plunged into the sea with the frightened maiden on his back and with her hanging on to his horns he swam to the island of Crete. It was on this island that she bore Zeus three children, Minos being the eldest, followed by Sarpedon and Rhadamanthys before Zeus married her to the mortal Asterion and made him the king of

Crete. At his mortal father's death Minos took over rule of the island and has ruled it since. He obtained the throne of Crete not with the help of my father, for Hera would not allow Zeus to help his son, but with the aid of the Sea God, Poseiden, and with the assistance of such a powerful God, Minos was able to gain control over not only Crete, but all the Aegean Islands. He had been portrayed throughout history as a powerful and just ruler who has earned the respect of not only father, but the respect of most of the Gods.

Minos although being the son of a powerful God didn't have all immortal blood and was considered only a lesser deity. He was mortal and would face death as all mortals must, but still I was surprised that he appeared old and frail, with long gray hair and beard. He must have been very old indeed, since divine blood slows down aging, allowing some of the children of the Gods to live for thousands of years. Minos, even though he was Zeus' son, looked much older than his father. The Olympians, like the Titans before them and the second generation Olympians, of which I am one, are immortal, and do not age once we reach maturity, but the children born of the lesser Gods or of nymphs are mortal and therefore are destine to die. Looking at the King's shriveled hands and bent body I thought that he must have ruled this island for centuries.

Completely contrasting the King was his bride Queen Pasiphae, the daughter of the Titan Helios, the Sun deity, and a minor Goddess named Perseis, Queen Pasiphae looked as if age would never touch her. She had pure white skin, almost translucent and thick brown hair that was pulled into a loose twist, allowing little wisps falling to frame her face. She had her father Helios' eyes, a light golden brown flecked with gold as bright as the sun itself surrounding the iris. She stood before me wearing a white gauze robe with colored ribbons around the waist, blowing in the wind. The fabric of her robe was sheer enough to glimpse her body beneath without really exposing it. She was extremely beautiful, and I knew why King Minos loved her, but I couldn't understand why she, who could have had any mortal of her choosing or even one of the Gods themselves, would chose a man who was old enough to be her father.

My father interrupted my thoughts by saying,

"Kore, Hades and I will leave you in the care of Minos, I have many things to discuss with him since we see each other only rarely". Zeus said, and seeing the disappointed look on my face, added, "Don't worry, I promise you'll see him tomorrow morning".

Hades walked over to me and whispered in my ear,

"I'll come to Minos' palace early tomorrow morning for you". With this, he quickly kissed my cheek and left with my father.

"I'll be waiting". I called out after them.

I sat within the king's gilded chariot and silently looked out the window at the passing huts until we reached the city walls, and as we approached the double gateway slowly opened to us, showing me the first glimpse of the city Knossos, the city that would be my home for the next year and a day. Once within the city the chariot stopped and the king, queen and I traveled to the palace on foot. The royal palace was at the heart of this splendid city surrounded by residences, the market and administrative centers, and as we slowly walked through the city streets I watched children run ahead as their parents pushed carts along the gravel roads. Wherever we walked the town folk stopped before us and soon silence filled the air as all bowed low to the King and Queen, and then to my surprise they bowed to me. We walked like this, for about half an hour before we reached the palace of King Minos, located on the southern coast of the island.

The palace was a massive structure with over a thousand rooms on three separate levels. Its passageways seemed to shift and twist even as you walk within them, causing many to get lost within the maze, thus helping to create the legend of the labyrinth holding its dark secrets deep within. Throughout the centuries this labyrinth within the palace was rumored to be the home of a terrible beast that ate only human flesh, a terrible monster with the body of a man and the head of a great bull; a monster called the Minotaur. He was the son of Queen Pasiphae and a great white bull that Poseidon sent to Minos to sacrifice to the Gods. It was ironic that Poseidon sent a magnificent white bull to Minos, since it was in this form that Zeus mated with his mother and conceived him. Why Minos refused to sacrifice this bull, instead sacrificing one of his own, I didn't know at the time. As punishment Poseidon enchanted the Queen so she would fall in love with the bull and with the help of the court magician Daedalus, Pasiphae was able to express her love and the child produced from this union was the monster named the Minotaur. Whether or not this is only a myth or based on reality I won't say here, I'll leave that tale for another part of my story.

Let me briefly tell you of the palace of King Minos, it was almost as impressive as my father's palace on Mount Olympus. The central court, located on the main level, was able to seat thousands of visitors. This court had huge stained glass windows that covered all four walls, illuminating the entire room as beautiful colors danced off the walls when the sun shone. At night this hall was illuminated by several candelabras that were suspended from the high ceiling, which was painted with images of the creation of the world and many scenes from what has come down through the centuries as only myths. It was here in this grand room that the King conducted all court business, sitting on his gilded thrown at the far end of the hall as the town folk gathered around presenting their cases to him.

Surrounding the central court were several halls each as impressive, some for dining, and dancing, and other for which I didn't know the purpose, one being a small room with light green marble walls and carved within the back wall of marble was a sculpture of a massive tree with branches reaching up to the heavens, each one reaching higher. On the end of each of these branches was a small shelf, and perched on each shelf was a single engraved jar. No two jars were alike, and I couldn't tell what these jars contained, for no one in the palace would speak of that room. It was only much later that I came to realize that these jars contained the ashes of the ancestors. I was surprised to learn this, since at that time in history, the dead were usually not cremated, they were buried. There were many other rooms that I didn't visit during my stay with the King and Queen, these included the kitchens, workshops and the servants' quarters located on the first level behind the central court.

In the central court, across from the king's thrown was a grand staircase that spiraled up to the second level of the palace. Here were the shrines to the many Gods and Goddesses worshiped by the royal family, along with the private chambers of the King and his three children, Androgeos, Ariadne, and Phaedra, leaving the third level entirely to the Queen and her numerous servants. I would be staying in one of the rooms belonging to her. She took my hand and led me up the stairs to the third level and showed me the chamber that would be my home for the next year. It was a small chamber compared to the one I occupied on Mount Olympus, but by mortal standards it would be considered very large. The Queen told me that some mortals' entire homes aren't as big as this one chamber. The room was dark when we entered, so the Queen walked to the only window in the room and opened the curtains letting the bright sunlight flood the room, causing me to cover my eyes until they adjusted to the brightness. Across the room was a niche with bright green velvet drapes covering the opening. She pulled the drapes open showing me the king-sized bed covered in the same color green silk and velvet bedding, with numerous pillows thrown across. The room was simple, decorated using the fresco technique, where earth pigments were brushed onto the plaster before it had dried, and the scenes were a mixture of life-sized murals along with miniatures portraying the lives of the Gods. There were no other decorations within the room; none were needed, except for the mosaic floor, which was made from various colored pebbles, again depicting scenes of the Gods.

"You must be tired after your long journey".

She said to me as she clapped her hands, signaling for several of her servants to enter. Immediately the servants pushed aside the curtains that concealed a second doorway and entered the chamber and slowly walked over to me. Without saying a word to either the Queen or I, the two servants took me by the arms guided me to a large stone tub located in the center of the room. In this tub the water was continually kept hot. Still, without speaking they started to undress me. One slowly reached for the broach that held my robe in place, and when she unfastened it the soft fabric fell to my feet. The servants lead me into the tub holding my arms to steady me as I slowly lowered into the warm water. While I was soaking another servant brushed my hair, and with a silk ribbon tied it up so it wouldn't get wet while I was bathing. Instantly the scent filled my senses relaxing me totally, and as I sat there, surrounded by warm water with my eyes closed one servant massaged my body with perfumed oil, while the other continued to brush my hair. I heard a lyre playing in the distance and this sound along with the warm water and the scents filling the air around me almost caused me to fall asleep.

This was the first time in my life that I was treated as a Goddess. Back home, on Mount Olympus, I was thought of as only a minor Goddess, and that is only because my father was the Great God Zeus. Had any other God fathered me, Hera would not have allowed mother and I to resided within the palace, our home would have been among one of the many cottages that surround the royal grounds, but since Demeter is not only a first generation Olympian, but also one of the most powerful Goddesses, Hera couldn't use her influence to keep us out of Mount Olympus, so we were tolerated within the palace. But, here on earth, in this simple palace, I was being treated if I was Hera herself. I dare not say that out loud, for fear that Hera would hear me: The Gods don't like others to boast of their good fortune.

After the servants finished bathing me, they dressed me in the finest silk robes of pure white with silver and gold embroidery along the hem, and one plaited my hair, pulling it off my face and securing it with several golden pins on the top of my head as other massaged perfumed oil into my skin. When they were finished dressing me, they led me to the canopied bed and helped me down. As I sat there one of the servants kneeled at my feet waiting for me to release her.

"You are free to leave, I'll call if I require anything". I said to them.

The servant who appeared to be in charge of the others picked up a small bell that was on the table next to the bed and handed it to me and bowed low before speaking,

"My Lady, we are here to serve you. If you desire anything, anything at all, all you have to do is ring this bell and one of your faithful servants will attend to your heart's desires".

As she said this, all three servants bowed low before quietly backing out of the room. I laid on the bed and thought about what had happened that day. Not only did I finally meet Hades, but I found out that I would soon be his bride, the arrangements were being made as I sat there, I was sure of it. For the next year and a day I would live here in this palace with servants attending all my needs during the day, and Hades to occupy my evenings with, and as my head filled with these delicious thoughts I instantly fell asleep.

IV
Demeter

    LET ME BRIEFLY interrupt my daughter Kore's story here, for there are many reasons I behaved the way I did; and even though it will be hard for mortals to understand my motives, let me do my best to try to clarify them here. But before I begin, let me introduce myself. I am an old Goddess, though I don't look it, my long flowing hair is a light golden blonde, the color of spun silk that was kissed by the Sun and my skin as flawless as a pearl. My body is still as youthful and firm as it was when I was still an innocent Goddess, many, many centuries ago. My name is Demeter and I am the Goddess of Agriculture and Fertility and it is through me that all life on earth continues. I'm one of the original Olympian Gods and have been around since before the creation of mortal life. I've seen many cultures develop only to be destroyed, then baring witness as yet another, more advanced culture flourishes in its place; a cycle that imitates my creation of the seasons, one spring fades away as the summer season waxes in strength before it too wanes as fall once again approaches, followed by winter, only to start all over again with the beginning of a new year; a new year filled with new promises.

    Throughout the centuries I've been in contact with countless Gods and Goddess, some whose stories you may have heard many tales about, and others that little to nothing has been written. I've known most of these Gods and Goddesses intimately and could tell many tales to you, but I won't relate these here. The only tale I wish to reveal to you is that which concerns my daughter Kore and her marriage to my brother, the Lord of the Underworld, Hades. As I said earlier, I have many reasons why I didn't wish for my daughter to marry Hades. Many will think the reason is that Hades is my brother, making him Kore's uncle, but this matters little to me. You see, incestuous relationships are quite common among the Gods, as you see my daughter Kore was fathered by my own dear brother, Zeus, and our parents, Rhea and Cronus were also brother and sister. Others may have heard that many years before Kore was born I was involved in an intimate relationship with Hades, and some say that he refused my amorous advances and that it was a fit of jealousy that swayed my decision, but this isn't so. I didn't want my daughter to marry Hades for one reason and one reason alone; Hades is the Lord of the Underworld, and I feared that she would not survive spending eternity within that dreadful place, so far from her loving mother and father.

Let me briefly describe to you the circumstances that occurred before Kore's birth, and only after you've heard these may you be able to better understand my motives.

I begin my tale during the war between the Titans and Olympians. At this time I was Zeus' lover, and the night after the Olympians finally defeated the Titans, while we were laying in bed together and I was in his arms he described to me some of the horrors he witnessed during his voyage to the Underworld where he free the Cyclopes and the Hundred Handed Giants who were held prisoners in the Dungeon of the Damned, Tartarus. I'll do my best to relate these horrors here. Though it was so many centuries ago I can still remember the story he told, the smallest details were burned into my memory, and no matter how hard I try, I cannot forget the look of terror on his face as he began relating these terrors to me.

Just days before his voyage into the Underworld, the Titans unleashed a terrible weapon on the Gods, killing many of them and Zeus fearing that they would soon overtake the remaining Gods traveled to the Oracle hoping to find a way of finally defeating our enemies. On his return he came straight to me and revealed what the Oracle had told him.

I held my breath as he spoke,

"The only way for us to defeat the Titans and to win this war is for me to travel deep within the Underworld".

I gasped, "You can't!"

"I must, and I must go alone".

"How will this help us win"? I asked, not wanting him to face the terrors that the Underworld held.

"The Oracle made it clear; the only way to win this war is if I free the prisoners within, and with their assistance we could finally end this war before it destroys the entire Universe".

Though I longed for the war to end; death is so unnatural for a Fertility Goddess, I feared for my dear brother's safety. I, along with the other Gods and Goddesses pleaded with him not to go, but he wouldn't listen no matter how we begged. That night, as I laid in his bed I held him within my arms and begged that he not go, but with the coming dawn he began dressing for his long journey, a journey that would take him to the depths of the known world. I didn't move as he dressed, I only sat there in his bed crying. He said nothing, and when he was finally ready to leave, he kissed me once on my forehead, and as the tears fell down my cheeks, he left the palace of the Titans. I thought that I had lost him for eternity, for I knew that no one, not even a God as powerful as Zeus would be allowed to leave the dungeon Tartarus.

He traveled for an entire day before coming to the River Styx, the gloomy river that surrounds the Underworld; and once there he gathered all his courage and stood on the river's bank and disrobed before plunging naked into the icy waters below. He took no weapons with him, for none would help him where he was destined to go. The current swiftly brought him to the main entrance of the Underworld where he was confronted by Grief, Anxiety, Disease, Old Age, Fear, Hunger, Death and Agony. Just beyond is a single Tree, a magnificent Elm tree growing just beyond his reach, the Tree of False Dreams, where every leaf holds a false hope and unrealized dream. Zeus passed by these without much difficulty, being such a powerful God, he was immune to the despair that would destroy mere mortals. Once past the entrance he came upon Cerberus, the three-headed guard dog who will let any soul within the gates, but will refuse them passage back to the world of the living. Zeus had no trouble passing Cerberus, but he feared the hound would prevent him from leaving and he would spend eternity within this dreadful prison. He was determined not to allow these fears from stopping him from entering; it was his destiny to free the prisoners held deep within the earth. He would have to find some way to escape once his task was complete, or he would perish in the attempt.

Once within the Underworld, the waters of the river Styx flowed into the River Acheron, or River of Woe, and Zeus continued swimming through the marshy waters, which weighed him down with despair, trying to pull him under. Gasping for air as the marsh plants twisted around his arms and legs preventing him from moving and dragging him down further into the bog, he thought he would drown. It took several hours before he was able to completely free himself from their grip. Once freed, he continued swimming until the river once again split, this time into two branches causing a whirlpool of swirling water and hot mud that smelled of the sulfur that boiled up from the center of the earth. The river leading to the right becomes the Pyriphlegethon, or River of Fire, which surrounds Tartarus, and to left the Cocytus, or River of Lament, which now leads to the Elysian Fields beyond. It is here, where the river parts that the souls of the recently departed are judged, those who lived a just life are directed to the left branch, to the Elysian Fields and those who committed sins against either the Gods or mortals were forced to travel the other way, along the River of Fire to Tartarus where their punishment would continue for eternity; that is unless their victims would released their souls and free them from their tortures. At this time, since mortal death was still unknown, the Elysian Fields were nothing more than a barren patch of land, and the only inhabitants of the Underworld were those who would not bow to our father Cronus, and were thrown into this dungeon. Those imprisoned within Tartarus couldn't even hope for freedom, for Cronus allow none to escape. Even after his death, they could not hope to be released, for Cronus' followers refused to release them, knowing that they would surly join the Olympians in the war and bring about the defeat of the Titans.

The Dungeon of the Damned was Zeus' destination therefore he chose the path to the right, where the waters of the Pyriphlegethon instantly turned from icy cold to boiling hot as lava bubbled up from the womb of the earth. Zeus, his skin burning from the heat of the river, continued fighting the urge to leave his quest and return to the safety of the other Olympians; he endured this terrible pain until he finally reached the first of three bronze barriers that surrounds the prison of Tartarus. Stepping on the filthy shore, he wiped most of the mud from his body before walking to the Iron Gate and the enormous pillars that mark the entrance to this prison. He stood in front of the gate, his naked body covered with sweat and mud from the river, and here he faced the beautiful Goddess Tisiphone, the Erinye whose name means 'Avenger of murder'. She sits alone day and night at the entrance guarding the gates from any who wish to pass.

At the sight of the beautiful Goddess, Zeus did what he does with all beauty, he tried to seduce her. Tisiphone was the most beautiful Goddess he had ever seen, with long blonde hair and skin as white as marble, but as he approached her with open arms, she began to grow in stature and soon she was towering over him. Thunder and lightening flashed behind her; Zeus watched in horror as her pure white robes became tattered and covered with the bloodstains of her victims. He stood there not allowing her to see his fear, as he watched a pair of broad gray wings slowly spring from her shoulders blades and open wide behind her and as her beautiful golden hair transformed into a mass of wiggling snakes, turning this once beautiful Goddess into a beast so hideous that he dare not look at her for fear of being turned to stone.

Zeus gathered all his courage and prepared to fight his way past this hideous Goddess, but was surprised to find that she stood to the side and held her hand out, gesturing for him pass through the iron gates and leave the flaming river that surrounds Tartarus behind him. You see, the Goddess Tisiphone looks deep into the hearts of all those who enter the Underworld and will not let any soul who is morally blameless enter into Tartarus; one of her functions as an Eriyes, or Goddesses of Vengeance and Retribution, is to avenge the shedding of a parent's blood. Since Zeus had not only killed, but also dismembered his own father, she moved to the side to let him enter freely. Zeus had finally reached the darkest depths of the Underworld, the dungeon where his father Cronus had imprisoned all who would not obey his rule, leaving them to suffer an eternity of punishments.

Once within this dungeon it took him a few moments to adjust to the total darkness that surrounded him, and once his eyes became accustomed to the surroundings he saw that he was face to face with the Cyclopes and the Hundred Handed Giants who he had come to free. As he stood there looking at them terror seized him, for the Cyclopes were giants at lest twenty feet tall, each with a single eye in the middle of their massive forehead, who were used to eating the flesh of others. The Hundred Handed Giants, well, as their name describes, they were semi-human giants but much taller that the Cyclopes, and each possessed a hundred arms all strong enough to crush a God, even one as powerful as Zeus. He was relieved to see that they were all chained to the far end of the wall with a magical chain that couldn't be broken by even the Gods themselves. Next to them stood the two sisters of Tisiphone, Megaira and Alekto, who continually flogged the captives, causing blood to pour down their backs.

After some persuading; Zeus being such a smooth talker, especially with Goddesses; he was able to convince the two sisters to leave him alone with the prisoners, and once alone with them it was easy for him to convince them to join the side of the Olympians and fight their brother Titans in return for their freedom. With the arrangement made Zeus walked up to one of the Cyclopes and tried with all his strength to break the chains that securely held the prisoner tight, but they wouldn't budge. He tried and tried but no matter how hard he pulled on the chains, he couldn't break them. Hope had left him and he was just about to give up when one of the Cyclopes, Steropes, quietly whispered to him,

"Near the entrance, just beyond the Goddess Tisiphone, there are several magical thunderbolts that were entrusted to her to protect centuries ago. Your father, Cronus feared that if his son were to possess these great weapons, he would one day use them to destroy him. It was foretold by the Oracle that if the youngest son of Cronus were to acquire these thunderbolts, he would be the most powerful God in the Universe".

Zeus looked up past the Goddess and when he saw the magical thunderbolts his eyes lit with desire to posses these.

"With your strength, you'll be able to use these weapons and break the chains that bind us to this prison, giving us our freedom".

Steropes said this as Zeus began to climb the stone stairs that spiraled up to the top level where the snake-haired Goddess Tisiphone sat watching as his neared. He tried several times to pass her, but each time one of the venomous snakes that were woven in her hair would lash out and sink long fangs into his skin, releasing deadly venom. With blood running down his face and the poison starting to affect his body, he fell backward, tumbling down the stone stairs, back into the pit Tartarus. Steropes, seeing that Zeus was in danger of the poison traveling throughout his body and soon paralyzing him, wiped the blood from Zeus' face and with a sharp stone cut into the skin over each bite and once the blood flowed freely, he pressed his mouth to the open cut and slowly sucked all the poison venom from his body. When the Cyclops was finished tending to each bite Zeus began to gain his strength back; he sat up and once again contemplated the situation. Upon seeing this, the seven Cyclopes became excited, wanting their freedom. They were shouting at him, but he didn't understand what they were saying. Finally Brontes, one of the other Cyclopes, neared him hissing in his ear,

"I know a way for you to pass Tisiphone without her even noticing you".

"How"? asked Zeus weakly

"There's a golden helmet that my brothers and I made for Cronus that will make any who wear it invisible. Cronus' spies would use this helmet to gather information that they would then pass to the Titans. When Cronus was destroyed and his blood mixed with the rivers of the Underworld Thanatos, the God of Death, was born and this helmet now belongs to him. He uses this while he is out hunting, and invisible he is able to sneak up upon his prey. This helmet cannot leave this place with anyone other than the ruler of the Underworld, but you can use it down here, and the second it touches your head, you will become invisible to Tisiphone and be able to pass her. You'll easily be able to reach the Thunderbolts and release us from our chains".

Using all his strength to get up, still weak from the poison, Zeus looked around the dungeon, straining to see in the dark. After scanning the dungeon for several minuets and still not seeing the helmet he thought it must truly be invisible. Suddenly as he turned his head back toward the Cyclopes he spied a glittering near the flaming river, instantly he know this must be the magical helment the Cyclopes spoke of. He once again climbed the treacherous stairs and upon reaching the top step he held out his hand, but no matter how hard he tried, the helmet was just out of his reach. More than once he lost his balance and almost fell within the river below as his feet slipped on the slimy mud that covered the rocks. One of the three Hundred Handed Giants, seeing him fail repeatedly feared that if he didn't reach this helmet they would never be released from their prison, so he picked him up and without any effort, tossed him against the wall. Zeus hit the rock wall hard, knocking all the air from his lungs, and as he was sliding down he was able to knock the helmet from its resting place before crashing to the ground with a loud thud. The helmet fell a few feet from where he landed. It took him a few moments to recover from this fall, and once he had he realized that the helmet was within his reach. Tisiphone also seeing the golden helmet jumped to her feet and tried to reach it before he could. She was too late; Zeus snatched the helmet and placed it upon his head, instantly disappearing from sight. It was easy for him, now invisible, to sneak passed the angry Goddess as the snakes in her hair tried to lash out and strike him. Once past her he easily took the Thunderbolts that once belonged to his father, and were now rightfully his. A deafening howl filled the dungeon as she realized that this God was now was in possession of the most powerful weapon ever created, and in a fury she held up her sword and started slashing in the air where she thought Zeus might be.

    Zeus, who was quick on his feet and was able to dodge her swings easily, ran to where the Cyclopes were and using the Thunderbolts easily broke through the magical chains that bound them and gave them their freedom. The prisoners were freed from their bounds, but now he had to figure out a way to leave this underground prison. It was only with the help of his new allies and much fighting all were able to finally pass from the world of darkness into the world of light. Once freed, the Cyclopes and Hundred-Handed Giants kept their promise and took their place on the battlefield all that is except one of the Hundred-Handed Giants, Gyes, who once freed joined his brothers, the Titans and fought against the Gods. After the war Zeus took great pleasure when he imprisoned this traitor back in Tartartus where he still is today.

After telling me of his decent into Tartarus, Zeus declared that he would never set foot in the Underworld again, for dreams of the horrors he saw there still haunt him. Zeus told me all this the night after the Olympians finally defeated the Titans, and it was during this night that I conceived my first child with him, a son who I named Iacchus. You couldn't imagine my surprise when a few nights later the Goddess Ananke was summoned to pass out our fate, and the anger I felt as she declared that my unborn daughter would be destined to spend eternity within the Underworld. I was the only one who objected to her decision, I hoped that Zeus would support me, not wanting to see his daughter dwell within this dreadful place, for he alone of all the Gods knew what horrors awaited her there, but he said nothing. None of the other Gods or Goddesses, my sisters and brothers would support me, and I alone decided that night that I would do everything within my power to make sure that my daughter would not marry Hades.

That night I wasn't aware that I was with child, and when I found out, I was sure that this was going to be the child that was destine to dwell in the Underworld. You cannot imagine my anxiety during the nine months leading to the birth of my first child, but when the night of the birth finally arrived I was relieved to find that Zeus fathered a son. I was determined that I would never have another child with him and stopped my intimate relations with him immediately. My sister Hera took advantage of the tension that grew between Zeus and myself by feeding his fears, and within a few weeks after I gave birth to my son, Zeus announced that he was to wed Hera. The despair I felt was unimaginable, I had not only lost a lover and future husband, for you see I was the fairest of the three Olympians Goddesses and should have been Zeus' wife, but I also lost my unborn daughter that night.

It was only later that I found out the real reason that Zeus could never support me; for after drinking from the waters of the river Styx, and swearing to accept the decision of the Goddess Ananke, Zeus feared that if any the six siblings disobeyed her ruling, all would suffer the consequences. Zeus didn't fear that he would die, being immortal, death didn't frighten him, instead he feared that not only would I lose my position of Goddess of Agriculture and Fertility, but that he would lose his position as God of the Heavens and be made

King of the Underworld as punishment for disobeying the Goddess of Destiny. He wouldn't let that happen, even if it meant sacrificing his daughter.

Knowing that I wouldn't allow him to father another child with me, Zeus planned a way of deceiving me. Many years after the birth of my son, I became amorous of a minor deity, a mortal named Iasion, a son of Zeus and a mortal woman, and it was in this form that Zeus approached me one night, and during our hours of passionate lovemaking I conceived my second child with him. When I found out about his trickery I became furious and fled from Mount Olympus. I went alone to the palace of my brother Poseidon deep within the oceans, and it was there that I gave birth to my daughter. I named her Kore for that was the word for Maiden and I hoped that she would remain a maiden forever. I wanted to keep her there, away from both of my brothers, Zeus and Hades, but Destiny would not allow this to happen.

After several years of living within his palace Poseidon fell madly in love with me. My feelings for him were not the same, and no matter how many times I told him this he wouldn't accept it. He followed me wherever I went. Finally to get away from his advances I changed my self into the form of a beautiful mare and hid among the horses of King Oncus in Arcadia, but this didn't discourage Poseidon, who just a easily changed into a magnificent steed and in this guise we mated.

This union produced not only one child, but two, a son and a daughter. My son by Poseidon doesn't possess human form, instead was born a magnificent stallion that I named Areion. Areion was a magical horse and like Pegasus had the ability to fly, but instead of being pure white as Pegasus was, he was a beautiful shining black stallion who not only conquered flight, but who could speak with both the Gods and mortals. I left Areion in the care on Oncus, who raised him and watched over him. Areion lived with many heroes and kings on earth, but now resides with the other magical creatures on Mount Olympus where I see him daily.

My second child born on the next night was a beautiful girl who I named Despoena. There are myths that say she was, like the Centaurs, a beautiful woman from the waist up on the body of a mare, and that she became the lover of Chiron, but this is not so. Yes, she did love Chiron, and they were together for many centuries before death took him and she vowed that she would never love another. It was because of her love for Chiron, which couldn't die with him, that she went deep into the woods to live alone. She became a mysterious figure who could be seen on nights when the moon is full, known to humans only as the Mistress, her true name could only be spoken in the Eleusinian Mysteries.

    I won't linger here on tales of my other children for I don't wish to distract from the tale my daughter Kore started. All I will say is that I left Poseidon's palace and with nowhere else to go, I returned to the palace on Mount Olympus. All the Gods and Goddesses welcomed both my daughter Kore and myself, but I announced that I would leave the palace again and never return if Hades ever sets foot on Mount Olympus. He tried to come shortly after our arrival, offering a gift to my young daughter, Kore, but I refused to allow him into the palace. I kept my daughter sheltered, far from where Hades was.

    While we were in the care of Poseidon, she became friends with many of the Sea Nymphs, and once I returned to Mount Olympus I would allow her to visit them on earth. Poseidon, still being in love with me promised that he would watch over her and not let her near our brother Hades, and I was foolish enough to believe him. Yes, I made many mistakes raising her, I should never have allowed her to leave my side, but then I was young and foolish, and one should learn to not live with regrets. Kore's fate was sealed that night so long ago, along with the other Olympians. I don't think that anything I could have done would have prevented her from falling in love and marrying Hades. She was destine to become Queen of the Dead.

    So you see, I have done everything within my power to keep my daughter safe from harm. I did this not to punish her, or Hades, as she still believes. All I ever wanted to do was to keep her from having to endure eternity living within the Underworld and to be parted from her only family. Any parent, who loves their child, would do whatever they could to ensure that their own flesh and blood were kept safe from harm, and I'm no different. I know that my daughter still does not understand my intentions, and for many years she wouldn't even speak to me, but throughout the centuries we have come to an understanding.

V
Persephone

    THE YEAR THAT I lived on earth with King Minos and his beautiful wife, Queen Pasiphae, was one of the happiest times of my life. During my brief stay with these mortals I tasted the life of a Goddess. This was the first time that humans worshiped me, and whether they showed me this respect due to the fact that they feared the wrath of my father, Zeus or not didn't matter much to me. Each day I would meet with my future husband early in the afternoon, spending the entire day on the island getting acquainted with each other, then just after sunset I would return to the palace where I was waited on hand and foot by my many servants. It did take a bit of getting use to, having servant constantly following me around, but soon I began to enjoy all the attention I was getting. Even when I was with Hades there were at least two servants watching over me in the distance, making sure to be far enough from us where they couldn't hear our private conservations, but always within sight of us. When Hades and I kissed, they did their best to not notice these intimate moments between us, but still I felt a little uncomfortable, and I'm sure that Hades felt the same.

    King Minos feared that if anything happen to me while I was in his care, Zeus would not only destroy him but his entire kingdom, so he made sure I was surrounded by his faithful servants day and night. The only time that I was alone with Hades was for the brief time I visited him in the Underworld, for not even the fear of Zeus would force King Minos to allow his servants to travel to the Underworld. He knew that no mortals who set foot into that realm would be permitted to leave, so the first time I went there; I traveled alone.

Mother visited me several times during that year, being an Earth Goddess brought her to earth daily and in her spare time she would come to the Island of Crete for a brief time. Before each of her visits Hermes would appear and warn us that mother was on her way. Hades would kiss me briefly before disappearing in a flash of bright light. I don't know where he went, but as soon as mother was gone, he would return. I thought that mother would wonder why I wanted to stay on earth, when I had all of Mount Olympus to enjoy, but father told her that he wished for me to live among humans so that one day I could assist her with her duties, and I went along with this story, making sure never to mention Hades' name when I was with her. She seemed pleased that I was becoming acquainted with the customs of mortal life. King Minos and the Queen were placed in an awkward situation. When Demeter came to his land, he and his wife were careful to not allow Zeus' deception be revealed in their words to the Goddess. Even though they feared Demeter's wrath, they feared Zeus' more, and though they never actually lied to her, they both did their best to avoid her altogether. Zeus wasn't the only God they feared offending, for even though Zeus was the most powerful God, Hades ruled the Underworld, and once there, not even death would release you from his wrath.

I was glad that mother didn't posses the ability to read others thoughts as both Hades and my father had, for she would have discovered our plan instantly and forced me to return to Mount Olympus with her. It was torture for me not being able to confide in her. Each day that brought me closer to my wedding, my anxiety grew. As a young bride to be I wanted nothing more than to plan my wedding with my beloved mother, but I knew that I must be silent. When mother would visit me I wanted nothing more than to jump up and down and tell not only her, but also the whole world that I was in love, but I couldn't say a word to anyone. Even though the servants knew that Hades and I were courting they dare not speak to anyone about it, I think that King Minos warned them that if any of the Gods overheard them they would instantly be dragged into the Underworld and face eternity in the Dungeon of the Damned.

The months passed quickly and the year was coming to an end and I had not yet visited the Underworld once. Both Hades and father agreed that I wouldn't be permitted to marry until I had seen for myself the palace I would spend eternity within. Father feared that once I beheld the horrors within the Underworld I would never agree to the marriage, and by my refusal, it would not be him, but me who went against Destiny. I must tell you that the first time I entered Hades' realm I was more than a little nervous. None of the Gods who lived on Mount Olympus ever visited the Underworld, except for Hermes, who as Psychompompus, would lead the souls of the newly departed to the river Styx where the ferryman Charon would guide them through the gates into the world of the dead. During this part of his duty he did not pass through the gates himself, he only guided the souls to the river's edge. The only time Hermes would enter Hades' Palace was when Zeus needed him to deliver a message to his brother, for Zeus knew that no other God would set foot in Hades' palace.

During the year between the times I had first glimpsed Hades emerging from the Underworld and when I spoke my first words to him I had questioned Hermes many times about what it was like in the Underworld.

"Why would you even ask of such a place, when you not only have all of Mount Olympus to fill your thought with, but with the entire earth"? Was all he would say to my many questions.

I felt as if I was being pulled in two directions at once, I wanted nothing more than to be Hades' wife, but I also dreaded the idea of spending eternity confined within the Underworld. No matter how hard I tried to convince myself that the Underworld couldn't be so horrible since after getting to know Hades I realized that he wasn't the terrible monster that I grew up believing him to be. I kept telling myself that if he could endure living within the Underworld for so many centuries alone, I would also be able to endure it, especially if he would be at my side. But no matter how many times I told this to myself I couldn't free my mind of the childhood stories of the terrible monsters that dwelled deep within the bowels of the earth.

When the time finally arrived for me to see the palace that I would spend the rest of my life in I was horrified. That morning, well before dawn, Hades came to the palace of King Minos and they spoke in hushed voices outside as I watched from the window of my bedchamber. I hurried and dressed, then waited for my servants to summon me to the main hall where I knew Hades would be waiting, but no one came. After what seemed an eternity, I left my chamber and hurried downstairs expecting to see Hades there, but he was nowhere to be found. I was perplexed. All that morning and afternoon I spent waiting, or should I say pacing in back and forth within the royal garden. I couldn't help wondering why he didn't come for me.

"What have I done to offend him"?

I kept thinking about the day before, did I say or do something wrong? My imagination continued to supply reasons for him coming to the palace so early.

"He came earlier than I expected, hoping to talk to King Minos alone, explaining that he wouldn't be returning, that mother would soon be arriving to take me back to Mount Olympus".

I don't know how many hours I was sitting in the garden in a trance, but when I finally looked up I noticed that it was almost dusk. I returned to the palace and prepared for bed, and as I laid down I felt the wetness of the tears as they began filling my eyes. I held them back as best as I could, but soon I felt single tear fall down my cheek. As I wiped it I heard one of my servants knocking on the door. Sitting up in bed, I made sure that I was presentable, and that no one would notice that I was crying.

"Enter", I said after I was satisfied

"Forgive me my Lady, I came to tell you that the God Pluton, Lord of the Underworld, is waiting for you downstairs". She spoke quietly as she entered the chamber. I jumped up and was about to run downstairs, when she stopped me, shyly saying,

"My lady, before you greet your Lord, let me plait your hair and anoint you with perfumed oil".

The few minuets I sat there as she made me up seemed like an eternity. I wanted to rush downstairs and find out why my love was so late in meeting me. When she was finished, I didn't even thank her, but ran out into the hall as fast as I could. I continued to run until I reached the landing above the great hall where I paused, not wishing for Hades to see me rushing to greet him. I knew instantly that something was wrong, for he didn't answer my questions. He took me by the hand and we walked outside to where his chariot, the one I had seen that first day spring from the earth, waited for us. He effortlessly lifted me up to my seat, then sat quietly next to me. I didn't know where he was taking me, for all I knew he might have been taking me home to mother. At first I thought my suspicions were confirmed when I realized that this was the first time we were totally alone, for none of the servants were accompanying us. Hades tried to calm me by talking in a sweet voice, as if he were trying to calm a frighten animal, but I didn't hear a single word that he said. I feared that I would never see him again.

"Kore, are you listening to me"? As he said this, I woke from my thoughts and I nodded that I was, so he continued,

"Kore, today I'm going to show you my palace in the Underworld. Your father and I have discussed this, and he feels that the time for you to see the Underworld has arrived".

As he said this, he grabbed the reins with one hand and with the other he cracked his whip over the heads of the six winged horses and instantly we were off. We rode swiftly across the sea to the land of Attica, then continued south past Thebes, past Delphi, past Thessaly until, after many hours we finally reached our destination, the river Styx. The journey from Crete took longer than I expected, and by the time we reached the river Styx the sun was almost completely set, making the sky a beautiful dark purple, the full moon the only illumination. On the far bank of the river the horses came to a slow stop and Hades jumped from the chariot, and before I could follow him he said to me,

"Wait here Kore, I need to speak to the ferryman, Charon, making sure that he'll allow you to ride across the river". I looked confused, so he continued, "It's his duty to ensure that no living soul other than I enter his boat".

As I waited I could feel the grief, anxiety, and sorrow that lived across the river and a cold chill ran down my spine. Though the moon illuminating the bank, there was still a gloominess about the place, a gloominess that I didn't think would go away even in the bright of the day. After speaking with Charon, Hades returned to the chariot and held out a hand to help me down. When my feat touched the muddy ground he whispered something to the lead horse and the chariot swiftly disappeared into the fog. We were alone I thought, but then I felt the presence of others and when I looked around I noticed that there were hundreds, no thousands of souls here aimlessly wandering the banks of the river; souls of those who didn't have the fee needed to cross the river; souls of those who were doomed to wander along the shore for at least a hundred years. They were nothing but phantoms, wisps of a form that only appeared somewhat human. I didn't know what these amorphous forms were made of, only that they looked solid, but suddenly this form would evaporate and in a swirling mist would dissolve back into the fog, only to be replaced by another of these phantoms. They passed through trees and other obstacles as they swiftly floated by, and though the bank was a soft mud, their feet left no impressions. I stood there transfixed at the sight of these shades. Hades, not wanting these phantoms to notice us, took my arm and tried to guide me away, but we didn't move fast enough. They had seen us and in a frenzy they began approaching and soon we were totally surrounded by thousands of phantoms hand, all reaching out and begging for the needed fare to cross the river. Even though not one of these phantoms possessed a human voice, their pleas filled my head and I thought the sound of their screams would cause my head to burst.

    Hades, sensing my fear, said to me

    "Don't fear my darling, nothing will happen to you as long as you are with me. I'm the ruler here, and all will do as I bid". As he said this he lifted his right hand, palm facing the shades and instantaneously a bright flash of green light flowed from his outstretched fingers, causing the phantoms to be both fascinated and terrified. As he closed his hand, both the light and the energy that came with it faded, and after a brief pause he spoke to these creatures in a voice I didn't recognize. Within seconds I felt a soft breeze surround us causing all of these phantoms to back away. Once the breath touched them, their gossamer forms began to swirl, breaking up into small specks of multicolored light, which slowly began to merge with the forest behind before disappearing altoghter. We were alone once again.

    "Are you alright, my dear"? he asked.

    I tried to feign a smile as I nodded, but I known I didn't fool him. He held my hand tight as we walked to the small boat that would carry us over the river Styx and into the Underworld. I knew that once I set foot within the boat there would be no going back, and even though the shore was only a few yards away the walk there seem like an eternity. When we finally reached the dilapidated boat Charon held out his bony hand gesturing for me to place an obolus, the coin fee for my passage across the river, in his grasp.

"Kore, I would like you to meet Charon. He ferries the departed souls across the river to the other side". As Hades introduced me I held out a hand to Charon, who said nothing to me. He waved his outstretched hand as if to tell me to enter into the vessel. Charon was not a god but still an immortal, being the son of Erebus, the Personification of Darkness and Nyx, the Night. He didn't always live within the Underworld, he lived on earth for many centuries, but after the death of his wife and children, for they were not immortal like he was, he relinquished mortal life and since he himself would never die he went to the Underworld where he was given his current position. Without a word, Charon picked up the oars and handed them to me. I looked a little confused so Hades explained to me,

"Charon doesn't row the boat, he only steers it. The task of rowing is given to the souls of the dead".

As he said this he took the oars from Charon's bony hands and set them down next to me. He waved his hand over the still waters of the river Styx, and as he did I watched with fascination as the water began to slowly oscillate causing the small boat to give way to the undulating current of the black waters of the river below and we began to gradually move. As I sat there I wanted to keep my mind busy so I wouldn't dwell on the fears that were starting to strangle my thoughts, I looked around at the surroundings, and when I looked at our ferryman, I noticed the horrid conditions of Charon, his dark robes tattered and covered with filth, hung loosely from his bony shoulders. I told myself that the stains on his robes must be from the mud of the river's bank, but they looked more like the stains of dried blood. His hair and long gray beard, at least I think the color was gray, being so filthy I couldn't be certain, looked as if they hadn't been washed in centuries. I brought my gaze up to see his face, covered in the mud or blood and I noticed that he was nothing more then skin and bones. He had the appearance of a corpse that had laid out for several days and decomposition had already started.

The only life I saw in his face was his blazing red eyes, which felt as if they were shooting a jet of fire directly into my core. I had to look away, fearing that his gaze would burn my soul. He didn't speak as he steered the small boat to the shore of the Underworld, and for this I was glad, for I didn't wish to hear his horrible voice.

During the short trip across the river my future husband held my hand tightly and when we reached the shore he helped me off the boat. I had barely set my feet on the shore when Charon silently started on his journey back to the other side where he would wait for his next fare. My first impression of the Underworld was as horrible as I had expected and I wanted nothing more than to return to the Palace of Minos. Not want Hades to know my fears, I began asking questions, hoping that the sound of his voice would comfort me.

"This isn't the only passage to the Underworld, is it"? I asked

"No, it isn't, there are many entrances to the Underworld, but I wanted you to see how the souls of those who are mortal and destined to die enter this realm. The other entrances are used only by myself and those who are brave enough to visit me in my palace". He replied.

On this side of the river there were no shades of the dead, and I was glad of this since their presence caused a chill to run down my spine. Instead, I soon found out, this side of the river held greater horrors. Here was the home of Grief, Anxiety, Disease, Old Age, Fear, Hunger, Death, and Agony. Limo was the personification of Hunger, Famine and Starvation and I couldn't look at her and not feel pity; her face was pallid, her eyes sunken, and her yawning mouth was filled with only a few rotten teeth. Filth covered the tattered rags that she wore as a robe. One breast was exposed, and I could see that it was drained of all life, it just hung down to the void that was once her stomach. The emptiness of this was emphasized by the protruding hipbones and bloated legs and feet. Next to her stood Akhlys, the hag of Misery, who was just as hideous as her older sister. Akhys' skin was a pale green and brown stains, from her blood tears ran down and discolored cheeks. She leaned on her sister, who was barely strong enough to support her, wailing continuously only pausing briefly to use her filthy robe to wipe the falling blood tears as they slid down her face. When I looked at her it was as if all happiness was sucked from my soul. I couldn't stand the sight, so I closed my eyes. When they opened I then saw Geras, the personification of Old Age sitting behind the two sisters. He sat on the bare ground, too weak to stand without the aid of others. As Old Age, he was a small shriveled up man who could hardly lift his head when we approached. He sat there oblivious to all that passed by, the only movement was the shacking of his wrinkled body. His sister, Akhys stopped her wailing long enough to wipe the drool that was falling from Geras' toothless mouth.

There were many others here whose job it was to suck the last life out of the mortal souls before they could continue their journey to their new homes. Even though I was a Goddess I could feel them preying on my senses, and I knew that no mortal would be able to withstand the draining caused by these leeches. The entrance gate to the Underworld, the place that only minutes ago I feared more than anything looked inviting now. I wanted to pass through it quickly, to get away from these horrid creatures before they would gorge themselves on my spirit.

"We don't want to stay here too long, or all hope and love will be drained from you". Hades said as he quickly led me away, he continued as soon as we were far enough from them so as not to feel their pull. "After living down here for so many centuries I've become accustomed to them, but even I sometimes feel as if I would welcome death in their presence. Let's move on, I fear that they are still upsetting you". As we approached the entrance separating the two worlds, the large brass gates slowly opened and a huge three-headed dog ran up to Hades and jumped up to greet her master. Hades scratched one of the heads as the other two started licking his face and her tail began wagging.

"This is my guard dog Cerberus". Hades said as he continued petting the dog. I held out the back of my hand with caution, letting the head nearest catch my scent before trying to pet her. Once I started scratching one of the heads, she jumped up, placed her front paws on my shoulders, almost knocking me down in the process, and started licking my face. I started to laugh as Hades and I played with this three-headed, overgrown puppy. Hades threw her on the ground and started scratching her stomach as all three heads playfully bite at her master's hands. When we tried to leave, Cerberus came after us biting at Hades' robes, no wanting him not to go.

Hades gave her a last pat on the head, then we continued on foot until we reached yet another riverbank. This part of the Underworld didn't seem terrible at all, but still I was fearful of going further into this dreadful place.

We entered another small boat, a boat that would lead us deep down within the earth to the depths of the Underworld, to where the palace that I feared seeing, the palace that would one day I would call my home, was located. As we moved along the Acheron River, which some mortals call the River of Woe, I saw the Elm of False Hopes, the only tree growing on the banks of this river, and hope suddenly began to fill me.

"Do not heed this false hope my dear, for on this elm each leave holds a dream that's just out of reach, and it's this sense of hope that pulls one deeper into the Underworld". Hades warned me and I nodded that I understood.

We soon drew to a fork where the river to the right became the Pyriphlegethon, or River of Fire, the river surrounds Tartarus and the left side becomes the Cocytus, or River of Lament. Here the two rivers meet with a whirlpool of boiling lava from the Pyriphlegethon, spouting mud and slimy sand into the Cocytus, forming on its banks the Wailing Marshes, where one could always hear the wailing of the lost souls. Here is where the souls of those who committee suicide would be condemned for all eternity. As we paused here I felt the heat of the lava as it flowed just feet from where our little boat was.

"We'll be taking the path along these marshes to my palace". Hades said to me as he pointed to the path on the right. He must have sensed that I was nervous, he took my hand and asked, "Are you alright, my dear"?

I nodded before asking,

"The other river leads to Tartarus, the depths where the wicked are punished"?

I couldn't help but hear the clashing rocks and the turbulent waters, which even though loud enough to fill the cavern, they weren't loud enough to drown out the screams of those who were imprisoned within that horrid prison.

"You'll never have any need to visit that place I assure you. I seldom visit that part of my kingdom myself, leaving Thanatos, the God of Death to watch over this dungeon". Hades assured me. I nodded that I understood, then quietly sat next to Hades.

As we continued along the Cocytus River, I could see a faint light, what looked like the dawn, which shone over the Marshes. As we moved along the river I noticed that the light slowly became brighter and I could start to see that the marshes were soon replace with green pastures speckled with what at first looked like nothing more than black spots, but soon I realized that the fields were filled with hundreds of coal black cattle grazing. I could see a small cottage behind the pasture where an elderly man was tending these magnificent creatures.

"That's Menoetes", Hades said to me as he pointed to him, "He's in charge of the care of my cattle".

Before I could answer, Hades continued,

"I have many servants here in the Underworld, Menoetes watches over the cattle; Ascalaphus is the gardener who tends the orchards that surround the palace; Aeacus, a son of Zeus who in life ruled the island of Aigina, was after his death appointed as one of the judges of the Underworld, he also holds the keys to this realm. Another Judge appointed to watch over the souls is Rhadymanthos, also a son of Zeus and the older brother of King Minos'. During his life Rhadamanthos was renowned for his wisdom and justice and because of this upon his death he was appointed to judge the souls of the dead sending only those who had committed horrendous sins to Tartarus. Not all who dwell here have come after their mortal life had passed by, many Nymphs and Daimons also serve me in the Underworld".

"Where is the light coming from, I thought the Underworld was only filled with darkness"? I asked.

"Only Tartarus is completely dark. My palace and the Elysium Fields, where the souls of heroes and virtuous people go after death, enjoy daylight. When I first became Lord here, I couldn't stand the constant darkness, so I asked Helios to create a small Sun that would rise in the Underworld when the Sun on earth sets. If you noticed when we started our journey on the river Styx the Sun was already starting its decent, night had just began on earth, but here my Sun is only starting to show his face".

As we continued along the river I was able to glimpse the palace in the distance surrounded by beautiful gardens and mountains on the right. With the Sun raising over these mountains the palace looked almost as beautiful as Mount Olympus to me and I thought that this couldn't possibly be the place that all the Gods feared. When we reached Hades' home it was like stepping into a giant geode, an enchanted land where the palace was carved entirely out of solid marble. Unlike the marble of the palace I grew up in, which was made by the Cyclopes talents, carving parian, a glistening white marble, into large blocks that were then used to build the structure. Hades' palace was different, the entire palace was carved within one huge slab of Pentelic marble, a beautiful marble that had traces of iron within and throughout the centuries these iron veins acquired a golden patina. The ceiling and walls were covered with these glittering crystals and gems and their many facets reflecting the light dazzled me. I then realized why some mortals called Hades by the name Pluto, which means 'the Rich One', for he not only rules the Underworld, but he also rules the inexhaustible richness of the earth. It is by this name, Pluto, that he became known to the Romans.

Upon entering this enchanted palace we came to the main hall, which was much smaller then the great hall of the palace on Mount Olympus, but still just as impressive, furnished with all the comforts one could wish for. Instead of being lit from the firmament as Zeus' palace is, here deep within the earth, the only source of light was several torches and candles. A fire was burning within the massive central hearth, and the torches positioned in the corners gave a romantic feel to the room. I sat down on a red velvet recliner and as Hades sat next to me I noticed that this chamber opened into a garden with beautiful flowers and trees. I was compelled to get up and slowly walk into the garden, noticing that one tree growing in the center was more beautiful than any other tree I had ever seen before. I walked up to this tree and as I stood under it I held my hand out reaching to touch its leaves when Hades, who was standing behind me, took my hand in his and whispered to me,

"Of all the trees within this garden, this one and this one alone is sacred to me".

I wondered what was special about this tree, but could tell from the look on his face that he didn't wish to tell me, at least not then. It wasn't until after we were married that I found out why this tree was so sacred, but I am getting ahead of myself here. Hades took my hand and without saying a word he led me away from this beautiful tree. We walked through the palace garden until we reached the banks of the Lethe River and the entrance of the Elysian Fields. These beautiful fields of soft green grass and flowers are where the souls of the heroes and virtuous people go after their death. Unlike Tartarus, the Elysian Fields, sometimes called the 'Island of the Blest', is filled with the souls of the heroes wrestling in the grass or playing games with each other, while others sing and dance to beautiful music. These shades, as the souls of mortal are called down here, appeared not as the phantoms who greeted us on the far banks of the river Styx, instead they retained their human form, being dressed in the finest cloths and appeared content.

"Do these souls remember their lives"? I asked

"As the souls of the newly departed travel to their home in the Elysian Fields, all are required to taste the waters of the River of Forgetfulness. Once this water touches their lips their former lives become oblivious to them".

"So all the shades within the Underworld have lost their memories of who they once were"?

"No, not all the souls. Those who are judged wicked and sent to dwell in the prison Tartarus will never taste this water, for part of their punishment is to remember their former lives, their families who they dishonored and especially their victims' pain".

We stood here watching the shades within the Elysian Fields for a few moments before walking through his gardens where I met many of his servants. Hades spent most of the day showing me the different areas of the Underworld, and just as I noticed that it was starting to get dark we headed back to his palace for the evening meal. We walked back in silence and as we were sitting at the magnificent marble table, I began to doubt what I was seeing. I had heard from all the Gods and Goddesses that the Underworld was a place filled with nothing but death and decay, where souls were tormented for eternity.

"*Was I bewitched? Had a spell been cast over me so that I wouldn't behold the true horrors of the Underworld*"?

Hades, reading my thoughts answered me,

"You're doubting that what you see is not real, only an illusion that I created to make sure that you'll agree to marry me".

"It's not that", I said, adding, "My entire life, I've been told that the Underworld is such a horrible place, that not even Zeus himself would dare to set foot into it, and when I finally do see it, it's almost as beautiful as the palace on Mount Olympus. How can that be"?

"Let me tell you, that before I was named ruler of this place, chaos ruled here. This palace didn't exist yet, it wasn't built until after the Cyclopes finished building Zeus' palace, and since there was no death until my father Cronos was killed, the Elysian Fields as they are now didn't yet exist; and as you already know there was no light down here, it was nothing but darkness, fear and death. My father created the Underworld as nothing more than a prison where horrible punishments would continue for eternity. When Zeus entered this realm to free the prisoners, he journeyed to Tartarus alone, he didn't extend his visit to any other part of this realm, and when he told of the horrors down here the other Gods didn't doubt his word. When I took over as Lord of the Underworld I thought that I would rather die than spend eternity down here. Since it was my destiny to dwell down here I decide that instead of just sitting back and accepting what Fate would hand me, I would do what ever I could to improve my situation. After allowing some light to illuminate the darkness, my spirits began to rise. Not wanting the souls of the righteous await their rebirth within the Dungeon of the Dammed, I created the Elysian Fields where they would dwell in comfort. After all that was finally complete I had this palace built".

"But why does everyone fear this place still"? I asked.

"Not everyone fears this place, as you can see, I have many nymphs who choose to live her and serve me, but growing up on Mount Olympus you were never exposed to those who have traveled here".

"I don't understand". I said,

"Zeus is the most powerful of the Gods, and when he speaks of the Underworld and shakes with fear, no God will question him. Now after you leave this place and return to Mount Olympus, would you in front of the others contradict Zeus and tell him that my palace could rival that of the great God himself"?

"No". I said, for I feared that Zeus would punish any who would doubt his word.

"As the others have all decided. Poseidon, Hecate, and Hermes along with others often visit me within this realm, but they never speak of it to anyone, especially Zeus".

"So all the horrors of the Underworld are just stories told to frighten those who would visit you"? I asked.

"No, they're true, there is the Dungeon of the Damned, Tartartus, where the souls of the wicked go to be purified. All the horror stories you have heard are tales of this Dungeon alone. Here Thanatos, the God of Death, rules".

"I wish to see this prison". I said.

"You don't need to, I assure you that it will never be required that you have anything to do with that dreadful place".

"I know that, but I must see this place for myself before I can decide if I wish to live here for eternity". I insisted.

After a short disagreement, Hades finally agreed to take me to Tartarus,

"Stay with me in my palace tonight, and in the morning I'll take you to the Dungeon of the Damned, I don't wish for you to see that dreadful place during the dark of night".

I agreed that I would wait until the morning. We spent the rest of the meal in silence, and that night, though I stayed within the palace, I didn't share Hades' bed, though that is where I would have liked to be; instead I spent the night with Daeira, a Nymph who resides in the Underworld as one of Hades' servants. Daeira and I spent most of the night giggling and telling each other our deepest secrets. I was finally able to tell someone about my feelings for Hades, how my heart melted when I first laid eyes on him. I couldn't tell mother any of this, and I seldom spoke to father; nor could I tell any of the servants of King Minos, for they didn't think of me as a young girl in love, I was a Goddess to them, so I kept my feelings tightly bottled up inside myself for almost a year. Once I opened up to Daeira, I couldn't stop and that night we formed a bond that would last for centuries. She became my dearest friend and constant companion within the Underworld.

Shortly before dawn came, Daeira left me alone, since I hadn't slept all day and most of the night had already passed by. I laid down, but fear of the following morning and my visit to Tartarus wouldn't allow sleep to come. Getting out of my bed, I walked to the window and as I looked out I saw in the distance the sky flashing with lightening, and I thought that someone must have angered father. I wondered who it was. I spent the rest of the night sitting at the window watching the lightening as it filled the sky, until I saw the first rays of this Sun illuminate Hades' palace grounds.

When Hades came for me, I was already prepared for our journey to Tartarus. He sat me down on the bed and then sitting next to me, took my hand and again tried to explain that there is no need for my visiting Tartarus, but I was insistent. We left the palace and took the Cocytus River up to where the Pyriphlegethon River meets but instead of continuing along in the small boat that would carried us along the river we continued on foot. Where we were going I didn't know, for I saw nothing but rock walls surrounding us. We walked to the eastern wall and suddenly I heard a slight rumbling noise that started to get louder and louder. I looked at the wall that was just inches from us and noticed that the rock wall started to quiver and split. Magically there appeared to be a door forming where seconds before was only bare rock. The minerals that formed the door began to groan and creek as it slowly opened exposing a small chamber constructed entirely of bronze. We stepped into this chamber and instantly the doors closed and soon I felt as if we were traveling.

"What is this room"? I asked.

"This is a special chariot which will transport us to Tartarus". Hades explained to me.

"I thought the way to reach Tartarus is by the River of Fire", I asked.

"That's how the souls of the dead enter, but Tartarus is very deep within the Earth, much deeper than my palace, it would take a long time for us to get there by boat. This chariot doesn't follow the winding path of the river, instead it goes down in a straight line through the center of the earth, stopping only when it reaches Tartarus".

As we continued to move, I could feel the hot air from the fires within, and I touched the bronze wall of this magical chariot and felt that it was warm from these same fires. When the chariot finally stopped only minuets after we entered the doors opened I faced the two giant pillars that marked the entrance of Tartarus. There a beautiful Goddess clad in pure white robes with long, thick, wavy blonde hair was sitting watch. She stood when she saw us, and Hades walked up to her, took her hand in his and raising it to his lips, kissing her hand before introducing her to me,

"Tisiphone, this is my future wife, Kore. Before we marry, she wishes to visit all of my kingdom, including this Dungeon of the Damned". He turned to me and continued,

"Tisiphone is the Goddess of Vengeance, it is her duty is to prevent any soul from leaving Tartarus before it has been purified".

With the introductions made, Tisiphone bowed slightly to me and moved to the side allowing us to enter as she said,

"As you wish my Lord".

As we entered, the stench of excrement mixed with that of burning flesh began to fill my senses. This dungeon was crowded with thousands upon thousands of souls of those who were damned. Vermin scurried around the floor looking for anything to eat. There was no light in here, except the light from the flames that burned the sins from the wicked, and as my eyes adjusted to the dim atmosphere I began to make out some details of this dungeon. We were standing at the top looking down into the pit of despair and I could see a stairway that was carved into the rock walls that separated this place from the rest of the Underworld. Even if the poor souls could free themselves from their bonds, break the chains that held their wrists and ankles to the walls, they would never be able to reach these stairs for a moat of flaming lava prevented any from passing.

As I looked into the pit, I saw a flash of light to my right and when I turned my head I saw a beautiful God approaching. He was dressed in a short robe with shining golden armor, a cuirass covering his torso with a linen layer extending below the waist and golden greaves giving his lower legs full protection. From his back two pure white wings reached out from his shoulder blades towering above him. As he walked the feathers of these beautiful wings brushed the floor. When he was near I saw that he held in his one hand a golden helmet that glittered from the light of the fires below, and in his other hand he carried a long sword. He had skin that looked as if it was carved from pure white marble, and with his short blonde curly hair he appeared as an angel. I knew that this could be no other than Thanatos, the God of Death, who is sometimes called the Angel of Death, for in his eyes I saw the blazing fires that consumed the souls of the living. Thanatos was the twin brother of Hypnos the God of Sleep and like his brother he came to mortals as non-violent death comes, his sisters the Keres are the Goddesses of Violent Death, and it is one of them that come to those who are destine to die in battle. Thanatos wears the golden helmet that hides him from his victims as he silently stalks them and sucks their last breath. He needs no food, nor drink, his only nourishment being the souls of his human victims. Hades told me that he is welcome to dwell within the palace, but that he prefers to stay in Tartartus, to be near those who are tortured, were he feeds off their suffering.

When he reached us, he looked at me then addressing Hades, said,

"My Lord, have you come to summon me"?

"Thanatos, I've come with Zeus' daughter Kore today. She wishes to see the Underworld and I am her guide". Hades said to him.

"Very well my lord, I'll leave you". Thanatos said as he lifted my hand to his lips and gently kissed it. I was surprised to see that the God of Death was as beautiful as any of the other Gods who lived on Mount Olympus, I expected him to be hideous, but then nothing I have encountered within the Underworld was to my expectations.

We were left alone and I was able to take a closer look at those whose screams I would never be able forget. Here the wicked were sent to purge their souls from the sins committed during their lives before finally being released to the Elysian Fields or to another earthly life. The worst of these criminals would spend eternity here, while others could hope for release in a few thousand years or so. I saw Tityus, Zeus' son, who was tied down while a vulture pecked at his liver daily, only to be rejuvenated during the night while he tried to sleep; his crime was that he fought against the Olympians during the war with the Titans, a crime that Zeus would never forgive and I feared that he would be down here for all eternity.

Tantalus, another of Zeus' sons born to a mortal woman, is also condemned to tortures here. He, at one time, was the most beloved of Zeus' sons and even though he had mortal blood he was allowed to dine with the Gods at Mount Olympus. But Tantalus became proud and thought that he was better than the great God himself, and in his self- confidence he murdered his only son by boiling him in a great cauldron, and if this was not bad enough, he then served this dish to the Gods to prove that they weren't as powerful as they thought. His punishment for these crimes is to be chained to a tree sitting in the middle of a cool pool of water continuously tormented by thirst and hunger. Each time he tried to lower his head to sip of the cool water, the pool would lower, and his chained hands couldn't reach the fruit that hung just over his head. The mortal Sisyphus who killed his brother, hoping to gain control of his property, along with his daughter was destined to roll a huge bolder uphill, only to watch it fall as he neared the top. His soul cannot be released until both his brother and his daughter absolve his crimes, and at that time the bolder will finally reach the top and his soul released.

"Don't pity these shades, for these wretched souls are not here for committing minor crimes. Here, only the most wicked of sinners will endure punishment until their souls are purified. This prison is home to murderers, rapist, and those who committed crimes against the Gods". Hades whispered in my ear.

There were many souls down here, some who were not as famous as the ones I mentioned before. I saw one man who was bound to a wheel naked, and as the wheel turned a demon would, using an iron rod, shatter the limbs over and over again. Like Tityus during the night when the demons would finally leave him alone his broken bones would mend, allowing the same torture to be endured day after day. Since these souls were already dead they couldn't even wish for death to release them from their tortures. In the middle of the dungeon there was a giant cauldron that held hundreds of screaming souls as they tried, clawing each other trying to free themselves from the boiling oil that burned the flesh from their bones. Along the walls of the prison some of the wretched souls were chained and branded with red-hot irons or flogged until their flesh was torn from their bodies. Still others were tied to a giant rack and stretched until their limbs would tear, causing a sound that I was able to hear even over the loud screaming and pleading of the many souls. One of the most terrifying tortures I beheld, was to smear a sweet honey mixture on a soul chained to the ground and allow a number of beasts, rats, dogs, snakes and worms to eat the flesh off their bones. Again during the night all wounds would heal and in the morning the tortures would start fresh.

    This dungeon contrasted sharply with that of the beautiful palace I had spend the previous day admiring. The heat of the fires were getting to me, I was starting to fell a little dizzy so I held on to Hades' arm to steady myself. The heat, along with the sight of the half eaten, decomposing corpses that filled the pit below, the smells of rotting and burning flesh and the sounds of bodies breaking along with the pitiful shrieks and cries of the shades condemned to this torture filled my senses and soon I lost consciousness.

VI
Hades

NO MORTAL CAN truly comprehend the desolation I felt when I saw my beloved Kore laying unconscious at my feet, just inches from the stairs that lead to the Dungeon of the Damned. I had lost her, I was sure of it. I tried to convince her not to visit that damnable place, but no matter what I said she wouldn't hear it. Over the last year as we were getting to know each other I came to understand that she had indeed inherited her mother's stubbornness. That's one of things that made me fall in love with her. Yes, I truly loved her. I loved her more than life itself, and the thought of loosing her was unbearable to me. Many centuries ago when I first took my position in the Underworld I believed that I'd go mad if I was to endure eternity alone, but with the passage of time I have become accustomed to being alone. Let me explain here, I was not seeking a consort to relieve my loneliness; I sought a partner to make myself complete. The Gods, like mortals, are not really whole until they can freely give their heart to another. Kore was not my first love. I've had many lovers here in the Underworld before her, but none have ever made my heart stop beating as it does when I am with her.

That day, almost a year ago, when I left my home deep within the Underworld, breaking free into the daylight, and almost running over the frightened young maiden who waited for me, seemed like only yesterday. I fell in love with her the instant our eyes meet. I still remember how nervous I was as I tried to speak with her. After spending so much time alone, I had almost forgotten how to communicate with others. I wanted so much to just look into her mind, to feel her thoughts, but I couldn't do that, fear wouldn't allow me to reach into her mind. After being hurt so many times, I've come to realize that reading other's thoughts isn't a blessing, but a curse. When she finally told me why she had come, I almost started to weep with joy.

Even though I despise mortals I traveled to earth daily this past year just to be with her. I wanted to take her back with me to my palace, our palace within the Underworld where we could be together forever, but I couldn't, not just then. Instead I walked among mortals who would scurry away from the sight of me as fast as they could. When they couldn't get away fast enough, they bowed to me not out of respect, but out of fear. Throughout the long centuries I've watched mortals worship my brothers and sisters, and yes I became bitter. I cursed the Goddess of Destiny, blaming her for all my troubles. I could've let my heart harden, and truly become the monster that mortals thought I was, but I didn't. Instead, I retreated further into the Underworld and had little contact with my brothers and sisters. I spoke only with the few Gods that were brave enough to visit me within my prison.

Years turn into decades, and decades into centuries and one day I woke to realized that I was totally alone. I wept for all my lost desires. I lived in misery for I don't know how long, until I remembered that so many centuries ago, I was promised a Goddess to relieve my loneliness. I called to Hermes.

"Hermes, tell Zeus I wish to speak with him about his daughter Kore".

"I don't think that's a good idea, not just now". He replied, adding, "Demeter's in the palace".

"I don't care. I'm only claiming what is rightfully mine". I barked at him.

"Give me a couple of days, I could create a drought on earth. That'll keep her busy, then you could speak with Zeus alone".

"I'll give you two days only. Tell Zeus that after that time I'll meet him at the palace just after dawn".

Hermes bowed before soaring away.

The morning of the second day came and when I reached the palace gates I saw Demeter there and I knew that I would be returning alone.

My sister Demeter is a beautiful Goddess, more beautiful then even Aphrodite, and at one time I loved her. All of us brothers did. That was many, many centuries ago. Like all the Olympian Gods, I was proud, and wouldn't take her to my bed. I knew that she didn't love me. Her heart belonged to Zeus alone. I don't blame her, Zeus can be very captivating, especially with Goddesses. Demeter only came to me in despair, knowing that Zeus would never settle for only one Goddess. As I mentioned earlier, I possess the ability to read other's thoughts; really all of the Olympian Gods and Goddesses have this ability to some degree. Hestia's is the most powerful; visions of other's thoughts instantly flash through her mind. Zeus, he's clairaudient; he hears the thoughts of both Gods and mortals alike. My gift is more subtle. When I choose to look into another's mind, their thoughts flood my emotions. I feel both their joy and their sorrow. I felt Demeter's pain that day when she came to me. I almost took her in my arms to comfort her, but I couldn't. If I were to take her, I'd have to know that it would be forever.

Unlike my younger brother, Zeus, who loved Goddess after Goddess, I couldn't give my heart so freely. Before I took my place within the Underworld, I could have had a number of Goddesses, but I choose to be with only one, a beautiful nymph. I would have been content to spend eternity with her, but she was mortal and all too soon death took her from me. Constantly surrounded by death, you would think that when her time came, I would understand. I didn't. A part of my soul died with her. After that, I did the only thing I knew; I retreated deeper into my world of darkness, and loneliness. I lived a half-life for so long, I didn't even remember the prophecy; that I would be given Zeus and Demeter's only daughter as a wife.

When I went to claim my bride, Demeter was waiting there for me.

"You're not welcome here Hades". Was her greeting to me.

I bowed slightly to her, and took her hand and kissed it before finally speaking, "My beloved sister, you look beautiful, as usual".

"Flattery won't get you anywhere with me. I know why you've come here".

"Demeter, I found it within my heart to forgive you, can't you forgive me".

"I've done nothing that deserves your forgiveness". She started to say, but then Zeus came and the three of us went to his private chamber to discuss the Fate of their daughter. Hermes was stationed just outside the chamber, making sure that none would dare disturb the discussion.

After much arguing, Demeter finally spoke, her words were a slap to my face.

"Hades, I can't believe how selfish you are. Kore is an Earth Goddess, she would wither being surrounded by death. If you love her, leave her to me".

I didn't know how to respond to this, I never wanted to hurt her, I only wanted someone to share my life with. I thought about Demeter's words and realized that she was right, I was being selfish. I turned to leave when Zeus spoke,

"Don't go yet".

"There's nothing to talk about". I replied as I flung the massive door open, knocking Kore to the floor. She was as beautiful, if not more so, than her mother. Demeter has beautiful golden hair, the color of sun kissed grain, but Kore inherited her father's dark hair, and as it fell across her face, I saw that she was indeed more beautiful than her mother. I held out my hand to assist her up and our eyes met. I felt a pain in my heart as I looked into her eyes. Demeter's words once again rung in my head, *'Kore is an Earth Goddess, she would wither being surrounded by death. If you love her, leave her to me'.*

Demeter pushed me aside and grabbed her daughter's arm, dragging her away from me. I left for the Underworld, and thought my heart would break.

For the next year I kept my sorrow locked deep within, speaking to no one about my feelings. Hermes came one morning, telling me that Zeus wanted to meet on the Island of Crete to discuss the marriage arrangements. I refused at first telling Hermes to make the trip in my place.

"I can not do that". He replied, and after a short discussion, I left for Crete, intending to tell Zeus that I would rather spend eternity alone than to force his beautiful daughter to be trapped so deep underground as my consort. When I broke free into the bright light of the world above, I couldn't believe what I saw. I blinked to make sure that it wasn't just my imagination. Right in front of me was my beloved. Hope filled me for the first time in eons. I hadn't won her heart yet, I had another year, but at least I had her by my side for now. As the year passed my love for her only deepened. Each night when I would leave her to return to my palace, I wept. Alone for so many years, I lived in my self-pity, keeping my emotions locked, but now that I was with her, my heart began to open once again. As the loneliness left, there was space open, and happiness began seeping in.

Time flew by, the year was coming near the end, and I knew that it wouldn't be long before I had to leave her forever. Two months left with my beloved Kore. I kept postponing her visit to my world, fearing that once she beheld it she would run back to her mother. One morning as I reached Crete I saw Zeus waiting for me on the shore.

"Hades, the time has come for you to take Kore to the Underworld". He spoke as we embraced.

"Do I have to take her so soon? I don't think she's ready yet". I wanted so bad to have more time with her, even if it was only a couple of days.

"She needs to see your world before she can decide whether to be your bride".

"I know". I said sadly as I nodded. "I'll speak with Minos and come for her later today".

All that day I thought about Kore visiting the Underworld. Maybe, I thought, if I kept her from visiting Tartartus she would agree to the marriage. I couldn't let her see that place, knowing that if she witnessed the horrors of damned dungeon, she could never agree to live in the Underworld.

I picked her up early that evening and as we began the trip I tried to prepare her for the horrors she would soon see. As soon as the chariot stopped near the river Styx, instantly I felt her fear. It consumed me. I tried my best to close my mind, not being able to bear the fear she felt, but I couldn't. Instantly, in a frenzy shades began circling us, begging me to allow them to enter the Underworld. Their preternatural hands grabbed at both of our robes and though no sound came from my beloved lips, her screams filled my soul. I let loose all my power causing the poor souls to shriek back in panic. They fled into the woods that surround the river and we were alone. I led her deeper into the Underworld, and my heart almost broke as she faced the personification of Grief, Anxiety, Disease, Old Age, Fear, Hunger, Death, and Agony. I used all my power to close my mind to her feelings, but again I couldn't. I knew that if we stayed too long all happiness would be sucked from her soul. We moved on quickly, and to my surprise, she wasn't afraid of my beloved pet, Cerberus. Cerberus usually instills terror in all who saw her, but Kore was like a little kid playing with a puppy. I smiled while I watched the two of them play. We continued and once she was safely within my palace, I relaxed, just a little. At least there was nothing disturbing here.

After showing her only the grounds that surround my palace we retired to dinner. All through dinner she seemed pensive. Instead of looking into her mind, I asked her,

"What's bothering you, my dear"?

She knew that I was hiding something from her. Yes, she faced terrors between the two worlds, but my palace is almost as impressive as that of Zeus'. I explained to her that she would never have to leave the palace grounds.

"My dear", she began after a long silence, "I must see all of the Underworld if I'm to decide".

I tried to talk her out of going to Tartartus, but I couldn't. Not wanting her to see the terrors that occur during the night, which even terrify me, I asked her to spend the night, and first thing in the morning I would escort her to the Dungeon of the Damned. That night I didn't sleep; worry wouldn't allow me any rest.

The morning came all too soon and Kore was waiting for me, ready for the journey that would take her from me. We proceeded to Tartartus and after seeing only a small part of that horrible place my beloved fainted. As I looked at her unconscious form laying there, I knew that my sister Demeter was right, I was only being selfish, how could I expect a Goddess so full of life live with the dead. I carried her back to my palace and when she awoke, I told her that we would be going back to Crete.

"What have I done wrong"? she begged me.

"Nothing, my dear". Was all I could answer, as I held her hand tightly, holding back my tears.

VII
Persephone

WHEN I WOKE I was back in Hades palace lying on the velvet recliner; the fire that burned in the hearth warmed me. *'What happened?'* I thought as I slowly began to focus on the events that brought me here. The last thing I remembered was looking down into the pit of despair, then suddenly everything went black. I looked around the room, hoping to see Hades there and was relieved that he was. I was about to speak, but he spoke first;

"Kore, it's time for you to return to the palace of King Minos, I have kept you here much too long". As he said this to me, I was sure that I heard his voice tremble. My first thought was that my fainting is what caused this, but no, the tone in his voice suggested that I had done something to upset him. I wondered what it might have been.

"I'm not ready to go back yet, I want to stay here with you". I pleaded but he said nothing.

"Please don't take me back so soon". I begged again, trying as hard as I could to keep the tears from pouring out.

"I'm sorry, but your father will be upset with me for keeping you here overnight. I should never have allowed you to stay here last night; I wasn't thinking when I agreed".

"Father doesn't care about me". I insisted but he wouldn't listen.

"I'm sure that when we reach the island of Crete we'll find Zeus already there waiting for us". He answered.

"I don't even think he knows that I left King Minos' palace. These last few months he hasn't once set foot on the island".

I tried to convince him that father really didn't care about me, but it did no good. He reached for my arm and after assisting me up he led me to the door where his golden chariot was waiting. As he lifted me into the seat, I knew that no matter what I said, I would have to return to father and it wouldn't be long before he would take me back to Mount Olympus, and I would never see Hades again. We barely were seated when the stallions took off, causing me to fall back into the seat. The chariot began to speed up and each beat of the stallions great wings caused the chariot to not only move forward, but up. Within seconds we were totally off the ground and heading straight up toward to roof of the cavern. I thought that we were going to depart from the Underworld by the route that we entered, but instead we were going straight up. I was sure that the chariot would soon crash. I couldn't help but scream, thinking that the stallions were going much to fast to be able to stop before hitting the glistening rocks that formed the ceiling of the Underworld. We were only a few feet from impact; I closed my eyes, not wanting to see as we crashed. I heard a thundering sound that reverberated through my head, making me tighten all my muscles, preparing for the impact as the chariot smashed into the rocks above. Nothing happened; I cautiously opened my eyes and instantly was blinded by a thin ray of sunlight as it peeked through a small opening within the quivering rocks. As the chariot neared the fissure began widening, letting the sunlight and scent of the earth flood in. I blinked; the brightness was overwhelming at first. I felt the earth tremble as the stallions pulled the chariot free from the world below. I knew that we had broke free of Hades' realm in the exact spot that I had first encountered him almost a year ago.

As we drove on I continued trying to explain to Hades that I didn't want to return to Crete, or Mount Olympus, that I only wanted to stay with him, but I don't think he heard a word I said. All I could think of was that I was going back to mother, and nothing I could say or do would stop it, and for the first time in my short life, I felt totally helpless. The tears started and as we flew over the sea my face burned as sea salt bite into my tear-stained cheeks. Hades was correct when he predicted that father would be waiting for us, and as we neared the island, I saw the greatest of all the Olympians standing alone on the shore. I tried to stop my tears, not wanting father to see me cry, but no matter how hard I tried, I failed; the tears continued. When we stopped, I didn't even set on foot on land before father spoke, and by the tone of his voice I knew that he was angry. I was expecting him to be angry with me, but he ignored me entirely and walked right up to his brother,

"Hades, you were supposed to bring Kore back last night before sunset. Minos was so worried when you didn't return that he summoned me". He barked at his brother,

"Then this morning, Hermes informs me that you kept my daughter overnight in the Underworld, this wasn't what we agreed upon".

"Forgive me father, for it was my fault. I didn't wish to leave until I saw the entire kingdom". I said timidly. Even though I was terrified of father, I didn't want him to blame Hades.

"That's true Zeus. Kore was determined to visit my entire kingdom, and no matter what I could say to her I couldn't change her mind".

"Yes, she is stubborn… like her mother". Zeus said with a little less anger in his voice.

Hades continued, "Since it was almost dark, I decided to wait until sunrise to take her to Tartartus, I didn't think that you would approve of her seeing the Dungeon of the Damned during the night".

"Well, yes I agree with you, I wouldn't want her to have seen that dreadful place at night, but you should not have kept her there without informing the King either. You should have known that Minos would have been worried, for I left Kore in his protection". Zeus replied.

"But now that you are back, I must return with Kore to Mount Olympus now, her mother wishes to be reunited with her".

"But father", I interjected, "You promised me that if after one year of staying on earth and getting to know Hades, and if after seeing the Underworld, that if I chose to I could marry Hades. Even though the year hasn't yet passed entirely, I have seen Hades' realm and I have made my decision".

They both stood there silently as I continued,

"I have made my decision, I will willingly live within the Underworld as Hades' bride".

I could see that my words surprised both Gods.

"Are you sure that you still wish to marry Hades"? Zeus finally asked, shocked.

"Of course I do. Tartarus is a horrible place and I wish nothing more than to never set foot there again, but I would face even that horrid place to marry Hades".

"Are you sure of this, for once you become my bride, you won't be able to return to Mount Olympus"? Hades asked me as he reached for my hand.

I couldn't understand why Hades didn't know my feelings since he was able to read my thoughts, and it was only much later that I realized that he didn't always look into other's minds, especially those who he cared for. After centuries of seeing either fear or repulsion in the minds of those he loved he closed his mind, not wanting to face the pain he knew he would find there. Zeus, on the other hand never shut out the thoughts of anyone, but that day I was simply ignored while he focused on the thoughts of his brother.

I looked into Hades eyes and with insistent determination, told him,

"I have never been so sure about anything in my life as I am about this".

Hades smiled and then lifted me into his arms and kissed me.

"Kore, return to Minos' palace and prepare for your wedding. Tomorrow morning as the first rays of the Sun emerge I'll return and give you freely to my dear brother, Hades". Father said to me with a smile.

I kissed Hades then rushed back to the palace of King Minos, where his attendants were waiting for me.

Usually the night before the wedding it would be the bride's mother who would prepare her, but since mother didn't approve of this marriage or even know of it for that matter, I looked to Queen Pasiphae to fill this role. That night I feasted with the Queen, her daughters and my servants and when we finished I was left alone while I prepared to make my offerings to the different Gods and Goddesses, who I thought of as family. The usual offering consisted of childhood clothing and toys, signifying the separation of the bride from her childhood and her transformation into the role of wife and mother, but I had none of these items with me, so instead I offered the few personal items I possessed on the island. My sacrifices began with libations to Hestia, Goddess of the Hearth, as was customary; followed by an offering to Hera, the Goddess of Marriage, to whom I offered the clothes that I wore on the day I met Hades in a brunt offering; to Artemis, Goddess of Virginity and Transition, I offered a golden bracelet that Hades had given me as a gift in hope that she would ease the passage from virgin to bride; and as I made my offering of a lock of hair to my mother, Demeter, the Goddess of Fertility, wishing for her blessings on this marriage, I sat in silence contemplating if she could sense it was her own daughter who was seeking her assistance this night. I spoke to her not as my mother, but as the Goddess that she was and as I put the lock of my hair into the flame a tear ran down my cheek. The only thing that would have made my marriage more perfect was if she could be there with me, sharing my joy. I lifted my cup in one last gesture to her and the other Gods and Goddesses before taking a small sip, then I poured out the remaining wine onto the bare ground as an offering to the Earth itself.

The ritual was complete; I hoped for the God's blessing on my marriage, but deep down inside my heart I knew that I would never have mother's. I laid down and tried to sleep, but in my excitement I tossed and turned until the night was more than half over, I looked out the window at the waxing moon and thought of my future with Hades until sleep finally came over me. I was awoken early, well before dawn by one of my servants,

"My Lady, we must prepare you for your Lord". She said as she helped me out of bed. I smiled at her as she guided me to the bath. Others servants, who I hadn't seen before came into the chamber one by one, each caring a silver vase decorated with scenes of a wedding procession, filled to overflowing with water from a local spring; water from this spring was believed to cleans and purify the body and was used before any ceremonies took place. I felt as if I was still asleep, dreaming, as they poured the warm water over my body, and then massaged perfumed oils into my skin until a glistening sheen covered me. I relaxed in the bath as the servant brought me some food and plaited my hair. The sky was still dark, with the first rays of sunlight only starting to peek over the sea and I heard the voices of the other servants as they prepared the palace for the coming celebration.

After the ritual bath two of my servants helped me dress in my wedding gown. It was a beautiful light violet gown worn in the Pepos Doric style. This style consisted of a rectangular piece of the finest silk about three meters wide, and as long as I was tall that was folded into a tube. One servant held the garment as I stepped into it, while another pulled it up to my shoulders and fastened on both sides with a beautiful golden broach. A girdle secured the robe while allowing the excess fabric to drape loosely across my breast and leaving my arms exposed. The embroidered hem just fell short of hitting the ground, showing off my golden sandals encrusted with precious jewels, a gift from King Minos. The same pattern that was embroidered along the edge of my robe was repeated on my matching shawl. My hair was plaited in a single braid woven with jewels, and then twisted around the crown of my head with wisps of loose curls framing my face. I looked into the mirror and was stunned by my transformation. To this day I still wear this style of dress when I'm in my palace with Hades. When I'm with mother on Earth I wear the styles of the day, but I have never felt truly comfortable in those.

As I admired myself in the mirror Queen Pasiphae entered the room and motioned the servants to leave. Once alone, she took my hand and placed into it a gift; a beautiful pearl and gold necklace that was given to her by her mother when she was wed to King Minos.

"I can't except this". I said "This should be given to one of your daughters on her wedding day".

"Please take this small gift from me, for during this last year you have become like a daughter to me. I have many other gifts for my own daughters when it is their time to marry". She said softy to me.

I allowed her to put the necklace around my neck, and then I turned around and gave her a kiss on her check.

"Thank you, for everything". I said as I gave her a hug, adding, "Without your help I wouldn't be marrying today".

As I said this I noticed that the Queen was crying, and then I felt the tears start flowing down my cheeks.

It was now time for me to be presented to Hades in the central court, but before this the Queen added the final touch to my wedding gown, a veil that covered my face, symbolizing my virginity.

We preceded down to the central court with the Queen in front, followed by her daughters, the servants and finally I was allowed to enter. There must have been hundreds of guests all waiting for me to enter, and as I stepped into the staircase that led into the great hall I felt a little faint, one of the servants held my arm tightly, holding me up. Then I saw my future husband seated next to my father and our eyes locked. Only longing to be with him filled me. He looked as beautiful as the first time I saw him, but instead of wearing his usual himation, he was dressed in short tunic of gold silk with a matching cloak. His long dark hair was pulled back into a single braid that fell between his shoulders with little wisps caressing his cheeks. His green eyes lit when he saw me; they were not the only eyes on me, for as I entered a hush filled the room and all stared as I began my descent down the stairs and took my place sitting between the two Gods, father on the right and Hades on my left.

It was traditional that wedding ceremonies last for three days, the first in preparation; the wedding feast, which would start on the afternoon of the second day with dining and dancing lasting all through the night; the third and last day is when the actual wedding ceremony took place, followed by a procession from the bride's house to that of her new home, where the feasting and celebrating continued. This feast was expected to last well into the night, and I wouldn't be alone with my husband until the end of the following night. I can't tell you much about the feast, for I was in a dream-like state. Sounds of music filled my senses while singers and dancers provided entertainment as the guests dined on delicacies fit for the Gods, even though there were only a few Gods in attendance; my father, Hades, Hermes and myself the only deities present. Father, not wanting it to be known that I was marrying Hades, knowing that if mother found out she would have done all she could have to stop the ceremony, didn't mention it to any of the residents of Mount Olympus other than Hermes. This mattered little to the guests who were drunk from the finest wine that father could supply. I wanted the day to end so that I could be alone with Hades but no matter where we went, guests were laughing, dancing and drinking.

The final day of the ceremony began, as father reached for the sistra that sat on the table and began rattling it, announcing to the guests that the ceremony was about to take place. The guests formed a circle around us as I stood facing my father with Hades at my side. Zeus took my left hand and placed it into his brother's and said,

"My beloved daughter and dear brother, I acknowledge the bond that is between you". He held our hands together and speaking not only to us, but to the all present, he continued,

"In front of these witnesses, I give my daughter Kore, to you my dear brother, Hades, to love and protect for all eternity".

This was the most significant part of the ceremony; it is only then that the bride is officially handed over to the groom.

Hades lifted my veil and around my neck he placed a golden pendant and after securing it he whispered to me,

"This pendant is a token of my love for you. Of all the precious metals I chose gold to give to you, since gold like my love for you cannot be destroyed".

He then kissed me, then spoke not only to me, but to all present,

"Today, I name you Persephone, for your new life as my bride, you will have a new name".

Mortals usually had only a personal name that was given to them at birth, and woman didn't change their names when they married as it is the custom now, but the Gods would take on different names as their roles within society changed, each name expressing their essence at that time, and since I was no longer the Maiden that I was once, I was given a new name to fit my role as consort of Lord of the Underworld.

Hades whispered, so only I could hear,

"Persephone means 'light-bearing face', and this is what I name you, since I saw your face, light has replaced the darkness that has filled my soul for so many centuries".

Since that day no one other than mother has called me by my former name.

We then kissed and the entire palace filled with applause. Father led us out to an awaiting chariot, which would take me to my new home in the Underworld. Hades lifted me into the chariot, and before he entered, father kissed me, then bent over to whisper in my ear,

"Persephone, farewell, for I won't accompany you to your new dwelling as is customary, Hermes will make that journey for me, and there he'll continue the celebration with you and Hades throughout the night".

I started to cry, and told him that I would visit him in Mount Olympus. He then turned to Hades,

"I'm trusting you to love and protect her". Hades nodded.

With that we were off. I wished that once we reached Hades' palace we could be alone, but this was the third and final day of the wedding ceremony, the celebration would continue for the entire day at the brides' new home. It was during this part of the celebration that wild dancing and loud music was performed throughout the night, intending to ward off evil spirits that might harm the new couple during their first night together. Once we were in the main hall with all the guests Hades offered me a Pomegranate, which I accepted as a symbol of the consummation of our marriage. From this time on, and continuing throughout the years this fruit has become a symbol of sexuality. I took this Pomegranate in my hand willing, and bringing it up to my mouth I bite into it and tasted its sweetness, then handed it to my new husband, who also allowed the sweet fruit to fill him. This symbol bound me to Hades, and was the only ritual that mother couldn't destroy when she tried to drag me back with her to Mount Olympus.

Just as the previous night, there was singing, dancing and feasting the entire day, going well into the night with Hades' servants, and the nymphs who lived in the Underworld. Both Hades and I tired, since we had been awake for two entire days, quietly left the celebration without anyone noticing and entered the bridal chamber. This was the first time since I met Hades that we were totally alone.

Although I have visited Hades in the Underworld just a couple of days ago, I didn't enter into his private chambers. Such a whirlwind I felt as I entered, it was as if I was walking into a dream. Veins of gold spotted with precious gems ran throughout the different minerals that formed the chambers walls and ceiling. The room was dimly lit, its only illumination a couple of candles. A slight breeze blew across the small flickering flames causing light and shadows to dance off the walls. The room was scarcely furnished with only a king sized bed; the curtains invitingly open, covered with several soft down pillows and a silk comforter, and a single dressing table next to the bed. Hades took me by the hand and gently guided me to a silver chalice encrusted with precious stones that sat alone on this table.

"This is the chalice that the Olympians drank from on the night each was given his domain". Hades said this as he held the chalice up, his eyes burning with desire.

"It contains water from the river Styx, and as I drink from this cup I promise that I'll tell you no lies, Persephone". He lifted the chalice up to his mouth and took a deep drink. When he finished, he lowered the cup down to place it back on the table, but before he could rest the chalice down I closed my hands over his and said to him with confidence.

"I promise, by drinking freely the waters of the river Styx, that I'll love no other". Then I let the cool water slide down my throat.

Hades lifted my hands to his lips and gently kissed them, and then he embraced me. We stood there for what seemed like an eternity, just looking into each other's eyes, and a shudder of anticipation surged throughout my body. I had wanted this moment to happen for so long and now that it was within my grasp I felt a little anxious, and a little shy. I lowered my eyes and Hades put his hand on my chin and lifted my face until our eyes met. He took my hand in his as he slowly leaned toward me, our lips brushing softly together in a kiss. His lips were soft and once I felt his mouth pressed against mine, I couldn't contain myself, I kissed him hard. He pulled back and smiled softly before kissing me once again, this time with a passion that burned through to my soul. As his tongue explored my mouth, his hands found the pins that secured my robe and slowly he unfastened them, letting the silk fall to my waist, and as he did this I reached down to my girdle and untied it. Instantly my robes fell to the ground in a pool at my feet. I was wearing only a thin silk undergarment and could feel my husbands' body pressing hard against mine as his hands gently caressed the curves of my body, resting momentarily on the fleshy part of my buttocks. I could feel his hands squeezing my flesh as his kisses became deeper and filled my body with a desire I hadn't known before. My entire body ached with this desire, and I wanted nothing else than to have him within me, bringing my attention to the moisture that was now between my legs. His hands slowly glided over the silk, feeling the curve of my waist, sliding up and stopping to cusp my breasts. Gently, using his index finger and thumb he pinched my nipple sending a shiver through my body that intensified in the area between my legs, as if a single nerve connected my nipples to this area. My legs began to quiver and I was sure that they wouldn't be able to support me for much longer.

Hades kissed me once more, and then in one swift movement, he ripped the silk gown from my body. I was entirely naked. His hands again found their way to my breasts, again pinching my nipples while he started nibbling at my ear. His kisses flowed down my neck, kiss after kiss, down my throat, kiss after kiss, until his mouth found what it was anticipating, my breasts. As his mouth closed over my breast I felt wave after wave of pleasure starting at the source and ending in that secret place between my legs. My legs started to give in, I was sure I was going to fall when he effortlessly lifted me up and carried me to his bed, to our bed. He gently laid me down among the soft pillows and I watched holding my breath as he slowly undressed.

The robes that were fashionable at that time in history left little to the imagination. I had seen much of Hades' chest and upper body since the first meeting, but as he started undressing, I wondered if the rest of his body would be as perfect, and as his tunic dropped to the floor I was overcome with desire. When I saw the size of what was hidden under his clothes I became more than a little frightened, for surely he would ripe me open as he entered me. He smiled at me and slowly lowered himself down on his elbows, keeping his weight off my body and I could feel how hard he was as he pressed into my thigh, and as he did this, he kissed me softly and said,

"I promise I'll be gentle with you".

"I love you". was all that I could say in return.

With that, he mounted me and thrust his manhood deep into the one area of my body that needed it the most. The wetness encouraged its entry and then I felt a slight pain and then a flowing from within.

"Am I bleeding"?

I though, but then I assured myself that being a virgin after all, blood would be expected. He slowly rocked his body back and forth, sending wave after wave of pleasure throughout my entire body. I raised my hips to meet his thrusts and when I did this I could feel him deep within me. As he increased speed the pleasure also increased, until I though I could no longer take it. I felt my nails tear into the flesh on his back and shoulders as my teeth sank into his neck to avoid screaming with pleasure. I wanted to stop but I couldn't. He grabbed my hair and pulled my head to the side and let his lips and tongue run down my neck. With each spasm of pleasure my breathing became heavier and heavier, until I felt him swell even larger and felt his testicles contract as his seed burst forth in an explosion filling my body with warmth.

He collapsed next to me. After a few moments, the blood still beating heavily through my body, he lifted himself up and kissed me and said,

"I love you".

I wanted to tell him that I loved only him, and that I was his now and would never leave him, but the only words that came from my lips were,

"I love you too".

It didn't matter that I couldn't tell him how I felt, for he was blessed with the gift of being able to read my thoughts, and for the first time since I met him, I wasn't embarrassed by my longing for him, for I felt that he truly longed for me also.

We both lay there in each other's arms whispering through the night. As we talked of our future life together I noticed there was a sadness that seemed to overtake him,

"What is it my love"? I asked as I wrapped my arms around him and he instantly turned his face away from mine. I held him tight and gently turned his head so he could face me, and when our eyes met I noticed that there were quiet tears forming in his eyes.

"Persephone, I want you to know that I would like nothing better than to give you a child, but when I accepted my destiny as the ruler of the Underworld, Lord of the Dead, I gave up the ability to create life. I can destroy life, but I cannot create it".

VIII
Demeter

IT IS I, Demeter, once again. I must speak to you directly, for only I can tell you how for one year I was deceived by not only my two brothers Zeus and Hades, but by my beloved daughter, Kore, as well and how I searched frantically for her for nine days and nine nights with no nourishment nor rest. No matter how much she wants to tell the story of her life alone, this part she cannot; for she can never understand the fear that consumed my soul, nor to what depths I would have gone to find her and return her to the land of the living.

As some may be aware, a select few of the Gods and Goddesses have the ability to read others thoughts, but I unfortunately do not possess that gift, of the six first generation Olympians only three of us, Zeus, Hades and Hestia, posses that ability. While my daughter was staying on earth with Zeus' son, Minos I was told by him that he wished for her to learn the customs of mortals.

"Since as the daughter of an Earth Goddess it would be wise for her to be acquainted with the ways of humans". He told that that day so many, many centuries ago. I agreed with him, thinking that it would be good for her to spend some time away from me. I had trusted my daughter and was sure that she wouldn't have been hiding anything from me, but alas, I was wrong. Even though I had visited her at the king's palace many times during her stay I had no idea that she was deceiving me, that she, along with her father Zeus, Hades and the mere mortals who watched over her were bound together in a conspiracy that would take her away from me for all eternity.

PERSEPHONE: QUEEN OF THE DEAD

Zeus knew that our sister Hestia and I were the closest of the Olympians, and if she were to find out about his plans she would have immediately inform me, therefore during that year he tried to avoid her whenever possible. When this was impossible and she was near him he would clear his thoughts of his intensions; therefore she was not able to disclose any of his plans to me. I don't think he even told his wife Hera of his actions, afraid that she would willingly tell me of his plans. It is a well known fact that Hera and I do not get along, even after so many centuries she still feels threaten by me and I don't blame her; I was Zeus' lover long before she, and if I hadn't refused him in my bed, I would have been his wife, not her. Zeus feared that if I knew his intentions of giving my beloved Kore to Hades in marriage I would rush to Crete and take her back and both of us would leave Mount Olympus for good, living on the earth. He was correct, for if I had known of his treachery I would have taken her to the ends of the world to keep her safely away from Hades and the Underworld.

When Kore was finally married to her uncle, Zeus came back from the celebrations drunk with wine and confident his plan was a complete success, therefore he wasn't as careful as he should've been, and failed to conceal his thoughts when he came upon Hestia as he walked through the Great Hall on his way to his private chamber. Immediately she understood the deception that had transpired and after bursting in my room and finding me relaxing, she told me of our brother's treachery.

"Demeter, my dear sister, I have horrible news I must tell you". As she exclaimed this I jumped up from my bed, shocked to hear someone, even another Olympian, address me in such a manner.

"What is it? What has happened"? I asked, not masking the dread in my voice.

"Zeus has just come back from the island of Crete where he gave your daughter Kore to Hades in marriage".

I didn't say a word. I couldn't. What she had said didn't register in my mind, so I stood there for a few seconds just looking at her.

Seeing my confusion, for I truly didn't believe what she was saying, she continued,

"Apparently King Minos and his wife were both in on the conspiracy. While you were visiting they hid their intentions from you, fearing Zeus' wrath enough to make them deceive a Goddess as powerful as yourself".

"I don't believe you". I cried. I desperately wanted to believe that Hestia was mistaken, hoping that my own brother Zeus, of all the Gods, wouldn't be able to do this to our beloved daughter, but deep down in my heart I knew that I had been deceived by him once again.

Hestia continued,

"When I encountered Zeus a few moments ago, I surprised him and not being quick enough to conceal his thought, images of the last year instantly flooded my mind. I have to tell you before it is too late. There is still time left, the third day of the ceremony has not been completed yet". She replied, adding, "If you hurry you may be able to find your daughter before she enters the Underworld".

"No, No!" I said, "Kore would never marry without telling me. You must be mistaken".

"Ask Zeus for yourself, he's in his chamber with Hera. I don't think he'll be able deceive you any longer". She replied as she held the door open for me to leave.

I rushed for the door, leaving Hestia standing in my room alone and as I ran through the palace anger started to fill me, so when I finally reached Zeus and Hera's private chamber I burst through the door without even knocking, accusing Zeus.

"Where is my daughter"? I screamed at him, and even though Hera tried to quite me continued yelling at our brother,

"I trusted you and you betrayed me. You know that I didn't approve of this marriage".

"Demeter", he attempted to reason with me, "We cannot fight destiny. You shouldn't be upset, for Hades, as Lord of the Underworld is more than a suitable husband for any Goddess". I tried to stop his words, but he continued, "An arrow from Eros' bow has pierced your daughter's heart and she is truly in love with Hades. I left the choice to her".

The shock of this whole deception washed over my body, I wanted to scream at him, to hit, to hurt him, but I was frozen on the spot. I didn't feel anything, I was numb, but then the wetness of the tears as they ran down my cheeks woke me and without thinking I ran from all that I loved. I left my son, my beloved sister, and the only home I had known; I left Mount Olympus and headed for earth and started my search for a path that would lead me to the Underworld, a search that would last nine days and nine nights; nine days and nights with neither nourishment nor rest. I would have faced any horrors I might have encounter within the Underworld to bring my daughter safely back home, but I was unable to find my way. Looking back on my actions, I now realize that I should've sought guidance from Hermes, for he is the only God besides Zeus who knows the path that leads to the Underworld, and the palace of that retched Hades, but the Goddess of Destiny would not allow my rational self to emerge, so bitterly I searched alone, my only illumination the torch I held tight. Exhausted and feeling defeated, I had no place to go, so I decided to seek the assistance of the one God that I knew would never betray me, my brother Poseidon.

Now, as I told you earlier Poseidon was in love with me, and I knew that I would easily be able to convince him to assist me in finding my daughter. When I reached his palace, deep within the oceans depths, I ran to him with tears in my eyes and as he held me tightly in his arms I explained everything to him through my sobs. I explained how Zeus, with the help of King Minos deceived me and stole my daughter, how I refused to step foot back on Mount Olympus until I was reunited with her, and how for the last nine days and nights I searched the earth in vain for the entrance to the Underworld. Poseidon listened to my pleas for his assistance quietly, then as he stroked my hair, he said in a soft voice,

"Demeter, you know that I would do anything to please you, for your happiness means everything to me, but I can't assist you. As you remember I too was there that day so many centuries ago when it was decided by the Goddess of Destiny that it would be your daughter who would marry Hades and live in the Underworld as his bride".

He paused here, and when I didn't respond, he continued,

"Hades is a strong God, almost as strong as Zeus. You shouldn't worry about Kore, I'm sure that he'll take good care of her".

I pulled myself from his arms and still sobbing, I spit out the words "You fear Zeus' wrath, that is the only reason you won't assist me". as a snake spits out its venom.

"I don't fear Zeus, Demeter. It is done; let your daughter go. If you don't wish to return to Mount Olympus you may stay here with me, you know that I love you dearly and would give all I have to keep you happy. To prove my love for you I'll punish Zeus' beloved son King Minos and the Queen for their part in this conspiracy".

"I wish for not only their lives, but for the lives of their family as well". I begged of him.

"I can't kill Minos, for he is a just ruler who has sought my protection, but I know of a way that we could destroy his entire kingdom".

And as Poseidon said these words, for the first time since I found out about my daughter's marriage, I felt relief from the pain that filled my heart.

That very night Poseidon appeared to King Minos in all his glory, cloaked within the mist of a dream. The mighty Sea God towered in front of the king, as the wretched mortal lowered his head. Poseidon bellowed in a voice that would make any mortal tremble:

> *"King Minos, you have insulted my beloved sister Demeter, Goddess of Fertility, by deceiving her and allowing her daughter to be taken to the Underworld as Hades' bride. She has informed me that she will hold back all growth on the Island of Crete until all your people die of starvation as punishment for your actions against her.*

Minos, in his dream, kept his face to the floor, for he did not wish to see Poseidon's anger.

Poseidon then spoke to Minos more gently.

> *Do not fear my son, for you have found favor with me and have been a faithful servant; therefore I will assist you in appeasing my sister's wrath.*
> *The only way to satisfy her anger is to sacrifice a bull, a bull that I will send to you on the night of the full moon; a bull as white as the waves of the sea that it rides on to greet you on the shore of your kingdom. Sacrifice this bull to her in a lavish ceremony that is dedicated to the Demeter, Goddess of Fertility, on the night of the new moon and she will forgive you your transgressions. This is the only way you can appease her wrath".*

Minos woke instantly and after wiping the sweat from his brow he looked out the window. It was still the middle of the night, but he couldn't wait until morning to tell his wife Pasiphae of this horrible dream so he went to her private chamber, and without knocking he burst through the door going straight to her bed. She had not wakened when he entered, so he gently sat on the edge, holding his head in his hands as he rocked back and forth weeping. The movement woke the queen, who spoke in a half-sleep, "Who is there"?

"My dear Pasiphae, I must speak to you".

"What is the matter, my dear"? She said as she slowly opened her eyes and saw her husband sitting there, his face buried in his hands. He told her of his dream and instantly she was struck with the horror that soon their entire kingdom would be destroyed, by either me, or by Zeus. I don't know which of us they feared more at that moment.

"My Lord", Pasiphae wept, and through her sobs, she continued,

"We must sacrifice this bull to appease the Goddess Demeter, for if we don't our entire kingdom will become barren and all your subjects will starve, even though I fear that after this sacrifice is complete we will surly have to face Zeus' wrath. I fear for our future".

"We have no need to fear Zeus' wrath, we did nothing to betray his trust in us, we are his faithful servants; he is a just God and would never punish the innocent".

Minos replied to his wife as he placed his hand on her chin and gently lifted her face and as their eyes meet, he gently wiped the tears that ran down her cheek. Even though he tried to comfort her, he know that she was right, nothing they could do would prevent the destruction of his kingdom.

I stayed with Poseidon until the full moon rose, and just as he had promised, that night I watched as Minos stood alone on the coast of the island Crete, looking out to the sea. In the distance there was at first nothing more than a mere white speck above the water, and I watched as a magnificent white bull emerged from the depths of Poseidon's palace, and gliding over the waves effortlessly, without even causing a single ripple in the water as he came to the island and once on land he lowered his front legs in a bow to the King. Now all who saw this magnificent creature knew that this was no ordinary bull, but surly a gift from the Gods. None wished to see the king sacrifice this bull, but wanted to take it to the palace where it would mate with the royal herd producing cattle that would be the envy of the Gods themselves. Instead of sacrificing this bull, his servants told him he should substitute one of his own bulls, for surly Poseidon wouldn't want such a magnificent creature destroyed. For days they continued to try to convince the king to spare the mystical bull, but Minos would not hear of it, Poseidon wanted that bull sacrificed to Demeter on the night of the new moon, and he would see to it no matter what his subjects thought. He had no other choice, knowing that if he didn't I would bring a famine that would destroy not only his family, but his entire kingdom.

Now during the weeks before the new moon, my dear brother, Poseidon sent a madness over Queen Pasiphae, and she desired nothing but this bull. She would neither eat nor sleep, spending her waking hours either in the stable or in the meadow petting and speaking softly to this creature. Daedalus, the court magician, was in love with Queen Pasiphae, and even though she didn't accept his love, he couldn't stand by watch her pine away for the love of this beautiful creature. With no where else to go, she turned to the only person she thought would be able to assist her; she went to Daedalus' chamber and knocked softly before entering. As she walked to him, he bowed to her.

"Rise". She said, and when he did their eyes met for the briefest second and during that time he was able to see the pain she felt and he held out his arms to her. She fell into his outstretched arms and cried and cried before she slowly backed away from the magician. After a brief pause she softy spoke to him.

"Daedalus, I have no one else to turn to, therefore I come to you. I know that you alone can assist me".

"I will give my life for you, my Queen. Ask what you wish and if it is in my power I will gladly give it to you". He replied.

She paused once again, ashamed of her request, but her heart wouldn't allow her to keep silent.

"I wish to have the White Bull".

"I don't understand, you want to keep the Bull"? He asked.

"I can't stop my husband from sacrificing the bull in a few days, but before he is killed I wish to make love to it". As she said this she lowered her eyes in shame.

He alone understood the pain she felt, for he loved her so dearly, and would have given anything to her. He softly spoke, "I'll do what I can to assist you".

Pasiphae ran to him and once again began to cry in his arms. He kissed her forehead once before leaving her alone in his chamber and immediately went to work in his workshop, spending the entire night constructing a mechanical wooden cow which he then hollowed out and covered in the skin of one of the cows from the herd, creating a heifer so life-like that he was sure that not even the Gods themselves could tell it was an imposter.

The night before the new moon came, and as Daedalus watched the sun set, he went to the queen's chamber and knocked softly on her door. There was no reply. He knocked again, this time a little louder.

"Go away, I don't wish to speak with anyone". Her voice quivered from behind the closed door.

He knocked once more, this time calling out to her,

"My Queen, it is I, your faithful servant Daedalus, I have found a way to assist you".

She ran to the door and when it opened he saw that her eyes were red and swollen from days of crying. He held her in his arms as he told her of his plan. She didn't even change, but rushed with him to the stables in her dressing gown, feet still bare. Before they reached the stables she saw the White Bull in the meadow and just stood in place thinking that her heart would break. Daedalus took her hand and walked with her to the stables where he lifted her up allowing her access into the wooden creature from an access door that was concealed on its back and once shut inside the wooden creature, he wheeled it to the meadow where the magnificent bull was grazing. Poseidon guided his bull to approach and couple with the mechanical cow, and as Daedalus watched from the distance his heart felt as if it were breaking for the love he felt for his queen.

Once the bull was finished mating, and while the queen was still concealed within the wooden cow, Poseidon lifted her madness and instantly as if her eyes were just open she realized what she had done. In shame she ran back to the palace, hiding in the shadows, hoping that none would discover her disgrace. But Poseidon had not yet finished with her, nor with Minos. The next dawn, the bull was sacrifice as was planned, but Pasiphae couldn't bring herself to participate in the ritual, her shame of this unnatural love for this magnificent bull had overwhelmed her and as the people of Crete celebrated, thinking Demeter would finally be appeased by the sacrifice and would no longer hold back her fruits of the land, the queen stayed in her chamber alone and cried. She wouldn't even allow Daedalus to comfort her this time.

After a month when Pasiphae found out that she was with child, fearing that it wasn't her husbands, she went to Daedalus once again for help. Together they traveled to Delphi, for she wouldn't allow him to go alone to consult the Oracle, and once within the temple of Apollo her fears were confirmed, her unborn child wasn't her husband's son. She didn't need to ask who the father was, for she knew what the answer would be.

The Priestesses of the Oracle sat on her tripod, her head down and eyes closed as the vapors filled the chamber. Pasiphae began to tremble, the noxious fumes getting to her. Daedalus held her tight as the Priestesses, once within her trance called out to the God Apollo. His answer came through.

> "Your shame will destroy the kingdom that your husband, King Minos, has created. The child that you carry will be born in the form of a creature neither man nor bull, but both; a man with a bull's head who will taste only human flesh.
> This creature must be hidden within the dungeons of the palace at Knossos and fed a sacrifice of fourteen youths every year. If this sacrifice is not presented to him, he will ravage the countryside bringing fear and death to all the people of Crete".

As she heard these words Pasiphae fainted. Daedalus carried her outside the temple where the fresh air would allow her to think clear, and when she came to she realized that there was nothing else for her to do but to tell her husband the truth, knowing that he would find out once the child was born that it couldn't possibly be his son. The queen rushed back to the palace planning on telling her husband everything, begging for his forgiveness

Once alone with Minos, she began, "That night you dreamed the God Poseidon came to tell you about the White Bull, I feared that we would be punished by the Gods, and now I see that my fears were not in vain." She lowered her head and could not stop the tears from flowing. Minos lifted her face and she found the words, "I have found out that I am expecting a child".

"A child, that is wonderful news, I see this as the Gods blessing us, not punishing us". He said as he kissed his wife.

The tears fell and she couldn't speak, even though she knew she had to tell her husband everything.

"The child isn't your". She finally said, then added, "I fear that it will be this child that I carry that'll be the destruction of our kingdom".

"Who is the father"? Minos fumed, thinking that his wife had been unfaithful to him.

"I cannot tell you that, I am too ashamed". She said through her hands, which she held up to cover her face.

"It's Daedalus, I am sure of it. I've seen the way that he looks at you. I'll destroy him".

"No, it's not Daedalus". She sobbed.

"Then tell me who it is, so I could kill him". He demanded.

"He is already dead". She said softly.

"Tell me woman, who fathered your child!" he shouted at her.

"It was…the Bull that you sacrificed". She finally said the words that she dreaded to speak. Once these words were out, she couldn't stop and told her husband everything. Upon hearing his wife's confession, Minos was very understanding, for he knew that it wasn't his wife's doing, but the will of Gods that possessed her. This was their punishment for hiding my daughter and the blasphemy of allowing the marriage ceremony to take place within their palace walls, but I wouldn't stop here, I was determined to destroy not only their marriage, but the entire kingdom as well. That night Minos prayed to his father Zeus to assist him in his time of need.

"Zeus, father, I pray that you will lift this curse from my family and my kingdom". Instantly in a bright flash of light Zeus appeared to meet his son Minos.

"My son, don't blame yourself, for your kingdom is suffering because you have assisted me with my request of housing my daughter. Poseidon will not harm you, for you've found favor with him, but he won't ignore Demeter's request either. I am afraid that Pasiphae will give birth to a monster, a creature who will feed only on human flesh. This creature is destined to destroy your kingdom, I cannot stop this, but I'll protect you and your wife Pasiphae from all harm. I wish that I could do something more, but I can not, for even the Gods cannot change destiny, and it is destiny that directs the destruction of Crete".

I wouldn't let Zeus' love for his son spoil my revenge of Minos and Pasiphae. What did he care about the love that I felt for my daughter when he gave her away in marriage to our brother without my permission? I would see justice. I gave myself to Poseidon in passion that night in return for his assistance.

"Dear brother, I cannot forgive Minos and Pasiphae for giving my daughter to Hades, and will only be appeased after their beloved son, Androgeos is with her in the Underworld".

I asked this of him only after we had made love the entire night, knowing that he wouldn't be able to refuse me then.

"Sister, what you ask is a trespass against innocent blood, Androgeos is innocent of his parents doings".

"I don't care, for my daughter was also innocent". I said bitterly.

So that night Poseidon arranged for Androgeos' death.

Androgeos excelled in all athletic sports, and was at that time in Athens participating in the sporting event of the century, the All-Athenian games, in which he won first place in every contest, with a little help from Poseidon, of course. During the night Poseidon sent a fear into the king of Athens, King Aegeus' heart, making him believe that Androgeos wouldn't be satisfied with the awards he won but would not stop until the entire kingdom of Athens belonged to him, and so the king spoke with the other athletics shaming their performances and in a fit of jealousy that was inspired by none other than my dear brother, they laid in wait of Minos' only son. When morning arrived and Androgeos was walking to the boat that would carry him home to bring glory to his country, fifty of the athletes ambushed him and only after a fierce battle and the lose of many lives was the youth finally killed. His remains were taken back to his parents on Crete, and it was only then that I truly felt avenged. In his anger Minos declared that the King of Athens was to send him fourteen of their children, seven maidens and seven young men, every year to be sacrificed, for this is what the oracle at Delphi requested after all and it would only be fitting for the youths destined to be sacrificed would belong to the race of those who killed his only son.

Eight months later Queen Pasiphae gave birth to a hideous creature, a perfect human child from the shoulders down, but with the head of a mighty bull. Even though she loathed the sight of the child she couldn't forget her passion for the beautiful bull and when she looked at his eyes, she saw the love she felt for his father, and no matter how much she tried, she couldn't deny her motherly instincts. She named the child Asterion, but it wasn't by this name that he became known. Throughout the centuries, the myths call him only the Minotaur, a name that translates as "the Bull of Minos", and it was this name alone that he would be remembered by. Within a week of his birth he was fully-grown with a huge appetite. Now the fourteen children who were sent from Athens were kept prisoners within the palace and were fed to this monster at the rate of about one per month. During the years that followed many innocent victims were given to the Minotaur, and it wasn't until three years later that I would finally allow his death to occur, through one of Poseidon's sons, a boy named Theseus.

Theseus was destined from birth to become king of both Crete and Athens and it was his bravery when facing the Minotaur that would lead him to this goal. Just before the third group of youths destined to be food for this monster, were to leave for Crete, Theseus, whose mortal father was King Aegeus, arranged that his name would be pulled from the lot of those allegeable for the sacrifice, and when his father heard that he would be sending his only son to his death he wept.

"Don't fear for my safety, father, for I intend to return home and as your heir one day rule the land". Theseus said to his father as he prepared for the long journey to Crete.

Once there he, along with the other young victims was imprisoned and it was in a cell in the dungeons under the palace that he met Daedalus, who had been imprisoned there by Minos three years earlier. Daedalus' cell was right next to Theseus, and during the long nights, when all were asleep they developed a plan to not only destroy the Minotaur, but to destroy the entire kingdom of Crete. Pasiphae couldn't forget the assistance Daedalus had given her and even though the king forbid it, she visited the magician daily for the past three years and it was his love for her that kept him alive so long. The queen didn't even question him when he asked her for some herbs, herbs that he mixed together creating a love potion that he sent with her to give to her daughter Ariadne. Once this potion touched her lips, Ariadne fell madly in love with Theseus. That night both mother and daughter came down into the dungeon and when Ariadne's eyes meet those of Theseus she fell to her knees and offered her assistance to him, knowing full well that with her help he would destroy her father's kingdom. In return she asked that when he leaves the island he would take her with him, for she knew that after all that was to happen she would no longer be able to live within her father's palace. He pledged that he would obey her request.

Ariadne arranged for Theseus to be taken to the Minotaur the next day, and before he was to depart she was able to present him the sword that he would use to kill the Minotaur along with a ball of thread, explaining that the corridors within the dungeon can be misleading, even to the palace guards, therefore he was to unwind the thread as he was lead through the dungeon. Poseidon made sure that the palace guards wouldn't notice the sword under Theseus' robe, nor the thread he carried by placing a veil over their eyes, allowing him to enter into the cell that caged the Minotaur armed.

Within seconds of shutting the youth in the cell, the guards heard terrifying cries and screams, but these they ignored assuming the screams were from the poor boy as he was being eaten alive; all the victims screamed when they saw the hideous monster, not once did they think the screams might be coming from the beast itself. With the Minotaur dead, Theseus easily followed the thread back to his cell and freed Daedalus, and with Ariadne he left for the shore where a boat was waiting for them.

"Daedalus, you must come with us". Theseus said as he saw the magician ran toward the palace.

"I cannot leave without Pasiphae". He replied as Theseus and Ariadne boarded the ship.

Daedalus ran through the palace, calling out to Pasiphae. Finally, after almost an hour he found her alone in his old cell crying. When she saw him tears fell from her eyes.

"I thought you left with Theseus and my daughter". She said in between kisses.

"I couldn't leave without you".

They both knew that it was no longer safe to stay on the island, Minos would destroy them both when he found out what they had done.

"Come with me". Daedalus whispered in the queen's ear.

Over the last three years she had opened her heart to the Magician and she knew that she would be able to find happiness wherever he was, so she left the island with him.

I should have been satisfied knowing that Minos lost his son to death, was deceived by his favorite daughter and abandoned by his wife, but I wasn't. I wouldn't be satisfied until his entire kingdom was destroyed, and this occurred shortly after Minos left his palace at Knossos in search of his wife Pasiphae and Daedalus. Poseidon, being not only the God of the Seas, but an Earth Shaker as well, struck the island with his mighty Trident causing the worst destruction in Crete's history. Poseidon waited for Minos to leave, for he couldn't destroy one who was not only Zeus' son, but a man who had found favor with him, so I also waited patiently. Once Minos was safe from the island, Poseidon struck the earth with his Trident and a massive earthquake occurred, destroying the entire island. With his kingdom left in ruins, and nowhere to go, Minos searched for years for Daedalus and his wife but no matter how long he searched he couldn't find them.

Years later, while in the town of Camicos, Minos heard that a great magician was living in the palace of King Cocalus. Thinking that it could only be Daedalus, Minos went to the king and after explaining who he was and the reason for him coming, the king took him in. It was here that I finished my task of destroying Minos, for that very night I sent a fear into the king's daughters making them believe that this visitor only came to the palace to kill their father, King Cocalus, and take over his land. In their loyalty they devised a plan and in the morning when Minos was taking a bath, they poured boiling oil on him, thereby killing him and sending him to the Underworld to keep my daughter company.

My revenge on Minos was complete, but it didn't leave a sweet taste in my mouth, for after his death Hades and my daughter paid Minos great honors for his assistance; they made him one of the Judges of the Dead. Minos' brother, Rhadymanthos upon his death was appointed the Judge who ruled over the Elysian Fields, and Aeacus, another judge was appointed to hold the keys to the Underworld, but Minos held the highest position, being the judge who made the final decision on where the souls of the newly departed would stay while in the Underworld. I couldn't continue to punish Pasiphae or their children any longer, for they weren't really to blame, so after years of tormenting them, I finally left them in peace.

IX
Demeter

    I LEFT POSEIDON'S palace long before the destruction of Minos' kingdom was complete, for I knew that once the wheels were set in motion, what was to come would; even Zeus himself could not save his beloved son. For his help I will never forget my dear brother Poseidon, but I had to leave, I couldn't stay with him, nor any of the other Gods. I cut my long beautiful golden hair as was customary for women when in mourning and dressed in a black torn robe and veil that covered my tear stained cheeks, and in this state I walked on the face of the earth alone in my grief, devising a way of getting even with the Great God Zeus for his treachery. After several weeks of wandering alone an inspiration hit me, just as if Zeus himself struck me with one of his thunderbolts. I knew that I could do nothing to harm Zeus, for he was much too powerful a God even for me, but I being the Goddess of Fertility could withhold the fruits of the earth and not allow any grain to sprout nor allow any mortal births to occur until the humans who Zeus so loved were totally destroyed. To mortals I was known as Birth, but soon I would become Death.

    To ensure that my plan succeeded I needed assistance and this I easily acquired. I left my black robe and dressed in my most seductive gown and went to visit Boreas, the God of the North Wind and was easily able to convince him to let loose his son, Zephyrus, the Personification of Strong Winds and Storms, bringing a cold wind over all the lands, a wind that would make the leaves fall from the trees and all the crops to wither and die. I didn't have to persuade him, for he felt pity for me, knowing how much I loved my dear daughter and he answered my prayers instantly. That evening just after the sun set, Zephyrus came in the form of a wild gray stallion ravaging the countryside unleashing a cold wind as was never known before, a tremendous wind that blew across the earth bringing icy rain and snow wherever it touched. Humans sought shelter within their homes as Zephyrs rattled at their doors and tapped on the windows, tap...tap...tap, seeking entrance. His sought out even the smallest crevice only to blow out the fires of their hearth. Zephyrus' breath, like a tornado ravaged the land causing destruction wherever it touched. On that first night alone more than one-half of all life on Earth was totally destroyed.

The Goddess of Destiny, Ananke gave the fertility of the entire earth to me when I was declared Goddess of Fertility, therefore I had no need to call upon any other God or Goddess to assist me in cursing the land. I looked up into the sky and saw the clouds part and the cold light of the full moon shining down on me. I stood alone, with only the moonlight as my witness, and slowly I raised my arms to the heavens and called out to the Universe. I called out to the energy of the Earth itself to fill my body with power. Facing the East I began my curse:

> "I call to the elements of the East, to the Spirits of the Air, the Sirens, take my prayers and lift them to the four corners of the Universe".

Turning to face the South, I continued:

> "I call to the elements of the South, to the Spirits of Fire, the Dragons, let your breath bring power to my words, giving them a life of their own".

Another quarter turn, now facing the West,

> "I call to the elements of the West, to the Spirits of Water, the Undines, let my body be receptive to the powers I call upon, allowing their energy to flow into and throughout me".

Finishing my curse facing the North;

> "I call to the elements of the North, to the Spirits of the Earth, the Gnomes, take my words deep within the Earth and unleash their power".

As I said these words, I could feel the energy flow up from deep within the earth itself, entering my feet and slowly building as it pulsated throughout my entire body. With each beat of my heart I could feel the power intensifying until I felt that I was completely full and could take in no more. I stood for several moments, allowing the power of the Earth itself to consume me. My body, not used to this much power, began to quiver; and I felt as if I could conquer the Universe itself. It took all my will to focus this surging energy into my hands and when I looked down at them I saw the red glow of all the sadness that had consumed my soul since I lost my beloved daughter Kore. In despair, I lowered my hands, palms down and directed all of my hatred, my anger, and all of my grief into the depth of the earth. As I did this I watched as the energy crackled and sizzled as if exploded from my hands, and once touching the land the red energy serge is a massive wave, branching out in all directions until its power reached the four corners of the earth. Once freed of all my sorrow I staggered back, thrown off balance by the power that I had unleashed. My curse was complete; my heart empty.

For the next year, the amount of time that I was deceived, I wouldn't allow any crops to grow or births to occur on the earth. I had become Death, and I must admit that in my bitterness I took pleasure as I watched as all mortal life began to slowly wither and die. During this year there were many prayers and rituals dedicated to me, begging that I lift my curse from the lands, but just as Zeus refused to hear my objections when I forbid my beloved daughter from marrying Hades, I was deaf to their pleas. Once my curse was complete I once again dressed in the black tattered robes and wandered the once rich fields that were now as barren as my life. I assumed the shape of an old woman, for in my heart I was old and weary and wanted to find death myself, but being immortal that was not possible, so in the shape of an old woman, bent over in weariness, I wandered the earth alone; sadness and regret were my only companions.

I took the name Deo, for it was impossible for me to travel with my birth name, and in my wandering I found no humans who welcomed me. All were starving and none wished to share their last meal with a stranger so near to death herself, so I traveled the civilized lands alone, until I reached a small village in a remote corner of Attica, a town named Eleusis. It was a poor city, all the people had left for the neighboring town Athens and I was surprised to find that the king of this village, Celeus and his wife Metanira welcomed me. They took me into their meager home and only after offering me food and drink, they asked me where I was from, knowing by my dress that I was not from their kingdom.

"My name is Deo". I quietly said to them making sure my head stayed bowed, fearful that they would instantly detect my disguise if they would see the power in my eyes. "I was born many decades ago to a noble family in Crete".

I then made up a story of what I thought my life would have been if I were born a mortal. I told them how I traveled over the sea for many months from my home in Crete not willingly, but as a captive on a pirate ship, explaining that the pirates wished only to sell me at market as a slave. I explained that one night when the ship I was held prisoner on was at the shore, I was able to sneak out of my cabin, since I was such an old woman, the pirates didn't think it necessary to chain me, and once freed from their ship I ran into the woods and hid. There I waited until their ship had set off and I could no longer see the sails on the horizon. I wandered alone for days, for no one would offer me food or shelter, until I met the King's daughters by the well as I was trying to get a drink. Even though there was little food throughout Celeus' kingdom, I was given a banquet fit for the Gods, and in return for their hospitality I made sure that their land alone would produce grain, and their livestock would not be barren, so no one within this household tasted death during my year of vengeance.

Shortly before I cursed the lands, Metaneira gave birth to a beautiful son who she named Demophoon. He was less than a year old when I entered their home, and she feared that he wouldn't survive the famine,

"I would do anything to protect my dear son". She confided in me one night as we sat by the hearth.

"You have no need to fear, the Gods will watch over him". That night I promised myself that I would not let this innocent child die, for it was in him alone that I was able to give the love I felt for my lost daughter. The months that I stayed within the kingdom tending Demophoon, I felt as if he was my own child, and I couldn't stand the thought of him growing old like his father only to one day taste death, therefore I let him nurse from my breast, and with the sweet milk of a Goddess he began to grow at an astonishing rate, much faster than other children. Soon he was able to stand on his own and he was walking within a couple of months since my arrival. When the time came for him to eat solid food, I started feeding him the food of the Gods, Ambrosia, and at night while he slept I would place this child who I so loved within the hearth and while holding him over the fires that burned there, I prayed to my dearest sister, the Goddess Hestia,

> *"Hestia, Goddess of the Hearth, and my dear sister, you who are worshipped in every house, even above the great God Zeus, hear my pleas. Just as the hearth is the religious center of the home, you are the religious center of all life. I beg you to make this child, Demophoon, immortal. I could not bear to see Death touch his soul".*

The ritual of burning the mortality from a mortal child normally lasts three nights starting on the first night of the new moon, and I had almost completed the ritual when on the last night, I was sure that Demophoon would soon be immortal, and as I held him in the fire, I forgot to enchant him making sure that his cries would not wake his parents. Metanira hearing her son's sobs as the fire licked at his naked body was awaken instantly. She rushed into the chamber and beheld the sight of her son being held by this old woman within the hearth as the fires burned around him. Without hesitation she snatched the child from my arms as her screams alerted her husband. The King entered the chamber within seconds and found his son lying on the floor crying while his wife, the Queen was accusing me of trying to kill their son.

"We have taken you in and given you food and shelter, and this is how you repay us, by trying to kill my beloved son".

I didn't say anything in my defense at first, only standing there while she accused me. The spell was broken, I could do no more; Demophoon was destine to grow old and one-day die, all because of his mother's lack of trust. Once the reality of the situation set in, I, in a fury revealed myself to her as the Goddess I was, and she seeing me in all my glory fell at my feet with tears in her eyes, begging for my forgiveness.

"I would have made your son immortal, like the Gods themselves, but because of your foolish behavior, he will not be able to escape the God Thanatos' grip. Death will one day find him". I said to her as I lifted her to her feet.

Through her sobs, she begged me,
"Forgive me, for I only wished to protect my son from harm".

How could I not forgive her for trying to protect her beloved son, was I not also only trying to keep my daughter from harm? I did forgave her, but I could no longer stay within their house, so I left the next morning after instructing the King to build a great temple and dedicate it to me. He agreed, and I promised that I would return when Demophoon reached manhood, and show him the mysteries of the Gods, and this I did not forget, for when Demophoon came of age I came to him and taught him my Mysteries, and every five years, at the end of September all the people of Demophoon's kingdom would celebrate the Festival of Demeter, a elaborate affair which took place over a period of nine days and nights.

Now during my yearlong absence from Mount Olympus, Zeus was beginning to worry about the havoc I was bringing upon the mortal world. His beloved children, those who were mortal from his many lovers, were dieing and he was unable to offer them any assistance, for no matter how powerful he was he wasn't able to lift the curse I had laid upon the land. Hades also wasn't pleased with my vengeance, for the Underworld was becoming overcrowded, and since I, also being a Fertility Goddess, wouldn't allow any births to occur he couldn't send any soul back to an earthly life, so his palace was soon overflowing with phantoms of the dead who allow him no rest.

Thanatos, the Messenger of Death, who was once a beautiful God with short curly blonde hair dressed in shinning golden armor and beautiful white wings that would transport him swiftly to the dying to release their souls, feeding off their last breath became bloated after several months of gorging on the sick and dying. Soon his armor was no longer able to fit his swollen body and he took to wearing a tunic for he no longer needed armor for protection, for since his weight increased his wings were barely able to lift him and he became sluggish and was no longer was able to bring death swiftly to those who suffered. The dying no longer scratched and clawed at him as he sucked their last breath, for after several months of waiting for him, waiting for his kiss, they welcomed his touch with open arms.

After a year of this destruction Zeus finally had enough of watching helplessly as two-thirds of all mortal life was destroyed, for the cries of those who still lived would not allow him rest. He sent Iris, the Goddess of the Rainbow and the messenger between the Heavens and the earth, between the Gods and mortals, to find me and bring me back to Mount Olympus and finally put an end to the curse I had brought upon the earth. I was sitting in one of my temples, near Eleusis, where I would sit alone day after day waiting until I could be reunited with my daughter, when Iris finally found me. Before speaking, she bowed slightly to me, showing her respect for a Goddess as powerful as myself, and I almost for a split second became transfixed by the sight of her multicolored tunic, which was woven from the thread of a single spider's web. This tunic, at first glance, appears bright white, but then as the sun shines on it, it suddenly takes on a yellow hue with a touch of saffron, but then a second later, you would see a fiery orange, blending with a purple sheen, until all the colors of the rainbow had appeared transfixing the gaze. This tunic was embroidered with jewels that gleamed like the stars and only after a few seconds of looking at the Sun reflecting off it I understood how mortals could easily become transfixed by the sight.

Her words brought me back to the moment.

"Demeter, Goddess of Fertility, I have come here to beg you to return with me to Mount Olympus, for your dear brother Zeus wishes to speak to you".

I noticed that her words were sweet but I knew they were laced with poison, for if I were to return with her to Mount Olympus I knew that Zeus would surely punish me.

"I am sorry, but I can't. I vowed that I wouldn't return to my brothers and sisters until I can be reunited my daughter, Kore". I said as I turned away from her.

She cleared her throat, letting me know that she wasn't through with me. I turned only my head to look at her.

"I fear for you if you don't agree to accompany me back to greet your brother and the other Olympians". She said to me, adding. "Zeus misses you dearly".

"I won't return with you". I said again, this time more firmly, then I once again turned away from her gaze.

I knew that she was becoming frustrated, she didn't expect me to refuse Zeus' message, for no other God or Goddess has ever dared refused him.

"Zeus is angry with you for allowing the land to become barren, but he has agreed to forgive you if you return with me to the palace at once". She said.

We stood there at a stand off as I watched the sky slowly darken as the Sun traveled through the heavens, allowing the moon to awake from her daily slumber and illuminate the night sky. We stayed within the temple throughout the night. I was very firm; stating that I wouldn't set foot back on Mount Olympus unless it was to welcome my daughter each time Iris spoke. Finally as the night started to wane and the sky slowly began to glow with the first light of the Sun peeking over the horizon, Iris asked me once more to return with her,

"Please, Demeter... please, I beg you. Don't make me return to Zeus alone".

"I would like nothing more than to be back home with my beloved brother and sisters, but I cannot return unless I come with my daughter, Kore".

This was my final answer.

She bowed to me and said farewell, and I watched as she flew into the coming dawn. I was alone again, but not for long, for it wasn't even midday when I felt the presence of another God, and as I turned I saw Hermes, Zeus' personal messenger approaching the sanctuary. He didn't speak, waiting until I spoke first.

"Hermes, if you came here to try to convince me into returning to my brother's house you're wasting your time, for you know I cannot return with you. There is nothing you can say to me to make me change my mind".

He paused before he replied as if he were trying to find the right words to say to me; Hermes, the God of Communication, chooses his word carefully so as not to be misunderstood.

"If you refuse to return with me and greet the other Olympians, I will have no other choose but to make the long journey to the Underworld, where I will speak with your daughter Persephone and her husband Hades and arrange a meeting between mother and daughter at your brother's palace. If your daughter agrees to meet with you, will you return then"?

"I will return, only if Kore is there without Hades, for I wish to speak to her alone." I replied.

"I'll return to Mount Olympus with her, and at dawn tomorrow Zeus and your daughter will be waiting to welcome you home". He said as he swiftly departed for his long journey to the Underworld.

Joy filled my heart for the first time in almost a year. I would soon be reunited with my beloved daughter; tomorrow morning I'll be able to hold her in my arms and tell her how much I loved her and how for the last year I have thought of nothing but my longing to see her.

****

The following dawn I was at the gates of Mount Olympus as the first rays of the Sun started illuminate the sky and as I glimpsed up I saw my daughter waiting at the top of the stairs. I started to run towards her. I was half way up to the palace when she saw me, and she too started running to greet me with tears in her eyes.

We embraced for what seemed like an eternity.

"Mother, I have missed you this last year. I have so much to tell you". She said to me once I finally let her out of my embrace. Her words brought tears to my eyes, and I held her and kissed her forehead. I couldn't believe that she was really there, she was in my arms and I would never allow her to leave me again.

"Let us enter Mount Olympus and take our seats next to your father". I finally said to her.

"Mother, before you enter the gates, I must tell you that I didn't come alone. My husband, Hades, is here with me".

She paused here, seeing the expression on my face made her stop for a moment before she could speak again. "He's within the palace speaking with father".

You couldn't imagine my anger; Hermes swore to me that he would not bring Hades with him, knowing that I wouldn't return unless my daughter was there alone. I didn't know if Kore had picked up the gift of reading others thoughts from Hades during the last year of living with him in the Underworld, but as if she knew the reason of my anger she answered me.

"Don't blame Hermes mother, his message was clear that you wished to speak to me alone, but you must understand that Hades is my husband now and that I love him. This hatred between the two of you cannot continue without causing me grief. I love you both and refuse to take sides".

The war between the Olympians and the Titans seemed like a squabble between two children compared to the fight that took place just outside the palace. I flatly refused to set one foot through the gate, and after hours of holding my ground Zeus brought out our mother to speak to me, for when the three brothers were fighting for their domains, it was Rhea alone who was able to reach an understanding with them. All stood quiet as Rhea stood there contemplating the situation. Finally she spoke.

"My children, there has been fighting between all of you for too long now, we must accept what the Fates have given us and find peace within ourselves. I will no longer stand by watching as my children try to destroy not only each other but the earth as well".

"But mother, all I wish for is to be reunited with my daughter". I interrupted her, trying to explain to her why I behaved the way I did.

"Silence! Demeter, your daughter is no longer a child and must be able to stand alone and make her own decisions. She is in love with Hades and gave herself willingly to him in marriage, it is time for you to let her go".

"I cannot. I fear that no one understands my grief". I shouted back at her.

"Since Demeter will not give life back to the land until her daughter is reunited with her, I will propose a compromise". All stood quiet as she continued

"Persephone will spend one-half the year in the Underworld with her husband, Hades and during the other half she will live here, on Mount Olympus with her mother Demeter and the other Gods and Goddess".

Kore, speaking to her grandmother Rhea pleaded,

"But grandmother, why are you punishing me, I did nothing wrong".

She took Kore's hand and held it as she spoke softly to her, trying to comfort her favorite granddaughter.

"Persephone, it isn't I who am punishing you. You see many centuries ago it was decided by the Fates that Hades' wife would spend one-half the year in the Underworld as Queen of the Dead, only to return to the land of the living for the other half of the year. This is the only way I can see of convincing your mother to lift her curse from the land".

"I will compromise also", I said, "For if my daughter is to spend one-half the year in the Underworld, I will curse the land for this amount of time only. When she is returned to me I will again allow the grains to sprout and grow and the animals to reproduce, but when she departs for the Underworld I will call the winds to bring a cold breeze across the face of the earth destroying all the fruits that I have given".

I spoke this pledge not only to my mother Rhea, and to Zeus, but to all the Gods and Goddess present, I spoke this pledge to the Earth itself.

"Very well, Persephone will live with her mother Demeter and the other Gods and Goddesses on Mount Olympus from the Twenty-first day of the Third month of the year, which will be known as Kathodos, the time that Persephone as symbol of the seed, goes down into the Underworld, to the Twenty-first day of the Ninth month, which will be known as Anodos, when life once again returns to the earth after its long slumber. On these two days the amount of time for night and day will be equal, for the rest of the year, as the hours of the night increase, so will the cold".

Instead of running to me, as I thought she would do, Kore ran to Hades and buried her face into his chest trying to hold back her sobs. I walked up to her smiling, but the look in her eyes told me she wished for nothing but my death. I took her hand and tried to pull her from Hades, and she turned to me and said,

"Mother, I can never forgive you for trying to destroy my happiness".

I tried to explain to her that I didn't wish to destroy her happiness, that I only wished to protect her, but she wouldn't hear me. As she said her goodbyes to Hades through her sobs, I saw that he too shed a tear, and as I watched them together my heart began to melt and sadness crept into my soul. Was I wrong to try to protect my daughter from an eternity within the Underworld? I was only acting as any mother who loves her daughter would act. Hades placed one final kiss on his wife's forehead and entered his chariot and soon was out of sight, Zeus then took Kore's hand and lead her to me, and I thought then, for the first time, that maybe I was wrong, maybe I should've welcomed my daughter's happiness. I wished that I could lift the curse from the land and release her to live the rest of her life with my brother, Hades, in the

Underworld, but being a Goddess I couldn't. My words, once spoken, could never be taken back.

I'd promised that I would release the land from my curse once I was reunited with her, and so I did. I once again lifted my arms to the heavens and called to the Universe to fill my body with the energy of the four elements and once filled with their power I called to the God of the North Wind, Boreas,

"Boreas, I beg you to hold back your son Zephyrus from destroying the land with his cold breath".

I paused here until I was certain that he heard my call, and then I spoke again.

"I call to the Earth mother, to Gaia, begging her to once again allow life to spring forth from the land".

I was surprised to see that almost instantly the trees, as if they waited only for my words to be spoken, finally releasing them from their long slumber, began to sprout buds. Spring had arrived after a long, bitter winter and it didn't take long before the land was offering up its life everywhere, and as I walked along the earth, the feel of the damp grass against my bear feet comforted me. But even this did not relieve the sadness I felt in my heart, for I didn't truly get my daughter back until many, many seasons later.

X
Persephone

MOTHER, LIKE ALWAYS, has felt the need to interrupt my story once more, saying that I could not possibility have known her reasons for her holding back the fertility of the earth after she found out that I married Hades; explaining that it was only feelings of sadness and longing after losing her beloved daughter to a God that she didn't approve of as a suitable husband that caused her destruction of two-thirds of all life on the planet. She told of how in desperation she searched for days, and unable to locate the entrance to the Underworld, and how she conspired with her brother, my uncle Poseidon, and with his help alone she was able to destroy the island of Crete, and the Kingdom of Zeus' son Minos as punishment for his assisting both Gods in their plot to take me from her. With the bitter taste of the revenge she instilled on King Minos still on her lips, she sought a way to get even with Zeus since he, in her eyes, instigated Hades to capture me. What mother didn't tell was how her actions affected my new life as Queen of the Dead; how it affected the other Gods and Goddesses, the lesser deities, and most of all; how it affected the poor mortals who would suffer the most. I will pause here briefly to retell the events that mother had already explained, for I feel that my perspective needs to be expressed to clarify any misunderstandings the reader may have.

During the first couple of months of my marriage I was the happiest I had ever been in my life. Everything was perfect, but as time went on and Hades and I became acquainted with each other I started to feel that something was missing from my life. I soon realized that even though I loved Hades deeply and had made many new friends here in the Underworld, I missed the other Gods and Goddesses I had grown up with, and I especially missed mother. One night, about seven months after we had married, as we sat quietly at dinner Hades, knowing my feelings, suggested to me that I visit Mount Olympus the next day. At the thought of seeing mother I became excited,

"Will you accompany me home? Now that we are married mother couldn't refuse you from entering the palace".

"No, I'm content here in the Underworld, now that your here by my side there's no need for me to leave".

The tone of his reply suggested sadness to me… a sadness that I couldn't understand. I didn't know then that he too longed to be welcomed by his brothers and sisters, but he couldn't stand the thought of their rejection. He had spent many centuries alone in the Underworld, and those long years have made him cautious of interacting with not only mortals, but with the other Gods as well.

The next day as Hades helped me into the chariot, he said to me,

"Don't stay too long that you forget that I'm here waiting for your return".

"I promise that I'll be back early tomorrow". I said to him before kissing him one last time.

It is a long journey from the Underworld to Mount Olympus, with mortal beasts it would take many months, but with the six immortal steeds that pull Hades' gilded chariot, the trip takes less than half a day, bringing me to Mount Olympus at just after dawn. The Gods can also use magic and appear at certain places by their will alone, but this takes a tremendous amount of energy, and only the most powerful Gods can travel this way without becoming weakened. Most travel by chariot as the mortals did, the only difference being that magical beasts were used to pull the chariots instead of mere horses. As I flew across the land I though about how much I had missed mother, and the closer I came to Mount Olympus the greater my anxiety grew.

"Would mother forgive me for deceiving her and marrying a God that I knew she disapproved of"? I though, reassuring myself, *"I was married now, so even if she did there was nothing she could do about it".*

When I finally arrived at the base of Mount Olympus I exited the chariot and looked up at the towering palace. I felt a chill run up my spine, but put it out of my mind, blaming my excitement at seeing my family after so long. Walking up to the lead stallion, I petted him for a moment before whispering in his ear, telling him to return to the Underworld and return for me early the next day. I began the long walk up the hill to the palace, but before I even I set foot on the grounds I knew that something was terribly wrong. The Goddess Season, who usually sits at the front gates allowing only the Gods and Goddesses entrance to the palace, was no where to be found.

I called out to her... there was no answer.

Waiting patiently, I felt a cool breeze blow across my face. Nothing happened... I called out to her once again, and still there was no answer. I was about to leave when I saw the curtain of clouds that obscure the gate to the palace began to slowly part, allowing me entrance into the palace grounds. I walked slowing in; caution made me pause as the scent of death filled my senses. Even though I had been the consort of the Lord of the Underworld for a few short months, I couldn't mistake that scent.

I called out to the servants... again there was no answer. Looking around the garden I noticed that it had not been tended for weeks, weeds were starting to strangle the beautiful flowers that Zeus was so proud of, they were now withered and the sweet smell they produced, a smell that as a child I took for granted, no longer filled the air. It was replaced by the strong scent of death and decay.

I stood just inside the gates, and was aware of a strange quietness that surrounded me; I didn't hear the usual bubbling of the water as it flowed down through the garden, nor the singing of the many birds that usually took shelter within this sanctuary. I walked to the stream and when I looked down at it, expecting to see the flowing waters, instead the water was still, as if some force greater than it held it magically in place. I reached down to touch it, and was surprised to find that it no longer held the properties of water, but had somehow become solid; it had turned to ice. Confused, I stood up and walked toward the palace but as my feet touched the once green grass I heard a sound that I couldn't explain,

"Crunch….Crunch…Crunch…"

Looking down I saw a sight that at the time I couldn't comprehend, for it was totally foreign to my senses; the usually lush green grass that was a blanket in the garden was no longer green, but yellowed and now covered with piles of dead leaves in various shades of browns, gold and oranges, and as I stepped on these dead leaves they made a strange crunching sound and crumbled into nothing more than debris.

I wanted to reach the palace and for father to tell me that everything was as it should be, but I knew that he wouldn't, for when I finally entered the main hall I couldn't believe what I beheld. The cold wind bite into my face and as I looked around I saw that all of the servants had the skins of animals wrapped around their bodies, apparently they had adapted this style of dress to keep warm, but it wasn't enough, for they stood around a great bonfire that filled the center of the great hall, it's smoke rising to the heavens above. There wasn't the usual music, the voices of the Gods debating as they snacked on ambrosia, nor the chattering of the birds as they flew over the palace, only the sound of the crackling fire and the hushed voices of the servants. Being a major deity, the cold doesn't affect me as much as it would those who were only minor deities, but even I felt the bite of the cold air and a shiver ran down my spine. The warmth of the fire drew me closer and as I moved toward it trying to warm myself, one of the servants ran to me,

"Persephone, I am glad that you are here. You must do something to stop this destruction your mother, the Goddess Demeter, is causing".

I didn't have time to address her, nor to ask what destruction was she talking about, before Zeus' voice bellowed out my name,

"Persephone, come into my chamber immediately!"

I ran to his chamber, even though I was a married Goddess now, I was still terrified when he used that tone of voice with me.

"Father, what has happened here"? I said to him as I entered into his chamber, just from his expression I knew that something terrible must have occurred.

"Your mother," He began... "In her anger she has convinced the God Boreas and his sons, the four Winds to blow a cold breeze over all the lands of not only the earth, but the Heavens as well, causing death and destruction throughout their path".

As he said this I noticed that his voice was not filled with anger, but tinged with a tremor that suggested fear. I had never seen the slightest fear in father before and didn't wish to discover what it was that freighted him so.

"Why would she do this, she is a Fertility Goddess, it is her duty to bring life, not death to the land"? I asked, suggesting that must he was mistaken.

"She's blaming me for your marriage to Hades, saying that I conspired with him and that you didn't submit willingly, but that your uncle abducted you by force. In her mind, you screamed and pleaded with your uncle Hades, Lord of the Underworld, not to take you to that damned dungeon, but your screams were unheard by even the Gods themselves. When she found out that you were in the Underworld, she stormed out of the palace and went to the depths of the seas, to Poseidon, where he helped her plot revenge on both Minos and Pasiphae".

Before he could finish, I interrupted him, "She didn't kill them, if she did I would have surly seen their shades entering the Underworld".

"No, Poseidon wouldn't allow her to kill Minos, he is his faithful servant of his, but Poseidon was to play a major part in your mother's wrath and in the coming destruction of Minos' kingdom".

Seeing that I didn't understand what he was telling me, Zeus retold the events that mother had already explained to you, therefore I will not bore you with retelling them here.

After he finished, I jumped from my seat and exclaimed, "Where is she now, I must see her and explain that you didn't force me to marry Hades, that I willingly chose to live in the Underworld".

He didn't answer, no one did. The Gods present all looked at me, as if I was the only one that could possible know where mother could be found. Finally, Hermes broke the silence,

"Demeter has been wandering the earth disguised as an old woman, but she is very swift, for even with my winged sandals I can't keep up with her trail".

Zeus interrupted,

"That's not all that she's done, once the cold winds were released the land became covered with snow and ice, destroying the crops and causing the mortals to slaughter their work animals for food and to wear their skins for warmth".

As he said this I thought of the sight of the nymphs in the main hall all wearing furs draped around their bodies. I was disgusted by the idea of killing poor innocent beasts to drape their skins over the body. Zeus continued.

"Demeter has cursed the land and will not allow any new crops to grow, nor will she allow any mortal births to take place, I fear that soon all mortal life on earth will be destroyed if she is not stopped, and stopped immediately".

We spent the entire night debating on where she could be and how we could convince her to remove her curse from the lands, but with the coming of dawn we were no closer to an answer. Since I was of no help there, that is until mother could be located and I could go to her and try my best to explain why I had deceived her, Zeus decided that I would be more service back in the Underworld where soon the souls of those condemned to die of starvation would be arriving in the thousands. I left immediately and when I reached the Underworld, I was surprised to see that the first victims of mother's wrath had already started to arrive, and within a month Hades and I were no longer able to keep up with the new arrivals. Entire families soon came to our gates, and a sadness filled my soul, when I looked at the children who were not destine to die so young, all I could think of was that this was mother's doing and I hated her for it. I was able to understand her anger for being deceived, I could even justify the revenge she inflicted on King Minos and his family, though I still felt pity for them, but I couldn't understand how she could allow innocent children watch as their parents die of starvation before the God of Death finally came to end their pain and suffering.

Soon Chaos filled the Underworld.

Thanatos, the God of Death, usually wore the helmet of invisibility that Hades gave to him as a gift when traveling among the mortals and silently he would seek out those who were destine to die, those who the Goddess Atopos, one of the Moirai and daughter of the Goddess Ananke, the Goddess who cuts the thread of life has decided that the end of their life has come, and with one touch of his lips to theirs he would suck their last breath. No mortal worshiped him; instead all feared his touch, which was known as the Kiss of Death. Soon, he was no longer feared, but welcomed by those who had watched as their loved ones had suffered many months before finally dying, waiting until Thanatos' kiss would finally release their soul from it's pain and suffering. It wasn't long before he became lethargic and was unable to keep up with Atopos' list and those who suffered started begging and praying to him to come to them and administer his kiss to them in their sleep.

There are many rituals that all souls must follow before being allowed entrance within the Underworld, and the souls of those whose earthly families for one reason or another do not follow these steps are doomed to wander the earth for eternity. After Thanatos delivers the Kiss of Death and releases their soul, the family of the deceased is to arrange for their burial, for without a proper burial no soul is allowed within the Underworld. Instead they were destined to wander near the home of their loved ones, or along the banks of the river Styx. It was at the funeral that Hermes would greet the newly departed soul and in his role as Psychompompus, the 'Accompanier of Souls' he would lead them to the river Styx, where the ferryman, Charon waited to guide them across the river to the Gate of the Underworld in return for the two obolus that were placed upon their closed eyes. Without these coins, Charon wouldn't allow entry in his boat and without another way to cross the river; their soul would have to wander on the far bank until they could find the needed fare. Now Charon didn't posses a welcoming personality to begin with, and since entire families were dying, many were buried hastily, without any thought for the obolus, while some were not buried at all. Soon many of these wandering shades came to the river without the needed fare and caused Charon's normally bad temper to explode, causing an eruption that could be heard all the way back to Mount Olympus. Those souls lucky enough to have the proper fare were thrown into his dilapidated boat and whipped as they rowed across the river, while thousands were left wandering the bank screaming endlessly.

Once within the Underworld, those who were lucky enough to pass through the marshes would be presented to the Judge Rhadymanthos, who guides the soul to a narrow bridge that leads to the Elysium Fields. Each soul, believing that he led a just life will try to cross this bridge, but only those with a pure heart will be allowed to pass while those who have committed sins would fall into the River of Fire, only to be swept by the swift current to the banks of Tartarus. Those who found passage across the bridge to the Elysian Fields were then instructed to drink from the River of Forgetfulness, where their former lives become only a dream to them, and oblivious to their past, they would live happily within the Underworld until it was decided by the Fates that they were to be reborn again and the three Goddesses would begin spinning a new thread that would be their life.

Any soul who committed crimes against either the Gods or mortals would stumble on this bridge and plummet into the fiery river below and once there they would fight the current until reaching the shore of Tartarus. There they were to stand naked in front of the Goddess Tisiphone, while she looked deep into their soul and those whose crimes were horrendous were graciously welcomed by her with open arms to their new home, where she would stand watch over them until their punishment was complete. The souls who are in Tartarus are not allowed to taste the water from the River of Forgetfulness, for it is part of their punishment that they endure their tortures while reflecting on the sins that had brought them there.

Many of the myths that have been passed down through the generations state that Minos, not Rhadymanthos, was the judge who decided the fate of the souls entering the Underworld. This is true, once King Minos died and entered the Underworld Hades appointed him this honor for his hospitality to me during the year that Hades and I courted. But the time I am speaking of was while King Minos still lived, and at this time it was his brother Rhadymanthos who was the judge who held this responsibility. After King Minos took this position, Hades transferred Rhadymanthos as the judge who watched over the Elysian Fields.

With the increase of those entering the Underworld Rhadymanthos was not able to keep up as shades wandered past him, leaving many not judged at all while others were misjudged. Many who were destined to spend eternity within the dungeons of Tartartus wandered the Underworld freely, and some entered the Elysian

Fields instead, causing those whose lips never touched the waters of the River of Forgetfulness to revolt. Anarchy soon filled the Underworld and since Hades couldn't send any soul back to earth until mother lifted her curse, the Underworld soon became overrun with souls wandering freely. The only peace I found was in our bedchamber, but this soon faded as the order that once ruled in the Underworld decreased and chaos increased, so did the growing tension between Hades and myself wax.

We weren't alone, for all the deities of the Underworld experienced this tension, but since I was still a new bride and didn't yet know what my role as Queen of the Dead was, I looked to Hades, my Lord, for answers. These did not come. Hades knew that I had no part to play in mother's little game. If I did he would have discovered it before we married, as you remember he possesses the ability to read other's thoughts. Even though he knew that I was blameless, he still felt that I was somehow responsible for mother's actions, and soon not only did he start to regret our rushing into this marriage, but I too felt that it would have been best if we waited a little longer. Maybe then mother would have given us her blessings.

Each morning I would wake to find I was once again alone in our bed and when I walked to the window I'd see Hades standing beneath the beautiful tree that sat alone in the center of the garden. I watched as he spoke to this tree in a whisper, then waited patiently as if for an answer, all the while feeling as if he was more attentive to it, a tree, then to his own wife. I was feeling more than a little jealous of this tree, but I couldn't explain why. It was only a tree, while I was Hades' wife. Then one morning as I sat in my bedchamber with Daeira, who since our first meeting had become a close companion of mine, especially during this period I felt as if she was the only friend I had. She brushed my hair as I sat looking out the window, watching Hades in his morning ritual of talking to the tree, when Daeira, hesitatingly spoke,

"Persephone",

The sound of her voice pulled my back from my thoughts of jealousy. I looked up at her and answered.

"Daeira, I'm sorry but I was lost in my thoughts. Did you say something to me"?

"It was nothing, never mind".

"I sense that there's something you want to say to me. Please, you've been my only friend these last several months, please speak freely to me".

She pretended that it was nothing, but I insisting that she tell me what was on her mind. After a long pause, she reluctantly began to speak.

"I don't understand why you haven't had that tree cut down, I wouldn't let it stand in my garden".

"Why should I destroy that beautiful tree". I replied, not knowing what she meant.

"I couldn't sit by and watch my husband spending every morning with that tree, giving all his attention to it instead of his wife".

I wanted to ask her *'Why should I be jealous of a tree?'* but I couldn't seem to form the words, I knew that it was foolish to feel this way, but I couldn't stop it. I didn't want to admit it but I was jealous, jealous not only of this tree, but jealous of the time that Hades would spend in the garden away from me, and I was jealous of the fact that he could freely speak to that tree but not to me, his own wife.

Daeira could tell by my reaction that I was upset by my husband's behavior, but that I didn't truly understand the details of how this tree came to be within the garden, she asked,

"You don't know anything about the origins of that tree, do you"?

"No".

I replied, and wanted to ask her if she knew, but right then I didn't wish to hear her answer, and I sensed that she didn't want to be the one to explain the significance of this tree to me. Since she was a close friend to me she felt that I needed to know where this tree came from, and what it meant to Hades. Hesitating before speaking, she began,

> "This tree was once a Nymph like me, a daughter of Oceanus and Tethys, a beautiful maiden named Leuce, the 'White One', for her skin was as white as marble. She was the most beautiful of all of Oceanus' daughters and many of the Gods fell in love with her. Hades was one of them. It was long before the war between the Olympians and the Titans was over when Hades and Leuce became lovers, and once he moved here to the Underworld he was able to convince

her to join him in his kingdom. Here they happily spent hundreds of years together, but since she was not immortal, soon she started to grow old; her hair turned as white as her skin, her body soon became bent over and wrinkles appeared on her face, but Hades' love for her never faded".

Daeira paused here, not wanting to continue, but I pressed her to finish her story,

"As her death came near, Hades knew that there was nothing he could do to prevent this, Zeus wouldn't grant her immortality for it was destined that Hades was to marry the daughter of Demeter, but he couldn't stand the thought of her shade drinking from the River of Forgetfulness, and wandering the Underworld blind to his feelings. Instead of allowing death to take her from him, he changed her into a white poplar tree, which he then planted in the center of his garden. Here he could see it upon awaking, and every morning since then he comes to this tree. Some mornings before you came to the Underworld, he would spend the entire day just sitting under that tree".

If I was depressed before finding this out, it was nothing to the melancholy that filled my soul after learning that Hades not only loved another women before me, for this I could forgive, but it broke my heart that his love for her still endured. I knew that Hades was destined to marry me, and after hearing this story doubts of his love for me filled my soul. I was sure that he never truly loved me, but only sought a Goddess, who immortal like he, would relieve his loneliness.

"I'm sorry that I had to tell this to you, but I feel that you should know how much that tree means to Hades". She said to me as she took my hand.

"I can't stay here any longer". I said as I pulled my hand from hers and stood.

"Where are you going"? she asked me, alarmed.

"I don't know". I said, then added,

"Please don't say anything to Hades, I don't want him coming after me. I need time to think about what you've told me, about everything that has happened over the last few months".

"I promise, but please don't tell Hades it was I who told you about this".

Daeira pleaded with me and I assured her that I would never betray her honesty. Since she was the only friend I had in the Underworld, I didn't wish to do anything to jeopardize that, but I was a little upset that she didn't tell me this story earlier, but I couldn't blame her, I wouldn't want to tell a young bride that her husband had a previous lover, a lover whom he couldn't forget. I left the palace without even thinking of where I would go. Since mother had destroyed the island of Crete I couldn't return there, and I didn't know where Queen Pasiphae and Daedalus had traveled to, therefore I couldn't go to her. The only place I knew where I would be accepted was back on Mount Olympus, so I packed up a few of my belongings and without saying a word to anyone, I began the long journey back home.

XI
Persephone

ONCE WITHIN MY father's palace I immediately I ran to Hermes, of all the Gods he was my dearest friend and I knew that he alone would understand the betrayal that I felt. Some myths state that when I found out about Hades and his love for Leuce I went to Hermes and as a way of getting back at my husband I had an affair with him. For the record, I almost did. That night I was in Hermes bed, in his arms, and as we laid there he started to kiss me softly. I kissed him back even though I knew I shouldn't have. Encouraged by this, he closed his lips over mine and as his tongue explored my mouth, his hands slowly caressed by body, finding there way to my breasts. I moaned slightly. It had been so long since my husband touched me like that, the tension between us growing over the last few months, and I missed the feeling of being wanted, of being loved for who I was. Taking my moan as further encouragement he cupped my breast and let his tongue move slowly down to my neck, then continuing down between my breasts. At that moment I wanted nothing more than to make love to him, I truly loved him ever since I was a child, and before that day when the sight of Hades lit the flame in my heart that melted my soul, I wanted to be Hermes' lover, I dreamt of us laying together in bed, just as we were. I let his kisses fill me with desire, and then I opened my robe to him allowing his mouth to find its way to my breast.

I expected to feel the pleasure that I felt when my husband kissed me like that, but instead of feeling pleasure sadness filled my heart. I knew then that I could not make love to him that, nor any other night. I realized then that I only wanted to give myself to him not because I loved him but as a way to betray Hades, as I felt he had betrayed me. I don't even think I consciously thought about this, all I knew was that I couldn't allow myself to make love to him. I cared too much for him to use him that way. Even though I felt betrayed by my husband I knew that deep down I still loved him, no matter how I much wanted to deny it just then. Hermes brought his mouth up to kiss mine but I turned my face, his kiss falling on my cheek.

"Your so beautiful", Hermes said to me, continuing, "You don't know how long I waiting for this moment".

I was surprised by this, growing up in the palace of Zeus, none of the Gods ever showed any interest in me.

"Don't look so surprised, Persephone. I, like the other Gods, knew that you would one day belong to Hades, and none of us wanted to risk his wrath by being the God who would defile his young bride". As he said this, he let his kisses flow back down to my breast.

"No, I can't". I said as I pushed him off me.

"Why not, Hades doesn't need to know, I can teach you how to block your thoughts from him. I, the Trickster God, know how to deceive even the Great God, Zeus". Hermes said with a smile, and then he lowered down and started kissing me again.

"I can't", I paused trying to hold back my tears. "I still love him". I said as a tear ran down my check.

I knew then that my heart belonged to Hades and I couldn't betray his trust. On our wedding night, as I drank from the waters of the river Styx, I stated that I would not betray Hades love, and I wouldn't no matter what. Hermes wiped the tears that filled my eyes, and then spoke softly to me,

"Persephone, I love you and always have, but I won't do anything to hurt you. I'll be here for you as long as you need me. I'll hold you in my arms and comfort you, and even though I have longed for your touch, I promise that I'll control myself".

I couldn't answer him, the tears that I had tried to suppress for so long now began to flow and nothing I could do would stop them. The rest of the night I stayed with Hermes and he held me in his arm and gently stroked my hair and wiped the tears from my cheeks. It was mid-day before I allowed sleep to come over me and release me from the pain of my breaking heart.

****

I stayed on Mount Olympus with my brother, Iacchus, in the chamber that we used to share for almost a week, and each day Hades would make the long journey to the palace to try to speak with me. He would come to my room, knocking on the door, hoping that I would finally agree to see him, but I refused to even hear his explanations. I wouldn't leave my chamber, fearing that he was still somewhere within the palace, so while I was staying on Mount Olympus I spoke only to my brother, and the only nourishment I received was the few scrapes that Iacchus brought back to me. Not once during that week did I leave our chamber, and on the morning of the sixth day Hades knocked on my door once again,

"Persephone, please speak with me".

I didn't answer him.

He knocked once more, before speaking once again, very quietly. I had to strain to hear his words,

"I'm not asking you to return to the Underworld with me, but I'll be leaving Mount Olympus tonight and will not be returning. Please," he begged, "I must speak to you before I leave".

I still didn't answer.

He continued,

"You don't have to return with me if you don't want to. I won't force you, but I hope that you can at least find it in your heart to forgive me".

There was a few seconds of silence and then I heard his footsteps walking away. I hesitated for a split second, then the fear that he was leaving me forever filled my soul and I throw opened the door. Hades, who was at the end of the hallway, stopped and turned around to face me, and as I stood there looking at him, tears filled my eyes and I ran to his outstretched arms and buried my face in his chest.

"I'm sorry if I hurt you". He said to me as he placed his hand on my chin and lifted my face so that our eyes finally meet. We looked into each other's eyes for what seemed like hours before he gently kissed my forehead.

"Why didn't you tell me about her... about that tree"? I asked, through my sobs, "On our wedding night you told me that you would never lie to me".

I turned and led Hades back into my room not wanting the others to hear us, then I sat on my bed and Hades knelt down in front of me and took my hands in his before speaking,

"I didn't tell you about Leuce for fear that you couldn't understand my feelings for her, feelings that I can't push aside". He paused, then added, "I never wished to cause you pain".

"Did you not think that I would find out"? I asked

"On our wedding night I did promise that I would never lie to you and I didn't".

I tried to tell him that he did, but then I realized that he really didn't lie, he just failed to mention certain facts about that tree, and I not wanting to increase the tension that mother had inflicted on us, never really asked. I wondered if I did ask, would he have told me the truth.

"Yes, I would have told you everything." He answered my thoughts.

He continued, 'I intended to tell you everything right after we married, but when the time came I found that I couldn't, I couldn't for fear that you would become jealous and leave me. The fear of you leaving me has consumed me these last few months. You don't understand, I don't think I could continue living within the Underworld knowing that I would be alone for eternity".

Here I did interrupt him. I had to know the real reason he married me. "Did you only marry me because it was destined that I share your loneliness with you"?

"No, I married you because I love you".

"I don't believe you. If you loved me, you wouldn't have kept any secrets from me".

"I know that I was being selfish for not telling you about Leuce, but if you'll listen to me now I promise that I'll tell you everything and from now on I won't keep any thing from you".

I nodded to him, acknowledging that I would at least listen to what he had to say.

"After hearing my reasons for deceiving you, I hope that you'll be able to find it in your heart to forgive me, for if you don't I don't know what I'll do".

He paused before beginning.

> "You cannot know the loneliness I felt for the millennium I have lived within the Underworld. My bothers and sisters wouldn't even visit me, and all mortals feared even saying my name, calling me Pluto instead. Gods and mortals alike think the Underworld is a horrible place, and because I'm the ruler of this dreadful place, I too, must be a terrible monster. All feared me, and since I didn't have anyone to share my feelings with, I kept them locked deep inside, and soon they started eating away at my soul until I thought I would go mad. My only salvation was the thought that I too would someday have a wife to share my loneliness with, but I didn't know when that would be, for you weren't born yet and Demeter refused to have another child with Zeus, hoping to cheat me of my bride. Your mother had many reasons for not wanting you to marry me, some which I didn't wish to tell you about, but if you are to understand my motives, I must tell you now".

I interrupted, "I know that mother didn't want us to marry, I don't want to hear the details now", I paused, then I continued, "What I want is for you to tell me about this Nymph, the one that you still love".

"The two stories are related, and to understand one, you must understand the other. I promise I'm going tell you everything". He said, continuing, "Please be patient with me and let me tell you the story from the beginning".

I nodded for him to continue.

> "During the war between the Olympians and the Titans five of the six Olympian Gods lived in Cronus' palace, Hera being the only one who didn't participate in the war. Your mother, along with all the other Goddesses wished to marry Zeus since he was the most powerful of the Gods, but his

heart belonged to Hera alone. Yes, he had many affairs, and yes some of these affairs hurt Hera deeply, but he couldn't deny his love for her. During the war he sent her away to protect her from harm, and the other Goddesses took advantage of her absence. Now, as then, Zeus wouldn't refuse any beautiful Goddess to spend the night in his bed, and he and Demeter spent many nights together. After several years of being Zeus' mistress, your mother demanded that Zeus marry her, and if he didn't she would leave him. He refused. What else could he do? In her anger Demeter turned her attention to me hoping to make Zeus jealous, but I knew her intentions, and since I was enamored with a Nymph, a Nymph named Leuce, I didn't encourage her. Night after night she would offer herself to me, and after several weeks of my refusing her, she in a jealous rage stripped both Leuce and myself of the ability to create life, being a Fertility Goddess, this was her right.

Demeter could have turned her attention to Poseidon next, for she knew that he truly loved her, and still does, but she likes a challenge, and Poseidon would've given in to her too easily, so she went back to Zeus and he took her back to his bed. During the several weeks that she withheld herself from Zeus, she was devising another plan, a simple one that is still used by mortal women to this day, she would conceive a child with him and he would have to forget his obligations to Hera and marry her instead. In the last few weeks of the war she would spend each night in Zeus' bed, and it wasn't until she found out that it would be her daughter that would marry me that she stopped sleeping with Zeus altogether, for after hearing this she refused to conceive a child with him. I was the only God that refused her, and she was still furious with my rejection. If she couldn't have me, she wouldn't allow her daughter to.

Once the war was over Hera returned immediately to the palace, she was then, as she still is, very jealous of Zeus' affairs and didn't want to be away any longer then was needed. It was only a few weeks after each of the three brothers were given their domains that Demeter found out she was carrying Zeus' child. Even though she didn't wish her child to marry me, the though of being Zeus' wife filled her, and so she told him she was expecting his child, hoping that he would finally marry her. He was overjoyed with the thought of their having a child together, though Hera was not. Your mother begged Zeus to marry her now, but still he refused her. It wasn't that long after that Zeus announced to the entire palace that since the war was finally over, he planned to marry. Tension filled the air, both Demeter and Hera were glaring at each other, each one hoping that Zeus would announce her as his new bride.

Zeus finally spoke,

"The King of the Heavens shall have a Queen, and this Queen shall be my beloved sister, Hera". Hera and Zeus embraced as those present applauded, all that was except Demeter; distraught, she left the palace immediately.

That night was the last night I would stay within the palace, the next day I would take my place as King of the Underworld. I spent my last night on Mount Olympus with Leuce. I couldn't allow her to dwell in the Underworld with me and since it was to be out last night together I wanted her to know my feelings. As the sun rose the following morning I took her in my arms and kissed her for what I though would be the last time. She cried as we parted as I spoke to her.

"I promise, I'll return to you whenever I can, that is if you still want me".

"Of course I do, I will wait till the end of time for your return".

For several hundreds of years I would split my time between organizing the Underworld and visiting Leuce on earth. Even though I can read other's thoughts, not once did I look into her mind, fearing that I would be torn apart by her rejection, so you can imagine that I was slightly surprised when after hundreds of years, she told me

"My love, I can't be parted from you any longer. Please allow me to return with you tonight. I don't fear what the Underworld has to offer, for I know that you'll protect me".

You can't imagine how I felt, at that time the Underworld was truly a horrible place, nothing like what it is now, and I didn't wish for her to spend eternity there, but she insisted that she would willingly spend the rest of her life there with me. She accompanied me home that night.

We lived happily for a couple more hundred years and she assisted me with the many changes that made the Underworld livable. But alas, she was not immortal like we are, and soon age crept up and she was no longer the young nymph that I fell in love with. Now don't get me wrong, I still loved her dearly and told her this each morning when we awoke, explaining to her that I still loved her and would continue to love her. No matter how many times I told her this, she wouldn't believe me, and each night she would beg me to change her into a tree, a beautiful tree that will never grow old and wither as her mortal form was.

"Please", She begged me, "The only way I can find happiness will be if you grant me this one request".

"I can't". I told her as I took her in my arms.

"Please, transform this dieing mortal form into a beautiful tree, then plant it within the garden I helped you create. There you will see me each morning and remember me as I once was".

At first I couldn't do this, I did love her with all my heart, but too soon the time came when I knew that she would be dying within a few days, I could smell the death and decay of her mortal body, and I almost died myself. I couldn't stand the thought of watching as her soul wandering through the Elysium Fields oblivious to my love for her. With no other choice, I agreed to transform her.

She said goodbye to me and I kissed her one last time before I called to the Powers of the Universe and instantly after hearing my plea, a thick fog emerged from the depths of the earth and within seconds surrounded us. I stood there looking at her as if I were looking at her through a veil. I took a deep breath, breathing in the mystical fog, allowing all the energy that was building in the ground just below my feet enter into my body and soul, allowing this energy to pulsate through me building in power as it continued up through my legs, my torso, my arms until it finally reached my head. Once I knew that I was filled to capacity with this primal energy I wiped a single tear that ran down her cheek. I took both her hands in mine and focused all this power, the power of the Earth itself, into my hands and when I felt them tremble with the surging power, I directed all that energy to flow from deep within the earth, through my body and into her, all the while concentrating on the image of a beautiful tree.

She shook, slightly at first, but then more violent, as this energy began consuming her. I held her hands tightly as I watched, amazed, as old age suddenly left her face, and within a short time, seconds only, she appeared as young and beautiful as when I first met her. I went to touch her face and as I did I noticed that her skin was no longer soft and supple as it had once been, but was beginning to become ridge and when I looked down I couldn't see her legs. Where I knew they should have been, I saw only a tree trunk with its roots starting their slow decent deep down into the ground. The ground began to quiver as it was forced back by the growing roots.

I watched as the bark that started at her feet slowly creep up through her legs and body and into her arms and finally as her face started to change, her last words to me were, "I love you." I didn't have the time to respond to her, to tell her that I too loved her. The metamorphosis was complete, there in front of me, where the woman I loved stood just a few seconds before, there was now only a magnificent tree. I knelt before her and started to cry, and after a few hours I was finally able to stand up and slowly I walked away. The next day I had one of my servants plant the tree in my garden below my bedchamber window where I can see her upon awakening just as she had wished.

Hades paused here, I think he was waiting for me to say something, but I didn't respond. After a moment of silence he continued.

"You have to understand that after she was gone, I had no one left. For thousands of years there was no one that I could talk to other than that tree that was once Leuce, so I would talk to the soul that I knew still dwelled deep within the white bark, and she would answer me. As a nymph there were things that I couldn't tell her, but as a tree I felt as if I could release my soul to her and throughout the years I did. When you were born, I told her about you and even though I promised that I would never forget her, I could see a shift in the leaves and from her bark I swear that I saw tears falling and the next day I noticed that her leaves had started to wilt. I didn't speak to her about you after that, and when you came to the Underworld for the first time and walked into my garden and reached out to touch this tree I realized that I couldn't tell you about her and cause you to feel the same pain that I saw in her. I promised that I would never forget her, and I haven't, each morning I would spend a few minuets alone with her, telling her my deepest feelings. Soon she began to accept you, knowing that though I loved you with my entire heart, I still couldn't overlook the feelings that we once shared".

He paused here and took my hand in his, then continued,

"I dreaded the day that you would ask me about this tree. It wasn't my intent to hurt you, and now that you know about my past love I hope that you can forgive me, though I want you to realize that I'm not asking you to forgive me for loving someone before you, but only to forgive me for not being totally honest with you from the beginning".

I did forgive him. I had come to understand over the past few months how lonely it could be in the Underworld. I had only lived in this world for less than a year, while Hades had spent several centuries there.

"I forgive you". I said and before I could say any more he wrapped me in his arms and kissed me. We left Mount Olympus immediately and once back in our palace, Hades lifted me up and carried me to our private chamber where we made love the entire night. This was the first time since mother had put her curse on the land that Hades and I made love, and after we were finished, I fell asleep within his arms. When I awoke the following morning I was surprised to find that Hades was still in bed with me, I was expecting him to be in the garden as was his custom in the mornings. He got up with me and as I dressed he waited for me in the main hall, and when I came down he took me by the hand and led me to the garden where we both stood under the tree that was his first love, and together we both acknowledged Leuce, and I spoke to her in my own words promising that I would never allow Hades to forget her. I have kept this promise, every morning Hades will spend a few moments under this tree. Some mornings I would join him, but most of the time I allow him to spend this time alone with his former love.

I was back in the Underworld where I belonged, but for the rest of the year and for many years to come, life there was chaotic. The souls of the mortals who mother condemned to die continued to flood our home, and when Demeter was finally found we hoped that I would be able to convince her to release her curse on the land. The Goddess Iris was the first to approach Demeter in her sanctuary in Eleusis, and when she realized that she couldn't convince her to return to Mount Olympus she sent Hermes to try. He was only able to convince her after promising that I would be waiting for her alone on Mount Olympus the next day.

"How dare you promise her that I'll return alone. I'm now married and I could care less if she approves of who I chose to marry or not, she has no right to prevent Hades from accompanying me". I shouted at Hermes. I couldn't help it, I was angry, angry at all the destruction she caused, angry at Hermes for promising her, angry at myself for allowing her to rule my life. It was about time that the two of them at least came to an understanding. I should've known that mother was too stubborn to admit that she was wrong.

Hades and I reached Mount Olympus well before dawn and Hades was in the palace speaking with his brothers and sisters, while I waited near the gates for mother's approach. Even though I was furious with her for her destruction of the land, I still missed her, having not seen her for almost an entire year. When I saw her coming, I ran down the path and into her arms.

"Mother, I've missed you so". I said to her as she held me tight.

"I feared that I would never see you again, my dear daughter". She said as she kissed my forehead.

"Before we enter the palace, I must speak to you".

"Let us return, as mother and daughter to the palace, then you'll have all the time to tell me of your pain". She said as she took my hand and started walking toward the palace.

"Mother, before you enter I must tell you that Hades is with me…" I started to explain, but was interrupted.

"How dare you!" She shouted at me. "How dare you, to bring him here! I told Hermes that I would return only if you were to come alone".

"Please don't blame Hermes, his message was clear, but Hades is now my husband and I feel that you two should forget the past and try to get along".

"I can't believe what I am hearing, you are telling me, your mother, what I should and should not do!" She hissed at me.

Demeter refused to enter the gates, and after a few minuets Zeus was summoned out to speak with her.

"Demeter, you must put the past behind you, what is done is done. It is now time to think about all the innocent lives you have committed to the Underworld".

She didn't reply to him,

"I order you to lift your curse from the lands!" Zeus barked at his sister and all the Gods present shook with fear as mother stood her ground.

"I will not! I swore that until my daughter was back where she belongs I would not allow any growth to occur…"

"But mother," I interrupted, "I am where I belong. I now belong with my husband".

After several hours of debating my grandmother Rhea came out and as she approached all became quiet. She began to speak.

"My dear daughter, Demeter, I offer a compromise. If Persephone is allowed to spend one-half the year with you and the other Gods and Goddesses, will you then restore life to the lands"?

At first my mother refused, but after some shouting, especially on my part she agreed, but under one condition.

"I will restore life to the land, but only during the time that my daughter is here with me, for once she returns to the Underworld, I will once again curse the land. No more will mortal life enjoy my blessings year-round".

I tried to speak to my grandmother, telling her that I didn't wish to leave my husband; that I willingly gave myself to him, to live with him in the Underworld for all eternity. Her reply was,

"Dear granddaughter, many centuries ago the Goddess of Destiny declared that you would marry the Lord of the Underworld, stating that yours would be a marriage built on trust and love, but not without a price. You would only be allowed to spend part of the year with your husband, and the other with the other Gods and Goddesses who dwell on Mount Olympus. I know that right now you feel as is your heart will break being separated from Hades, but soon you'll forgive your mother".

I did forgive mother, but it took several decades just before I was able to even speak to her during the spring and summer months that I spent on earth with her, but soon I realized that whatever her motives were, she was still my mother and nothing I could do would change that.

Part II

XII
Persephone

I HAVE INTRODUCED you to the Gods and Goddesses who I call my family; I have described the events that lead to my marriage to Hades, Lord of the Underworld; and I have explained how my mother Demeter, the Goddess of Fertility, withheld her blessings for almost an entire year causing almost two-thirds of all mortal life on earth to parish, and once reunited with me how she created the seasons that still exist to this day. I wish to now briefly explain to you the role I assumed within the hierarchy of the Underworld, and to tell you of just a few of the adventures that I have witnesses as both mortal men and Gods have ventured into the realm of the dead for one reason or another. Some of these stories you have probably heard, but the myths that have passed down through the ages are very different from the events that actually occurred. Throughout the many centuries each generation made trivial changes to these tales, not only to fit in with societies' ideals, but also to show their own heroes in a good light, in the process changing some of these stories forever. What follows are the tales as they actually happened.

Before I married I don't think mortals even knew I existed, if they did, I was thought of only as nothing more than the maiden Kore, daughter of the Fertility Goddess, Demeter, but during the first part of the year that my mother withheld her fruits from the land, mortals heard of the sorrow that mother felt for the loss of her beloved daughter, the maiden Kore, who was raped and dragged down into the Underworld by her uncle, the God Hades. But soon after she withdrew the fertility of the land, they began to stand up and curse her as they watched their loved ones slowly die of starvation. Soon, to my surprise, prayers started to flood into not her temples as I expected, instead all prayers were dedicated to me. Hades was the true Lord of the Underworld, but since mortals feared him, daring not to even utter his name, they addressed me hoping that I would intercede and deliver their prayers. Now that I was married to the Lord of the Underworld I had become mediator between the two worlds, that of the living and of the dead. The prayers of the sick and dying were not intended for Demeter, Goddess of Fertility, begging her forgiveness, and imploring her to lift the curse from the land and once again allow the crops to grow, but to me, as Queen of the Dead, beseeching me to not only keep the God of Death, Thanatos at bay, but to find mother and beg her to give her blessings back to the earth.

Although she still won't admit it, mother became just a little jealous of all the attention I was getting (all of the Gods and Goddess become envious when another received attention), and when we reunited after the year-long famine, she took me to the city Eleusis, the only place that welcomed her during her absence and continued to worship her while all the others gave up hope. It was there that she taught the people of this land the rituals that would ensure the fertility of their lands for eternity. These teachings were the first of the true Mystery Religions, and were known as the Eleusinian Mysteries. At the beginning the Mysteries were mother's alone, but slowly I began to steal her honor even here, for the people no longer worship Demeter alone, they began worshipping her as the mother of Kore, and soon I took on a duel role as not only the Queen of the Dead, but as the Goddess of Rebirth and Renewal.

Because of my increase in popularity, the tension between mother and I escalated during those first few years of my marriage, and I began to fear that Hades would also resent all the attention I was now receiving. I was surprised to find that didn't happen, after so many centuries of living without any contact with mortals, Hades became accustomed to the solitude of the Underworld. That was not the only reason, for he did not wish to deal with the responsibility that came with their prayers, a responsibility that I didn't have the luxury to ignore. Even though he warned me against getting involved with humanity, I still felt pity for some of the poor mortals who prayed to me to release the soul of a loved one, but once the Fates, the three sisters of inescapable destiny decided that the measure of the thread of life was at its end, and the Goddess Atropos finally cut the line, there was nothing I, nor any of the Gods could do. It was only a few years after I settled into my new role as Queen of the Dead that I was so moved by one man, whose love for his wife wouldn't allow her to die, that I tried to outwit the Fates. I will briefly tell you his adventure now.

****

Orpheus was the son of the Muse of Lyric Poetry, Calliope, and a mortal man named Oeagrus, and as the son of a lesser deity he was not an immortal, but mortal like his father. He grew up not within the Palace at Mount Olympus nor on earth with his mortal father, but in one of the smaller dwellings within the grounds of Zeus' palace with his mother and her sisters, the Muses. Of course being the son of a Muse, Orpheus was guaranteed to possess many talents, and Apollo took him in when still a young boy and presented the lad a gift of a Lyre, teaching him to play the most beautiful music ever heard. Orpheus was welcomed within the Palace daily where he would sit in the center of the great hall for hours playing on his Lyre while singing enchanting songs that would bring tears to the Goddesses' eyes. All the Goddesses and Nymphs would have willingly given him their heart, but he never looked at them, his music was his only love; that was until he met the Dryad, Eurydice, and Eros shot him with one of his arrows, as he did when I beheld Hades for the first time. The Dryads are Nymphs who dwelled on earth in wooded areas and frolicked within the trees, and one day while Eurydice was in the forest playing with the other Nymphs high up in the trees she heard Orpheus' music and the melody enchanted her. She began to sing. Orpheus, hearing her sweet voice stopped playing…the beautiful singing also stopped. He began playing and once again her song enchanted him. Continuing to play, he followed the sound until he was standing under a large Elm tree. When he looked up Eurydice tried to hide within the leaves, but their eyes meet for the briefest of seconds and Orpheus felt a pang in his heart and he knew that he would not be able to live without her love.

It was not long after that that Orpheus convinced the Nymph to marry him, and soon the Palace on Mount Olympus was filled with wedding preparations. The day of the wedding arrived and early that morning Hymenaeus, the God who would lead the wedding procession arrived, along with several ominous omens. First, while Eurydice was dressing a picture in her room fell from the wall, the noise startled the bride causing the mirror she held within her hand to fall and brake into several pieces. All present in the room stood in silence, fearing that trouble was near, for they knew that if a picture should fall from the wall upon which it hung, death was near, and the breaking of a mirror guaranteed misfortune to the one who broke it. Eurydice thought of postponing the ceremony until a more favorable time, but she feared that if Orpheus heard of the ominous signs he would call the wedding off entirely.

"Please don't say anything to my beloved Orpheus, for I will die if I can not marry him today". She begged her attendants to a vow of silence.

They promised to say nothing, but it didn't matter, for as Eurydice walked down the center of the great hall as Orpheus and all in attendance watched, she knew that the Gods would never bless this union, for she stumbled not once, not twice, but trice. As she approached Orpheus her heart felt as if it was breaking in half, she loved him so much, more than life itself, but she knew this marriage was destined to cause misfortune to them both and she couldn't bear the thought that she might cause her love pain.

"Should I speak of the ill omens that have visited me this day? If I do, would my love still marry me"? she thought as she continued her way to Orpheus' side.

Her mind was made up, she had to tell him that she couldn't marry him that day, but it was too late; Hymenaeus had begun with the ceremony. She decided to kept quiet, telling herself that it was only nerves that caused her clumsiness. About half way through the service sparks flew from the torch that stood to the right of Hymenaeus, causing silence throughout the great hall. After several moments, hushed voices began to fill the air and Hymenaeus called out for all to be silent.

"I cannot continue with this ceremony, for it is obvious that this marriage will be doomed from the beginning".

The finality of Hymenaeus' words struck her like a slap to the face and she couldn't stop the tears from flowing. The guests started to speak, and even though they spoke in whispers, soon the Great Hall was again filled with the sound of their voices. Orpheus tried to speak, but couldn't be heard over the din. He shouted over the crowd, and only when silence filled the hall he spoke.

"I will not postpone the wedding ceremony. I have come here today to marry Eurydice and I will not leave until we are wed".

Eurydice listened in disbelief, even with all the ominous omens predicting that this marriage would cause misfortune; Orpheus still wanted to marry her. Before she could reply to him his mother, the Muse Calliope, approached them both and took her son's hand and said softy so that only he and his bride to could hear her words,

"My dear son, the Moirai have decided not to bless this marriage, don't incur their wrath by challenging their decision".

"I swear to the Moirai; to Clotho the Goddess who spins the thread of life; to the Goddess Lachesis who appoints man's lot in life; and to Atropos, the Goddess who cuts the thread of life, that not even they can stop this marriage. I will risk their wrath, for my love for Eurydice is greater than my fear of the Moirai". Orpheus announced to all the guests and as he spoke these words the sound of their gasps filled the Great Hall.

"My love, we don't need to cancel the ceremony, only to postpone it until we could consult the Oracle and make the proper offerings to the Moirai". She said to him hoping that he would agree.

"I will not wait! Hymenaeus, I beg you to continue with the ceremony. I refuse to leave until Eurydice and I have been wed".

Hymenaeus reluctantly agreed to continue with the ceremony and after Orpheus kissed his new bride on the cheek, they left the Great Hall in silence. Instead of the two-day celebration that usually followed the ceremony, the two lovers departed to their new home in silence. None of the guests thought it wise to celebrate a ceremony that was destined to only cause misfortune to the new couple.

That night as they laid in bed together Orpheus tried to convince Eurydice that everything would be fine, that they need not fear the Moirai, their love could withstand any difficulties that came their way; and even though she didn't believe his words, she smiled a soft smile and gently kissed him, all the while hiding her tears. They didn't make love that night, instead Orpheus held her in his arms and comforted her throughout the night, and when Eurydice awoke in the early morning she felt as if all her fears were lifted, a beautiful new day had began and so too would their new life together. They had held their ground against the Moirai, and they made it through the night, maybe Orpheus was right she thought; maybe there was nothing for them to fear. They would face whatever obstacles the Moirai threw in their way together.

Seeing her dear husband lying on the bed still asleep Eurydice thought that it would be a nice touch if he awoke to the smell of fresh flowers, so she draped a robe over her nightgown and quietly opened the door and stepped into the garden. Once surrounded by the beautiful flowers, she instantly forgot her fears from the previous day and as she bent to pick a rose, she jerked as a sharp pain filled her left ankle. At first she thought it was only a thorn that pricked her skin, but when she looked down she saw a bright green snake slowly slithering away. Her scream woke Orpheus and he ran out to her without taking the time dress and held her to his chest.

"Don't worry my dear, everything will be alright". He said to her as he stroked her hair.

She didn't respond, knowing all to well that her life was soon to be over. He helped her back into their home and after assisting her into the bed he looked at the wound. He knew then that she was right; he would soon lose her to death. Within hours her foot was swollen twice its normal size and the fever made her fall in and out of consciousness. Orpheus called Asclepius, the mortal son of Apollo, who had been raised by the Centaur Chiron and learned the art of Medicine from him, to tend to his beloved wife Eurydice. The healer came immediately and used incantations to ease the pain and applied salves to reduce the swelling, but nothing he could do would save her, for the Goddess Atopos wouldn't allow her to live. By nightfall she was in a coma and Orpheus thought that his beloved was already dead and called to me begging me to release his wife's soul.

"Persephone, Queen of the Dead, I beg you not to take my dear Eurydice, for I cannot live without her". He shouted as he stood next to his unconscious wife.

I didn't answer his prayer; what could I do but wait until the Goddess Atropos finally cut the thread that was her life and greet her shade as she entered into the land of the dead. Orpheus took my silence as a refusal to assist him in his hour of need.

He took one of the horses from the stables and rode for seven days and seven nights in utter madness, not stopping for food or sleep until he came to the river Styx, marking the entrance of the Underworld. He wandered through the fog, following the bank of the river until he saw the ferryman Charon waiting in his boat. At first Charon would not allow him to enter, for no living soul other than one of the Gods of the Underworld was allowed to cross the river, but Orpheus persisted. He took out his lyre and played a song so beautiful and touching, that soon even the ill tempered Charon shed a tear. He still would not allow Orpheus to ride in his boat, fearing Hades' wrath, instead he turned his head for the briefest of seconds, allowing the mortal to dive into the icy water of the Styx and swim through the marshy waters to the other side. Once there he felt the coldness of the shades of the dead, and at first he thought it was only his wet cloths that chilled him, but soon he felt the coldness reach down into his very soul. Again he took out his lyre, which was tucked in his robe for safekeeping, and began to play and sing so tenderly that the personifications of Grief, Anxiety, Disease, Old Age, Fear, and Hunger stopped to listen to his song and while he played they forgot their misery for a few moments and allowed him to pass in gratitude. Once away from their negative energies his soul soon began to warm up, that is until he reached the Elm of False Hopes; for at the sight of this massive tree a sadness consumed him. Instead of hope filling him he saw what his life would have been had he waited until the Moirai would bless their union. He stopped here and fell to his knees and began weeping for all that he lost.

After what seemed like an eternity to him, he pulled himself up and tried to follow the path that lead to the entrance of the Underworld, but the fog was too thick and he couldn't see more than a couple of inches in front of his face. He wandered through the fog for hours until he finally reached the pillars that mark the entrance to the

Underworld. Once at the gates Cerberus, the guard dog, came charging after him, but again, his beautiful music calmed her so much that she lied down all three of her heads and was soon fast asleep. He had passed through the mists that separate the world of the living from that of the dead. Even though he had made it farther than any other mortal, he still had a long way to go before he finally would reach our palace. He trudged through the marsh that followed the Cocytus River and all the while he played his music hoping to ease the pain of the pour souls who were destined to dwell within these marshes. His journey through the Underworld lasted the entire day, and as night fell he finally reached the doors of our palace.

Orpheus was brought before Hades and I as we sat upon our thrones. Upon seeing us he fell to his knees and with his head to the floor he begged our forgiveness for intruding. He then began to address not Hades, the true Lord of the Underworld, but to my surprise he addressed me, pleading that I release his wife. His words were so beautiful; they touched my heart.

He spoke thus to me,

> "Persephone, the raven haired Goddess of the Underworld to whom all must submit to one day, I beg you to hear me out. I haven't traveled for seven days and nights without food or rest to try to release the souls of those who are imprisoned in the dungeon of the damned, Tartarus; I have not entered your world to test my strength against Cerberus, the three-headed guard dog who protects the entrance; nor did I come to free the shades who dwell down here in the Elysian Fields. I don't seek glory for myself; I traveled to your kingdom only to free my wife Eurydice, whose life was cut short by the fangs of a poisonous viper.
>
> It is my love for Eurydice alone that has brought me here, to kneel at your feet and to beg your assistance, for it has been told that you also have fought many obstacles to secure your love. I implore you to have pity on me and call the Goddess Atropus and pled with her, for me, to unite the thread of Eurydice's life. I don't ask you to pardon her for eternity, for all mortals must sooner or later pass through your gates and dwell within your world, but I beseech you to

allow her to fill her term of life, and then I will willingly give her to you.

I must warn you, if I am denied, I cannot return to the world of the living; the Gods will have triumphed in the death of us both".

I didn't know what to do so I turned to Hades hoping that he would guide me, instead he moved his head close to mine so that only I could hear his words and whispered in my ear,

"We can't get involved with the death of a mere mortal".

I couldn't believe what I had just heard. I thought that my husband was a caring God but just then I was shocked by his indifference to this poor mortal. Now as I look back I realize that after many centuries of being alone in the Underworld could cause any God to withdraw and not allow mortal life to touch their soul, but then I was just a young Goddess who had spent only a few years here. I turned from Hades, determined to assist if I could and motioned for Orpheus to stand up and come closer to me. When he was right in front of me I took his hand and said,

"I cannot free your wife, for I rule over those who have already died and have no power over the Moirai. The Goddess Atopos, in her wisdom has decided it was time to cut the thread of Eurydice's life, and nothing I say to her will stop this", as I said this I could see that his heart was breaking at my words.

"If you can't return her to me, please grant me one more day with her, one day so I may be allowed to tell her that her death was my fault and to beg her forgiveness. She pleaded with me to postpone the wedding, knowing that the omens present forbid us to marry that morning, but I, being the son of a deity, believed that I couldn't be touched by the Fates". He begged me, and I could see his eyes filling with the tears he tried so desperately to hold back.

"I'll send you back with one of our stallions, he'll be able to return you home in less than a day, but you must hurry, Eurydice doesn't have much time left to her. Once you return, I'll make sure that you have one last day with her, and then I must claim her soul".

One of my servants brought the fastest of our stallions, and when Orpheus was mounted, I spoke once more to him,

"Orpheus, I promise that I'll do whatever is in my power to assist you".

He thanked me and kissed my hand in gratitude before the horse took off carrying him back to his wife. When he was no longer within our sight, Hades looked at me and said softly,

"My dear, please don't try to assist these mortals, you will soon go mad if you allow their pain to touch your heart".

"I wouldn't be able to forgive myself if I didn't even try to give him one day to say farewell to his beloved". After saying this to my husband, I called to the Goddess Atropos to plead with her to allow Eurydice one more day.

Atropos didn't appear, but soon her voice filled the room,

"Persephone, consort of Hades, Goddess of the Underworld, why do you suffer for this mortal man"?

"I too was once young and filled with love and thought I would rather die than live without my beloved. I know what it feels like to be betrayed by someone who you thought could not possibly hurt you. I can feel his sorrow and pain, and though I cannot give him his wife back, I can at least try to give him one day with her, one day only, so he may beg her for forgiveness before saying his final goodbyes".

"I will honor your request this one time and allow her one day more, but at the stroke of midnight tomorrow night, I will cut the thread and sever her life. Once she enters the Underworld you may do with her shade as you please".

Silence filled the room.

Hades took my hand and said to me.

"You must learn to not get involved in the prayers of the living, you won't be able to endure eternity down here if you do".

"Haven't you ever been so touched by a plea that you at least tried to honor their request"? I asked.

"No", he replied sadly, "Mortals have never prayed to me. During the centuries I have lived in the Underworld, I have always been misunderstood. I am thought of as only the cruel God who snatches mortals in their sleep to deposit their shade in the Dungeon of the Damned. No mortals even dare to speak my name aloud, for fear that I would then turn my grasp on their life".

When I heard these words, I felt pity for Hades, for how alone he must feel. It was then that I decided that I didn't wish to be feared like he was, so as Queen of the Dead, I greeted each new soul as they passed through to our world and tried to ease their transition to their new life within the Underworld.

When Orpheus reached his home, Eurydice was sitting up in bed waiting for him, and when he saw her, he ran to her and let his head fall into her lap. She stroked his hair and the tears that he was suppressing for so long began to flow and would not stop.

"My dear, don't cry for me". She said softly.

"I can never forgive myself, I should have listened to you. If I did you wouldn't be leaving me now".

"Don't blame yourself, I could've stopped the ceremony if I really wanted to. I didn't because I feared that if I did I would lose your love".

"Can you ever forgive me"? he said as she held him.

"I don't want our last night together to be spent with regrets, I wish to spend it with you in love". Orpheus kissed her and they spend the entire night holding each other. When the appointed hour came, Orpheus held his beloved, Eurydice tightly in his arms and kissed her one last time as she closed her eyes and took her last breath.

The next night, her shade passed through the gates of the Underworld, and I was standing there on the banks of the river Styx to greet her. Once Charon's boat stopped and she stepped on to the bank I could see the confusion in her face. I took her by the hand and spoke softly to her shade,

"Don't fear, everything will be all right".

Instead of leading her to the River of Forgetfulness, I lead her to my palace instead. You might think it was cruel of me to keep her soul here in the Underworld while she still longed for her former life, and for her love of Orpheus, but I had a plan. Each night she would cry for her lost love, and I would feel her pain, and I too thought my heart would break. After several days, I called once again to the Goddess Atropos, and once again only her voice came and soon it filled the room,

"What do you wish of me now!" the voice said with irration, "I have granted Eurydice one day for Orpheus to say farewell to her".

I could tell by her voice that she was losing patients with me.

"I thank you", I said, then added, "I could have asked you to release Eurydice from the thread of destiny, but I did not. I asked for one day only".

"I would've refused your request if you had asked for more than one day". The cold voice said.

"Yes I know that. That's why I asked for one day only, I know that you would never release those whose life has been deemed complete, but I also know that you, as a Goddess of Destiny, cannot take any soul before the allotted life has expired".

"And your point is". She replied coldly.

"Eurydice's life was cut short... cut short by you for vengeance against her husband's harsh words against the Moirai". I said.

"It is Destiny that decides when to cut the thread of life, and I am Destiny". The voice said, louder than before.

"I'm not asking for you to free her soul, I know that you would refuse me, I have called you here to ask you to give her husband over to me, allow them to live together here in the Underworld".

"For insinuating that I'd allow personal feeling to influence my decision and to take a soul before their time, I don't think I should grant your request...." Atropus blustered, but then the voice continued at a more quiet tone,

"But, since you are a noble Goddess and are only doing this out of pity for lost love, I believe I will grant your request. But... under one condition".

I agreed and she continued,

"The condition is that I'm allowed to chose how Orpheus will die".

I didn't have the time to thank her, for before my words came out, I felt her presence had departed.

The next day while Orpheus was out walking in the forest where he first met Eurydice, he stopped and sat under the same tree that he had when he glimpsed the lovely Nymph that would steal his heart, and sadness once again filled him. As he sat, his back against this tree he tried to suppress his sorrow. He wasn't alone for long, for soon a group of young women came across him and knowing of his skills on the lyre, asked him to sing for their enjoyment. He refused and they, in a frenzy that was caused by the Goddesses of Destiny, attacked him. With their bare hands they torn Orpheus to pieces and each took one of the pieces and tossed it deep into the forest, ensuring that a proper burial couldn't possibility take place thus committing his shade to wander the forest for eternity.

The Goddess Atropos gave her word that she'd allow Orpheus to die, but she had no intention of allowing his soul to enter the Underworld to be reunited with his wife. I was furious! How dare Atropos try to destroy their love for each other! That night, just after sunset, I appeared in the woods and searched until I found Orpheus' shade wandering aimlessly looking for the remains of his body. I approached his shade, and reached out to him I took his hand and personally guided him back to the Underworld with me, and to the Elysian Fields where Eurydice was sitting alone morning for her former life. Once Eurydice saw her husband, she cried, but this time her tears were not tears of sorrow, but tears of joy. When he saw the shade of his beloved wife, Orpheus ran to embrace her and as they kissed I turned my head and went back to the palace. Of all the shades within the Elysian Fields, only Eurydice and Orpheus have not tasted the waters from the River of Forgetfulness, and to this day I can hear Orpheus playing the lyre and singing so beautiful to his wife, that tears still fill my eyes.

XIII
Persephone

AS I HAD said earlier throughout the long centuries that I have lived within the Underworld there have been many mortals who have risked their lives to enter into the realm of the dead begging me to release the soul of a loved one, but none were so bold as the Lapith Prince Pirithous, son of King Ixion and half-brother to the Centaurs. The young prince inherited his father, Ixion's, pride. Even though Ixion was married to a beautiful princess named Dia, he believe that he was blessed by the Gods and therefore he deserved no mere mortal princess as a bride, instead he thought that he deserved a Goddess as his wife. Of all the Goddesses to choose from, he picked none other than Hera, wife of Zeus the greatest of the Olympian Gods to be his new bride.

Hera was flattered by the attention she was getting from this mortal and when she was angry with her husband, usually because she had found out he had been unfaithful to her once again, she would run to the king's palace and tease him, hoping that this would make Zeus feel even the slightest jealousy. Now even though she would tell the king that he was worthy of her affection she had no intention of becoming his lover, she was only using him to get back at her unfaithful husband. Her plan worked and soon Zeus thought his wife was having an affair with a mere mortal. Instantly he became furious and decided to put an end to his wife's new love interest.

"How dare you give yourself to the mortal!" Zeus shouted at his wife.

"You've slept with many mortals, both men and women". Hera shouted back.

"That man is a beast!" Zeus bellowed as he took one of his thunderbolts in his hand and was preparing to leave the palace, to strike the mortal down when Hera begged,

"Please Zeus, don't destroy him. Nothing has pasted between us, I swear to you". Hera said to her husband as she opened her mind to him.

Instantly he was assured that nothing had passed between them, and he knew that his wife was only using this mortal to make him jealous. This made him smile.

"I won't destroy him now, but I swear that if I find out that anything passes between you I'll not only destroy him, but you as well".

He stayed his weapon and spared the mortal's life, but he couldn't let Ixion go unpunished for one of the most heinous of crimes, the crime of hubris. It took several days before he was able to devise a plan that would not only punish the mortal, but also to teach his wife a lesson. He stretched out his arms into the sky and searched until his fingers grasped a large white cloud. He drew this cloud back to the palace and hid it until night when he was certain Hera was fast asleep. Zeus looked at his wife's beautiful face as she slept, and all the anger he had toward her vanished, only the love he felt stayed behind. He almost gave stopped what he was going to do, but then he remembered the look on Ixion's face when he looked at the Goddess. Using only his bare hands alone, he shaped this cloud into the likeness of his wife, Hera, and once satisfied that Ixion would be convinced that it was the Goddess herself, he let his breath fill the form with life. Instantly the form opened its eyes and was filled with life. He instructed this reflection of his wife to go to the king. That night the image of the Goddess entered the king's palace and went to his private chamber. Ixion thought that the Goddess Hera herself had finally given in to his passion. Without uttering a single word, he took the cloud that he thought was the Goddess and instead of making love to it, he raped the image he held in his arms, and it was from his lust and the seeds he sent forth into the magical cloud that the Centaurs were born.

Let me stop here for a moment to distinguish between the Centaurs who were born from Ixion with the most famous and wisest of all the Centaurs, Chiron. Chiron was not related to Ixion at all, his father was Cronus who took the form of a stallion as he made love to his mother Philyra, one of the daughters of Oceanus, making him of the same generation as the Olympians, and like the Olympians he was immortal. Chiron lived in Thessaly and not only befriended Gods and mortals alike, but became mentor to a number of heroes. The Centaurs who were descended from Ixion were monstrous beings, half man and half horse, who were mortal. They lived in the mountains and forests, far form any civilization; their food was raw flesh and their behavior bestial. No mortals except the Lapith people would even speak of these creatures.

The prince Pirithous was not born from this union, instead he was born to Ixion's wife, the princess Dia, making him only half brother to the Centaurs, and while he was growing up he heard the story of how his half brothers were conceived and thought that he wouldn't be as foolish as his father by allowing himself to be tricked by the Gods, he would succeed where his father failed; he would marry a Goddess. King Ixion had other plans for his son, he wished for Pirithous to marry the daughter of Adrastus, King of Sicyon, therefore joining the two kingdoms in an alliance. The arrangements were made when his son was still a young boy and it would be many years before the marriage would take place, so the young prince thought little about his future wife and allowed his fantasies to take over. When Pirithous became a young man his father started to discuss the marriage plans, and since he had no intention of marrying King Adrastus' daughter Hippodameia he left his home and family spending many years at sea.

In his travels he had come to city Athens where he meet Theseus, who had just been crowned as King for his bravery in defeating the Minotaur and freeing the people of the land from the threat that loomed over them for the past four years, and instantly the two became good friends. Theseus, on his way back from Crete with Ariadne, the daughter of King Minos, left her on the island of Naxos.

"My dear Ariadne, you know it's for the best that you stay here". He said to the young girl as she held her tear-stained face against his chest.

"But I love you". She sobbed.

"You deserve someone who will give you his entire heart".

"But I have nowhere to go".

"The Gods will take care of you". He said as he kissed her forehead and stepped onto his boat. The reason Theseus left the princess Ariadne at Naxos was because he was in love with the child who would one day grow up to become the most beautiful woman in the world, Helen, and he knew that though Ariadne was beautiful, he would never be satisfied with anyone other than the child who had stolen his heart. He told this to Pirithous one night as they were both drunk from the finest wine his kingdom could supply. While listening to his friend, Pirithous devised a plan.

"Theseus, we can leave tonight for Sparta and bring back Helen as your bride".

"My friend, this is foolish". Theseus replied, though he secretly hoped that they would.

"Why? You don't think yourself worthy enough for Helen"?

The two friends spent the entire night discussing their plans and within a week they both set off for Sparta. Several weeks earlier Helen had her first blood, and she along with several other girls were to perform a ritual dance in a couple of days to announce to the entire village that they were no longer children, but had become women. The two men found Helen, along with the other girls just outside a temple dedicated to Artemis rehearsing their dance. As they hid behind some shrubs and watched the young girls dance, Theseus knew deep within his soul that this was a mistake, but he did nothing to stop his friend's plan. They stayed concealed until the dance was complete and the girls were preparing to leave, and with luck on their side Helen stayed behind, having trouble changing back into her daily robes, and as she tried to catch up with the others Pirithous grabbed her from behind, placing his hand over her mouth to prevent her companions from hearing her screams and fled into the cover of the forest, dragging the young Helen behind. Once near the shore, Pirithous' hand slipped and the frightened child let out a scream that instantly alerted the others. "Help! Help me!" She cried.

Her companions, hearing her screams turned toward the beach and started to run only to reach the shore too late. They watched as the small boat carrying the scared Helen sailed into the darkness of the night.

"Look, the shore is empty". Pirithous said to his friend, not seeing her companions. "I told you no one heard her". He continued.

"The others might not have heard her, but I fear that the Gods have".

"Nonsense! You have nothing to fear". Pirithous tried to reassure Theseus. Seeing that his words had no effect, he came up with a different strategy.

"We can turn around and take Helen to your mother Aethra. She can watch her until she can become your bride. That way, even if they suspect you took Helen, they won't be able to find her. They can search your entire kingdom, but they'll never find Helen".

"No matter where we go, the Gods will know". Theseus said with a tone of hopelessness. Even thought he knew this would not save them, they turned their ship around and headed for his mother's home in Attica.

What they didn't know was that the other girls who had followed them to the shore reported what they had seen to Helen's brothers, Castor and Pollux, who immediately set out to save her. I don't know how they knew that their sister was in Attica, but one of the Gods, probably Artemis, informed them, for it is sacrilegious to hurt any mortal while in a temple dedicated to any of the Gods. Two weeks after the young Helen was brought to Aethra ships were seen on the horizon.

"Look!" one man shouted, "Battleships". The men ran to the city to warn others and soon the entire town was prepared for battle. The people of Attica had no idea why they were being attacked, but still they fought bravely and it wasn't until many souls were guided to my palace that the two brothers and their companions were able to rescue the scared child Helen. It was several months before the news of Helen's rescue reached Theseus during which time Pirithous had returned to his father's land.

Once reunited with his father, Pirithous could no longer postpone his marriage to Hippodameia, so he agreed to allow his father to make the wedding arraignments, and it wasn't until the day of the wedding when Theseus arrived that he found out what had happened to Helen.

"Helen's brothers, Castor and Pollux, destroyed Attica. My mother barely got away with her life".

"They took Helen back with them"? Pirithous asked, pretending to share Theseus grief, but it didn't matter to him, he had assisted Theseus and knew that he was bound to assist him in the future.

The wedding took place and during the last day of the celebrations Pirithous' half brothers, the Centaurs, who don't usually tolerate alcohol became drunk and when they saw the dancers, they grabbed them and dragged them kicking and screaming towards the nearby woods. They had no intention of returning the maidens, for after their lust was satisfied, they would then satisfy their appetite. Both Theseus and Pirithous immediately started to fight the Centaurs, and one of them, a powerful dark brown and white Centaur named Eurytion became so enraged at his half-brother's nerve to protect the maidens, he snatched the bride Hippodamia and started to flee with her, causing the battle between the Centaurs and the Lapiths that was told about in myths and images adorn many vases and urns.

Even though their marriage did not start out well, soon Pirithous grew to love Hippodamia and they lived together happily for many years. Just after their son, Polypoetes was born, Pirithous began to long for the sea again, and soon he set sail for Athens to visit his old friend Theseus. That first night while they were drinking he convinced Theseus to leave his kingdom once more and go to the seas again like they had when they were young.

"Theseus, don't you miss the adventure of the sea"? You've been trapped here in Athens for so long."

"I'm much too busy to enjoy myself, I have a kingdom to rule". Theseus said with a sigh.

"We won't be long, I promise".

"What do you have in mind"? thinking if it was only a short trip he could find someone to rule in his place.

Pirithous told his friend, "I want to travel to the Underworld".

Theseus chocked as he repeated, "The Underworld. Why would you want to travel there"?

"You remember when years ago I assisted you with the capture of the young Helen". Theseus nodded, he had indeed remembered, "Well, I want us to travel to the Underworld were we'll release the Goddess Persephone from her prison".

"Your mad with drink". Theseus told his friend, adding, "We'd never succeed in such a plan".

"You know as well as I do, that the Persephone wouldn't agree to marry the Lord of the Underworld unless he placed a spell over her. Once we enter the Underworld and free her from his spell, she'll protect us".

It didn't really matter, since he had assisted his friend when they kidnapped Helen, Theseus couldn't refuse Pirithous' request no matter how ludicrous he though this plan was. He did at least try to convince his old friend to return to his wife and son, knowing that she was a good woman, but Pirithous wouldn't listen to him.

They set out the next morning, and after many months of traveling, when they were almost ready to give up hope of ever finding an entrance to my kingdom, they came upon a cave near Mount Cyllene where they planned to take shelter for the night. A storm was growing outside and they were confined within this cave for an entire day. As they searched for another exit they traveled deeper and deeper in the cavern, and it was there that they accidentally found an entrance to the world below. This entrance didn't bring them through the main gate, but was a back door to our world, letting them out in the middle of the mountains that are between Hades' palace and the Dungeon of the Damned, Tartarus, and once within our world the gate they came through suddenly slammed shut, instantly trapping them there between the two worlds.

Hades knew of their plans from the beginning, and I believe that it was he who secretly led them to seek shelter within that cave, and once there it would be easy for him to make them accidentally stumble upon this hidden entrance to the Underworld, and once they were there he made sure that they wouldn't be allowed to leave. The mountains near our palace are cold and inhospitable, and the two would have died from exposure if Hades had not secretly guide them to the Elysian Fields, and once there it was easy for them to locate our palace. I also knew that they were coming for my dear husband Hades explained to me their mission before they even set out on the expedition, and when they finally arrived both Hades and I were sitting on our thrones waiting for them. Theseus bowed low to us showing us the respect that we deserved, but Pirithous stood proudly and looking directly into Hades' eyes he said without any fear in his voice,

"I am Pirithous, son of King Ixion".

Not following the usual customs when greeting a deity, where the God or Goddess is addressed first by acknowledging their status, followed by a statement of telling how you have worshipped them, and only then stating the reason why you have come. Pirithous was not showing Hades the proper respect that a God as powerful as he deserved.

Hades overlooked this rudeness, and politely greeted them,

"What brings you two mortals here to the Underworld"?, Hades said, pretending that he knew nothing of their plan.

"We have heard that the Goddess Persephone was abducted by the Lord of the Underworld, and forced to spend one-half the year in this prison as your wife".

Pirithous addressed Hades, and as he said this I thought that this must be the story mother is still telling. Even though I had already spend several decades here within the Underworld, and have explained to her that I was happy living as Hades wife, she still couldn't accept the fact that I fell in love, telling everyone that I must have been abducted and dragged against my will.

"And where did you hear this story from"? I asked.

"It is common knowledge that ever since you were abducted by the Lord of the Underworld, the great Fertility Goddess Demeter has decided to withhold her fruits from the earth while you are kept in this prison, and only when you are released and returned to Mount Olympus, will she allow any growth to occur". He replied to me.

"And you two heroes have come to free her and remove Demeter's curse on the lands". Hades responded to them with a smile on his face.

"No", responded Pirithous, boldly stating, "We've come to take the Goddess Persephone, daughter of the Goddess Demeter and the great God Zeus as my new bride, where she will live among the mortals and rule with me in the kingdom of my father".

"And what makes you think that I'll allow this"? Hades asked.

"As Lord of the Underworld, it is told that you are a just ruler, and as a just ruler, you must know that your wife would be much happier living with me in the world of the living".

"And what do you think of this, my dear"? Hades asked me, leaning closer and whispering to me to go along with what Pirithous proposes.

"My dear husband, during these long years of living within the Underworld I have grown found of you, but I must admit that the offer this mortal makes is tempting. I do miss the company of the living". I said to all.

"Very well, Persephone, you are free to leave with Pirithous…but before you leave I have one request of you". Hades said, pausing for a moment before continuing, "I hope that you and your new husband-to-be would agree to have a farewell dinner with me".

Before Pirithous or Theseus could respond, I said, "I wouldn't dream of leaving without a farewell dinner, for throughout the years you have been very kind to me".

Hades clapped his hands and a servant arrived and led the two men to one of the chambers where they were provided with fine robes to change into since their cloaks were torn and wet from their long travels. Once alone, Theseus tried once again to convince Pirithous that this had to be some type of trap,

"My friend, you know that the God of the Underworld would never release his bride, not even to the great God Zeus. Aren't you at all suspicious that he had agreed to release her to a mere mortal".

Pirithous was as foolish as his father was and wouldn't listen to his friend's advice.

"The God of the Underworld knows that I am correct. Persephone will be much happier living as my Queen, then she ever could be here surrounded by death".

Hades and I dressed in our finest silk robes, embroidered with gold and silver threads and were already seated in the dining area when our two guests entered. Hades bid them to take the seat of honor across from where we were, and once the two mortals were seated the arms of the chairs, which were carved serpents, instantly opened their red eyes and came to life. Neither of the men noticed this, nor did they notice as the snakes started to slither up, very slowly winding around their ankles, continuing up their legs. When they did finally realize what was happening, it was too late; the serpents had already bound them tightly to their seat. Both men struggled to free themselves, but the harder they fought, the tighter the serpents wound around them.

A purple mist soon began filling the room and I watched as both men looked in terror as their skin started to lighten, as if all the blood were being drained from their bodies, and gradually they turned turn almost pure white. Their struggling seemed to slow as the color faded and soon I saw that they were no longer able to move their limbs, and I knew that the transformation was almost complete, within seconds they would no longer be mortal men, but only statues of their former selves. Once complete, the look of terror was frozen on their faces as they sat and sat for the next four years. They would have both sat there frozen for eternity, but the hero Hercules came to the Underworld as one of his twelve labors and found his cousin Theseus sitting in the "Chair of Forgetfulness" and begged us to release him.

Before I continue, let me briefly tell the tale of hero Hercules.

Many years ago Zeus had found another mortal woman name Alcmene that he had become infatuated with. Though Alcmene was beautiful, she was married, and did whatever she could to discourage the awestruck God. Zeus tried all of his tricks, but none worked, so when her husband Amphitryon was away on an expedition he took his shape and came to Alcmene.

"My beloved, I've missed you so". Zeus said.

"Amphitryon, your back early". Alcmene replied to the disguised god, all the while thinking it was her beloved husband.

"I couldn't bear being parted from your loveliness for any longer". He said as he took the beauty in his arms and kissed her. She giggled as he effortlessly lifted her and took her to her husband's bed where made love all day, and when the evening arrived, Zeus knew that Alcmene's real husband was near, so he excused himself, telling her he has some business to complete before night fell. Zeus kissed her forehead, and when he did this he was assured that she had conceived a son. It was only a few hours later when the real Amphitryon came home,

"Alcmene, I'm home".

"Were you able to complete what you needed"? she asked, still thinking that her husband was gone only a couple of hours.

"What are you talking about? I've just come back".

It was then that she suspected some type of treachery, so she pretended that everything was as it should be, saying nothing of his appearance that very afternoon. That night her true husband made love to her and she conceived a second son, this one fathered by her mortal husband. It wasn't until she found out that she was expecting that the seer Tiresias explained to her what had happened that day, telling her that one of her sons was fathered by the great God Zeus, and would be remembered throughout history as the greatest hero who ever lived, while the other would be destined to be forgotten. Alcmene didn't want her husband to find out, for if he did, she was sure he would kill her. Zeus, not wanting to cause trouble in his lover's domestic life came to Amphitryon that night while he dreamt.

"Amphitryon, your wife has conceived two boys". Zeus' image spoke. In his dream, Amphitryon fell prostrate on the floor, knowing he was in the presence of the most powerful of the Gods.

"Stand". The mortal did as he was bid. Since Zeus was cloaked within a dream, his form glowed, but he had no fear of his presence destroying the mortal.

"Amphitryon, the first son born to your wife will not be your son, but mine."

Amphitryon looked at the God, and Zeus knew that he thought that his wife had been unfaithful to him, so Zeus told him how he had assumed his shape and as her husband, he made love to Alcmene. Zeus continued.

"Don't blame Alcmene, she had done nothing wrong".

Amphitryon woke, and he knew that there was nothing for him to do, except love both children as if they were both his own.

Eight months later, Alcmene gave birth to twin boys. It wasn't long before Hera found out about her husband's affair and she swore that she would curse the life of the son that was to be bore from that union, sending many dangers and trials across his path. A lesser mortal would've given up hope and accepted his fate, but Hercules was no mere mortal, he was the son of the greatest of the Gods, Zeus, and he was able to keep one step ahead of Hera. Once he became a teenager, he left his mortal family, not wanting anything to happen to them and for the next ten years he moved around continuously, not staying in one place for more than a couple of weeks.

While he was approaching the city of Thebes a lion crossed his path. Thinking nothing of it, he continued walking, but the beast attacked him from behind. Hercules easily killed the lion. What he didn't know was that this same lion had been causing destruction in the land, and as a reward the King of Thebes gave Hercules his youngest daughter Megara as his bride. Tired of moving around, Hercules decided that he would no longer run, so he took Megara as his wife and for the next several years they lived together peacefully in Thebes. Soon Hercules thought that the Goddess Hera forgotten her hatred for him, and during the time that Hercules stayed in Thebes his wife Megara gave birth to three children. Hercules loved his children dearly, and if he had any notion that Hera hadn't given up, he would have left his family immediately to protect them, but he knew nothing of Hera's plans.

Hera wasn't through with Hercules though, and one night while the happy family was sleeping, the Goddess sent a madness into him. He awoke with a fear in his soul that he couldn't explain. He didn't know what power was taking control of his body, only that some force greater than his own made him take the oil lamp near his bed in his hands and open it. He tried to stop himself as he held this lamp above his innocent children and poured the oil over there sleeping bodies, the oldest being only three years old. The boy stirred while he slept, but did not wake. Hercules tried with all his might to stop what he was doing, but he couldn't fight this madness. He tried to scream, to wake his children and alert them of the danger, but no sound came from his mouth. After struggling for a few moments, his hand reached into the hearth and lifted a burning log; the heat burning his hand. The pain shot up his arm, and he thought he would pass out from it. "Good", he thought, "if I pass out, I won't hurt anyone", but he didn't. Time seemed to stop as he struggled with himself, and as if in a dream he watched as he held the burning log over his innocent children. A single sound, a screech, slipped from his mouth as he dropped the fire on his sleeping children.

I made sure that the three children died instantly without much suffering, and I personally greeted their shades when they entered the Underworld doing whatever I could to console them, but as I did so a hatred filled my heart, not a hatred for Hercules, for he was only an innocent victim of Hera' wrath, but a hatred of the Goddess herself. When Hercules realized what he had done, he almost killed himself; I don't know why he didn't, maybe Hera wouldn't allow him to escape her wrath by taking his own life. Instead, he left his hysterical wife and wandered for months, only to find himself one day at the Oracle of Apollo. Here he asked the Gods for their forgiveness, and after sitting there alone for hours with no answer, he stood up and was about to leave, when a voice filled the room telling him,

> *The Goddess Hera, the wife of Zeus, has condemned you from birth, and through her you have killed your children. The Gods will forgive you, but first you must give your wife Megara to your nephew Iolaus to live as his wife for the rest of her days. After this is done, you must travel to Argos and seek out your cousin, King Eurystheus. He will give you ten labors to complete. When you have completed these ten labors, and only then will your sins be forgiven and will you be allowed to live the rest of your life in peace.*

"I can't marry Iolaus, I'm married to you". Megara said to her husband when he told her what the Oracle told him.

"Don't fear, Iolaus will take care of you".

"But it's a sin to have more than one husband". She said as she tried to suppress the sobs.

"The Oracle wouldn't tell me to give you to Iolaus if the Gods didn't want you to be with him". Hercules said as he took her hand and placed it within his nephew's, then he looked at Iolaus and said,

"Iolaus, please take care of her". Without another word, he turned and walked away, never seeing his first wife again. Within a month he reached Argos and when he met with his cousin he bowed to Eurystheus. When his eyes meet his cousin's he knew that Hera had already been there. Hera had instilled a fear into Eurystheus, a fear that the hero would destroy him. She had whispered the tasks into Eurystheus' ear, hoping that the labors would be too great and destroy Hercules.

For his first task, Hercules was to kill the Nemean Lion, a monster that was ravaging the land and devouring the inhabitants of Nemea. Eurystheus demanded proof of the death of the lion, requesting that he bring back the lion's skin. At first Hercules thought this would be an easy task, had he not already killed a lion that threatened the people of Thebes, but this lion was not an ordinary beast, and Eurystheus knew it, this lion was a mythical beast whose hide was impervious to any mortal weapons. Hercules shot the lion with his arrows, but these only bounced off him, then the lion, angered by this, pounced on the hero and as he fought to keep the lion's mouth from his body, he pulled out his sword and tried to stab the lion, but the sword only broke in two. He thought that the lion would soon kill him and at that time he welcomed death, but death was not to come to him, at least not yet. He heard a voice and at first thought it was the voice of the God of Death, calling to him.

"Death, come and take me!" he shouted.

The voice came again, a little louder and he knew that it was his father, Zeus, speaking to him alone,

> "Don't fight this beast as you would a normal lion, for mortal weapons can not hurt him. Stop fighting and let your body go limp. The lion will think you are dead and will momentarily loosen his grip. When he does, you are to jump onto his back and with your entire strength grasp the lion's neck and strangle him. This is the only way to kill this beast".

Hercules did as he was told, and after a long struggle with his bare hands around the lion's throat, he felt the beast slowly lose its strength, and finally give in to death. Once he was sure the lion was dead, Hercules tried with all his weapons to skin the beast, but no blades would penetrate the beast's hid, finally it occurred to him that if mortal weapons couldn't kill the beast, then he would have to use something that wasn't made my mortal hands to skin it.

"*Use the* claws". He didn't know if this was his thought, or if Zeus had spoken to him once again. He grabbed the massive paw and using only one claw he ripped through the magical hid. Once finished skinning the beast, he threw the hide over his robe and retuned to his cousin.

Eurystheus' next task was for Hercules to destroy the Lernaean Hydra, a giant serpent with seven heads and breath that was venomous. Hercules traveled to the swamp where this creature lived and saw only a gigantic tree that grew within the marshy land. Shooting arrows into the swamp, near the base of the tree, he felt the ground began to tremble slightly. He knew he had found the Hydra's lair. After several more arrows, the serpent rose from the marshy water angry at the intrusion. Hercules struggled with this task, for each time he would cut off one of the heads it would immediately grow back, and after awhile the poisonous breath began to make him dizzy and he feared that he would soon loose consciousness. Again Zeus assisted his son, this time by taking the form of Zeus' nephew Iolaus, who was acting as charioteer for his uncle during this task. Zeus' breath surrounded Iolaus, and instantly he was asleep. As Iolaus the God came to Hercules who was fighting a loosing battle with the Hydra; Zeus knew that without his assistance, the hero would be totally destroyed. Iolaus, who was holding a flaming torch, yelled to Hercules,

"Uncle, don't let the beast's breath get to you".

"Iolaus get away!" Hercules shouted to his favorite nephew.

"Cut off the nearest head". Iolaus shouted.

Hercules did this and before a new head could sprout from the severed neck his nephew thrust the torch into the bleeding stump, searing it and preventing a new head from growing in its place. One head was destroyed, followed by the second, the third, fourth, fifth, sixth and as the seventh head was finally cut, the beast died, its massive body crashing down at Hercules feet.

Zeus, still in the form of Iolaus then took several of Hercules' arrows and dipped them in the Hydra's blood, knowing that these arrows would contain venom so powerful that whatever it touched would die. He gave these arrows to his son hoping that he'd be able to use them in one of his other labors. When Hercules returned to his chariot he was surprised to see his nephew fast asleep, but he was too worn out to give it a second thought. Hera, once again came to Eurystheus and whispered to him that Hercules didn't kill the Hydra alone, but was assisted with this task; therefore he would not agree to accept this as one of the ten labors and another labor was devised for him.

Next, Hercules was sent to Mount Erymanthus, were he was to capture the Erymanthian Boar and bring his body back to Eurystheus. Once completed, he was instructed to bring back the Hind of Ceryneia, a deer that was sacred to Artemis. Eurystheus thought that when Hercules killed this sacred deer, that he would anger the Goddess Artemis, and she'd destroy him, but Eurystheus failed to request that he wished for the body of the Hind of Ceryneia, so after many weeks of trying to capture this beautiful deer, Hercules finally succeeded and brought back the deer alive. Eurystheus, angry that the deer was alive, had it put in the stables and was planning on killing it himself the next day. That night Hercules called to the Goddess Artemis and told her of his cousin's plan and Artemis came and freed the animal, and as a reward for not hurting her beloved deer, she assisted Hercules in his remaining labors.

The fifth labor was for the hero to kill the Stymphalian birds. These predatory birds lived near the shore of Lake Stymphalus in Arcadia and had multiplied to the point of becoming a plague by ravaging the crops and attacking the local residents. Hercules was able to kill of few of these birds with his arrows, but after several hours he didn't see much progress. Artemis called on Hephaestus, the God of Fire, who created a giant rattle that she than gave to Hercules, and by using this he was able to frighten the birds away. Each time the hero returned Eurystheus became angrier and angrier that he couldn't think of a way to destroy his cousin, so the next labor was designed as a way to humiliate the hero by ordering him to clean the stables of Augias, in one day. These stables had not been cleaned in several decades, and it would be impossible to clean them in one night, so as Hercules sat contemplating what he should do, Artemis whispered to him in the wind,

> "Hercules, don't give up, for I know how you can finish this labor before the sun rises. Go to the Alpheus and Peneus rivers and divert the flow of both these mighty rivers, causing the waters to flow through the stables taking all the filth with them".

In the morning when Eurystheus saw that all of Augias' stables were completely clean, he couldn't believe his eyes, but then once again Hera whispered to him that the hero was again assisted by one of the Gods, so he wouldn't accept this labor either.

His next tasks were to capture the Cretan Bull; bring back the mares of Diomedes, four beautiful mares which fed only on human flesh; followed by going to the Amazons where he was to capture the girdle worn by the Queen of the Amazons; then to travel to the Mediterranean where he was to capture the cattle of Geryon and bring them back alive to Eurystheus, finally he was to travel to a sacred grove in the land of the Hesperides and steal the golden apples that Gaia had given to Hera as a wedding present, but to complete this task, he had to kill another multi-headed serpent who was guarding the apples. Eurystheus knew that if the hero succeeded, Hera's wrath would only increase since these apples were precious to her. All these labors Hercules was able to complete without much difficulty, and when he returned he was confident that the Gods would soon forgive him.

While Hercules was away on the eleventh task, which took almost an entire year, Eurystheus conceived a plan that he was sure would destroy the hero. The final labor required Hercules to gather all his courage, he was ordered to descend to the Underworld were he was to capture the guard dog Cerberus and bring him back to the upper world, either dead or alive. Again the Gods assisted Hercules. Zeus ordered Hermes to show his son the path to the Underworld and with Hermes as his guide he reached our palace within a few days, and once there, he bowed to us as Hermes introduced him and explained why he was sent to the Underworld. Reluctantly Hades agreed to allow Hercules to borrow Cerberus, but only because he knew that Zeus would be angry if he didn't.

"I'll allow you to take my beloved pet Cerberus, but you must promise me that no harm will come to her". Hades finally said.

"My Lord, with your blessings I'll have Cerberus back to you within a week". Hercules answered as he bowed low.

"Tell your cousin, Eurystheus that if Cerberus is harmed in any way, I'll personally come to his palace and drag his shade to the prison Tartarus for eternity". Hades explained.

As we were leaving the palace Hercules noticed Pirithous and his cousin Theseus in their petrified state, and asked,

"Forgive my curiosity, but this man is my cousin Theseus, King of Athens. Four years ago he set out to sea with his friend Pirithous and has not been heard from since". He paused here, then continued, "Please tell me what crime they committed against you".

"Pirithous inherited his fathers pride." Hades answered, "He had the nerve to come here with your cousin Theseus expecting to take Persephone back with him as his bride".

"I beg you my Lord, allow me to return with Theseus". Hercules said as he bowed to us.

"My dear", I said to my husband, "Theseus came with Pirithous unwillingly, you've seen this in his thoughts, I implore you to let him leave with his cousin, during these last four years he has paid for his crime". Hades nodded to me, then spoke to Hercules,

"I'll allow Theseus to return with you only after you return Cerberus".

Hercules went down on one knee and kissed Hades' hand in gratitude, this shocked him, since most mortals, and even most of the Gods feared the Lord of the Underworld. We left the palace and went to the Entrance of the Underworld where Hades spoke softly to Cerberus assuring her that Hercules would bring her back home in a couple of days, she walked up to him and gently licked his hand. Hades then called to Charon to bring the ferry across the river, and once there he had to order him to take Hercules and Cerberus to the other side.

Once he was back in his cousins' palace and Eurystheus saw the size of the hound that accompanied Hercules, he ran in terror and hid in a large jar and refused to come out until the beast was taken back to the Underworld. Three days later, Hercules returned with Cerberus, and thanked both of us again for allowing him to return with his cousin, and with that Hades clapped his hands once and I watched as the life slowly came back into Theseus' body changing his skin from white marble to soft flesh once again, while the serpents once more open their red eyes and slowly began their descent, uncoiling from his limbs, allowing him to once again move. Once freed Theseus knelt in front of us, then he spoke to me,

"Persephone, Goddess of the Underworld, consort of the Lord Pluto, please forgive me for my foolishness, I should've tried harder to convince Pirithous that his plan would only cause his death".

"My husband, Hades, knew from the beginning of your adventure that you came unwillingly, and it is for that reason alone that you are allowed to leave the Underworld, but I'm sad to say that your dear friend, Pirithous, will spend eternity with us".

Theseus nodded that he understood, then he took my hand and kissed it softy before leaving.

Hercules returned to his cousin's palace and once Eurystheus saw him he demanded that another labor was needed.

"I won't accept your last task as being complete. I asked for the Hound of the Underworld to be given to me. Since you have returned Cerberus I've no other choice but to devise another labor for you to complete".

At these words Hercules' head lowered, he was so tired and the thought of another labor almost destroyed him. He was about to speak, to ask what his next task would be when Zeus instantly appeared in a great flash of light and spoke to his beloved son,

"Hercules, my son, you have succeeded in not only the ten labors that were agreed upon, but you have completed two extra labors that Eurystheus had given you, therefore you have been forgiven of your crimes".

Eurystheus stood shaking in the corner as Hercules bowed to his father,

"Father, I don't think I could survive any longer if the Goddess Hera continues to torment me".

"You have no need to worry; because of your bravery, even my dear wife, Hera has decided that she will offer you her forgiveness and will lift her curse on you".

XIV
Persephone

AFTER FOUR YEARS of being trapped within the Underworld Theseus was finally freed and upon his return to Athens he found that the only woman he had ever loved had died while he sat motionlessly as our un-invited guest. Knowing that Pirithous' plan was foolish, he told no one where he was going when he set off with his old friend, so when he disappeared, those who loved him had no idea where to look, so after a few months they gave up hope of seeing their king again. Theseus' lover wasted away for many moons before finally giving into death, hoping to be greeted by Theseus at the gates to the Underworld.

When the king finally returned a great festival filled the streets of Athens. As he walked among the cheering crowds he tried his best to appear pleased to be back home, but in his heart he couldn't forget the pain he felt. His brief stay within the Underworld had changed him forever. It was his fault that his lover died and no matter what anyone could say, he couldn't deny his role in her death, so he withdrew into his palace and drowned himself in his loneliness. Sorrow and regret; regret for so many things he should have or should not have done soon consumed him. What he should have done was marry her, but it was much too late for that now. It wasn't that he didn't love her that prevented him from marring her, the reason being that she was no ordinary woman but a priestess of the Amazons and he knew that his people could never accept this woman as their queen, so he kept her hidden within the palace as his mistress only. He hated the fact that he was king, had he been an ordinary mortal he would have been free to marry the one who stole his heart, but as king he had to think of his subjects before his own happiness.

He sat alone within his chamber remembering the first time he saw the only woman who he would ever love, and cried. It was eighteen years ago while he was out at sea with Pirithous on one of their many voyages together. Their ship approached the shore of the island of the Amazons, and when the men on board saw the beautiful Amazon women swimming naked in the clear water they became wild with desire. Theseus watched as the men jumped into the sea fully dressed and smile came across his face as he too began feeling these same urges. He started to undress. Throwing his clothes to the side he stood on the deck of the ship naked, ready to join his crew in the cold water when he saw one of the Amazons posed on the shore with her bow held ready. He stood still, the sight of her made his heart stop and watched as she let her arrows fly, and as if one of these arrows touched by Eros love potion, had pierced his heart and filled his blood with the poison, he instantly fell in love with her.

Theseus ordered the crew back on board and when they were all accounted for he demanded that the ship go back out to sea. The men were not happy about the decision, but Pirithous ordered their return to sea. After several hours the Amazons thought that the threat of these men had passed and soon they relaxed guard. That night, while the ship was hidden, Theseus made sure that the men were all asleep, he walked to the deck and dived into the dark, cold waters. Silently he swam alone to the shore determined to find this strange woman who had stolen his heart. He searched the island for hours and had almost given up hope of finding her; the sun was being to lighten the sky and he knew that he wouldn't be able to hide from the Amazons keen sight during the day. Defeated, he started the long journey back to shore when a twinkling light in the distance suddenly caught his attention. At first it was small and hardly noticeable, but as he slowly approached he could make out a fire burning in the distance. Stealthily, he crept through the forest, using the woodlands as cover, until he was close enough to see the Amazon women dancing around the fire. Searching their faces, he looked for his love, this woman who now owned his heart, but there was no sight of her. Thinking she must be elsewhere, he was about to leave to continue his search on another part of the island, when something brought his gaze up and there in the distance he saw a lone woman sitting on a fallen log just outside of the circle of dancing women. This figure stared directly at him without showing any fear. When their eyes meet, he knew that she would be the only woman he would ever love, and was determined that he would never let her go.

Hippolyta, for that was the name of this Amazon priestess, also felt the tip of Eros' poison arrow pierce her heart as their eyes locked for the first time. Her intent was to wait for the stranger and when she spotted him she was going to alert the others and kill the intruder, but alas, her heart would not allow this. She quietly left the safety of the group and walked into the woods alone, knowing that the intruder would follow. Theseus did follow, and when he finally caught up she was waiting with her sword drawn. She didn't cry out for help, instead she fought him as bravely as any man would've, but Theseus was stronger and after a long scuffle he was finally able to capture her.

"Please, kill me". She begged, for she couldn't betray her sisters, especially for a man, but he wouldn't. She didn't scream out to the others, her dishonor in losing in battle could be forgiven, but not her feelings for this strange man. The Amazons' were raised in a society run entirely of women. No men were allowed on the island, so every ten years all the maidens would travel to a far off land where they would find a suitable man to mate with. All male children would either be killed at birth or be sent back to their father's land. Only the girls would be raised, and within a society like this, it's no wonder Hippolyta didn't trust this stranger. Without a word she lowered her head in shame as she slowly followed her capturer back to his ship and to Athens.

Over the years Hippolyta's love for Theseus grew and not too long after she arrived in Athens she gave birth to a beautiful son. Theseus held his newborn son Hippolytus, named after his mother as was the custom of the Amazons, and smiled.

"I can't give him up". She cried to her lover Theseus, knowing that raising a son would go against everything she believed in.

"No one asks you to. We'll raise him together". The King replied as he held her in him arms and kissed her tenderly on the lips. She smiled back and slowly lowered their son to her breast.

Hippolyta was Theseus' only love, and she alone shared his palace in Athens. He wished only to spend the rest of his life with his Amazon priestess and make her his Queen, the Queen of Athens, with their son Hippolytus as his heir, but alas, the Goddesses of Fate would not allow this. Talk of this foreign princess soon filled the land and Theseus knew that his subjects would never accept her as their Queen. As King he didn't have the luxury of choosing his own bride, nor remain unmarried, and since he couldn't have the only women he loved as his bride, he decided that he would marry Phaedra the daughter of King Minos and unite the kingdom of Crete with that of Athens, as was his destiny. So only five years after bringing the Amazon princess back home with him, he set out once again for Crete and once there he joined Phaedra and took rule of Crete. Once married, Phaedra thought that she would return with her new husband to Athens where they would rule together, but was surprised when he requested that she stay on the island of Crete.

"Why must I stay so far from you"? she pleaded with her husband, for she did love him at that time, but Theseus would not allow her to come to Athens, no matter what she said.

"You must stay here in my place and rule the lands. I can't govern both Athens and Crete alone".

"But I want to be with you". She said as she kissed him tenderly, hoping that she could change his mind.

"I promise, I'll come so often that soon you'll beg me to stay away". With that he left her in the beautiful palace that he had built for her on the land that her father's palace had stood only a decade earlier

Each night before retiring she would cry herself to sleep, longing to be away from this prison that reminded her so much of her former life. Her only happiness was the few times that Theseus would visit her throughout the year. Each time he would leave after only a few days, and soon her depression would consume her. Even though Theseus lied to her and told her that he loved her, Phaedra knew that he did not. She thought that maybe if she would give Theseus a son, he would feel obligated to stay with her, so she called to the Gods, "Please let me conceive a son.", and within the year she was expecting. When Theseus found out he was excited, and at first Phaedra thought that her plan worked, but at the end of the week her husband kissed her as he left once again for Athens. That night as Phaedra lay awake she thought about killing herself, but the Fates wouldn't allow her to escape her destiny. For the next fifteen years Phaedra lived as a prisoner in her own kingdom and throughout the years her love for her husband was replaced with loathing. She didn't even seek him out during the four years that he was trapped within the Underworld, instead she ruled the kingdom herself as she had become accustomed to.

When Theseus returned after those four long years and found out that his beloved Hippolyta was dead, Theseus took their son, Hippolytus, who was sixteen at the time and almost a man, back with him to Crete. He couldn't stay within the palace that held so many memories of his Amazon Queen. When he reached the island of Crete Phaedra greeted them and when her eyes meet Hippolytus she fell instantly in love with him; you see, this was Artemis' revenge for Theseus' abduction of one of her priestess, for the Amazons were dedicated to the worship of Artemis, and though many years had passed, Artemis never forgive Theseus, even though the Amazon priestess did. Phaedra knew that she should suppress her feelings for her stepson, but no matter how hard she tried, she couldn't deny the burning desire that filled her soul. She would neither eat nor sleep, blaming a headache as the cause of her suffering, and soon Theseus became worried for her health, she lost weight, and would sit in her chamber alone speaking to no one, not even her husband. Days turned into weeks and still there was no change in her condition.

After more than a month of watching his wife pine away Theseus finally called to Asclepius, the same Asclepius who tended Eurydice, to heal his wife. Many years had passed since then, and when he arrived it was not the young man that tried to save Eurydice, but an old man with gray hair and beard who walked hunched over, assisted by a cane. Asclepius used drugs, incantations, and other magic potions to free Phaedra of her headaches but nothing would relieve her suffering, for the cause of them was her burning desire for her stepson. Asclepius tended her for almost a week straight, and when nothing seemed to help he decided to return to Athens to collect a certain herb that only grows there, hoping that this would relieve her suffering. Shortly after the healer left Phaedra sat in her room, her head clouded by the incense that surrounded her; she walked to the window hoping to get some fresh air when she saw her stepson, Hippolytus, sitting alone in the garden below her room. She dressed in her most seductive gown, a gift from her husband Theseus and hurried down to the garden to speak with him.

"Mother, I see that you are out of bed, has the great healer Asclepius cured you of your headache? I've heard that his skills in medicine match those of the Gods themselves". He asked when he saw his step-mother approaching.

"I feel much better now, thank you". She replied shyly.

"I don't think father would want you to be up so soon; you should return to your chamber until he returns".

"I just needed a little fresh air to clear my head, the cloud of incense in my room is only making me feel worst. You don't mind if I sit here with you for a few moments, do you"? She asked. He motioned for her to sit across from him, but she took a seat right next to him.

"Hippolytus, it is such a beautiful day, and yet you sit here alone in the garden, don't you know of any young women with whom you may spend time with"? She asked this as a way of finding out whether or not Hippolytus had given his heart to another.

"I've dedicated my life to the Goddess Artemis, as my mother had done, and her mother before her, and like Artemis I plan on keeping myself eternally pure". He said to her, not liking the tone of voice she was speaking to him with.

"How could you say that," his step-mother replied, "the Gods didn't make humans to be like themselves, we were made to enjoy the gifts that the Gods allow us to have, and love is the greatest of those gifts. You are insulting the Goddess Artemis by trying to be like her".

After saying this Phaedra took her step-son's hand and kissed him on the cheek. He didn't move, at first thinking that his step-mother was only giving him a peck on the cheek, and when he didn't pull away, as she thought he would, she raised her hands to his face and let them caress his smooth skin. He reached up and gently pulled her hands away but as he did this she leaned in and kissed him on the lips. When he realized what she meant he grabbed her by the hair and pulled her away but she began to threaten him,

"Please do not refuse me, I can't stand my longing for you any longer. If you don't give in to me, I think I shall die". She said to him as she moved closer to him.

"I can't! You're my father's wife. It would be an insult to him if I were to make love to you". He said thinking that she would be offended if he told the truth, that he was repulsed by the thought of making love to her or any other woman for that matter.

She screamed at him, "If you don't consent to my wishes, I'll tell your father that it was you who seduced me, and I'll watch with a smile as he destroys you!"

Hippolytus slapped her face and in the struggle that followed Phaedra's gown was torn and her hair pulled loose and fell around her face. She ran to her room in tears. As she waited for her husband to return, her tears were replaced with anger at her step-son's rejection. Theseus came to her room to check up on her that night just after sunset as he usually did since her headaches began and upon seeing his wife with a torn gown and a bruised face he asked,

"Phaedra, what has happened to you"?

"Please, don't blame him, for it wasn't his fault". She said, hoping to sound innocent.

"Has someone done this injustice to you, tell me who it was and I will kill him". Theseus demanded.

She tried to hid her tears, but Theseus thinking that someone had made her cry demanded that she tell him who did this to her.

"Please, I beg you, don't hurt him, it wasn't his fault, the Gods must have sent a madness over him causing him to behave as he did, for it's not like him". She replied through her sobs.

"Woman, tell me who did this to you, and let me handle it!" Theseus shouted at her as he grabbed her and shook her violently.

"It was your son Hippolytus". She said through tears.

Theseus didn't know what to do, Hippolytus was his favorite son, he reminded him so much of his mother, but as king he couldn't allow an injustice to his wife go unpunished. He threw his wife on her bed and stormed out of the palace. He went to the shore where he stood looking out to the sea thinking about what he should do for what seemed like an eternity. As the clouds parted he saw the moon's reflection on the waters and instantly he knew that he had no other choice, but to call to his father, the God Poseidon, to assist him in cursing his very own flesh and blood. It was a night just as this, many, many years ago when Poseidon had promised Theseus that he would fulfill three requests, and Theseus had used only two of these. He had one request left, and he knew that his father would not be able to refuse him, so he called out to the God.

"Poseidon, God of the Seas, your faithful servant and son Theseus has come to you to beg for your assistance one last time".

Pausing here to wait until he saw a sign that Poseidon was listening to him, and continuing only after seeing a great wave form deep in the ocean rise in the form of a majestic horse and slowly come towards him, bowing as the waves broke up at the shore.

"A great injustice has been done to me, and I ask that you punish the person responsible".

Poseidon's voice came from the water horse,

"Theseus, my son, tell me who has dared commit an injustice to you, King of both Athens and of Crete. I assure you that I'll destroy him".

Theseus couldn't bear to see his son killed, but he also couldn't allow him to go unpunished, so finally he spoke his name to Poseidon,

"It is my beloved son, Hippolytus who has caused this injustice on me".

"Hippolytus is dedicated to the Goddess Artemis, and a faithful son to you, I don't know what he could have done to insult you". Poseidon replied.

As Thesues began to tell the God that his son, flesh of his flesh, tried to rape his wife and queen, his compassion for Hippolytus was soon replaced with anger.

"Hippolytus has dishonored me, his very own father, by trying to rape my wife and queen while I was away. He deserves to be punished".

Hippolytus knew what Phaedra had told his father, one of the servants had warned him and as soon as the sun set, he snuck into the stables and took one of the palace horses, and was planning on leaving his father's kingdom to return to the land where his mother had grown up, the land of the Amazons. It didn't matter to him wither the Amazons would accept him or not, he had no place else to go.

Poseidon knew that he couldn't refuse Theseus' request, for once a God makes a promise, he must fulfill it, so Poseidon unleashed a horrible sea monster. Waves crashed into the shore breaking up the form of the horse that appeared to Theseus, as he left the shore for the safety of his palace. The weather began to turn as the winds picked up and waves continued to crash into the shore. Hippolytus, sensing the danger, tried to ride his stallion faster, to get as far away from the shore as possible but it did no good, for the sea monster reached out his claw and struck the shore with such force that the horse the youth was riding reared up in terror. Hippolytus fell and catching his foot in one of the reigns, was dragged all the way back to the palace. The servants found the boy, near death, at the entrance to the garden. They brought his body into the palace and though they did their best to care for the wounded youth, he died before morning. Upon waking Phaedra heard that Hippolytus was dead, at the hands of his own father Theseus no less, she went to her room and fell to the floor crying. Unable to face her guilt, knowing that it was her accusation alone that caused Theseus to call to the God Poseidon, she tied a rope to one of the ceiling beams in her room and stood on a stool as she fitted the rope around her neck. Once she was sure the rope was securely tied she kicked the stool out from under her. As she fell her neck snapped and she died instantly, feeling no pain.

Once Artemis heard of the death of Hippolytus, she called to Asclepius, the healer,

"Asclepius", she said to him, "A faithful servant of mine has been killed unjustly and being a Goddess it's forbidden that I revive him, but I beg of you to use your power of healing and release the shade that was once Hippolytus from the clutches of the Underworld".

"Artemis, Goddess of the Moon, forgive me, but I do not possess the power to raise the dead". Asclepius explained to the Goddess as he slowly lowered his aged body in a slight bow.

"When the Gorgon Medusa was killed, I was given her head, and from it I drained all the remaining blood. The blood from the left side of the head is a deadly poison which causes instant death to any mortal who touches it, but the blood taken from the right side has a miraculous effect, being able to not only heal any disease, but also to revive the dead".

She held up a vial containing a thick brownish liquid and when Asclepius looked at the liquid he realized that with this he would be able to not only revive Hippolytus, but to heal all disease.

"Take this blood and while it is simmering over a low fire, stir in magical herbs…" before finishing her sentence, Asclepius interrupted her,

"Which magical herbs do you wish me to use"?

"Asclepius", she said a little impatiently waving her hand, "I'm no physician, I leave that up to you, for I trust in your abilities as a healer. Now, while the mixture is simmering you must sing an incantation while stirring", and before he was able to interrupted her again, she waved her hand at him ignoring his questions, and continued, "and only then will the potion be able to return Hippolytus to life".

After taking the vial from the Goddess, Asclepius bowed as low as his aged body would allow and thanked her once again. He went straight to the palace kitchen and ordered all the servants out, and once he was assured he was alone he began to prepare the potion as requested. A large cauldron was set on the hearth and into this he poured seawater and once the water began to boil he added the rancid brown liquid that was in the vial. When the liquid touch the water a mist rose and the smell almost made him gag, but he didn't stop stirring the potion. Only after he felt that it was mixed thoroughly did he add any and all herbs that had healing qualities and as the mixture simmered he called to the Universe to give him the power to revive Hippolytus. After the potion simmered for an hour and he was confident that he had done all that he could, he went to the main hall where he saw not only the corpse of Hippolytus, which was lying in the center, but to the right he saw the corpse of the Queen, Phaedra. Theseus was seated on his thrown with his hand over his face, trying to hide his shame and his grief.

"King Theseus", Asclepius said as he bowed to the king, "I have been blessed by the Gods and given a magical potion that will allow me to bring your beloved son back to life".

"I have heard that you are a great healer, Asclepius, and if you are as good as the people say and bring Hippolytus back to life, I would gladly give you my kingdom". Theseus said to him as he hugged the healer.

"I wish not for your kingdom, I'm only doing this because the Goddess Artemis has asked it of me".

After saying this, Asclepius went to the corpse and with the magical potion in a silver chalice that he held tightly, he opened the dead boys mouth and poured a little of this magical potion in while once again calling to the Universe to revive the youth.

Nothing happened.

He took out his sistrum, a rattle that was used in rituals to raise energy and began slowly shaking it over the body. As he did this he could feel all the atoms in his body begin to vibrate at the same speed of the rattle and after a few minutes he felt as if he had absorbed as much energy as he could for he no longer felt like an old man, he felt twenty, no fifty years younger. Filled with this new power, he waved his hands over the body of Hippolytus, directing all the raw energy into it while he began to cry out to the Gods;

> "Artemis, the beautiful Goddess, I call to Thee to breath your power into my body. I call to Thee to once again start this heart beating".

As he said this he held his hands over the youth's heart.

> "I call to Thee to let the pulse of life once again flow through Hippolytus' body. I call to Thee, Artemis...to make my words come true and give this poor lad his life back. You have blessed me with the power of Life and Creation".

Asclepius fell to his knees, exhausted by releasing so much energy, for he now felt as old as he really was. He waited... nothing happened. He put his hands to his face, trying to hide his shame. He had failed, he thought... but then slowly Hippolytus opened his eyes and began to speak,

"Forgive me father", but Theseus, who was standing right next to his son, put a finger upon his mouth and said,

"No, it is I who must ask forgiveness of you, I should've known that you were innocent. You would never have done what your stepmother accused you of".

Before another word was spoken, the sound of distant thunder filled the room and all present looked out at the sky as it instantly turned a dark gray. All stood silent when suddenly there was a bright flash of light that illuminated the heavens as a single lightening bolt came through the open window and struck Asclepius in the center of his chest, causing him to fall to the floor dead. A single scream filled the room, and before anyone could react another crack of thunder filled the room and a second lightening bolt came in, this one striking Hippolytus. Theseus seeing that his son was killed a second time fell to his knees and started to cry. Zeus had let his weapons loose, not because he was angry with Asclepius for bringing Hippolytus back to life, but because he feared that now that a mere mortal knew the secret of reviving the dead, Asclepius would upset the natural order of the Universe and the great God Zeus could never let that happen. That night I greeted not only the shade of Hippolytus, but that of Asclepius as well, and when he neared me he addressed me,

"Persephone, Goddess of the Underworld, I come to spend eternity within your embrace".

I was surprised to great Asclepius, since I remembered a prediction that the Oracle had made to the Thessalian King, Phlegyas, his grandfather many decades ago.

> *You must entrust this child, born from the seed of the God Apollo, to the Centaur Chiron to raise. He must grow strong, for both health and life shall be his. One day he will acquire the secrets to give life back to the departed souls, and for this he will fell the pain of Zeus' bolt. A second chance will come, and now divine he shall fulfill his destiny.*

I knew tha Asclepius was to become the greatest healer the world would know, but his had not yet come to pass. Yes, he was the greatest healer that Athens knew, but the world was much larger than that. I recalled the words of the Oracle and anger filled my soul, father had destroyed this mortal, his only crime was that of saving a life. I wasn't the only one who felt that Zeus was being unjust, for soon mortals began to grieve for the departed healer. The Gods also felt the loss, for you see he tended not only to mortals, but also the Immortals. I took Asclepius' hand and I tried to comfort him as we walked to the River of Forgetfulness, where I made sure that he took only the slightest sips of the cool water, knowing that not all his life would be forgotten and that when the time was right I would be able to restore his memories to him.

It wasn't even a week before mortals began praying to Asclepius' shade. Never before had mortals prayed to a shade, but soon the temples were filled with offerings to not one of the Gods or Goddesses as was usual, but to the mortal man who wouldn't refuse to help another, Asclepius. It was then that Zeus realized that he might possibility have made a mistake, and he summoned both Hades and I to Mount Olympus. We left the Underworld immediately and after the two brothers greeted each other, we were escorted to Zeus' private chambers, where they began talking about how to handle the situation. They talked about what had happened and discussed possible ways to appease the mortals without even noticing that I was in the room. When I finally offered a suggestion, father ignored me as usual, but Hades stopped to listen.

"Father, when Asclepius was an infant his grandfather when to the Oracle and it predicted..." I started to say, but Zeus stopped me,

"I don't care what the Oracle predicted about his man's life!" He said to me, speaking to me as if I were still a child. This was one of the Great God, Zeus' failings, if something didn't relate to his life, or one of the Gods' he didn't pay attention to it. I'm sure that he, knowing all, had heard the same Oracle that I was referring to, but he didn't give it a second thought.

Hades spoke to his brother, "Zeus, be patient and allow Persephone to finish".

I was surprised that Hades spoke so to Zeus, but then I realized that the original Olympians didn't fear Zeus as the rest of the Gods did.

"Continue". Zeus said sharply to me.

"The Oracle said that both men and Gods will owe their health and life to Asclepius, and that because of this gift, he shall one day be destroyed, but he would not enter into the realm of the dead. Now neither Hades nor I possess the ability to revive the dead, but you, as Greatest of the Gods do". I said.

"You are wasting time, you know as well as I do that it is forbidden for the Gods to restore life".

I couldn't believe that father had not realized that he wouldn't be going against Fate, that he wouldn't be raising Ascelpius from the dead, but would be transforming his souls.

"I'm not saying that you restore his life as a mere mortal for that is forbidden. What I'm suggesting is that you can request the Goddesses of Fate to make him immortal". I saw that both Zeus and Hades were contemplating this, so I added,

"If you fear that he'll continue to revive the dead, I promise you that since he has already tasted from the waters of the River of Forgetfulness, he won't be able to remember how to mix the magical potion needed".

"But then he'll also have forgotten his skills in healing". Hades added a little disappointedly.

"Don't worry about that, Chiron could once again teach Asclepius what he has forgotten, and as a God, it'll much easier for him to master the healing arts". Zeus said, and without another word he called to the Moirai and instantly all three of the Goddesses were bowing in front of us.

I was amazed to see how easily he was able to get the Goddesses into releasing Asclepius from the Underworld, but then as I had mentioned Zeus had a smooth tongue, especially with the Goddesses. The Moirai agreed to allow father to revive Asclepius, not as a mortal, for this was forbidden, but only as a God. Before this could happen his shade must be brought to Mount Olympus and be purified by washing in the waters of the River Styx. Zeus himself had to be present, for of all the Gods, only he possessed the power to transform a mere mortal into one of the immortals. Since Zeus would never set foot in the Underworld to perform the ceremony there I was instructed to make the long trip alone and return with Asclepius. I returned to Mount Olympus the following dawn followed by the shade of the healer, and were greeted by all the Gods and Goddesses present.

All stood forming a circle around Zeus and the shade of Asclepius. Silence filled the room. Finally after what seemed like eternity, Zeus lifted the chalice with the water I brought back from the River Styx and poured the cool water over Asclepius. As the water flowed over his shade, the three Goddesses of Destiny softly spoke an incantation. Their chanting began quiet, but as it continued it increased until the Goddesses were shouting,

"From corpse to divine, twice you shall know your destiny".

Within seconds a white mist began to rise from the ground and soon filled the entire hall. Thought I was near, I could hardly see Zeus though the haze. Again silence filled the hall, but soon it was replaced with Zeus' strong voice as he called to the Heavens, drawing all the energy of the Universe within his body,

> *"I am a King, son of a King.*
> *I am a God, son of a God.*
> *I am he who is known by many names*
> *and in many forms.*
> *I am the most powerful of the Deities.*
> *Only I possess the needed power*
> *to give life back to this soul.*
> *Transform this shade into a God!*
> *Asclepius lives as the God of Medicine".*

Suddenly through the mist I could see a glowing aura of the brightest red light surround Zeus, and for a second it looked as if he was consumed within a giant flame as the light flickered in the increasing power. There was so much energy within the palace that I'm sure all present felt it. I could feel the energy surging through the center of my body, swirling within my soul, causing a tingling sensation that filled every cell of my being. I watched transfixed as Zeus held up his hands to the sky and white lightening shot out of his fingers into the heavens. He did this several times until he was satisfied that he possessed the needed energy. Slowly he lowered his hands over the dead body of Asclepius as sparks flew from his outstretched hands into the form that was laying on the alter. The Moirai continued to chant, softly now, as Zeus forced all his power into the shade of Asclepius.

The corpse twitched once, then stopped as all watched the great God Zeus breathlessly. I know that for the next few moments I held my breath as Zeus removed his hands and the shade laid still. The only change was that the shade of the healer was no longer than of an old man. Zeus had restored youth once again to Asclepius. Not satisfied, Zeus held his hands up to the heavens, and this time bright purple lightening came down from the sky and entered into the God. He stood in place convulsing as the energy filled him. Once again, he placed his hands just over the corpse and the purple energy instantly few from the God to the shade. This time Asclepius' shade began twitching almost instantly, continuing to do so even after Zeus removed his hands. It was only a matter of seconds before I saw the life slowly returning to Asclepius. Soon he was able to move and he sat up looking around at those present. He was no longer the mortal Physician Asclepius, but Ascelpius, the God of Medicine, and now divine he could fulfill his destiny.

Of all the Gods, Zeus alone possessed the power to bring the dead back to life, but this gift dose not come without a price, for when Asclepius took his first breath, one of Zeus' mortal sons took his last. None of the Gods know this at the time, in fact it was many years later before any realized the consequences of restoring life. If father had known this earlier he would never have restored any other back to life, but then I'm getting ahead of myself.

XV
Persephone

THE BEAUTIFUL PSYCHE to whom Eros is married to was not born immortal as was the God of Love, but her devotion to the God could not die, and it was this love that transformed her into one of the Immortals. It was her beauty that drew the young God to her, but it was this same beauty that brought the wrath of Aphrodite, the Goddess of Love. I tell her story here, because during her mortal life she willingly traveled to the Underworld to seek my assistance in reuniting her with her true love.

****

Psyche was the youngest of three daughters born to a wealthy family, and even though her two sisters were already wed to kings of powerful lands she, even though nearly twenty, was still unwed. The reason for this was because of her unnatural beauty, you see the men of the nearby villages admired her beauty and even began to worship her, but none had the nerve to approach her as a suitor. Now as you can imagine, Aphrodite, the true Goddess of Love, was not pleased with this situation. There can't be Love without Jealousy, and jealousy is the Goddess Aphrodite's weakness. She couldn't allow mortal men to worship a mere mortal girl, so she called to her son Eros to assist her in destroying Psyche. The handsome young God appeared to her instantly.

"My dear son, I have a small task for you". She said to him as she kissed him tenderly on the cheek.

"Mother, you know that I'd do anything for you, just tell me what you desire and it'll be done instantly". Eros replied.

"There is a mortal girl who on her birth the Fates decided to give her beauty that should belong only to the Gods. She isn't married, for the mortal men only worship her from afar. I wish for you to watch her and when a truly ugly man approaches I want you to shoot both of them with your arrows, making them fall madly in love with each other".

Eros agreed to assist his mother, for he truly enjoys a little mischief, and immediately left for Psyche's village. When he reached her parents small cottage he hid high within a tall tree that grew it the front yard, out of sight from all. From his lofty perch he watched her all day while she did her chores, all the while waiting for a truly ugly man to approach, but no one came. It was a hot summer day and she was dressed in a thin gauze robe; as she worked within the garden, the God of Love was able to glimpse her body as the fabric clung to her every curve. Her long dark hair was pulled up in a tight bun, but several strands had fallen and framed her beautiful oval face. As Eros sat there watching her, her beauty touched his soul. The day was more than half over, and Psyche was just about to go inside to assist with the evening meal when the God of Love noticed the court fool approaching.

"Finally, I can have a little fun". He thought to himself as he reached for one of his arrows and for a second he became distracted by Psyche's beauty and accidentally pricked his finger. A single drop of blood formed from the prick as he held his finger up. Without thinking he lifted it to his mouth and licked the blood that appeared from the small wound. Instantly a burning desire filled his soul, a sensation that he would allow others to feel, but one that he never thought he would experience. When he saw the young man that he was about to shoot his hands trembled; he couldn't do it. His arrow still aimed at the young fool's heart, he tried once again to let his dart fly, but he couldn't go through his mother's plan. In shame, and still feeling the burning desire that filled his soul, he left the tree and flew back to Mount Olympus where he approached his mother.

"Have you finished your task so soon"? She asked with a slight yawn, as if she was already bored with the situation.

"Forgive me mother, but I couldn't allow that beauty to waste her love on a fool". He said as he sat down and lowered his head in guilt.

"What did you do"? She demanded of her son.

"Forgive me, but when I saw her beauty I became distracted…"

"What happened"? Aphrodite demanded.

"… I pricked my finger".

"Don't tell me that you were foolish enough to taste your own blood". She snapped at him.

Eros only nodded, then added, "When I looked up and saw her I instantly became filled with a longing that I've never felt before. I must have this woman, mother".

Aphrodite stormed from the room, and for the next few weeks Eros did nothing but sit and contemplate his love for the mortal girl Psyche. Aphrodite grew more and more angry at her son's clumsiness and decided that it was time for her to take matters into her own hands. Determined to destroy Psyche, she visited her parents while they slept. Whispering into their dreams, she spoke:

> *Your daughter Psyche is destined for no mortal man. It has been decided by the Fates that she is to be the bride of a hideous monster. A monster who lives high upon the mountain just beyond your village. You must dress her in her bridal gown and deliver her to the top of the mountain on the first day of Spring, and there she will wait alone until her husband takes her.*

That morning her parents discussed their dreams with each other, and since both had the identical dream they were assured that it was one of the Gods who had spoke to them. They had no intent on leaving their daughter alone on the mountain to meet this horrible fate, but Psyche had overheard them, and not wishing to cause her family any pain she approached her parents,

"Mother… Father… I'm not afraid to meet my destiny". She said as she looked her parents directly in their eyes.

"Psyche, what did you hear"?

"If the Gods have decided that I'm to wed a monster, then I shall be the bride of a monster". She said without showing any of the fear that she felt.

The first day of spring arrived sooner than she had wanted, and as she was dressed in a beautiful wedding gown she held back her tears, not wanting her beloved mother and father see the sadness that filled her soul. It wasn't until the veil was placed over her face that she would allow her tears to be shed. The procession to the mountain looked more like a funeral than a bridal train, with her parents and sisters weeping at her side. Her sisters each held her hand tightly and cried as they proceeded to the mountain. Myths portray her sisters as evil and jealous, but this isn't so; they loved Psyche dearly and the night before they sat up with her and even though she didn't shed a single tear, they shared her pain.

When they finally reached the top of the mountain her parents kissed her one last time,

"Don't morn for me, mother". She said to her crying mother as she embraced her one last time. Her mother didn't respond; her tears consumed her. Psyche then said her goodbyes to her father and her sisters, and turned as they slowly walked away.

She was alone. Not knowing what to expect, she stood there waiting for her future husband, the horrible monster, to come for her. She waited and waited…but nothing happened. Hours passed and the sun started to fall in the sky, and still nothing happened. Being wore out from a sleepless night she laid down in the soft green grass and instantly fell asleep. Aphrodite intended to let loose the Chimera, a monster with the foreparts of a lion on the body of a goat with three serpents for heads, hoping that it would devour her while she slept. But Eros couldn't let his mother's jealousy destroy the only woman he ever loved. He called to Zephyrus, the God of the West Wind, begging the wind to lift the beautiful maiden up in her sleep and gently bring her to his palace. Zephyrus came to her and let his breath gently caress her sleeping body, slowly lifting her off the ground. Taking care not to wake her, he swiftly carried her to a valley far, far away.

Several hours later, she awoke to the sound of chirping birds and at first didn't know where she was. She remembered falling asleep on the mountaintop, but she was no longer there, she was in a valley with a magnificent palace less than a hundred yards away. She heard a soft voice calling to her,

"Psyche, I'm the one who is destine to be your husband".

The voice didn't sound like that of a monster, she thought. It was soft and when he spoke again, she was almost hypnotized by the sound of it. Looking around, she saw no one near.

"Where are you, I can't see you"? She called out.

"Go into the palace, for this will be your new home. There are servants there to do your bidding". The soft voice spoke again.

"And will I see you there"? She asked, wanting to see the man whose voice alone caused her to fall in love with him.

"No, I have some errands to attend to, but I promise that I'll return tonight just after sunset. Wait for me". The voice said.

"Who are you"? She asked, but there was no answer.

She went into the palace and there a servant bathed her and dressed her in a beautiful silk robe embroidered with gold threads, a robe more beautiful then she had ever seen. Admiring herself in the mirror, she heard footsteps coming and instantly thought it was her new husband. Running to the door, she threw it open only to be disappointed, it was only the servant.

"My lady, it is time to dine".

She was led downstairs and seated in the dinning area where she feasted. She hadn't eaten the day before and was famished and finished everything offered to her. The rest of the day was spent wandered through the many rooms of the palace, looking for some sign to explain who her new husband was, but she couldn't find any. When she reached the third level, she opened the first door and within the huge room she saw a large bed. She was so tired, all she wanted to do was lay there for a few moments, but as soon as her head touched the pillow she fell asleep. It was past midnight when she was awoken by the soft voice that spoke to her that morning.

"My dear, I've returned".

She reached for the lamp, wanting to see who this mysterious man was, for she was sure he wasn't the horrible monster she was warned about, but as she touched the lamp his hand grabbed her wrist and he said in a stern voice,

"I'll give you anything you desire, all you need do is ask it of me. But… you must promise that you will never look upon my face". The mysterious voice said to her.

She agreed. Doubts began filling her. *Is he really the monster to whom she was destined to marry?* Even though she was terrified that her new husband would kill her after he had his way with her, she was determined that she would show no fear. The young God crawled into the bed next to her and held her in his arms and stroked her hair until all her fears slipped away, and before the dawn she gave herself willingly to him. That night they made love and after they finished she didn't care if he was this monster, she had fallen in love with him. For the next couple of months each day was the same, she was alone in the palace during the day with only the servants to attend her every want, but then once night approached she was once again reunited with her love. Each night she would try to wait up, hoping to catch a glimpse of the mysterious figure as he came home, but no matter how hard she tried she would always fall asleep only to be awoken by his soft voice.

Even though several months had past her parents and sister were still mourning for her, thinking she was either dead or being tortured by a horrid demon. Aphrodite, still furious with her son for spoiling her plans, came to her sisters disguised as an old woman.

"Don't grieve for your sister", She said to the two women, "She hasn't married a monster, only a man who is the richest king on the earth".

"She is still alive". They both asked, hoping that they will be able to see her once again.

"Don't trouble yourself by trying to visit her, she's very happy and doesn't want to be reminded of her former life". The old woman said as she waived a hand.

"Tell us where she is". They pleaded, but all the old woman would say was that Psyche was married to the richest king the land ever knew, and as she spoke to them she planted a seed within each, a small seed that grew and grew, filling their souls, and within a few days both sisters were overcome with jealousy. Aphrodite is not only the Goddess of Love, but also of the Goddess of Jealousy, and when she wants she can fill anyone's soul with the green monster. The two decided that they must find their sister and see for themselves if she had indeed married this mighty king. They wandered through all the nearby villages asking everyone they met if they know about this king, and if they could direct them to his palace. No one know of who they were speaking of, and after several weeks Aphrodite once again disguised herself and when they approached her asking if she knew of the richest king in the world, she told them that if they wanted to find this kingdom they must travel to the same mountain that Psyche was left at and wait until night, and then they would be magically transported to the palace that their sister lived in. The next morning they rushed up to the mountain and waited and waited. Soon night arrived and both sisters, tired, fell asleep. Again the West Wind, Zephyrus was called, but this time not by Eros, but by the Goddess Aphrodite, and again he came and lifted the two sleeping women and set them down just in front of her son's palace.

When Psyche awoke, her husband was gone as he was every morning, so she walked to the window hoping to catch a glimpse of him as he was leaving, but instead of seeing her husband, she saw two bodies laying on the grass just under her window. She ran down the stairs and out into the garden and when she saw that it was her sisters she let out a shriek, thinking that they were both dead. Her screams woke them, and when she saw that they were alive, she ran to embrace them. Her sisters, seeing the beautiful palace and the fine robes Psyche wore were instantly filled with envy.

"My dear sisters, how have you come here"? She asked them as they sat on the grass looking at her.

"We have been filled with dread thinking you were married to a hideous monster, so in our grief we went to the mountain and prayed to the Gods. We fell asleep and must have been transported here while we slept". One sister said to her.

"Come in and see my palace". Psyche said as she helped them to their feet.

They embraced their lost sister and it was then that they noticed that she was with child.

"Psyche, you have truly been blessed by the Gods; tell us when your child is due".

"I still have four months left before he'll be born. Come in and I'll tell you everything that happened to me after I was left on the mountain".

When the two sisters saw the beautiful palace they knew that the stories they heard were true and envy consumed them. As they sat talking to their younger sister they asked her question after question about her new husband, hoping to find out something they could use against her. She explained to them that after her family left her on the mountain she fell asleep and when she awoke she was in the garden of this beautiful palace, just as they had found themselves.

"Tell us, dear sister, your husband must be a great king to live in such a beautiful palace. Tell us all about him"? the eldest sister asked with a false smile on her face.

"I wish I could tell you all about him, but I don't know anything about him at all. Only that I love him dearly". She said.

"Is he an old man with gray hair and beard, or a man still in his youth"? asked the other sister, hoping that he would be an old man near death.

"I don't know, I've not seen his face". Psyche had said quietly, her head lowered.

"If you've never seen him, how do you know that he isn't the horrible monster that was predicted you were to marry"? they asked, hoping to fill her soul with doubt.

"He can't be a monster, he is so tender to me. He gives me everything my heart desires. Would a monster do this"?

"My dear sister, you must behold you husband before your child is born to prepare yourself".

"Prepare myself for what"? she asked not knowing what her sister could have meant.

"If your husband is a horrible monster, then your child might also be born a monster. You'll need to know this before the birth".

Psyche was soon consumed with doubt. Was her innocent child, conceived in love, destined to live life as a mortal from the waist up but with the body of a giant snake? It was told to her that the horrible monster that she would marry was a dragon. How could she have slept next to a dragon for the last several months and not notice it, she thought? She had made love with him night after night and even though she never saw his face, she felt his body and it felt normal. But then, she thought she had never been with a man before, how could she be certain.

"We can help you". One sister said and when she heard her sister's voice she was brought back from her thoughts.

"How"? she asked, determined to find the truth out.

"Tonight before you go to bed, hide an oil lamp next to your bed and when your husband comes to you tell him nothing of our visit here. After you make love with him, do not fall asleep, only pretend to allow sleep to overtake you. Wait until you are certain that he is asleep, then take the lamp out from its hiding place and shine it on his face. You'll then know if he is this horrible monster or not".

"I can't do that, I promised him that I would never betray his trust". Psyche said as her eyes filled with tears.

"Do you want your child to be born a monster"? they said together.

With nothing else to do, she followed her sisters' advice. That night before dark she took the small lamp that sat in her bedchamber and quickly slid it under the bed. Her lack of trust filled her with fear, thinking that somehow her husband had seen her do this. She paced around the room, and only after she was certain that she was alone she undressed and laid down in bed stoking her unborn child and talking to him in a soothing voice.

"Everything will be alright, my little one".

Looking out the window, she noticed it was dark,

"Your father will be coming soon". She said as she patted her stomach. About half an hour after this she heard the door to the room slowly open and the footsteps of someone approaching the bed.

"My dear, is that you"? She asked even though she knew it could be no other.

Her husband came to her and kissed her tenderly on the cheek as he did every night, then he undress and laid down next to her. They made love for hours. She wanted to cry, she was filled with disgust at the idea that this man that she thought she loved was nothing but an imposter. Her husband knew that something was bothering her and asked her to tell him about her day, hoping that she would enlighten him to what it was the upset her so. She didn't speak of her sisters coming to visit her, instead she told him that she was sad only because she missed her family and hoped that she could see them.

"I don't think it is a good idea for you to see your family". He said to her as he wiped away the tears that began to fill her eyes.

"Why not"? she asked, thinking all the time that he really must be this monster her sisters were speaking of, why else would he not wish for her to see her family.

"Your sisters, even though they are both married to kings, would become envious of you because of your good fortune".

She told him that he was right and that she wouldn't visit her sisters, but secretly she planned on escaping home to her mother and father after she was assured that she had indeed been deceived. She didn't speak of it anymore and soon pretended that she was very tired, and fell asleep. She didn't move for fear that she would disturb her husband, and after several hours of lying still, not even breathing she was certain that he was asleep. She quietly got out of the bed and was just about to reach for the lamp when he stirred. She stood still, holding her breath until she heard his quiet snores once again. For a few moments she did nothing, thinking of all the good things her husband had done for her and of her promise that she made to him on that first night, but then as the unborn child kicked at her belly, she though of his fate and lifted the oil lamp that she was holding. She lit it and when she turned to her husband she didn't see the terrible sight she was expecting, instead she saw a beautiful God lying in her bed. She, in shock of the sight, let the lamp tilt slightly and a drop of the hot oil fell onto her husband's shoulder and he awoke instantly.

"Psyche! What have you done"? he exclaimed.

"I'm sorry, but I had to see for myself that you weren't the horrible monster that the Gods predicted that I would marry." She said as she sat down on the bed letting the lamp fall to the floor breaking into pieces and spilling the oil over the floor.

"You've caused me such pain". He said and before he could say anything else, she touched the skin on his shoulder, just above his glorious white wing and felt a blister forming where the hot oil dripped on him.

"The pain in my shoulder is nothing compared to the pain that I feel in my heart. You've broken your promise to me and without faith, I can no longer stay here with you". He said as he slowly sat up.

"Can you not find it in your heart to forgive me"? She said through her sobs.

He kisser her one last time and suddenly disappeared.

Psyche searched for her husband for the next two months, taking her across much of the civilized world and when in Greece she came to a temple dedicated to Demeter. She entered and finding herself alone, she walked to the altar and fell to the floor in tears. Mother, remembering how she searched for me for almost an entire year and feeling pity for her, appeared in all her glory.

"Psyche, I can't find Eros for you. You must seek his mother, the Goddess Aphrodite, and beg her for her forgiveness".

"How do I find the Goddess"? She asked through her sobs.

"Go into one of her temples, and once there make an offering to her. I'll speak with her and convince her to have pity on you. If she doesn't appear at first, you must not to become discouraged, stay there within her temple until she finally appears". Then in a bright flash Demeter was gone, but her voice came, "I promise I'll do what I can". Silence.

Psyche left Demeter's temple and even though she was weary already, and welcomed death, she walked, stumbling along the path until she saw a temple in the distance. Hope filled her, and with this hope, she found the strength to reach the sanctuary. Once inside she fell into a stupor, lying unconscious for hours. When she awoke, she approached the altar and with nothing else to offer the Goddess, she cut all her beautiful dark brown hair off, as a sign of mourning and burned it on the alter. As the smoke rose, she called out to the Goddess Aphrodite, letting both fire and air take her plea to the heavens. Aphrodite didn't appear at first, and though Psyche was discouraged, she didn't leave. She waited and waited. Days went by, three days to be precise, and since she was almost seven months pregnant she was weak with hunger. Pulling herself to her feet, she was about to give up and leave the temple when she heard footsteps behind her. At first she didn't turn to see whom it was, thinking it was either her imagination or one of the Priestesses who attended the temple, but then she heard the Goddess speak to her.

"Psyche, you have called to me"?

Psyche stood up and turned to face the Goddess and when she saw her she was overcome with emotion. Tears ran down her cheeks and for a few moments she couldn't speak. She fell to her knees at the Goddess' feet.

"Aphrodite, Goddess of Love, even though I am unworthy, I have called to you. I've called to ask a favor". She said as she lowered her head to the marble floor showing her respect.

"What do you wish of me"? The Goddess replied coldly.

"I beg of you to speak with your son Eros, and tell him that I cannot live without his love""

"I'll do this for you, but first you must earn my blessings". Aphrodite said with a slight smile.

"I'm your servant, what ever you ask of me I'll do". Psyche said as hope began to fill her soul for the first time in months.

"In the storeroom of this temple there is a small pile of a variety of seeds, I wish for you to perform as small task of your loyalty. Sort them for me into separate piles".

Psyche got to her feet and was hurrying to the storeroom where she could get started on this task, but before she reached the door Aphrodite spoke,

"To earn my blessing, this task must be complete by the time the sun rises tomorrow morning. I'll appear then and see if you have completed this small task".

Psyche wanted to thank her, but before she could the Goddess disappeared in a great flash. She ran to the storeroom eager to start, thinking that the pile would take her no more than a couple of hours to sort, but when she saw the seeds, she fell to her knees, overcome with despair. The pile filled the room and she knew that no matter how hard she worked she wouldn't be able to complete this task before dawn.

As she sat there crying a soft voice came to her,

"Sleep now, for you're tired. Don't fear, when you wake up the task will be complete".

She was so tired, not having slept since she entered the temple and as she laid down she let this deep sleep overcome her, hoping that death would come with it. When she awoke, just before sunrise she was surprised to see that there were several separate piles of seeds; to her right a small pile of poppy seeds, next to that there were peas and barley, and in the center of the room a large pile of sesame seeds. She stood there in amazement and just then Aphrodite appeared, hoping to be able to refuse Psyche her request.

"Have you finished your task"? Aphrodite asked, but before Psyche could answer she saw the separate piles of seeds and couldn't believe her eyes.

"I see you've completed your task as I had asked. But, before I give you my full blessings I have another small little favor to ask of you".

Psyche's hope disappeared, she knew that it was the Goddess Demeter that completed her last task and she couldn't expect mother to assist her a second time, so she gave in to despair.

"Have you given up before even hearing what I ask of you"? Aphrodite asked as her smile grew.

"Don't despair, I'll assist you once again". A voice seemed to fill the room and she was sure that the Goddess Aphrodite heard it also, but when she looked up she saw the Goddess standing before her waiting for an answer; she knew that she alone heard the voice.

"Aphrodite, Goddess of Love, I'm your loyal servant, ask what you wish of me and it will be done".

Aphrodite didn't expect this and it took her a couple of moments to gather her thoughts before finally speaking.

"Near the river there live some golden rams, I'd like to use their wool to weave my dear son, Eros, a cloak. I wish for you to go there and collect some of their beautiful wool for me".

Psyche rushed off, thinking that this would be an easy task and when she neared the river she saw the beautiful golden rams calmly grazing. Again a voice came to her,

"These rams are vicious and will tear you apart, don't go near them, nor let them catch your scent".

"But how will I be able to collect their wool then"? Psyche looked up to the heavens as she spoke.

"During the hottest part of the day these ram will scratch on the bushes near the bank, watch from a distance and when they leave to drink from the cool waters of the river you'll be able to collect the wool that has gathered there". The voice said to her.

She watched from on top of the hill, making sure that she was against the wind, and just as Demeter had told her when the sun was high above the rams approached the bushes and began scratching themselves, depositing some of their gilded wool in the process. A few hours later the rams, hot from the sun beating down on their thick coat, went to the river to drink. When Psyche saw them leaving she ran down the hill and as fast as she could she grabbed as much of the wool as she could hold. With her hands full she ran back to the temple to give Aphrodite the golden wool and when she entered she saw Aphrodite's smile leave her face. The Goddess didn't even allow her to speak,

"You've given me this beautiful wool and I'm thankful, but I'm very thirsty now and wish for you to fetch me a drink of water".

Psyche ran to the pitcher of water that was near the altar and before she could pour some Aphrodite spoke,

"The Gods never drink ordinary water, you must go to that mountain," she said as she pointed to a steep mountain that was in the distance. "I'll only drink water from the stream that is at the top of that sacred mountain".

Psyche took the pitcher and started the long walk to the mountain. She didn't know how long it would take her to climb that mountain, but she would either succeed or die trying. When she reached the foot of the mountain she thought that that task Aphrodite gave her was not so hard, the mountain was not nearly as high as it appeared from the distance, but when she looked up she prepared herself to face Death. On top of the mountain there sat a huge dragon whose bright green scales glistened in the evening sunlight. He was sleeping at the time, but Psyche knew that she'd never be able to pass this guardian without waking it. Just then Demeter sent a golden eagle that landed near Psyche and slowly approached her. She didn't know what the eagle wanted, but she was sure it was there for a purpose. It came right up to her and as she reached out to touch it she again heard the voice of the Goddess Demeter,

"*Give the pitcher to this eagle, he's a servant of mine. He'll easily be able to pass the dragon and fill the pitcher with the sacred water*".

Psyche held the pitcher out and the eagle took the handle in its claws and flew off. She watched as the eagle came near the dragon, which woke as soon as he heard the eagle's wings beating the air. With a loud roar fire filled the darkening sky and Psyche thought that the eagle had perished, but suddenly she saw a flash of white flying high above the dragon, and she was sure it was the eagle. She watched it as it flew higher and higher until she couldn't see it any longer, all the while the dragon continued to roar and shoot fire from its nostrils in anger. A couple of moments later she was once again able to see the golden eagle again as it soared back to earth. When it landed it let the pitcher down on the ground at her feet before disappearing into the sky. Psyche picked up the sacred water and hurried back to Aphrodite.

"Why are you back so soon"? Aphrodite demanded of her when she saw her.

"I've returned with the water you requested". Psyche said as she bowed to the Goddess then offered her the pitcher.

"I don't believe that this water is from the spring I spoke of". Aphrodite said a little impatiently.

Psyche told her of her route to the mountain and that there was a glistening green and yellow dragon with red eyes that guarded the top of the mountain.

"When I taste this water I'll know if you are lying to me. If you are, I'll destroy you". Aphrodite said as she lifted the pitcher to her mouth. As the water touched her lips she knew that it was indeed water from the stream she spoke of.

"My dear", Aphrodite said sweetly, "I've only one more task for you. It is only a simple task". She said when she saw the look on Psyche's face she added, "There's no need for you to look so alarmed".

"I've run out of my beauty cream and wish for you to fetch some more for me". Aphrodite continued.

"Where is this cream"? Psyche asked, not really wanting to hear the answer.

"This cream I speak of is being held by the Goddess Persephone in the Underworld". Psyche fell to her knees and started to cry, but before Aphrodite could say anything, she wiped her eyes and said,

"If I'm destine to die, I'll face my fate without fear. My love for your son will take me to the Underworld, though I fear I'll never return".

Aphrodite gave her a small wooden box and a note that she was to present to me, explaining what the Goddess requested. She then disappeared.

Psyche started on her trip to the Underworld. She climbed the stairs of the temple and when she reached the top she looked at the ground. It was high enough where a fall would surly kill her and her unborn child. As she was about to jump, Demeter once again came to her.

"Stop! I'm the Goddess Persephone's mother and I'll guide you to her kingdom".

"You may be able to guide me there, but once there I'll be trapped with the souls of the dead for all eternity".

"Trust in me and I'll ensure that you return safely".

Mother directed her to travel south through Greece, to the River Styx, taking with her two pieces of barley bead soaked in a sweet honey mixture and two obolus, one for the trip to the Underworld and the other for the return.

After several days of traveling Psyche came to an area that was marshy and even though it was early in the day, it appeared dark here. The cries of the dead that were destined to wander the banks waiting until they could obtain the fare to cross surrounded her and she knew that she was near the Underworld. Though she couldn't see any of these phantoms, she felt them trying to grab at the coins that she held tightly within her closed hand. She ran from their grabbing hands and didn't stop until her feet slipped on the muddy bank of the river and she almost fell in. She stopped and looked at the water, and could only see a few feet in front of her; the fog was so thick. Charon appeared suddenly from the fog only inches from her and she let out a scream. He didn't stop the boat sensing that she was no shade, and as his boat passed her by, she jumped in. Charon looked at her with his blazing eyes, then held out his bony hand and in it she placed one of the coins. He slowly closed his fingers over the coin, then handed her the oars. Demeter had warned her that she would be required to row herself across the river, but she failed to tell her that Charon would whip her while she did so. She endured this torture as she rolled across the river to the land of the dead.

Once she reached the other side, she jumped off the boat and fell to her face crying in pain. Broken hearted as she was, she didn't feel anything as those who waited on the other side of the river Styx tried to suck the remaining life from her, there was none left. She picked her self up and even when she saw the Tree of False Dreams, she didn't allow its promise of hope lure her deeper into the world of the dead. She was dead already, not physically, but emotionally. After a long walk she was standing before the gates of the Underworld and Cerberus had caught the scent of a living mortal and was approaching fast. Psyche knew she only had one chance if she was to survive. She quickly reached into her purse that was hidden in her girdle and pulled out one piece of the sweet barley bread and held it out to the monstrous hound. Cerberus approached sniffing the air and when she caught the scent of the barley she gobbled the bread up and instantly fell asleep. Psyche had no problem passing the guard dog by, but unlike the others who found their way into the world of the dead she had no intentions of leaving. She was determined that if she couldn't be reunited with her beloved, than she would willingly stay in the Underworld forever.

When she reached the Cocytus river she saw a small boat and in this she paddled her way through the swampy waters to our palace, ignoring the wails of the lost souls who begged and pleaded for her to take them with her. No matter how hard she looked she couldn't see these shades, she was only able to hear their voices and feel their pain. Finally after several hours of enduring their cries and feeling as if all happiness was drained from her body, she reached the end of the river and saw our palace in the distance. The rest of the way she walked, and when she was within the palace grounds, just feet from the entrance she finally passed out from the ordeal. It was almost night when one of our servants approached Hades and myself saying,

"I beg your pardon my Lord and Lady, but a mortal woman is approaching the palace".

"I don't have time to deal with the living". Hades said as he started to walk away.

"But how has she come here"? I asked.

"If you wish my dear, you may go find out what she wants, otherwise send her away". Hades said to me as he let go of my hand and turned to walk away.

"Don't be too long, my dear, I'll be waiting for you". He added.

I went alone to greet this mortal and find out what had brought her here, for no one came to the Underworld without a reason. The servants had carried the unconscious girl into the palace and once within she awoke and begged to speak to me. Leaving her at the door, the servant came to get either Hades or myself.

When I reached her, Psyche fell to her knees.

"Persephone, Goddess of the Underworld, your mother Demeter, Goddess of Fertility has sent me to you".

"Mother"? I said to her surprised, "What does mother want of me now."

"Forgive me, but your mother didn't send me, she only guided me here to your palace, it is the Goddess of Love that has sent me". She explained.

"Aphrodite", I said, "And what dose she wish of me"?

She tried to tell me why she had come, but once she started to speak the tears she was holding inside would no longer wait, and she put her head in her hands and started to cry.

I saw that she was expecting, and it would be only a couple of weeks before the child would come. "Come inside". I said to her as I put my arm around her and guided her into the palace and near the warmth of the hearth. She entered the palace, but would neither sit nor take any food or drink that was offered. I wasn't surprised since mortals believed that if you ate or drank anything while in the Underworld you would never be allowed to leave, and since the release of the hero Theseus I'm sure that she feared that if she sat she would forget her former life and stay here oblivious to everything as a statue.

"My dear, tell me why Aphrodite has sent you here to the Underworld"? I said to her.

"She is punishing me for hurting her son".

She could tell that I didn't understand, so she began to explain what had happened to her over the last eight months; how she thought she was married to a monster; how he made her promise that she would never look at his face; how she fell in love with him anyway; and how once her sisters planted the seed of doubt in her she betrayed his request causing him to leave.

"In my wanderings I went into a temple to the Goddess Demeter, and she appeared to me and told me that the only way I could reach Eros was to beg Aphrodite, the Goddess of Love, for her forgiveness. She has already given me many tasks, and without your mother's help I wouldn't have been able to complete them, but now she has sent me here to you". She then handed me the note that Aphrodite wanted me to have.

I opened the parchment:

> *Persephone, Queen of the Dead, I've been up for many weeks now tending my wounded son Eros. I've not been able to sleep and wish for you to give this mortal girl a small bottle of Stygian sleep to bring back to me. I'd ask myself, but you know that it's impossible for me to travel to the Underworld. Please put it in this box so its power won't affect her.*
>
> *Love Aphrodite,*

I left Psyche there as I went to Hades to show him the letter.

"Do you think this is some kind of trick"? I asked my husband.

"I think that Aphrodite wants this poor mortal dead, and instead of killing her herself she sent her here to spend eternity".

"Why would Aphrodite want her dead"?

"My dear, you know how jealous the Goddess of Love can be. That girl is very beautiful, and you told me that she said that she was Eros' lover. Aphrodite doesn't want to share her son with a mere mortal". As he said this it all began to make sense.

"What should we do then"? I didn't want her to spend eternity here, and I knew that she wouldn't be able to return without our help.

"Let me scan her thoughts, see if she knows more than she's saying". Hades closed his eyes and I knew that he was reaching down into her soul. Since Psyche had no idea of Aphrodite's plan and so Hades saw no trickery.

"She has no idea what Aphrodite wants, so let's give her what she wants, and you can guide her back to the world of the living. Maybe Aphrodite will have no choice but to reunite her with Eros once she gives her what she requests".

"Do you think we should give her something else instead, I don't know how Stygian sleep will affect her". I asked.

"No, Aphrodite will know instantly if its something else. This box will protect her". He said as he took the wooden box I held in my hand and we both went to Hypnos, the God of Sleep and twin brother Thanatos to fill it with Stygian sleep. Stygian sleep is a very powerful sleeping aid, and if given to mere mortals it would cause them to fall into a deep coma. I waited for almost an hour before the God of Death came back, handing me the small box, which was much heavier than before.

Hades didn't go with me to deliver the small box to Psyche, but before I left he whispered in my ear, "I'll be waiting for you, don't be long." Then he kissed me softly on the cheek.

Psyche was waiting where I left her and when she saw me return she lite up. Before handling her the small box I said,

"Don't open this box, for the beauty cream of the Gods cannot be touched by mortal hands".

Taking the box in her hand she thanked me, and then wishing to return to the living she started toward the door. Charon would allow mortals to enter the Underworld with the needed fare, but he would never allow any soul to leave. I took her by the hand and explained to her that she wouldn't be allowed to leave the way she came.

"But your mother, the Goddess Demeter, said that I would be able to leave the way I came".

"Come with me. I'll take you back another way, a way that's faster".

****

Once she was back into the world of light I left her and as she started her travels back to the temple where Aphrodite was she thought about the beauty ointment in the box that she carried.

"Surly, the Goddess Aphrodite wouldn't miss a smidgen of this ointment. If I were to use this, I would become as beautiful as her and then Eros wouldn't be able to refuse me'. She thought to herself, but then remembered my warning 'The beauty cream of the Gods cannot be touched by mortal hands'.

Curiosity finally overcame her and she opened the box and instantly the Stygian sleep slipped out and she was soon overcome by its power. She laid down letting sleep take over, and instantly she fell into a deep coma.

It wasn't long before Eros found out what his mother had done to his beloved, and he went out searching for her. After several days he found her body laying in a meadow in Southern Greece, and when he saw her at first he thought she was dead. His heart ached as he thought that he had not only lost his love, but his unborn child. In tears, he lowered his head to kiss her one last time, and as he did he felt a slight breath coming from her parted lips. He instantly lifted her limp body and flew back to Mount Olympus and to my father. Zeus at first felt no sympathy for the God since Eros was fond of shooting his divine heart causing him to explain his actions to his wife, Hera, and face her wrath, but then a thought occurred to him. 'Maybe', he thought, 'if the God of Love was happily married he would be too busy to visit the other Gods and Goddess stirring up trouble', and so he agreed to bring Psyche back to life.

As Psyche lay on the floor at Zeus' feet he used all his powers to lift the sleep that had overtook her and instantly she opened her eyes. At the sight of her beloved she started to cry. Eros embraced her but before he could kiss her his mother entered the room,

"I won't have my son marry a mortal woman".

"Don't worry", Zeus said to Aphrodite, "when I revived her I also made her immortal. She will be a faithful wife to Eros".

Aphrodite started to protest, but Zeus waved a hand for her to be quiet.

"Aphrodite, I don't want you to hurt this girl any more. I have given her in marriage to Eros".

Psyche isn't one of the Gods, but because of her undying love, she was made immortal. To this day, she still sits faithfully at her husband's side along with their daughter, Pleasure.

XVI
Persephone

I HAD SPENT many decades living within the Underworld and even though I never regretted my decision to marry Hades and loved him dearly I felt as if there was something missing from my life. I felt as if I was grasping for something just beyond my reach and no matter how hard I tried my fingers just couldn't find what they were looking for. My first thought was that the longing in my heart was because I missed living in father's palace on Mount Olympus with the other Gods and Goddesses, but soon I realized that couldn't be the reason for the longing I continued to feel within my heart; for if you remember I split half the year between staying there and accompanying mother during her duties on earth, and even when I was in the company of the other Gods and Goddesses I felt this ache in my heart. It wasn't until the Goddess of Love, Aphrodite sent Hermes to deliver a message to me that I realized what I truly longed for.

Hermes kissed my hand as he handed me the scroll.

"What's this"? I asked.

"It's from Aphrodite". Was all that he would say.

I unrolled the scroll, not knowing what Aphrodite could possible have wanted from me. The message was simple.

"Meet me in Syria. I'll be waiting, please hurry".

"Hermes, what could Aphrodite possibly want from me"? I asked, and he assured me that he had no idea; he was just delivering the message. I went to tell Hades that I would be leaving the Underworld for a short time,

"My dear, the Goddess Aphrodite has requested that I meet her in Syria". I started to say, wanting to ask if he had any idea what she wanted.

"What does she want of you"? He asked, not liking the thought of me leaving the Underworld.

"I don't know, I was hoping that you might have some idea". I said, and when he assured me that he didn't either, I added, "I promise I won't be long".

I hope that I'm not confusing the reader here when I tell you that Hades had no idea what Aphrodite had wanted after telling you that he has the ability to read other's thoughts when he wanted to. You see, there is a limit to all the Gods and Goddesses powers and for Hades, or any of the Gods who possess this ability, they have to be within a certain distance of those whose mind they want to delve into. Aphrodite was on Earth, and Hades ability was confined to those who were within the Underworld alone.

"Do you want me to accompany you"? He asked me as I prepared the stallion.

"No, I'll be back in a little while". I said, knowing that he hated leaving the Underworld unless he absolutely had to. I mounted the swiftest of his horses and before I left, he took my hand and pulled me close to him for one kiss before saying,

"Be careful, I don't trust Aphrodite".

"I promise, I'll be back before night". I said before kissing him back. The stallion started at a gallop as it began flapping its giant wings and within seconds we were off to the world of the living.

I had no idea why Aphrodite wished to speak with me, we weren't the closest of friends, in fact I hardly ever saw her. Like so many of the Gods she never venture into the realm of the dead, and when I was on Mount Olympus she was either with her lover Ares, or with one of her numerous mortal boys on earth. You can imagine my surprise when I finally reached Syria and saw Aphrodite holding a newborn infant in her arms. I dismounted the horse and bowed slightly to her, showing my respect to an elder Goddess, then I spoke,

"Aphrodite, Goddess of Love, I've been summoned here to meet you".

"Persephone, Goddess of the Underworld, my dear". She said returning my greeting with the slightest of bows. She took my hand before continuing.

"Thank you for coming on such short notice. You might be wondering why I called you here".

Before I could answer, she continued, "I called you here because I desperately need your assistance".

When she paused, I interrupted, "Whose child is this"?

"This child belongs to no one. He was given to me to raise, but alas, I just don't have the time to care for him". She said trying to sound as if she really cared for the Fate of this child.

"Why are you even involved with this child if he has no parents"? I asked, knowing all to well that she must be somehow responsible for the child being alone.

"Your dear father, Zeus thought that since this child was alone, I'd be willing to either raise it myself or find one of the other Goddesses to look after it". She said, than added, "and all the Goddesses that I've asked are either much too busy or refuse to raise a mortal child. It was your dear mother, Demeter, who suggested that I try you next".

"Why would she think that I'd be willing to take this child"? I asked, wondering what mother was up to now.

"I don't know, maybe she knows the longing you feel, wanting to have a child of your own, and since Hades can't father any she thought you might be willing to assist me". I hated the fact that mother found it necessary to discuss my and Hades personal life with the other Gods on Mount Olympus. It wasn't any of Aphrodite's business to know why Hades and I didn't have any children, but I'm sure that after my marriage to Lord of the Underworld, it became common knowledge that mother stripped Hades of his fertility many, many centuries ago.

"Why has this child come to you, doesn't he have any mortal relatives to care for him"? I could tell by looking at the infant that he was completely mortal, he wasn't even fathered by one of the minor deities. If I was to agree to take this child, I needed to know all the circumstances of his birth.

"It's a silly misunderstanding. You don't need to know the trivial details". She said a little impatiently.

"If I'm to take this child, I must know everything". I said very firmly.

"Oh, alright". She said a little impatiently as she handed me the tiny infant. "It's all my fault that this child is alone in this world and your father felt that since I'm responsible for him being alone, I should raise him, but I just can't take him. You know how jealous Ares is, he'd never understand, and I'm sure that he would only destroy this poor helpless child".

Aphrodite then explained to me the events the surrounded the birth of this child, which I'll briefly relate to you now.

Theias, King of Syria had only one child, a daughter, who was a beautiful girl named Myrrha. Any mortal man would have wished for her to be his bride, but her father was greedy and wouldn't give her to any man, but only to one who was willing to pay the high bride price he demanded for her hand. She was already almost eighteen years old and most of her childhood friends were already married, some even with children, and she longed to start her own family. Now Myrrha prayed to Aphrodite each night before she went to bed, begging the Goddess of Love to have pity on her and allow her father to agree to one of her suitors' offers. Aphrodite heard her prayer and sent many young men, men who were more than worthy of Myrrha to her father's palace, but alas he was too stubborn to reduce his bride price, and soon they became discouraged and left the palace. After many months of seeing her father refusing all these suitors, she decided that she'd no longer pray to a Goddess who was deaf to her pleas. During the daily rituals performed at the palace Myrrha honored all the Gods and Goddesses, all that is except for Aphrodite.

Now on Mount Olympus, Aphrodite started fuming. She was doing all she could, sending men who were worthy of Myrrha, she even appeared to her father, Theias, in a dream insisting that he accept the offer of the next suitor and when he woke he thought about what the Goddess had said to him and for a few moments he was ready to consent to her wishes, but then he thought of the amount of money he'd get when the right man finally appeared and ignored his dream. It's a mistake to ignore the Gods. Aphrodite was furious at the disrespect that Theias was showing not only her, but all the Gods, so she decided that she'd find a way to punish him. After a little while she came up with a plan where she could get revenge on not only the king, but also his daughter, Myrrha as well. Even though the girl was innocent, it was her father who went against the Goddess' wish; Aphrodite couldn't accept the fact that Myrrha had stopped her devotion.

That night while Myrrha was asleep the Goddess came to her room and stood at the foot of the bed watching the young beauty sleep. Aphrodite walked to Myrrha, and slowly lowed herself to just inches above the sleeping beauty and placed one hand on her forehead. Myrrha stirred slightly, but didn't wake. The Goddess lifted her other hand to her pursed lips and blow Myrrha a kiss and a purple mist flew from Aphrodite into Myrrha's heart and instantly the young girl's heart was filled with a burning desire for none other than her own father. Smiling, Aphrodite kissed her forehead once before vanishing. As soon as the Goddess was gone, Myrrha opened her eyes and knew something was terribly wrong. She tried to sleep, but she couldn't stop thinking of her father, and the heat she felt when she thought of him caused her to flush. Days passed, but this unnatural longing for her father continued, so she hid in her room and spoke of this to no one. After a few days her father became concerned that she must be ill.

"My dear daughter, what is bothering you"? his concern clearly showing, as he said down on the side of her bed.

"Nothing father". Myrrha replied as she turned her head, not wanting to look into her father's eyes.

"Are you ill"? he asked, but she would not speak to him, nor even look at him.

This went on for a few more days before Aphrodite grew impatient, her plan wasn't working as she wished, so to speed things up a little, she compelled Myrrha's servant, Hippolyta, to approach her.

"Myrrha, please tell me what is bothering you, I couldn't help but noticed that each time your father enters into your presence you become agitated and suddenly leave. Has your father done anything to hurt you"?

On hearing her servant's words the tears she was holding in for so long could no longer be contained. She buried her face in her servant's chest and began to cry and cry. Hippolyta held her, and finally when there were no more tears left in her, she wiped her swollen eyes and spoke,

"Oh, Hippolyta, I've tried so hard to hide my shame, but I've failed".

"Myrrha, you've done nothing to be ashamed of, why should you leave the presence of your beloved father"?

"It's true that I haven't committed a sin, at least not with my body, but in my heart I have committed the most heinous of crimes". She paused here to wipe her eyes once more, as Hippolyta waited to hear her confession,

"I've committed the most horrible of all sins". She repeated, before continuing. "I've lusted after my father, and every time I see him a tingling sensation fills my body, and I have to leave his presence for fear that I'll offend him with my lust".

Hippolyta could have done nothing to assist Myrrha, but Aphrodite made sure that she would be a major actor in her scheme.

"Myrrha, you need not be ashamed of your feelings, it isn't a sin to committee incest, do not the Gods themselves love their brothers and sisters".

"Yes, it's true that the Gods have incestuously relationships, but they have forbidden this practice for mortals". Myrrha replied sadly.

"They've only forbid this so mortals may not be like the Gods. If you were to consummate your love for your father, any child born of that union would be more than a mere mortal, he would be like the Gods themselves, and it's for that reason alone that the Gods forbid humans to committee incest". Hippolyta explained, continuing, "I have an idea, I know a way that we could deceive your father".

"How"? Myrrha asked, and for the first time in weeks hope filled her heart.

"I'll tell your father that there is a young woman I know who happens to be infatuated with him, and that if he pleases, I'll arrange to have her meet him in his private chamber after dark tomorrow night. Since your mother died, your father hasn't been with a women and I'm sure that he'll be more than willing to meet with you".

"That'll get me into his room, but once he sees me he'll recognize me and instantly turn me away in disgust". Myrrha sobbed as she buried her face in her pillow.

"Don't worry, I'll make sure that he has plenty of wine to cloud his vision, and to ensure that you're not recognized, I'll remove all the oil lamps from his room, and since there'll be no moon in the sky there won't be any light in the room and he won't be able to recognize you".

The following day Hippolyta entered Myrrha's room and saw her sitting alone by the window looking out thinking about her father's love.

"Myrrha, while your father is dining, I'll make sure his wine glass is kept full. You are to prepare yourself then wait for him in his chamber. You'll have the entire night with him, but remember you must leave his presence before the sun rises and he recognizes you". Myrrha nodded that she understood.

During dinner Myrrha was absent once again, but this night her father didn't even notice, she had missed dining with him for more than a week already, and in his excitement about the thought of a young maiden waiting for him in his chamber he didn't even notice her absence. It had been many years since he lost his wife and he missed the touch of a woman's hand upon his body so much. Hippolyta made sure that Theias had more than enough wine, each time his glass was half filled, she would immediately refill it, and when the time came for him to retire for the night, she had to help him upstairs.

"I'm alright!" he shouted at the servant as she guided him to his chamber. Hippolyta bowed before leaving and Theias staggered into his room When he saw the young woman dressed in a beautiful red robe laying in his bed desired filled his soul. Slowly, he walked closer to her and spoke softly to her, "Please, remove your veil, I wish to behold your beauty".

"I mustn't, it's not proper for a maiden to show her face to a man".

Theias went to light one of the lamps but to his surprise he couldn't find it. He started to slowly walk to the other side of the room, to another lamp, but he became a little dizzy from all he had drunk. He paused and at that moment Myrrha stood up and started to undress, and he could do nothing but look at her beauty. After several moments of just watching her as she consciously removed layer after layer of her red silk garments, slowly exposing her body, he walked up to her and tried to remove her veil himself so that he could kiss her. Myrrha lifted the veil just enough for his lips to touch hers, but she refused to remove it once during the night, fearing that if it slipped he would surly recognize her. As her father's hands explored her body, she whispered in his ear,

"I have dreamt of your touch for so long now, I feared that it would only be that, a dream to me".

His hands followed the curve of her body up to her breasts, and when he held them she let out a soft gasp. Her hands were on his waist, and she slowly raised them over his robe up to his shoulder where she unfastened his robe, which fell instantly. When she saw him naked, she fell to her knees and started to cry, still ashamed of her feelings for her father. He took her hand and lifted her up, thinking that she was afraid of him, this being her first time with a man, so he spoke softy to her,

"Don't be afraid". He whispered in her ear. She buried her face in his chest and only cried more. "I promise that I'll be gentle with you, and would never do anything that would hurt you".

As he said this her tears increased, she wanted to tell him that she wasn't crying because she was afraid of him hurting her, but that she was crying because she was his only daughter, flesh of his flesh, and she knew that he would be repulsed by her if he knew the truth. That first night they didn't make love, she laid in his arms as he comforted her, and as he held her she became so relaxed that she almost fell asleep. It was almost morning when the sound of a dove cooing started her; she jumped up from the bed and told her father that she must leave at once. He tried to stop her, but she grabbed her clothes and ran out of the room and into her own chamber before he was even out of bed.

"Oh Hippolyts, I'm more miserable now, than I was before". Myrrha cried to her servant, "My father was so kind to me, not knowing that my tears were for my embarrassment, but thinking that I was afraid, being my first time with a man, he did nothing but hold me in his arms, comforting me the entire night".

"I'll arrange for another night, tonight. Get some sleep now, I'll be back in a couple of hours and wake you". Hippolyts told Myrrha as she left the chamber.

That night was the same as the first, and it wasn't until the third night that they spent together that Theias finally made love to his daughter. The following morning she told her servant Hippolyts and asked if she could arrange another night. Hippolyts arranged for nine more nights instead and on the twelfth night Aphrodite appeared in Theias' chamber, in spirit that is, making sure that neither Myrrha nor Theias saw her and watched as they made love for hours. Just before dawn, when the sun was just starting to peak over the horizon, the Goddess slowly lifted the veil from Myrrha's face and when Theias saw that he had made love for the last twelve nights to his beloved daughter, a rage he had never known before filled him. He grabbed at his sword, which lay on the floor next to the bed and started screaming,

"You wrenched girl, I'm going to kill you!"

Myrrha ran from her father's chamber without dressing and he, also naked chased after her with his sword held high screaming,

"I swear, I'll kill you!"

Myrrha ran behind Hippolyta, hoping her servant would protect her, but Theias grabbed the servant by the hair and threw her to the ground. Myrrha ran out of the palace and her father didn't follow her, at least not right away. He screamed at the servant who laid on the floor trying to scurry away from his grip.

"You witch, I can't believe what you've done to me".

"Please", Hipployta tried to speak, but the king let his sword fly, slashing at her while she tried to protect her face and neck from his blows. Blood spattering the walls. She tried to grab at him, to stop him, but she was too weak from blood lose and soon fell unconscious. Theias kicked her unconscious body to the side so that he could find and destroy his daughter. He felt no pity for poor Hippolyta, blaming her for the predicament he was in; he left her to there to slowly bleed to death. His encounter with Hippolyta had given Myrrha a head start and she had made it out of the palace and into the garden, but she knew that her father would soon catch up to her, so instead of running, she fell to her knees and began to pray to both Zeus and Hera, pleading for their protection. Her prayers were not only heard, but answered and as she saw her father approached her she knew that she was under the protection of the Gods. Theias stood in front of his daughter and held his sword ready to strike, but he couldn't move; the sight he saw was too horrible, and he could do nothing but watch as his beloved daughter's once beautiful body started to twist and contort while her white skin slowly became dark and wrinkled and her once long slender arms stretched out as if they were trying to touch the heavens, slowly transforming into the branches of a tree, a myrrh tree. Her tears, as they fell were transformed into the resin that to this day is named after her, Myrrh.

Hera then let her grace fill Theias causing him to realize all that had happened. He fell to his knees at the base of this tree that was only moments ago his daughter, and lowered his face into his hands and started to cry. After a couple of hours kneeing under the tree crying, crying for the lose of his only daughter, crying for his own foolishness, and also crying for the death of the servant Hippolyta, Theias picked up his sword and held it to the heavens as he spoke to the Gods, "Forgive me!" was all he said before he took the blade and with once swift movement he cut his throat, letting his blood spill onto the tree to mingle with what was left of his beloved daughter.

Aphrodite was finally satisfied, but this was not the end of Myrrha. Nine months later as a wild boar was wandering through that same garden, overgrown with weeds, it approached the tree and with its tusks it bore a small hole in the bark. This small hole soon started to increase in size until the entire side of the tree burst open and an infant fell to the ground crying. Zeus, knowing all that occurs in both the heavens and on earth, had seen this and since he knew that Theias killed his daughter's servant before committing suicide he knew that there was no one on Earth left to look after this child. Both Zeus and Hera took pity on the infant, remembering Myrrha's prayers the day they transformed her. They appeared in the garden and Hera picked up the newly born infant while Zeus summoned Aphrodite. Instantly she arrived.

"Aphrodite, Goddess of Love, you have succeeded in destroying the lives of not only one innocent mortal, but three".

Aphrodite started to interrupt, to protest her innocence, but Zeus wouldn't allow her to speak.

"Silence!" He shouted at her, and when she bowed her head in respect, he continued.

"I won't allow you to destroy this infant's life as well. Since it was your actions that caused his birth, and since it was your actions that resulted in his not having any family to look after him, it will be your action that'll ensure that he is raised properly".

"But Zeus, you can't expect me to raise this mortal child, I am far too busy".

"Too busy destroying innocent lives". Hera said.

"And how many innocent lives have you destroyed"? Aphrodite said to Hera as her eyes narrowed.

"I'll not tolerate this bickering, I've made my decision!" Zeus barked at Aphrodite.

"But…" Aphrodite started to say but Zeus stopped her,

"I'll release you only if you can find a suitable substitute to raise this child". After saying this Zeus and Hera were gone in a flash of bright light, leaving Aphrodite alone with the infant. Aphrodite called out to various Goddesses but none would agree to raise the child, then she called to Demeter, who also refused, but before leaving she suggested that I might be willing to raise this abandoned child, since Hades was unable to produce children and she knew that I was longing for my own child. Aphrodite's calls couldn't reach me in the Underworld, and she wasn't about to enter into the realm of the dead herself she begged Hermes to deliver a message to me to meet her in this garden.

Now after hearing the story of why this child was without any family, I felt pity on him and agreed to take him back with me to the Underworld where Hades and I would raise him as our own, without even thinking about what my husband would say. Once I returned to the Underworld and explained to Hades the circumstances involving this child's birth and that I wished to raise him, I could tell that he didn't agree with my decesion.

"My dear, what would you have me do, leave this innocent child to the wild animals, haven't I greeted enough innocent lives here in the Underworld". I said to him as I tried to suppress my tears, you see in my heart I longed for a child and in my arms I held an infant who I was sure would die if I didn't give him my love.

"Persephone, it's not that I don't want you to have this child, I've known for a long time that you've desired a child, and you may think I'm being selfish, but you must realize that I'm only looking out for your own good".

I couldn't believe what I was hearing and was about to interrupt Hades, but he put his finger to my mouth, then continued,

"This is a mortal child, and while it is young and under your care all will be fine, but what are you going to do when he becomes an adult and decides to leave the Underworld, for you of all people should know, this is no home to the living. I can't bear for your heart to be broken".

"Don't all parents have to face this one day when their child, whether mortal or immortal decides to leave". I answered, continuing. "Didn't I break my mother's heart when I left her and decided to live here in the Underworld with you"?

He paused for a few moments thinking about what I had said before continuing,

"I've watched as a mortal that I once loved grew old and slowly withered away, and I only wish to save you from that pain. I know that you have been longing for a child and I now realize that I have been selfish. I can't father a child, but your mother's curse hasn't touched you. I'll not stop you from having your own child, a child that'll be immortal".

I wanted to tell him that I didn't understand what he was saying to me, but like so many times before he read my thoughts and answered before I could even open my mouth.

"I know how you feel about Herme",

I tried to stop him, to tell him that while I did have deep feelings for Hermes, I didn't love him, but he wouldn't hear me,

"Don't worry, I know that your love for Hermes is different from your love for me. I have to admit that when we were first married I was more than just a little jealous of him, but throughout the long years we've been together I've learned to accept your feelings for him. But, I also know that Hermes has wanted you since you were a child, and I don't blame him, for you are so beautiful". As he said this he put his hand up to my face. "He thinks that he's fooled me by blocking his thoughts when near me, but I'm a powerful God and one who's not so easily fooled. If you wish to have a child, I won't blame you if you ask Hermes to make love to you".

I didn't know what to say and just stood there for a moment while a single tear ran down my cheek, finally I answered,

"If I the Goddesses of Destiny will not allow me to have a child with my husband, than I'll have no child".

I turned to walk away but Hades grabbed my arm and pulled me into his arms and held me while I cried, and after I calmed down he spoke,

"If you don't wish to take my advice, I won't force you. Since you have your heart set on raising this child, I'll not stop you".

You can't imagine my surprise when I heard this, I kissed Hades over and over and told him that we would name the child Adonis, and I would be the best mother. I nursed the child from my breast and feed him ambrosia when he was old enough to eat solid food, and he grew at an astonishing rate. While he was young, I told him about his mother and father, and how he came to live with us in the Underworld and sometimes when he was depressed by all the death that surrounded him, he would go to Syria and sit under the tree that was his once his mother, and I couldn't help but feel sad. Hades was right, Adonis was only fifteen years old, and was a beautiful child, but I knew that he wasn't happy living in the Underworld, and every time he would leave me I knew that some day soon he wouldn't be returning. That day came sooner than I had hoped for.

Adonis was sitting in the garden where he was born, thinking of his mother when Aphrodite happened to be passing by and saw a beautiful young man sitting alone in this unkempt garden.

"Why are you here alone"? The Goddess asked, causing Adonis to waken from his thoughts.

"My mother died on this spot". The youth said as he bowed to the most beautiful Goddess he had seen.

Instantly she realized that this must be the child that Myrrha had given birth to sixteen years ago. When she looked at his face, she was immediately smitten and it wasn't hard for her to convince Adonis to leave with her.

Several days passed and still I heard nothing of my son's whereabouts and I became worried and set out to look for him. He was nowhere to be found. I sent for Hermes to assist with the search, and after a week, Hermes returned with news that my dear Adonis was with Aphrodite. I was furious and left immediately for Mount Olympus to speak with father. After he heard me out he summoned Aphrodite, who didn't come right away, but made us wait for a couple of hours before strolling into the palace with Adonis at her side. When Zeus demanded her to explain why she had left with Adonis, she pleaded with Zeus,

"Zeus, you know that the Underworld is no place to raise a child. I realize now that I should've never given Adonis to Persephone in the first place". She said to all, continuing by stating that since she had seen her error, she was willing to make up for it by taking over care of the child now.

"You're correct, Aphrodite, the Underworld is no home for the living." Zeus said, "But I'll leave the decision of Adonis' fate to him". He then turned and addressed the young boy for the first time,

"Adonis, the choice is yours, will you return with the Goddess Persephone to the Underworld, or will you spend the rest of your life with the Goddess Aphrodite"?

"I know the judgment of the great God Zeus is just, but please don't make me decide. The Goddess Persephone has been the only mother I've known and I love her dearly and wish to cause her no pain, but I must admit the Underworld is no place for a young man to live his life, I long for the fresh air and to be with other mortals who I can speak with".

"I'll spare you the pain of making this decision, and I'll decide for you, but before I do I must ask both Goddesses to swear to abide my decision". Zeus said.

Both Aphrodite and I agreed.

"Adonis, you'll spend the summer with the Goddesses Persephone, and her mother, Demeter, traveling between the earth while they attend to their duties as Goddesses of Agriculture and Rebirth, and Mount Olympus; and during the winter months when the Goddess Persephone returns to my brother Hades in the Underworld, you'll be free to live with the Goddess Aphrodite".

I think Aphrodite was more upset by the decision than I was, since I was used to splitting the time I have with those I loved, but since it was winter and Adonis was to leave immediately with her, she wasn't too upset.

"I beg you to allow me to say goodbye to the God Hades, he's been very kind to me and it's not my intent to offend him". Adonis asked Zeus as he bowed to the God.

Aphrodite sighed, as if we were wasting what little time she had left with her new lover, but Zeus agreed, and Adonis accompanied me back to the Underworld one final time to say his goodbyes to Hades.

"Father, I don't wish to leave you, and I hope that you can find it in your heart to forgive me, but I can no longer live here surrounded by only the shades of the dead". He said to the only father he had known. Hades took his in arms and father and son embraced.

"I've nothing to forgive, I understand what it is like to be young and stuck in the Underworld, and I don't blame you". He kissed Adonis on the forehead and watched as he left the palace, and I am sure I saw Hades' eyes watery, as if he was holding back tears. It was then I realized that Hades was right so many years ago when he tried to convince me to find a mortal home for Adonis, my heart was breaking. When Adonis was gone, Hades took me in his arms and held me tight as I cried.

When the Spring Equinox finally arrived and I greeted mother on Mount Olympus, I was surprised that Adonis wasn't there yet, and it wasn't until a couple of days later that Aphrodite finally allowed him to meet us there. That spring and summer Adonis accompanied mother and I while we attended our duties on earth, and it was the first time since my marriage that I was actually happy to be with her. Now don't misunderstand me, I love mother dearly, but during that period of my life I still resentment her. Fall arrived sooner than I would've liked and when I said goodbye to mother and Adonis I sobbed, holding back the tears.

"My dear daughter Kore, this is the first time that I've seen you cry when we part, does this mean that you've finally forgiven me". She asked, and I didn't want to hurt her feelings by telling her that the tears that fell were because I was to be parted from my beloved son, Adonis.

"Mother, you know that I've forgiven you". In reality I had forgiven her many years earlier, I just didn't want her to know that. I thought that the sadness I felt deep within my heart was caused by the fact that I was parted from my son, for I regarded Adonis as a son, but through the fall and early winter I couldn't stop the growing anxiety that I would never see my only child again.

****

Let me explain to you now what occurred during that winter. Aphrodite was married to Hephaestus, the God of Fire and Blacksmiths but she never loved him, she was force to marry him by Zeus. You see when Hera gave birth to Hephaestus he was deformed and when she saw this hideous infant she discarded him to the island of Lemnos where he was raised by the Nereids. It was on this island that the Kabeiroi, the dwarflike blacksmiths who worked in a subterranean forge deep within the earth taught him the art of blacksmithing. Years later when Hera saw some of her son's beautiful creations she asked that he return to Mount Olympus, recognizing the beauty that he did not possess physically but could easily create with his bare hands. Hephaetus, who never forget his mother's lack of love, agreed to return to Mount Olympus. When he entered the palace he presented Hera with a beautiful golden thrown as a gift.

"Mother, this thrown is for you alone". He said as all present admired the craftsmanship.

"My dear son, not even Zeus has a thrown as fine as this". She said as she slowly sat down in it. Instantly magical chains bound her arms and legs. Not even Zeus could break these chains. Zeus begged the God to release his wife and Hephaestus agreed only on the condition that he would be given the Goddess Aphrodite as a bride. Zeus agreed without even asking the Goddess of Love and when she saw the hideous form of her husband to be she pleaded with Zeus to reconsider. It was too late thought, Zeus had given his word and was bound by it.

The Goddess of Love wasn't faithful to her husband and never once considered his feelings when she took lovers. Her heart belonged to the War God, Ares, who she would spend most of the year with. No matter how many lovers she took, she always discarded them when the novelty wore off and returned to her true love, Ares. The time that Adonis was with her, she neglected Ares, who soon became envious of the relationship between Aphrodite and her mortal lover, and with a little bit of encouragement from Hephaestus, Ares decide to take matters into his own hands. Adonis was to go hunting in Lebanon with some of the Nymphs, and like me, Aphrodite had a strong feeling that he shouldn't go. She begged him not to go, but he was young and foolish I suppose, and didn't listen to her pleas. While in the woods, Ares lead Adonis away from the others and in the guise of a wild boar, he attacked Adonis and gored his thigh, and within a few minutes my beloved son had bled to death, alone in the woods.

I didn't know what had happened at the time and it wasn't until many years later did any of the Gods speak of this tragedy to me. The only thing I remember that day was that I'd received word that there would be a new arrival to the Underworld and I prepared, as I had so many times before. I dressed in the ritual robes I'd normally wear when greeting those shades who were new to the Underworld and went to the river Styx where I saw Hermes approach followed by a shade. When the shade entered the boat I saw Charon hand the oars to the poor soul, I felt pity for him knowing how intimidating Charon could be, but then I noticed something that seemed odd to me, instead of leaving as Hermes usually does after leading the departed soul to the gates of the Underworld, he flew across the river on his golden sandals to greet me.

"My dear Persephone," he said as he took my hand, "I can't express how hard it is for me to tell you what I must".

At first I thought that something must have happened on Mount Olympus, but just then the small boat that Charon guided reached the shore and I saw the shade of Adonis step foot on the bank.

"Dear mother, I have come to spend eternity with you". He said, and continued speaking, but I don't know what he said. I lost consciousness.

I awoke in Hermes arms back in my palace.

"Where did you take my dear son, Adonis"? I asked through my sobs.

"Hades came and led his soul to the Elysian Fields".

"Please tell me that he didn't force my beloved son to drink from the River of Forgetfulness, I can't bear to see his shade wandering here in the Underworld not knowing who I am".

He didn't answer me, and from his silence I knew that Hades had indeed taken him to the River. I can't tell you how hard it was, and still is to see my dear Adonis wandering with the other shades unknowing to who I am and our relationship, and when I do see him I remember the words that Hades spoke to me so long ago, when I first brought the helpless infant home and realized that he was right, he was only trying to spare me the pain that I felt in my heart. I was thankful that my husband had the strength to perform the rituals needed to bring Adonis into the Elysian Fields, for I could never have accomplished them myself.

XVII
Persephone

APHRODITE WOULDN'T BELIEVE that it was her lover, Ares, who was responsible for Adonis' death; that he took on the shape of a wild beast and in a jealous rage killed her young lover. Since there were no witnesses to the event she blamed me, stating that I wished to keep Adonis for myself for the entire year, and no matter how hard I tried to explain to her that I couldn't bear seeing the shade of someone I had loved so deeply wandering through the Underworld, she wouldn't believe that I was innocent. By the time I had left Hades for my annual return to Mount Olympus I had thought that Aphrodite had forgotten her anger with me, since it was already several months since Adonis was killed and I'd not heard anything from her but I was mistaken. She had spent the entire winter planning her revenge on me.

Her plan was simple; she would do whatever was in her power to destroy my marriage. I wasn't even away from the Underworld for a week when she put her plan into motion. Being the Goddess of Love, Aphrodite used her power to enchant a mortal named Minthe, causing her to fall madly in love with Hades. Now this mortal girl, Minthe, was not chosen randomly, but was carefully selected by Aphrodite because she resembled me, with long dark wavy hair, pale skin and bright green eyes. Aphrodite might be the most beautiful of the Goddesses, but she's not among the brightest, this plan she devised was almost exactly the same as the one she used on Adonis' mother Myrrha, and I'm surprised that Hades didn't become suspicious. In a way I don't blame him, he'd spent so many centuries alone in the Underworld knowing that the other Gods feared him, he never thought that any of them would be bold enough for such treachery.

Once Minthe was enchanted she left her family and traveled far away from her home. Each day as the sun rose she would go to the same field that I had first spied Hades in so many years ago as he left the Underworld to meet my father. She had no idea of what compelled her, only that food or drink wouldn't satisfy the burning desire she felt within her soul. Under the same tree that I sat by she would pass the day and night waiting for Hades to appear. She would've waited until the fall and I returned and still not have seen the Lord of the Underworld, for Hades seldom leaves the world below, but Aphrodite had other ideas. Hermes was sent to deliver a message to Hades informing him that his brother Zeus wished for his presence on Mount Olympus.

Hades mounted his chariot and departed for Mount Olympus as soon as he read the message, for Zeus wouldn't request him unless it was for a reason, and when Hades' chariot emerged near Attica he nearly trampled the poor girl as she sat there half asleep. Hades stopped, and for a second it was as if he had stepped back into time, the sight of Minthe sitting there surrounded by the wildflowers so reminded him of our first meeting that he dismounted and approached her. This was just what Aphrodite was hoping for, and as he held out a hand to help her up, just as he had offered to me he asked,

"Are you alright"?

"Yes, I'm fine". She replied and Hades started to walk back to his chariot but she called out to him,

"I beg your forgiveness, but I have been waiting here for so many weeks hoping that you'd appear to me".

Her words were chosen very carefully, being almost the exact words that I had used when I first met Hades, but he wasn't fooled, he knew that she was there for a reason, although he had no idea of who had sent her or more importantly, why.

"Do you know who I am"? He asked her.

"Yes, you are the God Pluton, Ruler of the Underworld." She used this ritual title instead of Hades, mortals feared speaking his proper name, and instead they called him Pluton or Pluto, which means "the Rich God".

"I'm not used to meeting mortals, especially those who have no fear of me, but I'm on my way to meet the great God Zeus and I can't keep him waiting." This was a polite way of saying that he wouldn't waste any more time with this mere mortal, so he mounted his chariot and left as Minthe stood there watching him depart.

"I'll be waiting until you return". She called out to him as he rode away, and he knew that she was speaking the truth, reading only longing for him in her thoughts.

Hades was not surprised at all when Zeus greeted him, asking,

"What brings you to Mount Olympus, my dear brother"?

"You have summoned me". Hades replied, becoming more suspicious.

"I don't know what you are talking about, I haven't requested your presence here". Zeus said.

"I'm sorry for disturbing you, but I think I should be leaving now to return to the Underworld".

"Don't leave so soon. We seldom speak to each other. You need not worry, Demeter is on earth with Persephone and she won't even know that you were here".

Even though I had been married to Hades for over a hundred years, my mother still hadn't changed her feelings for him and would be furious if she knew that he had set one foot on Mount Olympus.

"I dare not stay, for I sense trouble". Hades responded.

He rushed back to the Underworld and was expecting to find the young women waiting for him where he left her, knowing that it was her intention to wait until he returned, but he was surprised to find the field empty. He paused only a second before the earth began to rumble, opening up to the dark world that was his home, and within seconds he was once again in the world below. Once back to the safety of his palace, which seemed to be exactly the same as he had left it, he felt relieved, thinking for a moment that maybe he had imagined everything. Sitting down on his thrown he picked up the scroll that Hermes gave him and read the message again, trying to deduce which one of the Gods was responsible, but was soon interrupted by Hermes,

"Hades, I found a young maiden waiting for you at one of the entrances to the Underworld as I was departing for Mount Olympus and thought that she would make a good servant for you and your dear wife Persephone".

"You didn't bring her down here did you"? Hades asked, not waiting for an answer knowing all too well that Hermes indeed did and that she was already in the servant's quarters.

"She didn't seem to fear the Underworld and since it is hard to find servants willing to live here, I brought her back with me. I hope you don't mind". He said, trying to sound innocent.

Hades scanned Hermes thoughts and didn't see the treachery there, Hermes had learned so many centuries ago to block his thoughts when around those who had the ability to read the minds of others. He didn't want such a powerful God to know his feelings for his wife, so when he was near Hades he'd do his best to conceal his thoughts. Hades knew that the young God possessed this ability, but still he didn't become suspicious, Hermes had always been a loyal friend to both of us and Hades couldn't imagine why he'd wish to deceive him.

"Hermes, why don't you stay here with me for a few days, it's so lonely when my dear wife is away".

Hades asked, hoping that Hermes might slip up and reveal what he was up to, for he was sure that Hermes was up to something, but he was too smart for that. Hermes, as I had already mentioned was a Trickster God and he had plenty of tricks up his sleeve.

For the next few days Minthe stayed with the other servants who started to show her around the Underworld, while Hermes talked Hades into allowing her stay as a servant. Hermes is not only a Trickster God, but also the God of Communication and when he wishes he could convince even Zeus to listen to him, so I wasn't surprised when I found out that Hades agreed to allow Minthe to stay. Minthe took on the role as Hades personal servant, and even though she would see my husband daily, she didn't revel any of Aphrodite's plan to him, and since she was oblivious of the Goddess' enchantment, Hades was unable to pick up anything from her thoughts. She was nothing more than a puppet whose strings were pulled by either Aphrodite or Hermes.

After a few days Hermes left the Underworld, but he returned frequently to make sure that Aphrodite's plan was working. A couple of months had passed and Minthe became more and more depressed fearing that she would spend the rest of her life as nothing more then a servant in the Underworld, so one night as she was getting ready to serve Hades his evening meal, Hermes approached her,

"Minthe, don't serve Hades tonight, let one of the other servants do this".

"Please allow me to serve him, the only happiness I have is when I see the God Pluton, don't take this one pleasure away from me. I fear that I'll pine away here in the Underworld if I'm denied this". She begged Hermes.

"Go to your chamber where one of the other servants is waiting to dress you in one of the Goddess Persephone's robes, and wait there silently until I call for you".

Minthe did as Hermes requested, and during the meal Hades was surprised to see another of his servants bringing the evening meal for he had become accustomed to Minthe. When he saw her he would feel the same love that he felt for his dear wife and some of his loneliness would disappear, at least for a little while.

"Where is Minthe, is she well"? Hades asked the nymph as she poured him a glass of wine.

"No, my Lord, she isn't feeling well tonight, and is in her room resting".

She then turned and filled Hermes' glass. As she started to leave with the bottle in her hand, Hermes grabbed it and placed it on the table. Now normal wine has no affect on the Gods, but Hermes had added some herbs that he knew would make even a God as powerful as Hades soon drunk, and was careful not to drink too much of this wine himself, he needed to have a clear mind if he was to succeed with his plan. While the two Gods sat and talked, Hermes made sure to keep Hades cup filled to the top, and reminded Hades of his love for his dear wife, Persephone.

As Hades became more and more drunk he started to feel the loneliness that for the last few months he had tried to suppress, and soon he decided to retire for the night. When he went to stand up, he almost lost his balance and fell against the wall. Hermes jumped up and held out a hand to steady him.

"I don't know why, but I feel like I'm drunk". Hades said as Hermes assisted him to his chamber.

Hermes guided my husband to our chamber and assisted him as he laid down, his head swimming from the wine.

"Are you alright"? Hermes asked.

"I'll be alright, I just need to clear my mind".

Hermes left Hades alone and as he lay on the bed, the room continued to spin, so Hades closed his eyes and soon fell asleep.

In the mean time Hermes went to the servant's quarters and called out to Minthe,

"Minthe, the time has come for you to express your love for Hades, the God of the Underworld. You're to go to Hades in his private chamber and pretend to be his wife, the Goddess Persephone."

"I can't do that, it's blasphemy to disguise myself as a Goddess". She replied in horror.

"It's the only way that you'll get Hades to love you". Hermes replied and the young woman started to cry.

"If it's the only way, I'll do what you wish. But I fear that the Gods will strike me dead for my actions". She said wiping her tears.

"When you enter the chamber, tell Hades that you have missed him dearly and was able to sneak away from your mother, making sure to tell him that you only have a short time to spend with him. He is so drunk that he'll think that you are his wife and will willingly make love to you". Hermes assured her.

"But won't he know that I'm deceiving him by my thoughts". She asked, knowing that Hades had the ability to read the thoughts of others.

"He's much too drunk to be able to read your mind, but still you must be careful of what you say to him".

Minthe entered the chamber and her fear overwhelmed her; she was about to leave when she saw Hades lying naked on the bed.

"My dear husband", she said in a whisper, "I've returned from my mother to be with you".

Once Hermes heard these words, he left the Underworld and with his winged sandals he flew to where mother and I were staying, confident that the plan was working.

When Hades saw Minthe standing in the shadows dressed in the same robe that I wore on our wedding day, he thought that I had indeed returned. Since the first year of me having to split my time between mother and my husband, I've always greeted Hades in that robe when I returned home.

"Persephone my dear, is that really you". He said.

"It is I, your dear wife. I've missed you so much that I had to return". As she said this Hades got up and tried to greet his wife, but he stumbled back into the bed.

"Come here to me, I'm too drunk to come to you". And Minthe came to Hades' open arms. She took his hand and he pulled her onto the bed, next to him.

"I've missed you so much". He said as he kissed her passionately. "I'm so glad that you've returned to me tonight".

"I don't have much time, the Goddess Demeter will soon notice that I'm missing". She replied, as Hades' hand slid up her robe to the broach that secured it in place, and slowly removed it. Her robe fell exposing her breasts and as he kissed her, his hands moved to her breast causing her to let out a slight groan.

"I want you so much". Was all that Minthe could say to him.

Hades ripped the robe off her and let his mouth follow the curve of her body, kissing first her neck, her breast, then her stomach, and with each kiss she would sigh slightly. Slowly he followed the kisses back up to her mouth and lowered himself on her and when he finally entered her, she moaned with pleasure. They made love for hours and when finished Hades rolled over and instantly fell asleep. If Minthe knew of Aphrodite's plan she would've left Hades' chamber immediately, but she didn't, so she stayed there in Hades' arms afraid that this would be the only time she would be with the God, and soon she too fell asleep.

****

It didn't take long for Hermes to find mother and I, he already knew our location, and after briefly greeting us he said to me,

"Persephone, you must return with me to the Underworld at once. I don't think Hades is well".

"You still have a few more weeks with me, you can't return to the Underworld yet". Mother said to me.

I wondered if she had known of Aphrodite's plan if she would've wanted me to return and catch my husband in bed with another.

"What's wrong with Hades"? I asked Hermes, but he didn't answer. I wasn't too concerned at first, so I kissed mother than said to her,

"I won't be gone long", I promised, adding, "I'll make the time up if you wish".

While we were traveling back to the Underworld, I asked Hermes again,

"Is Hades alright"?

"Hades didn't actually send me, but I don't think he's well". I was confused by his words, because you see the Gods and Goddesses don't get suffer from illnesses like mortals do, so I couldn't think of any reason why my husband wouldn't be well.

"What do you mean that he's not well"?

"I don't know what's the matter. I was having dinner with him tonight and he had only a few glasses of wine, and he seemed to become quite drunk. I've seen Hades drink far more then he did tonight and not appear intoxicated at all". He began and when he saw the concern on my face, he continued, "When he got up, he could barely stand straight, I had to help him to his chamber."

I began to become concerned, this didn't sound like Hades. I rushed back, worried about my husband and when I finally reached our palace, Hermes told me that he left Hades in his chamber. I opened the door slowly and to my surprise instead of seeing my husband alone in bed as I expected, I saw him naked, laying next to a young mortal woman. I don't remember saying anything, or screaming, but I must have because both jumped up startled and for a moment Hades looked confused. He called out to me, but I didn't answer, I ripped the golden pendant that I've worn since we married and throw it into the hearth and in my anger I held my hands up to the heavens and allowed all the hurt and anger I was feeling concentrate in my body. I could feel the energy swirl throughout my entire body before it surged within my hands and within seconds I held a whirling ball of bright red energy. I held the whirling mass in my left hand knowing that if it were to hit the poor mortal, she would die instantly. I didn't care. I threw it at her. She screamed for a split second as the flaming ball came towards her. Her screams stopped the second the energy hit her. She was instantly turned into a pile of dust. Hades tried to get up, calling out to me,

"Persephone"?

But he was still drunk and as he struggled to get out of bed, I ran out of the room. Hermes was waiting for me outside in the garden, and when I approached he spoke,

"What's the matter"?

I didn't answer him. He grabbed my arm, turning me to face him.

"Are you alright? What was all that commotion in there"?

Again I didn't answer him.

Instead of rushing to him with my grief as he thought I would, I went this time to mother. I thought for sure that she had some part to play in this, and I was determined to confront her and make sure that this time she wouldn't get her way. As I was leaving the Underworld, Hermes followed,

"Persephone, where are you going? What's wrong"?

Finally, I answered him, "I'm going to back to mother".

I didn't travel the way that I usually traveled, that is by chariot, instead I traveled the way that only the most powerful Gods do. Gods as strong as Zeus can call on the powers of the Universe to dissolve their physical form and instantly carry the particles that make up their bodies to their destination, and once there they just call to their bodies to once again form. Only the most powerful of the Gods travel this way, and even they don't always, you see this takes tremendous energy, so it is used only rarely. But that day I was so filled with rage, that I had this power within and I didn't hesitate to use it. Within seconds I was standing next to mother.

XVIII
Demeter

I MUST INTERRUPT my daughter one more time to expand on her story before she can continue. I promise that I'll be as brief as possible, allowing her to continue. Kore returned to me only a few hours after leaving with Hermes and I was surprised to see her so soon. The instant I saw her, I knew that something had to be dreadfully wrong. I had no idea what the cause of the trouble was and since the Gods never suffer any illnesses, I wasn't at all concerned with Hades' health. I was just about to ask my dear daughter what had happened in the Underworld, what made Hermes summons her back, but before I could say anything, she walked up to me and slapped me hard across the face. I was in shock. I couldn't understand her behavior, since I had done nothing to cause her pain.

"My dear daughter, what have I done to deserve this"? I said as I held my hand up to my face.

"Mother, can you not accept that I love Hades. Do you still wish to destroy the only happiness I have left? I hate you for what you have done to me". She shouted at me.

"My dear, I don't know what you're speaking of". I said to her before she slapped my face a second time, this time much harder than the first. She then started screaming at me,

"I've forgiven you for trying to destroy the only happiness I ever had by taking me away from my husband for half the year, I've forgiven you for not welcoming my husband in your home, I've even forgiven you for stripping Hades of the ability of having children, but I can never forgive you for what you've done to me today".

"I don't understand what you are talking about, I would never do anything to destroy your happiness". I said to her, but she was deaf to my words, she continued to scream at me.

"You've sent a mortal woman to seduce my husband while I was away, and then when Hermes told me I must return to the Underworld right away, you even pretended that you were angry for me returning early, hoping that I would think that you're innocent". She paused here only a second to catch her breath before adding,

"How many years have you been tempting Hades while I was away? Was this your plan all along, to keep me away from the Underworld while you send young mortal women, who were enchanted by your magic, to tempt him"?

I stood there in disbelief. I couldn't believe what my daughter was suggesting, I had never thought about destroying her marriage. I knew that she was upset, but I couldn't understand why she was so angry with me, you see the Gods unlike mortals are not usually faithful to their spouses, with marriages like hers unusual. You might think that we are cruel, but mortals cannot even begin to understand how hard it is to be faithful to only one partner for all eternity. I don't mean to say that we no longer love those who've been dear to us, and once we tire of them we discard them as one would an old toy, it is just that over the many centuries our feelings, like mortals' do change, and sometimes it is better to walk away from one you love than to start to resent them. But then, my daughter was still young, and I can understand how she felt; the first God I loved was Zeus, and I remember how I thought my heart would break in two when he announced to the Gods and Goddesses that he would marry our sister, Hera instead of me. Anger filled my heart, my entire body, only to soon be replaced with the pain of lose. I don't know how many centuries I resented Hera, but even my hatred of her slowly disappeared. Time truly cures all broken hearts.

After a few moments of silence, while I was reflecting on the past, I finally said,

"I don't understand what you are talking about, I've been with you all summer, when did I have the time find a young woman, let alone enchant her, that isn't the type of magic I'm used to using? I'm a Fertility Goddess not a Love Goddess".

She couldn't answer me, and I realized that she didn't really blame me, she was only letting her frustrations out, and

I happened to be there. The anger she was feeling soon change into feelings of loss and rejection just as it did with me so many centuries ago when my dear brother broke my heart for the first time. I took her in my arms and held her close as she cried and cried. I tried my best to comfort her, but nothing I could say or do would make her forget the sight of her husband in bed with another. As I held her I thought about what she had said, about that mortal woman being enchanted, and knew that one of the Gods had to have been responsible; no mortal woman could fall in love with the Lord of the Underworld without magic, and since all mortals feared the Underworld, I knew that none would dare enter the World of the Dead of their own free will.

"Kore, over the years, I've come to regret my actions when I found out that you married Hades, but believe me I never intended to destroy your happiness". She tried to stop me, but I put my finger to her lips, then continued,

"Everything that I did, I did only to protect you, and during these long years that you've been married, I've seen you grow into a Goddess as powerful as I am. I'm proud that the mortals worship not only me, but also you during the Eleusian Mysteries, and I'd never do anything to destroy the relationship that we've only began to rebuild".

"Mother, I'm sorry for blaming you". She said to me through her tears, "It's only that I can't imagine how a mortal could fall in love with Hades, most mortals fear him, so of course I thought that you were responsible, that you must've enchanted her".

"You're right to believe that the poor girl was enchanted, I'm sure that she was. I'll do what ever I can to help you find out which of the Gods had done this to you, but first you must return to the Underworld and speak with your husband".

She looked at me with astonishment. I continued,

"Don't look so surprised, I'm only looking out for your best interests. I've known Hades much longer than you have, and I don't believe that he'd ever do anything to hurt you. You must find out what occurred while you were gone".

"Mother, I don't know if I could go back just yet, I fear that I'll say or do something that I'll regret later".

"You must go back now, the longer you wait the harder it'll be", I paused here, before adding, "Trust me".

I would have accompanied her back to her husband, but I've never entered the Underworld and even though Kore had explained to me how different it is from the stories I've heard, I still feared entering into that world.

When she returned she went straight to their chamber and to her surprise Hades wasn't there, instead Hermes was waiting for her, sitting in their bed.

"Where's Hades"? she asked him.

"Back at Mount Olympus. He thought that you'd return there, so he went to meet you. He'll be back shortly". He said, continuing with, "He asked me to wait here in case you returned".

"Hermes, I must know why you brought me back to the Underworld, did you know that Hades would be in bed with a mortal woman"? She asked, not truly wanting to hear his answer.

"Persephone, I swear to you that I didn't know. I had found that girl waiting by one of the entrances to the Underworld shortly after you had returned to your mother, and brought her down here to be only a servant. I had no idea of what was going on down here during the summer. I was away most of the time". He paused here for a second, noticing a single tear run down Kore's eyes. He reached out to wipe it, but she turned her face away.

He continued, trying to sound innocent. "Tonight Hades became very drunk on only a few glasses of wine, and I was concerned about him. He must have, in a drunken stupor thought that that young mortal was you, you see she resembled you very much, and I could see that each time he looked at her, he longed for you".

"Hermes, I've always loved you, but if I find out that you had anything to do with what had happened here tonight, I swear to the Gods that I'll never forgive you".

Kore left the Underworld and once again came to me. She told me what Hermes had said to her and I agreed that he must have played a part in this deception, for he is a Trickster God. I accompanied her back to Mount Olympus, and when we arrived there we found Hera sitting outside her private chamber.

"Hera, is Hades in there with Zeus"? I asked.

"Yes, he's very angry though, I wouldn't go in there if I were you. He's blaming you for what happened." She said with a slight smile. Even though my resentment of Hera waned throughout the centuries, she could never allow her feelings of jealous die, and her hatred for me continued to consume her for many more centuries. Kore pushed her aunt out of the way and flung the massive door open, and when we stepped in we could hear Hades voice. He was shouting at his brother.

"Zeus, I swear that I won't return to the Underworld without my wife". Hades spoke to his brother in a tone of voice that I'd never heard him use before; it held the same type of power that Zeus possessed when he was angry.

Zeus interrupted, trying to calm his brother,

"Hades, you must return, I assure you that I'll find out who is responsible for enchanting that poor girl and I promise that I'll punish them. But in the mean time you must return to your kingdom".

At first they were so engrossed with their conservation that they didn't realize that we had entered the chamber.

"When I agreed to take over as Lord of the Underworld, I did so under the condition that I'd be given a wife to share my loneliness with, and now that that is being taken away from me, I don't think I could endure the thought of living in the Underworld alone". Hades said with desperation in his voice.

Just then Zeus saw us, and motioned for his brother to turn around, and, when Hades saw us, he ran up to Kore and fell to his knees and took her hand,

"My dear, you must forgive me, you know that I wouldn't do anything to hurt you".

Kore didn't answer right away, so Hades continued,

"Please don't make me return to the Underworld alone, I would rather die than to endure the centuries without your love".

Zeus smiled and then interrupted,

"Hades, has the wine you drank tonight still blocked your powers to read Persephone's thoughts, even I could tell that she is angry, but not with you". He paused. "She is angry with the God or Goddess that is responsible for this deception".

With her eyes filling with tears, Kore finally said to her husband,

"My dear, when I saw you in bed with that girl, the first thought I had was that you had betrayed me. Then I thought about the many summers I have spent with mother on earth, and I thought about all the mortals you must have seduced".

Hades interrupted her,

"I've never touched another since we married. I swear to you that I thought it was you who was laying next to me. I'd never betray your love".

"Please let me continue", Kore said, "When I left the Underworld and returned to mother, I thought that she must have enchanted that poor girl, for she would never have fallen in love with the God of the Underworld unless enchanted. Now my dear, I'm not saying that no one could love you, for this isn't true, you know that I love you dearly, but it's only that mortals fear you". Hades nodded that he understood before Kore continued.

"I don't blame you, I know that one of the other Gods must be responsible, and I suspect that Hermes was a part of the conspiracy".

"I don't know why Hermes would do this, he's always been loyal to me". Hades said.

Zeus interrupted, "It wasn't Hermes plan to destroy your marriage, that belongs to another, but be assured that I'll personally punish him, for his part of this little trick".

Hades tried to interrupt but Zeus held up his hand to quiet his brother,

"Don't blame Hermes, his reasons for assisting were not malicious, his only desire was to have one night with Persephone".

"I'll destroy him". Hades said with anger in his voice.

"Don't touch Hermes, I assure you that I'll not only punish him, but that I'll punish the Goddess responsible". Zeus said.

"Father, please tell me which of Goddess has done this to me". I said to him.

"Have all of you allowed your emotions to overcome you that you cannot see what is plainly written on the wall". Zeus said as Kore looked at him confused.

I broke in then, addressing Kore,

"My dear, when you accused me of this, I explained to you that I'm a Fertility Goddess and don't posses the ability to make others fall in love, but I think you know which of the Goddesses possesses that ability".

Before I could reply to mother's statement, Zeus spoke up,

"You can't condemn Aphrodite, she's been jealous of you, my dear daughter for many, many years".

"What do you mean, she's been jealous of me, I rule over the dead, no other Goddess would wish for that position". I replied.

"She's not jealous of your position in the Universe, but as Goddess of Love she feels that the Moirai have been unfair to her".

"I don't understand your meaning".

"You and Hades have a marriage that is built on trust and love, none of her relationships have been built on either of these. The Moirai determined that she marry a God that she has never loved, and even thought there is one who owns her heart the Moirai won't allow her to totally possess him or his love".

I knew that Zeus was speaking of his son Ares, the God of War. It was a well-known fact that Aphrodite loved him dearly and would willingly have become his wife, but she was destined to marry Hephaestus, the God of Fire, and a God that she despised. Ares, though he too loved Aphrodite with his entire heart, he wasn't faithful to her. He had inherited his father's ways and since he couldn't possess Aphrodite totally, he'd often travel to earth and seduce both mortals and nymphs alike, not realizing how much his affairs hurt his lover.

Zeus continued,

"Aphrodite was born deep in the waters that control emotions, and just as love is blind and subjective to the emotions, so too is she controlled by her emotions. She has, like so many times before, allowed her emotions to influence her actions. But I've assured you that she'll be punished". He paused here than added, "If I find out that any of you try to hurt her or Hermes, you'll have to answer to me alone. Do I make myself understood".

We all nodded that we understood, even Hades.

Hades took Kore's hand and placed in it the golden pendant that he had given her on their wedding day, which she throw into the fire in anger, and closed his hands around hers and lifted them up to his lips and kissed her. She opened her hand and saw the pendant, and spoke,

"It looks as if it was untouched by the fire".

"Like our love, it can't be destroyed".

After securing the pendant around her neck, he said, "Let's return home".

Kore looked at me before answering her husband, knowing that she still had a couple of weeks before I'd allow her to return to the Underworld, with tear forming. How could I not let her return with her husband.

"Kore, that's a good idea, why don't you return home. I can finish taking care of whatever is left myself".

"You don't mind, mother". She said before kissing my cheek. They had reached the door and were about to leave when Kore turned around and spoke to Zeus,

"Father, please forgive me, in my anger I called the powers of the Universe, and once I possessed this power, I used it to turn that poor innocent girl into a pile of dust".

"Don't worry, I'll transform her remains into a plant which mortals will call Mint in her honor".

With this Kore and Hades left Mount Olympus and returned to their home in the Underworld, I didn't even mind that she was returning early, knowing that I'd see her soon.

I was alone with Zeus in his private chamber, and as he walked up to me, he said,

"Demeter, I see that you've forgiven Hades, but have you found it in your heart to forgive me also"?

Over the long years I had forgiven Hades, he has shown that he is a good husband and my daughter is very happy with him, and even though I didn't truly forgive Zeus for tricking me, I have come to an understanding that my daughter was destine to marry the God of the Underworld and nothing I could do would be able to change that.

"You need not answer", he said to me, "I can see that you understand that Destiny rules over even the Gods themselves".

As he said this he reached up and pulled the pins that secured my hair on top of my head, and instantly my long blonde hair fall down over my shoulders.

"You have such beautiful hair, I don't understand why you insist on wearing it up".

I didn't say anything as he ran his fingers through my hair to the back of my neck. As he did this, Hera walked into the room and gave me a look that would have killed a mere mortal. I thanked Zeus for his assistance and left. I didn't return to earth that night, though I should've. That night as I was lying alone in my bed, I heard the door open and saw my beloved brother, Zeus standing just in front of my bed.

"We were interrupted earlier this afternoon". As he said this he slowly lowered onto the bed and leaned over and started to kiss my neck.

"Please Zeus, don't". I begged him.

Even though I spoke these words to him I knew that he wouldn't stop, for deep within my heart I wished for him to continue. He let his kisses follow the curve of my neck up to my ear where he bite my earlobe gently before continuing to my mouth and when his lips touched mine, a shiver of anticipation ran down my spine, and I couldn't help but to kiss him back. I wanted to tell him to stop, but no words came out of my mouth. I knew that it wouldn't be of any use, Zeus could feel the same energy that I felt and I'm sure that he wanted me as much as I wanted him, so when he lifted the covers off me I didn't refuse. I longed for his touch for so many centuries. I said nothing as I watched him undress. I thought only about the first time I made love with him and I thought about how it would be if he took me right then as he did that first night so many centuries ago, but then I saw him standing in front of all the Olympians announcing that he would take a bride, and in my foolishness I thought that it would be me, the betrayal I felt as he announced that my sister Hera would be his queen. I knew then that he had never really loved me, but was only with me because he knew that it would be our child that was destine to one day marry our brother, the God of the Underworld.

"Demeter, I've always loved you". He started me from my thoughts, "Even though you weren't my first love, nor my last, it doesn't mean that I've loved you any less". He said to me as he sat next to me still holding me in his arms.

"You've had so many lovers during your life, I thought that I was different, someone special, but I see that I wasn't". I replied to him.

"Yes, I've had many lovers, both Goddess and mortal, but you must understand that I've loved each and every one of them with all my heart, and while they were in my arms, I loved them more than life itself. Demeter, I've never forgotten our time together, and yes I still love you today as much as I loved you then". He said as he kissed me tenderly on the forehead.

"If you loved me so, then why did you marry Hera, and not me"? I asked as tears filled my eyes.

He wiped a single tear that fell down my cheek before replying.

"It was my destiny to marry Hera, and even a God as powerful as I must summit to Destiny, you must know that by now my dear".

I could see that over the many centuries, Zeus hadn't lost any of his charismatic charm; he was still able to woo any Goddess. He knelt on the bed and reached out to me,

"Demeter, I'll honor your decision, if you wish for me to go, I will. I'll walk out of here and never return".

I didn't answer nor move, so Zeus took me in his arms and kissed me as I opened the front of my nightgown exposing both my body and soul to the great God Zeus. After so many centuries of denying my desire for him, once I opened that part of myself I couldn't stop the feelings that were rushing into me, filling my soul. I knew that I must surrender to these feelings or die. I kissed him back with such a force that he pulled back for a second, then he returned and let his kisses follow the curve of my neck while his hands cupped my breasts. I pulled away from his mouth and let my tongue run down his neck, down his chest and when my lips reached his nipple, I bite there softly as he moaned with pleasure. I kissed his nipple, then allowed my kisses to follow back to his mouth.

I had suppressed my feelings for him for so long, that now that I had him, I wasn't going to let him go. When he entered me I rose my hips up to meet him as he thrust himself hard into me and as the pleasure filled my body I dug my nails into his back. He moaned with pleasure at this, and continued to ride me hard. He moaned loudly when he came and I was sure that all of Mount Olympus would wake, but after he collapsed next to me all was silent. Now Gods, unlike mortal men don't tire after an orgasm, and within a short time my beloved Zeus was ready to love me once again. We made love the entire night and when the Sun God Helios was barely visible on the horizon he jumped from my bed.

"I must return before Hera decides to come looking for me, I shouldn't have stayed the night, but I couldn't deny my feelings for you".

As he dressed he added,

"It would be best if you returned to earth, I'm sure that Hera will become suspicious if you stay within the palace any longer".

I still had a couple of weeks left of my duties as an Earth Goddess, and though I didn't want to leave just then I knew that he was right, Hera would soon realize that I'd made love with her husband, she always did, and I was glad that I'd be away until she cooled off.

"I wish I could tell you to hurry back, but it's for the best that you don't". Zeus said to me as he kissed me one last time before he left.

XIX
Hermes

DEAR READERS, MY beloved cousin Persephone has told you much about my relationship with her throughout the centuries, and while most of what she has related is true, I want to explain my motives for assisting Aphrodite, the Goddess of Love, in inflicting her revenge on both her and Hades. She has insinuated that it was only a way to get her into my bed, and while I admit I'd do anything for one night with her, this wasn't the true reason. You see, as Goddess of Love, Aphrodite, possesses not only enchanting beauty, but charm as well, and I don't know of a single God, even Zeus himself, who is able to refuse her. When Aphrodite came to me, seeking my assistance, I at first told her that I didn't want to get involved. Hades is not only one of the most powerful of the Gods, but is also one of my dearest friends and I didn't want to betray his trust.

"Hermes, I can't believe that you won't do this one little thing for me". The Goddess pouted as she put her arms around my neck and let me briefly taste her lips.

"Can't you find another of the Gods to help you"? I whispered in her ear as I drew her into my arms.

"You're the only God brave enough to face the horrors that dwell within the Underworld".

I could feel the heat between us and at that moment all I could think about was taking her, body and soul. Backing away from my embrace, she gazed at me and I could see the desire in her eyes,

"Hermes, please. Please, do this little thing for me".

I didn't answer her; instead I took her in my arms and unfastened the single broach that held her robe in place. The silk fell, pooling at her bare feet, leaving her standing there completely naked. I kissed her passionately before whispering in her ear,

"What do I need to do"? She said nothing, but I knew by way she smiled that she was mine, at least for the night. I swept her up in my arms, and took her to my bed. That night the Goddess of Love and I were entwined in each other's embrace and we made passionate love the entire night, and from this union our son Hermaphrodites was conceived. As morning approached and still within her embrace, she told me of her plan, and how I was to assist.

Being a Trickster God, it wasn't only easy, but rather enjoyable for me to test my skills fooling Hades. As you already know Hades has the ability to read thoughts, so my first obstacle was to be able to conceal our plan when I was near him, I didn't have the luxury of avoiding him, for I had to be near him the entire season if we were to succeed. This wasn't difficult; I've been practicing for many centuries, but still, I had to be on guard. Before Hades was parted from his wife for the spring and summer seasons, I scoured the earth looking for a mortal who resembled Persephone. My search lasted many weeks and with only a few days before the Spring Equinox I found a young mortal that was the splitting image of Persephone. She was so beautiful that for a moment I forgot why I sought her and thought about taking her for myself.

When we finally reached her palace, I went to Aphrodite private chamber, leaving the mortal with her servants "What took you so long?" She questioned, not wanting to sound too annoyed; she still needed my assistance if she wanted her scheme to go as planned.

"I had to go to the other side of the world to find this one, but I'm sure that you'll be pleased with her".

"Did you bring her back with you"? she said more excited.

"She's waiting just outside". Aphrodite kissed me before turning to greet the mortal but I took her arm and drew her back to me,

"She can wait a little longer".

When Aphrodite finally saw her the mortal girl, she exclaimed, "She's perfect". as she took her arm and led her into her chamber.

"What's your name, my dear"? The Goddess asked with her most charming smile.

The girl bowed low to the Goddess and quietly spoke, "Aphrodite, Goddess of Love, my name is Minthe and I'm your servant".

I had told young mortal that I was bringing her to be one of the Goddess's maidens and she willing came with me; what mortal girl would refuse to be the Goddess of Love's servant?

"You must be tired after your long journey, why don't you come and lie down". Aphrodite guided her to the next room where the Goddess' bed was.

"I'll be back after you've rested awhile and introduce you to the other maidens".

That night while the mortal was sleeping the Goddess of Love quietly came into the room carrying a small glass jar. Once the jar was open I saw the purple iridescent crystals dancing within. Aphrodite poured a small amount of these on her open palm and instead of just laying in her hand, they swirled in their magical dance. Starting at Minthe's head the beautiful Goddess slowly sprinkled the crystals in spiral pattern ending just at her heart, speaking very softly at first but slowly raising her voice,

> *Let the Universe take note,*
> *for I, the Goddess of Love,*
> *have decreed that this mortal*
> *will seek only her soul mate.*
> *Without his love,*
> *she will pine away.*
> *Food and drink will not satisfy her hunger,*
> *only his love will nourish her soul.*
> *I, the Goddess of Love,*
> *have given a name to her lover,*
> *and his name is Hades, Lord of the Underworld.*

As Aphrodite spoke the last of the incantation, Minthe stirred slightly within her sleep.

The next morning I took the mortal to the exact spot where Persephone saw Hades for the first time, explaining that she will soon be united with her love.

For the next several weeks, I had nothing to do but wait until Hades left the Underworld and spotted Minthe. Aphrodite had sent several of her servants to summon Hades, but he paid no attention to the Goddess' request. He never really trusted her, and thought she only wanted to blame the loss of her latest lover, Adonis, on both him and Persephone, so he ignored her. Aphrodite doesn't like to be ignored.

"Hermes, I don't know how to get Hades to leave the Underworld. I've tried everything I can think of". I could tell by her voice that she was becoming annoyed. Aphrodite may bestow beauty and charm, but she's impatient. I knew that she was tiring of my hanging around, she would rather spend her time with Ares, her soul mate.

"Let me go to Hades", I began, as I took out parchment and quill and began a brief note, "I'll tell him this is from Zeus, that he wishes to speak with him. He won't be able to refuse".

Aphrodite kissed me for the last time as I prepared for the journey to the Underworld.

"Once Persephone sees Hades with that mortal, I promise that she'll come to you for comfort. You may do with her as you please". She said with a waive of her hand.

It was then that I realized the real reason Aphrodite wanted to destroy Persephone and Hades' marriage wasn't because of the death of Adonis, for she had many lovers, but because of jealousy. Yes, it was jealousy. Persephone is beautiful, but her beauty can't compare with that of the Love Goddess herself, and still Aphrodite is consumed with envy. As Goddess of Love, Aphrodite believed that it was her right to marry the only God she loved, Ares, but the Fates wouldn't allow this. While Ares never married, Aphrodite was destined to marry a God she despised, Hephaestus. Ares, the God of War, in a fury left Mount Olympus when Zeus announced that that his true love would marry the lame God of Volcanic eruptions, and since he couldn't possess her, he in a jealous rage would destroy those who would take her away from him. Though I can't prove it, I'm sure that it was he, disguised as a boar, that killed Adonis, just as Persephone has related. Persephone and Hades' marriage, a marriage of love, was like a slap to her face. No matter how hard she tried, she couldn't stop the envy from flooding her soul and drowning her.

Though I didn't want to betray Hades, I continued with the game. I don't know why, maybe it was true, I saw this as a way of getting Persephone, at least for one night, into my bed. The modern reader may be shocked by the lack of fidelity of the Gods, but it's natural for the immortals. While Persephone was growing up at Mount Olympus, I wanted her, but I couldn't take her before her marriage, so I did nothing. I waited, longing filling me. I thought that after a couple of years of marriage she would willingly give herself to me. When she found out about Hades' former lover she almost did. It was then that I realized her love for Hades was different; she would never willingly give herself to another God. I was obsessed with finding a way to change that. Throughout the long years of her marriage, I contemplated a way, and I came up with many plans, but in the end I couldn't go through with them. If I did, I would have destroyed her. You might ask, why, then did I go along with Aphrodite's plan? As I said earlier, I really don't know why. Maybe it was because the Goddess of Love used her charms to sway my decision; maybe I too was envious of Persephone's love for Hades. Does it really matter why I did it? What does matter though, is that I have regretted my actions. For many years, too many to count, Persephone wouldn't even speak to me. I had lost not only her love, but her friendship and through the long centuries I come to understand that her friendship meant more to me then I realized.

I went to the Underworld, note in hand.

"Hades, this is from Zeus".

He took it and without even opening it said, "What's this".

"Don't know". I tried to sound convincing.

Come to Mount Olympus, I must speak with you.

"Do you have any idea what Zeus wants"? Hades questioned.

I shook my head, "Sorry".

Hades left immediately. I knew that he couldn't refuse Zeus. A few minutes after he left I, by way of another exit left the Underworld and approached the field where Minthe waited. Sitting with her back to a tree, her hands covered her face, her tears freely flowing.

"What's wrong"? I asked her as I took her hand and lifted her up.

"I think I'll die without the Lord Pluton's love".

"Didn't you see the Lord of the Underworld"? I asked.

"He nearly ran me over". She said, still a little shaken by this.

" He didn't question you"?

"Once he realized that I was alright, he left without another word." Minthe said with tears.

"Don't worry. Come with me, I'll take you to his palace where you can await him". As I said this a smile brightened her face.

Minthe was in the Underworld. It was now entirely up to me to get her into Hades' bed. This was more of a challenge than I thought, Minthe resembled Persephone so much that I thought Hades would welcome her, and though I could see that longing filled him, he didn't act on these feelings.

I set the mortal up as Hades' personal servant, and during that spring and summer, I stayed at his palace whenever I could. I would speak to him about Persephone, hoping that he would become lonely and then I would summon Minthe to bring us some wine.

"She looks so much like your lovely wife, Persephone". I told Hades one night.

"Her beauty can't compare to my dear Persephone's", Hades said and I knew that I would have to come up with another plan.

Several weeks went by and still nothing happened. Aphrodite summoned me a number of times, but I refused to come. She has a way of making the Gods feel inadequate when she doesn't get her way. Instead I decided to take drastic steps to bring our plan to an end. I went into the servant's quarters and took an urn of the best wine and poured half out, replacing it with water from the River of Forgetfulness, knowing that even the Gods wouldn't be able to drink this without becoming intoxicated, along with several herbs that grew within the Underworld. That night at dinner I made sure Hades' glass was continually filled, and when I thought he would pass out if he took one more sip, I took him to his chamber. The rest is as Persephone has told, so I won't bore you, dear reader, with the details.

With Hades in bed with Minthe, I went to Persephone and brought her back to the Underworld. I waited outside their chamber, expecting her to run into my arms, but she didn't. A loud thundering came from within, I ran in to see what had happened in time to see the poor mortal Minthe as a flaming energy hit her, instantly evaporating her. All that was left was a pile of dust. Once the mortal was destroyed, Persephone in a flash disappeared.

"Hermes, what did I do"? Hades asked as he tried to get up from his bed.

"I'm sorry, I thought you were ill, so I called Persephone back. I didn't know you'd be in Minthe's arms".

Hades sat up and put his hands to his head, "My head is spinning".

"Don't try to get up…" I started to say, but was cut off.

"No, I have to go to Mount Olympus, to find her".

Hades left. I knew that Persephone didn't go to Mount Olympus, but I didn't say anything. I waited.

It wasn't long before she returned, and I really thought that she would run to my open arms, but she didn't. I knew then that I had lost her forever.

XX
Persephone

AS I MADE love with my husband that night, mother slept with Zeus, and when the morning dawned he knew that she was with his child, so he kept her away from Mount Olympus until his son was born, hoping that Hera wouldn't torment this child as she did with so many of his other children. For the next nine months Demeter lived on earth among the mortals in her temple at Eleusis. It was the night of the Winter Solstice when I received a message that mother was going into labor. I left immediately and came to her just in time to assist in the delivery. She sat on the birthing chair, breathing heavy as I held her hand, trying to calm her. I had assisted with bringing those who had passed on with their earthly life to their new home in the Underworld, but I had never witnessed the birth of new life. Mother screamed with pain as the contractions became more frequent and I was assured that it wouldn't be long before the birth. One of the assistants gave mother a sip from the chalice she was holding.

"This will ease her pain". She said to me as she handed me a cool rag and showed me how to wipe the sweat that was forming on mother's forehead. Mother gripped the arms of the chair and I saw that that chair had been well worn. I wondered how many births have occurred within it.

"Kore!" Mother screamed and I took her hand as the assistant encouraged her, "It won't be long now. Just one more push".

"Persephone, kneel in front of your mother, the baby is coming". I did as I was told and within seconds I was holding a small head, and I helped guide this life into the world.

I took the tiny infant in my arms and started to clean it, "I'll take care of him". The servant said as I held my brother, and I pulled back slightly, saying, "That's alright, I can take care of this".

After being surrounded by so much death, I was awed by the innocent life I held within my hands.

"It's a boy". I said to mother as I laid the infant on her lap. Instantly she lowered her robe and let the tiny mouth find it's way to her breast. For the first time since my beloved Adonis left me I was totally happy.

"I'll name him Zagreus". She said smiling as she held her newborn son at her breast. I stayed with mother for only a few days, making sure that she had all she needed before returning to my place amongst the dead.

When spring arrived I left the Underworld as I usually did and for that first year I happily took over mother's duties while she tended her son, Zagreus, and when fall arrived she didn't seem too disappointed when I kissed her as I departed for the Underworld. Wishing to return to the only home she knew, she left for Mount Olympus. She had thought that Zeus was being too cautious, Hera had never tried to harm any of her other children. She was confidant that the Goddess feared her strength so she was assured that Zagreus would be safe on Mount Olympus. At first Hera greeted Demeter with a smile, commenting on how beautiful her infant was,

"My dear sister, I didn't know that you were expecting, is that why you didn't return at the beginning of fall last year"?

"Since Zagreus will one day be a Vegetation God, I wished for him to be born on the earth among mortals". She lied to Hera.

It was obvious that a God fathered the child, so Hera asked,

"Who is the father of this beautiful child"? Knowing all too well that it was her husband, Zeus.

"His father is a powerful God, and he's promised to watch over his son and one day make him his successor". Was all that Demeter would say.

Hera pretended to ignore the child, as she did all of Demeter's other children, but for the next year she was secretly scheming to destroy the child.

Zagreus was almost two years old, which would be equivalent to a mortal child of about six or seven years of age, when Hera came into the nursery that was adjacent to Demeter's private chamber and gave the child some presents; colorful balls, dice, tops, a bull-roarer and a shinning mirror. Mesmerized with his shinny new toys Zagreus played quietly. As the small boy sat on the floor, admiring his reflection in the mirror, one of the Titans, Coeus, who was working under Hera's orders, crept into the room and approached the innocent child. The Titan silently came from behind and before Zagreus could scream, he covered the boy's mouth with his large hand, allowing no sound escape. He then wrapped the boy in a sack and not wanting to take any chances, hid this under his cloak until he was far from the palace. When Demeter came into the room only a few minuets later and saw the new toys scatted on the floor, and the broken mirror she called out.

"Zagreus, where are you". When he didn't answer she ran straight to Zeus.

"Zeus!" she screamed, "Zagreus is missing!"

Zeus instantly went to his wife suspecting her of foul play and interrogated her,

"Where is Zagreus"? He demanded.

"My dear, I don't know". She said, trying her best to sound innocent.

"Where is my son"? He asked again, this time the sound of his voice caused the entire palace to shake.

"Your son! You didn't tell me that he was your son". Hera said trying to buy a little time, insuring that her plan would succeed.

"Hera, you know damn well that Zagreus was my son, and I promised Demeter that I would protect him, now tell me where he is!"

Over the many centuries Hera had learned to conceal her thoughts from her husband, and that night she closed her mind totally to his prying gaze.

"I don't know what you are talking about". was all that she would say to his accusations.

"I swear to you, Hera, if that child is hurt, you'll wish that you were mortal and death would be able to release you from my punishment". After threatening his wife, Zeus stormed out of the room and he and Demeter started the long search for their son.

At first they searched for Zagreus within the palace grounds, hoping that he was still near, but while they were distracted with Hera, the Titan Coeus took the child to earth where his companions were hiding in the forest that surrounded Parnassus. Once concealed within the woods the Titan reached for the ritual knife and with one swift stroke he sliced the child's throat. He held the tiny body over their cauldron ensuring that every drop of his blood mixed with the contains held within, causing a black steam to rise from the boiling liquid. Only after they were certain the boy was dead, they torn his body apart with their bare hands, and threw the pieces that once were Zagreus into the boiling liquid, adding vegetables and spices to make a stew for their dinner.

They left the stew simmer several hours and the aroma started to fill their sense. One of the Titans took the meat from the cauldron and placed it over an open flame roasting it, causing the scent to fill the sky. Zeus and Demeter were on earth at this very moment, and suddenly Zeus sniffed the air and took Demeter by the hand and instantly they appeared in the woods, just behind the Titans, who had just started feasting on the roasted meat. Zeus in his anger let all of his lightening bolts loose at once, filling the woods with a great flash that was brighter than the Sun itself. A mushroom cloud filled the sky and it would be days before the area would be clear of the debris, but Zeus called to the Winds and they instantly came and gently blew the smoke away and within the hour Zeus and Demeter stood within the devastated forest. The bodies of the Titans were charred beyond recognition, causing Demeter to cry out. She didn't cry for the lose of their life, but she was assured that her son was dead. Zeus rushed up to the cauldron and snatched out the heart, which was still in the boiling liquid, and as Demeter cried for the loss of her son Zeus assured her that if she had faith, everything would be all right, so they rushed back to Mount Olympus.

Once back, Zeus went straight to his mother, begging her,

"Mother", he said bowing low in respect to her, waiting until she requested that he speak,

"Speak my son, for I sense that something is bothering you".

"Hera, in a jealous rage, has destroyed my child Zagreus". He held out the small heart for Rhea to see, and before he could say anything else, Demeter interrupted,

"Why are the Fates trying to take all my children from me"? She said as she cried in Zeus' arms.

"Mother, of all the Gods, you alone will be able to save Zagreus, for if you cannot, his soul must depart to the Underworld for sure". Zeus said as he held the tiny organ out to his mother.

"My dear son and daughter, I can not save Zagreus…" Rhea started to say, but Demeter again interrupted, this time screaming,

"I won't let him go, if he is destine to live eternity within the Underworld, I will depart with him, where I will sit next to not only him, but also my beloved daughter Kore".

"I can't save Zagreus", Rhea began again, "But, since you were cleaver enough to recover his heart, I can bring him back to life, born of another".

"Please mother, let me bear him again". Demeter begged.

"No, he must be born of a mortal woman, but Demeter do not despair, he will remember that you were his first mother, and when he has grown to manhood, and proven himself he will take the seat next to his father and mother as not only a God, but as one of the Olympians".

Both agreed, and Zeus gave Rhea the child's heart, which she held tightly. Once alone Rhea took the heart and laid it down on a white cloth; she waved her hand over it, drying it out instantly. When she was sure all the moisture had been removed she took the dried heart and placed it in a mortar and began the slow process of grinding it into a fine power. Once satisfied with the results, she mixed in other herbs and then combined this with sacred water making a magical potion. As the potion simmered, Zeus and Demeter came into the room. Rhea motioned for them to come no closer. Before they could move a great flash rose from the cauldron and Rhea poured out a brownish liquid. Handing the pungent liquid to Zeus, she spoke.

"Zeus, to bring your child back from the dead, you must drink this, for this is Zagreus' essence".

Zeus held the chalice to his lips and drank all the liquid within. Rhea spoke again,

"Go to one of the Priestess of the New Moon, a mortal woman named Semele, she'll be in the temple alone. Go to her invisible and tell her who you are, and that your presence will impregnate her. She is a Phyrygian princess, daughter of Cadmus and Harmonia. I'll inform them that their grandchild has been fathered by the God Zeus, making them swear that nothing will happen to the child".

Zeus left in a great flash, and a second later he was standing just outside the temple his mother had told him about. He looked in and there he found the young maiden kneeling in front of the alter alone, and instantly he fell in love with her. As he entered the temple, all the candles extinguished, making the small chamber Semele was in totally dark. Startled, she looked around and seeing nothing she thought it was the wind alone that extinguished the flames. Cloaked within the dark, Zeus let his spirit fill the room, and soon Semele knew she was in the presence of a powerful God. She lowered her head. A slight breeze, no a whispered tickled her ear,

"I'm the God Zeus, and I've come here to bless you". He could see that she was still afraid, so he tried to calm her,

"You've no need to be afraid, I haven't come here to hurt you, only to love you".

"But, I cannot love you, I'm a priestess of Artemis. She will surly destroy me if I make love to you here in her temple". She pleaded with Zeus.

"There is no need to fear Artemis, I ensure you that you'll be safe, I'll protect you from the Goddess' wrath".

After she was convinced that no harm would come to her, she gave herself to the spirit that filled the room and while he was inside her, instead of leaving his seed, he deposited the soul of his beloved son Zagreus.

"My love," he addressed her after the union was complete, "You are with my child".

"What am I to tell my mother and father"? She cried.

"Don't worry, they've already been informed that the child you carry will one day sit next to me on Mount Olympus". The voice said before finally leaving Semele alone once again. The mortal sat within the temple and cried the entire night.

For the next several months Zeus would visit Semele several times a week and each time before leaving her he would warn her not to trust strangers, telling her that his wife was very jealous, and would not hesitate to destroy her and her unborn child. Semele was almost nine months pregnant before Hera was able to find out which mortal woman Zeus was involved with this time, and once she discovered that Semele was about to give birth, she disguised herself as an old woman and came to Semele pretending to be seeking employment.

"My dear, I see that you are almost ready to deliver". She said to Semele with a false smile across her face.

"I have less than a month left". Semele replied.

"Then you and your husband will be needing someone to take care of not only you, but your child as well. I happen to be looking for a house to take me in, and would be happy to look after your family". Hera said.

"I'm not married, so I'll be needing all the help I could get, and would be grateful if you would join my house". Semele said with a smile.

After a couple of days, as Semele's time came nearer, Hera as the old woman asked her who the father was.

"The father is none other than the Great God Zeus". She said without pausing, since the old woman had came to her house, she had done her best to gain Semele's trust.

"My dear, I hate to be the one to tell you this, but you have been fooled". Hera said with a slight laugh in her voice.

"What do you mean"? Semele asked, not liking the tone of her servant's voice.

"Some mortal man has tricked you into thinking that he's the God Zeus only to have his way with you", Hera said, adding, "Has he given you any proof that he's really a God".

This made Semele think, why was it that every time she was with Zeus, he made sure that he was cloaked by the night, and wouldn't allow any candles burn within the room. Maybe the old woman was correct, maybe for the last nine months she was being made a fool of by some mortal man. Shame filled her.

"What is to become of me and my child"? She said to the old woman as she lowered her head in disgrace.

"Next time your lover comes to you, ask him to grant you a wish, swearing on the waters of the River Styx. Once he agrees, and only after he agrees to this are you to ask him to show himself to you in all his glory. If he isn't Zeus he'll try to change your mind, saying something like 'no mortal eyes could bear the sight of the great God.' But, you're not to be persuaded. Insist that since he took an oath on the sacred waters, he cannot refuse you".

That very next night, as Semele laid in her bed, once again a wind came into the chamber and all the candles extinguished and soon she felt the power of Zeus within the room. She didn't rush to her lover as she usually did.

"My love", Zeus said to her, from behind a shadow, "Why are you so sad tonight"?

"My dear, I'll tell you what has caused my heart to break, but only if you grant me a wish first".

"Of course I'll give you anything you desire, but please tell me what is bothering you". He said sadly, feeling her pain.

"Promise me", she said, "No, swear to me, on the waters of the River Styx that you'll grant me one wish".

"I swear, I will grant all your desires". And as he said this a smile came over Semele's face.

"I wish only for you to show yourself, in your full glory, to me".

"I cannot do that." He said in a tone that Semele had never heard from her lover, he had always given her anything she had wished for. When he refused she thought of what the old woman had said, that if he refused her request she would know that he had been lying to her all the time.

"You swore on the waters of the River Styx, therefore you must obey my request". Semele said, knowing that both the Gods and mortals alike were bound to all oaths made on the waters of the river that separated the Underworld from the land of the living.

"You don't know what you are asking for, ask me for anything else, but don't ask this of me". He begged her, "If I show myself to you, my essence will consume you".

She wouldn't back down. He had no other choice, and at once he knew that his wife Hera must have been behind this, hoping to destroy the child. He kissed Semele one last time, than in a bright flash, he took on his own form and instantly Semele bust into flames, and as she screamed and fell to the floor, Zeus reached into her burning body and snatched the infant before disappearing. The child was almost full term and when Zeus saw the infant he knew that the child would survive. When he returned to Mount Olympus he didn't go to his chamber, instead he went to Hermes and instructed him to take the infant to Mount Nysa for the Mountain Nymphs to raise. The nymphs watched over him during the winter months, while he joined Demeter and I during the summers. For the next six years Demeter would happily tend to her son during her stay on Earth, and when he was old enough he began his schooling from the Satyr Silenus.

Now through the many generations that have passed, it has been told that Dionysus, which was Zagreus' new name was my child, since it was thought that his soul was once in the Underworld. Some of the old myths state that Zeus came to me in the Underworld in the form of a serpent and impregnated me, and that Dionysus was born nine months later, but this is not so. Let me pause my story here to explain that Zagreus' soul never entered the Underworld at all. Zeus snatched the still beating heart and therefore the soul of his son, and this was transferred into Semele who gave birth to the God a second time, making Dionysus both a Dying and Resurrecting God of Fertility and a God who was born twice. Since he was born of a human mother, and therefore half human, the mortals approached him to intercede to the Gods on their behalf, knowing that being half mortal, he would be able to better understand the problems of humanity, and therefore would willingly assist them.

Throughout the centuries Hera wouldn't allow Dionysus to live in peace, she harassed him as she did so many of Zeus' other children, and he like Hercules had to wander through the civilized world watching out for traps from the Goddess. Being born for the first time from Demeter, the Goddess of Fertility, Dionysus was also a Fertility God, and was considered by mortals to be the life force itself. Instead of cultivating grain, like his mother Demeter, Dionysus roamed through the wilderness, trying to keep ahead of Hera. Where ever he went he was followed by female worshipers, the Bacchants, spreading the art of cultivation of the vine and winemaking. The Bacchants was the name given to the women who were enchanted by Hera into madness believing that Dionysus was the Resurrecting God. These estranged women would follow the young God Dionysus wherever he traveled and in a frenzy they would tear both beast and man apart with their bare hands. After many decades of enduring Hera's wrath and traveling throughout the world alone, Zeus felt it was time to bring his son to Mount Olympus where he would join the other Gods.

Dionysus was summoned to Zeus' palace and once there, he saw that all the other Gods were present, including me, since it was not yet fall. Zeus rose from his seat when he saw Dionysus enter the Great Hall and everyone became quiet. Zeus spoke.

"I wish to invite my son, Dionysus, to join us as our brother".

Zeus said loudly, and at once Hera stood up in anger and screamed,

"I will not share Mount Olympus with the son of a mere mortal woman". And as she said this some of the other Gods who had never seen anyone stand up to Zeus started to whisper to each other.

"Dionysus was born to my sister, the Goddess Demeter, and therefore he is worthy of living on Mount Olympus". Zeus stated while looking at his wife hoping for her to question his authority.

Hera knowing that she couldn't disagree with Zeus, especially in front of the others, smiled and softy said,

"You are correct, my dear, Dionysus was born to a Goddess, therefore he is worthy of living on Mount Olympus, but since there are only twelve thrones here, he won't be able to rule with the other Gods".

Hera knew that without being able to participate as one of the Olympians, Dionysus would soon become bored with life within the palace and would leave for earth, but she was surprised when the Goddess Hestia stood up and said,

"You are correct Hera, but since I'm Goddess of the Hearth, I need no throne, and I will gladly give Dionysus my seat".

The look on Hera's face could not hide her anger at her sister and before she could say anything, Zeus announced,

"My beloved son Dionysus will no longer be only a mere God, he will be one of the Olympians, and will sit on my right side".

All applauded, but Dionysus stood, wanting to speak. He waited patiently until the hall became quiet, then spoke to his father.

"Father, I'm honored that you are willing to bring me to Mount Olympus, but before I can leave the earth, I have one request of you".

"Anything you wish, I will grant". Zeus said smiling.

Dionysus walked up to Demeter and held her hand and spoke,

"Demeter, Goddess of Fertility, you have raised me as your own son, and I'm grateful, I know that I was born from your womb first, and when I was killed, Zeus took my still beating heart and devoured it, preventing my soul from entering the Underworld. My soul was then deposited into the body of a mortal woman, Semele, who was killed by treachery". He paused here and then addressed to all present,

"Father, before I can take my seat next to you, I must be reunited with my mortal mother".

"No!" Shouted Hera.

"Silence woman!" Zeus shouted back, then walked up to me and spoke,

"Persephone, my dear daughter, do you know which shade is Semele"?

"Yes father". I answered.

"Go to the Underworld and tell Hades that I wish to make Semele an immortal, for she is the mother of one of the Olympians now".

Hera stood up and screamed at her husband,

"I said nothing when you made the mortal healer Asklepius a God, then I allowed you to make your beloved son, Hercules an immortal when he died, even though both were born from mortal women, I even allowed him to marry my daughter Hebe, but I will not stand by while you make this mortal woman one of us".

"You allowed me!" Zeus said to his wife, in a tone that made all present shake. "Remember one thing, I am the Great God Zeus, your husband, and you are to honor all my decisions".

Hera turned and walked out of the Great Hall and where she went none knew, but she was not seen on Mount Olympus for a couple of months.

"Persephone, go down and retrieve Semele's soul immediately!" Zeus shouted at me.

When I returned to the Underworld, Hades looked at me suspiciously, since the last time he thought that I returned early, it wasn't really me. I explained that Zeus was planning on making Dionysus' mortal mother one of the immortals and she would now dwell on Mount Olympus for eternity with her son. Hades allowed me to return with her soul, he couldn't disobey his brother, but he wasn't happy giving up one of his subjects, saying,

"I hope that Zeus doesn't decide to snatch souls from the Underworld again, it disrupts the delicate balance of life and death".

I went to the Elysian Fields and searched until I found the shade I was looking for. I took Semele's hand and tried to comfort her as I guided her back to our palace where Hades was waiting with our chariot. I was a little surprised that Hades accompanied me, wanting to be present for the transformation, but I was glad for the time we could be together. The entire journey, from start to finish took less than a day and I was back at Zeus' palace the same evening with Semele's shade. Dionysus took his mortal mother's hand and she only looked at him with a blank look and let him lead her into the palace. He knew by the look in her eyes that she was oblivious to fact that he was her only son. He guided the phantom to a chair that was situated in the center of the Great Hall and all the Gods and Goddesses stood in a giant circle waiting to see what Zeus would do next.

Instead of the Moirai performing the ceremony, as they did when Asclepius was made a God, Zeus himself raised his hands up to the sky and instantly storm clouds gathered over the palace. Thunder filled the main hall as lightening started flashing across the heavens, lighting the entire hall. A bright flash of lightening came down, striking Zeus, causing his body to twist in spasms as it filling him with the power to create life. All gasped as they watched the energy fill Zeus' body. After a few seconds all present saw his body glow with a white aura which became brighter and brighter as the single vein of lightening continued to pulsate through his body. Satisfied that he could take in no more energy he slowly lowered his hands and the connection of God and lightening broke with a loud sound of cracking thunder. All stood quiet, waiting to see what the God would do next.

Zeus turned to face the shade of Semele, and when she looked up at him, he placed his hands on her head and a strong wind filled the Great Hall. Thunder sounded once again and lightening flew, but this time not from the skies, it came from Zeus' hands. All the energy that was contained within the great God flooded into his once lover, Semele. Hades held my hand as I watched transfixed as her once transparent body slowly started to become solid; my father had been able to give her back her soul. Zeus removed his hands and staggered back as if he was drunk. Mother ran up to him, helping him stand and when he regained his balance he slowly walked up to the new Goddess and commanded her to open her eye. She slowly obeyed and when she did the first sight she saw was her son Dionysus. Dionysus ran to his mother, and as he took her hand, she a single tear fell as she spoke,

"My dear son".

XI
Persephone

ONCE DIONYSUS HAD entered the palace as one of the Olympians, his duties brought him together with mother and I as the Gods of the Eleusinian Mysteries. Considered a Fertility God, he was worshiped throughout his life, but it wasn't until he took his seat next to his father, Zeus, that he was able to participate in our Mysteries; before this time his only followers were the Bacchants. Most kingdoms forbid worship of him fearing the Goddess Hera's wrath causing a madness to overcome them. When he returned to his true home on Mount Olympus he was honored by all countries throughout the world as the God he was born to be.

I have spoken of the Eleusinian Mysteries, and most of modern reader cannot truly understand what these sacred ritual were. Throughout the centuries many have attempted to explain the Mystery Religions, but since those who participated within these rites transmitted their knowledge orally, and only to those who were initiated within the community, throughout the centuries many of the rites and rituals were lost forever. I'll try here to briefly explain to you how these Mysteries were practiced and how they continue to evolve to this day.

These sacred rites were named after the kingdom of Eleusis, and if you remember it was the King of this small city and his beloved wife, Metaneira, who took mother in during the long year that she withheld her fertility from the earth. The king and queen not only took her in, but also shared what little food they had with her, and to repay the only kindness she found during that long year, she taught their family these rituals in gratitude. These simple ceremonies honored not only Life, but Death as well. The Eleusinian Mysteries were the first of the Mystery Religions, and during the centuries that preceded the current era these mysteries grew and like a tree their many branches reached out into different directions taking root and forming a slightly different version wherever they touched. The Mystery Religions that were popular during their early history varied in which God or Goddess' were honored and the rituals used, but were common in that they not only honored both Life and Death, but promised to cleanse the sins of the initiated. These Mystery Religions were not concerned with the eternal life of the soul, instead they promised personal salvation. Unlike the modern era, most mortals living in the past centuries believed in reincarnation, and those who participated in one of the Mystery Religions believed that these sacred rites would break the cycle of birth, death, life within the Underworld, and rebirth. The human soul must spend at least three hundred years within the Underworld until they can once again be reborn. This cycle would continue until the soul was worthy of purification. For those who are initiated this cycle could be broken and the soul would join in the eternal company of the Gods.

Demeter as the Goddess of Grain and Fertility was considered the Life Force itself and I, as consort of Hades and Queen of the Underworld was Death, and throughout the Mysteries we were both worshiped as each a part of the whole; for there would be no life without death. The festival itself mirrored this duel aspect of both birth and death; the Greater Mysteries occurred during the month of September and honored both mother and I and were a thanksgiving celebration honoring not only us, but all the Gods for the harvest, while the Lesser Mysteries held in March were dedicated to me, as the Queen who must one day guide all souls to their final resting place, alone.

When the young Demophon, son of Metaneira, Queen of Eleusis, heard the story of how Demeter, Goddess of Fertility, had tried to make him immortal, and how his mother, only trying to protect her beloved son witnessed the ritual and in fear broke the spell, he was assured that the Goddess would one day come to him and reveal her mysteries. Each day after he was through with his daily chores he would sit alone in the Temple, the Temple his father built in the Goddess' honor, waiting patiently for her return. Day after day, for the next ten years he would sit and patiently wait until the Goddess would come to him. No matter how many days passed without any sign of the Goddess he didn't become discouraged, he knew deep within his heart that the Goddess would come. His sixteenth birthday had arrived, he was considered a man now and he knew that this would be the day he was waiting for so long.

It was a hot summer day and he broke off from the celebrations to go to the Temple where he began praying to the Goddess. Night was approaching fast, and for the first time disappointment set in.

'*Had the Goddess deserted me'?* He thought.

With the setting sun he stood up, turning to leave the temple when a great flash of light startled him at first. He didn't need to turn around to know that the Goddess Demeter had finally come to him, as she had promised. He looked briefly at her beauty, before falling to his knees and lowering his head in respect. Not speaking, he kissed her bare feet.

"Demophon, you may rise." Her voice was as beautiful as she was he thought when he finally beheld her.

"I had promised your mother and father for the kindness they offered me that I would return one day and teach you, their most beloved son, the Mysteries of both Life and Death".

Demophon who had been entranced by her beauty quietly spoke to her,

"Demeter, Goddess of Fertility, tell me now what these mysteries you speak of are, for I wish to honor you above all the other Gods and Goddesses".

Mother was pleased with his response.

"The rituals I will give to you will not only honor me, the Goddess of Grain and Fertility, but also my daughter Kore, the Queen of the Underworld, for as you know without death there would be no life. The seed must be planted deep within the ground where it will die. Buried deep within the earth, it will began it's new life and the following spring it will sprout up from the depths of the earth as grain.

The grain must also die, for if it is not harvested, there would be no food. These rites that I'll teach you will ensure fertility of both the land and the initiated, and a promise those who are faithful to me to break the cycle of death and rebirth".

The next couple of years mother spent the entire season teaching Demophon her rituals, and assisted him in establishing these mysteries to his people. After only a few years, mother took Demophon with her throughout the entire world where he taught the mysteries to all who listen. Within a few decades, temples sprang up not only in nearby kingdoms, but scattered throughout the entire civilized world, and soon people of all nations worshiped Demeter. She was no longer just a Fertility Goddess but became the Mother Goddess, the Giver of Life, who allowed the sacrifice of her beloved child to ensure that new life would sprout from her death, just as the seed was sacrificed to allow the grain to grow, and the grain then is sacrificed to allow mortal life to survive.

These mysteries were very complex; so let me start by explaining the Lesser Mysteries to you, since no one was allowed to participate in the Greater Mysteries until they had been initiated into the Lesser Mysteries for at least one full year and a day. These rituals were held in March at the time of the equinox, just after I left the Underworld to return to the land of the living, and were known as "Anodos" or "upcoming". All the rites were symbolic in that by performing them as I arose from the Underworld, so too the grain will rise from its yearly slumber deep with the body of the Mother Earth. On the night before the equinox the initiate would meet in Athens, where they would gather near Demeter's temple and from there would begin the fourteen-mile walk, along the Sacred Way in a grand procession to the river Ilissu, just outside of Eleusis where I would great each initiate personally. Each initiate would then bath in the cleansing waters of the sacred river as I blessed them. This baptism, like baptisms from other religions not only purified the soul but also allowed sins to be forgiven.

Only after they completed this baptism and were cleansed of their earthly sins would the new initiates be allowed to great the Mysteries. Blindfolded, they were lead to a nearby cave where they were to spend the next three days within the womb of the Mother Earth in fasting and silent meditation. Once within the cave the blindfold was removed, but no light was allowed to enter; they were alone, surrounded by nothing but darkness. Thought no food was brought to the initiates, they were allowed the sacred drink, a mixture of roasted barley water that contained ergot, a fungus that was a mild hallucinogenic, mandrake root, and poppies. This combination of fasting and the hallucinogenic drink caused the initiate to enter into a heightened sense of awareness. On the second day I would slowly lift the veil between the world of the living and that of the dead and those whose hearts were pure were able to briefly glimpse into the other side. Some of the initiates would see the shades of their loved ones, while others who weren't quite ready to see the dead would have spiritual visions that would answer the questions that burned deep within their souls. Each initiate's experience during this time of reflection was unique to his or her spiritual path.

On the third day the High Priestess would prepare to enter the cave and guide the new initiates to their new life. She would dress in a white linen robe, cover her hair and face with veils and perched on her head would be a golden crown that was filled with a small amount of alcohol. Once surrounded by the darkness of the cave the Priestess would ignite the alcohol and the crown would burst into flames. She would then enter into the chamber where the initiates were mediating.

"As handmaid of the Goddess Kore, I ask all to state their names". After this was done, she would hold her hands, palms facing the earth and breath in energy from the depths of the womb, imagining it rising up through her feet and into her body. The initiates would see a sparkling silver light flow around her, as she walked up to each initiate and place her hands upon their heads, speaking to each directly.

"In the name of the Fair Goddess Kore, I bless you with light and with love. So shall it be".

The one receiving the blessing would then hold her hands palms ups while the Priestess of Demeter would sprinkle water over their heads, speaking,

"In the name of the Goddess Demeter, I bless you with health, and with happiness. So shall it be".

The bright halo that surrounded the High Priestess was a symbol of the Goddess of Light and as thus she would take their hands and guide the initiates back into the world of the living where they were reborn as a Mystes and were welcomed by their new sisters. It was only after they were revived from their symbolic death that the celebration would finally begin. They were now welcomed as one of our followers, and each would greet the High Priestess and present her new name. It would be by this name alone that the other Mystes would know their sisters. Once I married Hades I was no longer known as Kore, the Maiden, but became Persephone, the Goddess of Death and Rebirth, and their new name symbolized their new life as a daughter of the Goddess.

It was only after one was a Mystes for at least a year and a day that they would be allowed to participate in the Greater Mysteries, known as "Kathodos", or "downgoing". This celebration lasted for nine days during the middle of September just before I would return to the Underworld and mother would let her sadness consume her, causing all life to wither and die. September 14th marked the beginning of the celebration, as a procession of hundreds of our followers traveled to the sea where they would camp out and wait until the first rays of the sun before bathing in the seawater to cleanse and purify their souls. Only after the participants were thus cleansed would they be allowed to make their offerings to Demeter, Goddess of Fertility, and then to me asking for not only our blessings for the following year but to ensure life and fertility for their families.

One by one, as the Mystes approached the altar with head lower showing respect, they would give their thanks to the High Priestesses who represented both Demeter and I and only after their silent prayer would they leave a small offering to us. The High Priestess would reply,

"In the name of the Goddess Demeter and the Goddess Kore, may your deepest desires grow and blossom. So shall it be".

Any personal item that had special meaning to them could be left as an offering; typical offerings included flowers, food, clothing or jewelry or any item that was made by the Mystes' own hands. Since the Gods have all that they wish for, we did not literally consume these offerings, instead they were given to the Priestesses who tended the Temple during the winter months as a payment for their services.

On the third day of the celebration two small pigs, which were thought to symbolically absorb the sins of the initiates were sacrificed by the High Priestess to Demeter. But, before the pigs were ritually slaughtered, each Mystes would walk up to one of the pigs and hold her hands over it while reflecting on their sins of the past year, praying for forgiveness, and only after each member had transferred their sins into the pig were they washed in the salt water of the sea allowing all the sins of the people be taken out to the sea where the power of both the Earth and of Water would cleanse them. Once this was complete, the High Priestess would hold up her ritual knife while loudly speaking,

"May the Goddess Persephone cleanse the sins of these pigs, the sins of our sisters". All present would reply, "Bless us Persephone!" while the High Priestess would slit the pig's throat making sure to collect all its blood into a chalice. The pig was then roasted over an open fire, while a few drops of the blood was mixed into the wine that was then offered to the Gods. That night after all within the group gave their thanks the High Priestess would hold up the offering of the first serving of both the meat and wine to the Goddesses, as the crowd spoke,

"May the Goddesses Persephone and Demeter accept this offering as a symbol of our devotion".

It was believed that part of our divine essence entered into this food as we took our offering and by tasting these offerings the Mystes were partaking of our body and blood, thus becoming one with the Gods. This was known as Enthusiasmos, allowing the person to consume part of the God or Goddess and keep this blessing inside them for the entire year.

The feast marked the beginning of the celebration, and since all their sins had been forgiven and the Gods accepted their offerings, the participates could now relax and enjoy the rest of the festival. Dancing and drumming would continue throughout the night as the Priestesses performed ritual dances accompanied by the singing and drumming of their sisters, and when all were exhausted they would sit by the fire while the eldest of the High Priestesses would perform divination. It was extremely difficult to train oneself to be an oracle; one had to allow themselves to be possessed by the Gods, so usually only the eldest and wises of the High Priestesses had this ability.

"Come my sister, tell me what you wish to know". The old woman would say as she took the Mystes' hand in hers and closed her eyes. Each Mystes would ask one question, and either mother or I would answer this through the High Priestess, who in a light trance would speak our words. When awoke from the trance the High Priestess wouldn't be able to remember what she had said, and in the morning those who didn't understand our message, which sometimes would be cryptic, they would go to her and she would interpret our words.

The following day, after the High Priestess had completed her services, several dramatic plays were preformed, each one telling one of the many parts of what has been passed down throughout history as the Myth of Persephone, or better known as the Rape of Kore. The first of these performances showed one of the Priestess, dressed as a maiden Goddess in a golden robe, picking flowers for her dear mother, while the stage below her began to shake allowing a small trap door to open, letting out the God of the Underworld.

"Do not fear dear maiden, for I come only to love you". The voice of the God of the Underworld would say as the Maiden Goddess would scream and try to run. Enraged, the dark God grabbed at her and dragged her back to the Underworld. Even though this was very different from what I had told you in this story, the mortals who participated in these rituals couldn't believe that I would willingly submit to marrying the Lord of the Underworld, instead they believed mother's story that I was raped and dragged into my current prison against my will.

In the next performance the Goddess Demeter, dressed in a dark tattered robe, head veiled and holding her lantern high searched for her beloved daughter. The Goddess would call out.

"Kore, my dear daughter, where are you"?

Each time she would call out, the audience would respond to her,

"Mother, I'm here in the Underworld, held against my will".

No matter how loudly they would cry out, the Goddess didn't seem to hear their cries.

With a little creative planning, the stage was changed into the kingdom of Eleusis. The Goddess would enter the stage, dressed in her black robes holding an infant to her breast. A fire burned in the hearth. She held the infant over the flames, crying to the heavens, "Dear child, let this fire consume your mortality".

Demophon's mother would then enter the stage, crying, "My child!"

A flash of light and the Goddess would tear off her dark robe, revealing the golden robe of the Goddess Demeter.

The scene changed once again, half the stage became Mount Olympus, the other side the Underworld. The audience watched as the Gods on Mount Olympus fought over my fate. The Priestess who portrayed Hades entered the side of the Underworld, speaking in a deep voice, "My dear wife, I don't wish to cause you pain. You may leave anytime you wish, but please take this pomegranate as a gift". The initiate that played me cautiously takes the pomegranate in her hand as the audience erupts with shouts telling her not to taste the fruit, "Don't allow your lips to touch the food of the dead." They would cry out, but alas, the maiden bites into the pomegranate sealing her fate. The final scene is once again on Mount Olympus between mother and I as she tells me my fate, that since I had tasted the food of the Underworld, I must therefore spend half the year there as consort to Hades, Lord of the Underworld. The two Goddesses cry and embrace each other. These scenes marked the end of the festival, and when finished all would pack their belongings and start the long procession back to Eleusis and their daily life.

****

Since it was thought that the Fertility God, Dionysus, had survived death he became assimilated within these rites, and as such he became a Resurrecting God associated with both Demeter and I in the Mysteries. While Demeter gave grain to the world her gifts gave life to all mortals, Dionysus' gift gave man pleasure through physical and spiritual intoxication through the vine, and thus wine. But just as wine can give man pleasure, it can also cause madness, and Dionysus, like me, was both honored and feared by mortals. For many years the Eleusianian Mysteries honored not only mother and I, but also Dionysus, my brother Iacchus and my half sister, Despoena, known only as "the Mistress".

As time went on and the Mysteries became more popular men wished to join in these rituals, hoping that they too would be saved in the afterlife. Now don't think that we didn't wish for men to participate, but the women who had worshipped us for so many years felt that if men were allowed to join, they would invariably corrupt the purity of the Mysteries. Fighting among the initiates occurred as some felt that both men and women were equal and therefore any should be allowed to participate within these sacred rites. Others didn't agree, causing a split, and the beginning of a new Mystery Religion, one that honored the God Dionysus alone. The Dionysian Mysteries, as this new cult was named allowed any who wished to honor the Gods to participate, both men along with the women.

Dionysus' cult was connected to the Eleusinian Mysteries in that it offered to the initiated the same benefits, forgiveness of sins, and a promise of a better afterlife, but instead of somber rites in which the participants made offerings and prayers to the Gods, in the Dionysian Mysteries the initiates would go into a temporary sacred madness caused by the wine, and in this intoxicated state, they would tear animals apart, reenacting the killing of the infant Zaagreus. Some would not only eat the raw flesh, but also drink the blood while it was still warm. By doing this they were consuming the God's essance and uniting with him just as when the Mystes consumed the ritual pig and united with both mother and I. These rituals soon became as popular as the Eleusinian Mysteries although both mother and I tried to convince the mortals that sacrificing the life of any living thing could never bring them closer to the Gods, they didn't stop these practices. Some my think that I'm being hypercritical since during the Eleusinian Mysteries pigs were sacrificed, but you see, these pigs weren't killed as a sacrifice only to please the Gods, they fed all the initiates. Dionysus' followers killed for the pleasure of killing alone, and what meat was not eaten was left to rot in the woods. We watched horror struck as our Mysteries mutated into these grisly rites. But as time passed and cultures were destroyed and replaced with new ones, these Mysteries also changed and evolved into other forms.

While the Dionysian Mysteries used wine, animal sacrifices and sex to unit with the Gods, allowing them to possess the worshiper, the Orphic Mysteries practiced an ascetic life, hoping to purge the evil that corrupted the soul. This Mystery Religion taught that the divine part of mortals existed within the soul, not within the physical body and after death the soul would enter into the Underworld where it would be judged. If they had lived a righteous life, they would live for the next three hundred years in the Elysian Fields and then be reborn into another life. It was taught that after three mortal lives the soul would finally be pure enough to be united with the Gods and live in paradise. If they didn't live a righteous life, their soul would be taken to Tartarus were they would remain until their sins were absolved. Because of this belief system, those who practiced Orphic Mysteries wouldn't kill any life, being strict vegetarians themselves, nor would they allow the lustful side of nature to drag them down to the Underworld.

They began praying not only for the living, but for the dead also, believing that their prayers would help to remove the sins of those they loved and shorten their stay within the Underworld. These mysteries were started by some of those who had heard our pleas, and even thought they still worshipped Dionysus, the rituals changed drastically. These rituals co-existed at the same time as the Dionysian Mysteries, and to avoid confusion Orpheus replaced Dionysian as the main God worshipped. Now Orpheus was not a God, nor an immortal, but because he had traveled to the Underworld and not only survived his journey, but was allowed to returned to the land of the living if even for only a brief time, he was thought of in the same light as one of the Dying and Resurrecting Gods. Since he was able to free his wife Eurydice from the despair of the Underworld, prayers directed to him were thought to deliver the soul from death.

Throughout the centuries, there were many others who became associated with the Mystery Religions, Attis was a man who was loved by the Mother Goddess, Mater Magna, and was castrated and died under a pine tree, rises and like Dionysus and Orpheus was another Resurrecting God. This cult was formed by the distorted myths that passed thought the years of Adonis. Attis was none other than my beloved son Adonis, and Mater Magna was my mother, Demeter. Adonis didn't survive death, but since he lived within the Underworld and was temporarily released to live as a mortal, he became associated with Dionysus, and just as Adonis was gored by a boar and bled to death while under a pine tree, Attis was thought to have castrated himself and willingly surrender to his own death, allowing life for others. This cult, like that of Orpheus believed that the body was corrupt therefore any act that gives the body pleasure must also be corrupt. All males who worshipped Attis practiced self-castration.

Attis was the Dying and Resuracting God of the Phrygian, but he was known as Tammuz in Babylonia and Dumuzi in Sumerian myths. In these myths he was not born a God, but only a mortal shepherd who the Fertility Goddess fell in love with. When he died, Inana, which was the name of the Fertility Goddess of Sumerian myths mourned for him and went to the Underworld to bargain for his return. Like me, it was told that he had eaten the food of the dead and would never be allowed to return to the world of the living. After much debating it was decided that he would be allowed to return for part of the year only if another would give up their life and sit in for him during the time he was allowed to return. No one would give up their life for Dumuzi, and Inana was about to withhold all fertility from the land, just as mother had. Finally Dumuzi's sister Geshtinanna came forward and agreed to spend one half the year in the Underworld. Inana allowed the lands to once again become fertile, but only during the months that Dumuzi was released, and once he returned to the Underworld the land once again became barren. The rituals for these Gods began with laments sung at a sacred cedar tree that not only marked the birthplace, but was also considered his mother, followed by a grand procession, which proceeded to the local river where all would wash their sin away.

In areas that were controlled by the Romans, Mithras was the God associated with the Mystery Religions. These cults were greatly influenced by the rites associated with Dionysus, but like the original Mystery Religions they allowed only one of the sexes, instead of women only men, who were thought of as the stronger sex, were the only ones allowed to enter into these rituals. Mithras was an Indo-Iranian Resurrecting Deity who was worshipped only in subterranean caves, symbolic of the Underworld, where the initiates would slay a bull and wash in its blood. This blood was thought to cleanse the sins of those who poured it over themselves. The initiates then consumed the bull and just as the followers of Dionysus had believed, they thought that by eating the flesh of a sacrificial animal they were consuming the God himself.

Of all the cults that based their beliefs on the Eleusinian Mysteries, the one that was the closest to our rituals were that of Isis and Osiris. During the time that these rites began Egypt had already been Hellenized, and Isis was associated not only with Demeter, Goddess of Fertility, but also me, Queen of the Dead. She was known as "The Giver of Seasonal Fertility", the "Mother of the dead, who takes them into her womb and rebirths them", and "the Goddess of Transformation." Hades was also turned into one of the Egyptian Gods, where he was known as Osiris, King of the land of the Dead. Slowly the Egyptian myths absorbed those of Dionysus, Adonis, and Orpheus and my dear husband Hades was worshiped as the Dying and Resurrecting God, named Osiris.

Some of the stories of Isis are remarkably similar to stories associated with both mother and I. Once such example is when Isis was searching for her husband Osiris.

According to the original Egyptian myths Osiris was originally a God of the Universe, but his brother Seth was consumed with jealousy and wished to destroy his brother and take over as ruler. Seth crafted a beautiful chest and when Osiris commented on the craftsmanship his brother said to all present,

"I will give this chest to who ever fits within it".

Knowing that only Osiris would fit. The other gods tried, but none fit perfectly, until Osiris came. Once inside the chest the evil God and his followers nailed the lid tight. Seth then threw the chest into the Nile where it traveled out to sea. It was not long before Osiris' wife, Isis, found out that her husband was missing. She searched for him for nine days without any sign, but on the ninth day a young child told her what he and his friends saw,

"We saw the God Seth, followed by many men, take a large wooden box and release it into the Nile River". The boy told her as he pointed to the direction the chest floated in. Isis followed the river until she reached the city of Byblos in Phoenicia where she was confident she would find her husband. She continued her search. Now during the nine days she was searching the chest reached the shore and miraculously a tamarisk tree grew around it.

This tree was so unusual and so beautiful that the king of Byblos had it cut down and fashioned into a pillar for his palace. Isis knew she was close to her beloved husband for she could feel his presence, but she still couldn't find him. In her despair she dressed in mourning clothes and sat by a fountain and began weeping. The queen's servants arrived to fetch water and found the Goddess sitting alone crying. They took her back to their queen, who had just given birth to a son. The Goddess was welcomed by the family and became nurse for the newborn.

Once she stepped into the palace, she felt her dear husband's pulse and knew he was near. That night, while the others slept she searched the palace and found the grand pillar, which contained the chest that concealed her husband's body. She didn't say anything about this, but each night she would go to the pillar and touch the wood and cry at the loose of her husband. The only happiness she found was when she tended the queen's infant son. She didn't feed him milk, but gave him the food of the Gods and each night she would place him within the hearth fire to burn away his mortality. One night the queen was awoken by the cries of her child and when she went into the nursery she saw the infant within the hearth. She screamed, and the spell was broken. Isis revealed herself to the queen and king as the Goddess that she was, just as mother had when she was in Eleusis. They fell to the floor and begged her forgiveness.

"I will forgave you, but you must give me something in return". She said to them as she lifted the queen to her feet.

"All that we own is yours". Both the queen and king answered.

"I wish for only this beautiful pillar". Isis said as she touched the wood and felt her husband's heartbeat. The following morning the king had his servants remove the pillar and once Isis touched it both disappeared in a great flash.

The setting was changed from Greece to Egypt, and the Goddess was Isis instead of Demeter. Isis searched nine days and nights, but not for her beloved daughter, instead for her husband. A king and queen took her in and she, as a reward for their hospitality tried to make their son immortal, but was interrupted on the final day, breaking the spell. Even with these modifications, it is hard to not notice that this is essentially the same as the story that mother told here. Once Isis freed her husband, he became Lord of the Underworld where he ruled the dead, with his beloved sister and wife Isis at his side.

.

untimes.com

LUANN

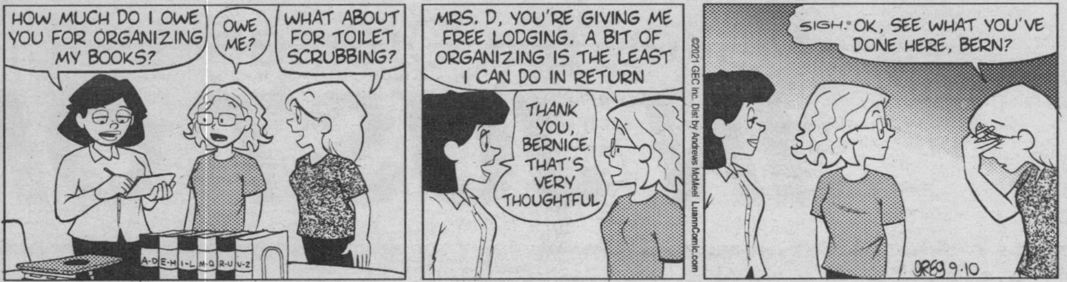

PEARLS BEFORE SWINE

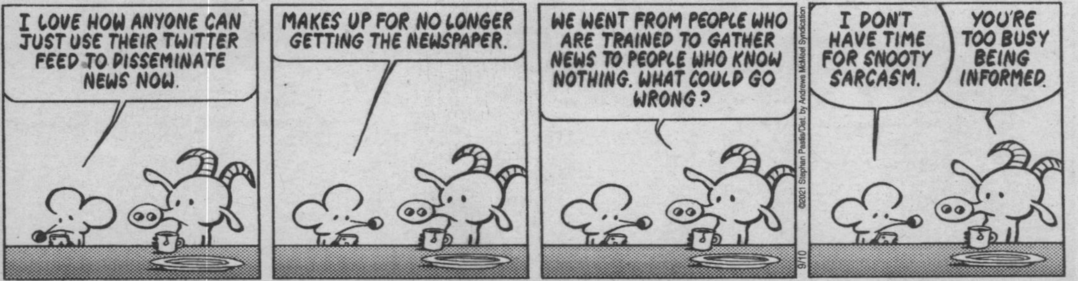

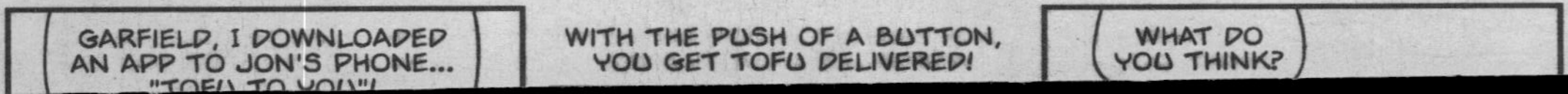

Make Your Ordinary Bathroom

IN JUST ONE
AS LITTLE AS

Part 3

XXII
Persephone

THERE WERE MANY other mortals who risked their lives by entering into the Underworld; some, like the heroes whose stories I have just told you were able to cheat the Lord of Death and return back to the land of the living, but other were not permitted to leave our realm. Most who dared set foot into the empire of the dead were destined to spend eternity there. The stories I have told you were about Greek heroes, but the Greeks were not the only people who were brave enough to risk their lives by making the long journey deep into the Underworld, there were men and women from all the civilized lands who would risk everything for one glimpse of the life that awaited them behind the veil. Look at the different myths from around the world and you'll find stories of heroes who journeyed to the Underworld to free a loved one, to cheat the God of Death of his prize, or to learn about the Mysteries of Life and Death. I won't bore you with any more of these tales, for I could tell many of their stories; instead, I will continue here by explaining how during the early part of the current Era Hades was transformed into the fallen Angel named Lucifer and became known throughout the Christian world as Satan, the enemy of their true God.

Hades was not the only God altered by the new religion; all of the Gods and Goddesses who lived on Mount Olympus went through some sort of transformation, but not all became demons, some became the many saints of this new religion. I won't lie and say that the Gods who lived on Mount Olympus didn't suffer; some were totally destroyed, while others slowly faded into nothingness. But, nothing could compare to what became of those of us who lived within the Underworld. We endured almost two centuries of existing as demons, and while we grew physically stronger, it was torture for me to look at my husband and see the monster that the Christians turned him into. You may wonder how the Gods, as powerful as we were, could allow their entire existence to be altered, and that is what I will explain here.

****

A little over two thousand years ago a new religion emerged and with it a new god, and this god, unlike those before him, wouldn't allow others to share his domain. Let me give you a brief history of the beginning of this new religion, which became known as Christianity. I call Christianity a new religion even though it has already survived almost two thousand years, and I suspect it will continue for many more, for you see I am much older than that and have seen many new religions begin and prosper, only to be replaced with a newer, improved version. Some of these cults are similar in their doctrines but many don't resemble the parent religion at all. Religions, like everything else in the Universe must either change with the times or slowly fade into nothingness.

Five thousand years ago Demeter was worshipped as the Mother Goddess of the Earth and Zeus as the Father God of the Sky by all cultures throughout the world. Each of these cultures had a different name for both Gods, too many to list here, and they would respond to them all. The other Gods and Goddesses were also worshipped since the beginnings of human civilizations. Each culture had a Goddess of Love, a War God, the God of Death, and a Trickster God; again they might not have had the names I have used in my story, but the faces were the same. The people who lived during these times weren't the primitive cultures that you are led to believe, they understood more than they are given credit for, they understood the laws of the Universe. Even though there were many different Gods worshipped, the people of these primitive cultures understood that even though their neighbor called their Gods by different names, and they might have been dressed differently, they were essentially worshipping the same deities, and they would respect the beliefs of each other. This religious tolerance continued for centuries.

The seeds of change were planted a little over three thousand years ago when a mortal man, the founder of Zoroastrianism, the religion of ancient Persia, was born. His parents named their first born son Zoroaster, and the wise men affirmed that the boy would grow to be a great man. As he grew, Zoroaster, sought all knowledge, listening to any who was willing to teach him. When he was still a young man, he began to question the faith of his people. This prophet believed that there couldn't possibly be hundreds of different Gods and Goddesses governing the various parts of the Universe, instead he began preaching the belief in only one God, the true God, who he called Ahura Mazda, meaning 'Wise Lord'. Again some believe that this was just another name for Zeus, and it might have been. Ahura Mazda was the God of both the Heavens and the Universe and was responsible for creating all life on earth; was not Zeus also the God of both the Heavens and Universe, and was he not worshipped above all the other Gods. Now I don't know if Zoroaster intended for Zeus to be the model of his God, but soon after this religion began Zeus was answering those who directed their prayers to Ahura Mazda.

At first this new religion had few followers and would have died with the prophet, but he was a clever man, just as the wise men predicted, and knew that for his beliefs to be passed on through the generations he would have to convert not only the few followers he currently had, but he must convert the entire nation. He approached the Persian Emperor Cyrus, bowing low before speaking.

"Just as there is one Emperor who was blessed by fate to rule over the Earth, there can be only one God, Ahura Mazda, who rules the Universe. It is by his grace alone that the Emperor received his power".

Cyrus liked this thought, and soon Zoroaster had the Emperor's support, and not long after that that Zoroastrianism was declared as the national religion of Persia. With only one religion and one god, and there was no room for the other Gods and Goddesses who dwelt on Mount Olympus, therefore Cyrus had to destroy them.

It wasn't as easy as Zoroaster thought to convert the common people, and though he had the Emperor Cyrus' army behind him, he failed to destroy the old Gods. With no other choice the prophet had to assimilated all the old Gods into his believe structure. The old Gods, the ones who are my family, continued to be worshipped, but they were distinguished from Ahura Mazda as lesser deities, whose only function was to serve as a link between the human realm and that of the Heavens, similar to Saints or Angels. They were not worshipped the same way the Ahura Mazda was, instead they were called upon only to deliver the prayers of the faithful to the Wise Lord. If one wished to bring love into their lives instead of praying to Aphrodite, the Goddess of Love, they would direct their prayers to the Angel who governed love, and he would then intercede on their behalf and deliver their message to Ahura Mazda.

Zoroastrianism outlived the prophet, and it became the first true monotheistic religion, but some who were forced to convert to this religion didn't want to let go of their old beliefs.

"If your god Ahura Mazda is all powerful and good, why then did he create so much evil in this world"? Some of the common people would ask. The priests had no answers at first, so more of their followers would soon go back to their old ways. The Zoroastrianism priests couldn't consent to the belief that Ahura Mazda was responsible for any evil, so again they modified his theology to fit into the beliefs of the common people. Zoroastrianism was no longer a monotheistic religion, but had evolved into a dualism religion, a religion were good and evil could never co-exist peacefully, as they had for so many centuries, but were now in a constant struggle for control of the entire Universe and the souls of all who lived on Earth. It was believed that Earth was nothing more than the battleground between good and evil, and mortals had the ability to choose which side they would support.

"Do not condemn your souls eternal suffering. The only guarantee to reach paradise after death is to fight with Ahura Mazda, and destroy evil". The Priests would lecture their people.

These changes were readily accepted, but again the common people started questioning the theology. If Ahura Mazda wasn't responsible for all the evil within the world, then where did it come from? The old myths were studied and after many years, the High

Priests had found an explanation. As I had said earlier Zeus was the model for Ahura Mazda, therefore it was only logical that Zeus' brother Hades, who dwells in a world filled with only death and decay would become the spirit of darkness, Angra Mainyu. Angra Mainyu as the personification of evil wasn't only responsible for discord among mortals, but it was thought that he took great pleasure in creating harsh weather, disease, poverty, death and all the evils throughout the Universe. The world according to Zoraster was created by Ahura Mazda, and evil came into the world when his twin brother Angra Mainyu, who was born only seconds after him, tried to overthrow his kingdom, and when he failed he decided if he could never rule the Universe, he would have to destroy it.

Of course since Ahura Mazda ruled from the Heavens, the evil god must have ruled from somewhere on earth, and since the dead would spend eternity buried deep within the earth it was only logical that this is where the evil god must dwell feeding on the souls of the dead. Thus the Underworld became the domain of Angra Mainyu and was now associated with everything that was evil. The Persians believed that at death, the soul of the departed would travel for four days until it reached the Cinvat Bridge, a long bridge, as narrow as a single edged blade that stretched between this world and the next, just as the River Styx separates the world of the living from that of the dead. Here three judges would each look deep within the soul of the newly decease and decide his fate. Once judged, the spirit was required to walk along this narrow bridge that suspended them over the lake of fire that contained the souls of the damned. Only those who had lived a just life and had a pure heart would be able reach Airyana Vaehjah, the land beyond death, or the Elysian Fields as I have called it; all the others would fall to the fiery pit below where their souls would be devoured by the flames. These flames couldn't destroy the soul, but only purge it of evil; therefore the poor souls who were thrown into this fiery pit had to endure this pain for all eternity. Even though for many centuries mortals feared Hades and the Underworld, neither was thought of as evil, you see death is a natural process. Once Zoroastrianism became the official religion the Underworld and all those who dwelled within it were considered totally evil and had to be destroyed.

The Persians, who couldn't explain the injustices of life, embraced these beliefs and soon all within the Empire were converted. As these people traveled throughout the Middle Eastern nations they took their beliefs with them, and these were absorbed by the many different cultures of the area. One particular nation, that of the Hebrew people, adopted these beliefs and immediately began making them their own, blending the original monotheistic beliefs with their belief system and created another new religion, Judaism. During the first few centuries Judaism was very similar to Zoroastrianism but instead of worshipping Ahura Mazda, the Hebrews named their God, Yahweh. As the years passed the two religions began to split and throughout the generations they grow further and further apart. The early Hebrews were true monotheistic, believing that all came from Yahweh, the good and the evil alike while Zoroastrianism continued to preach a dualistic religion.

Now as I had just said, the Hebrews believed that everything within the Universe, evil along with good was the doing of Yahweh, and Satan was only a servant of his, acting on orders when he brought evil into the world. Zeus answered to the name of Yahweh, as he did to all the other names of God, while Hades was thought of as nothing more than his servant named either Satan or Lucifer, who would punish mankind as his brother directed. The Old Testament refers to Satan as acting on Yahweh's orders when he causes misfortune to mortals.

Even though Judaism is today one of the three main religions in the world, it wasn't popular with the common people who lived in the Middle East three thousand years ago. Again it was hard to convert the peasants and most of them continued to worship the various Gods and Goddesses of the locale areas. The elders didn't approve of this and were determined to destroy the old pagan religions. Instead of transferring the old Gods into Angels like the Persians did and allowing them to still be worshipped to some extent, the Hebrews turned all the Gods and Goddesses into Demons and it was now forbidden to show them any respect. No matter how hard they tried, they couldn't stop the common people from participating in one of the many different Mystery religions that were abundant within the Middle East during this period in history. The Jewish Elders tried in vain to destroy these Mystery religions, stating that they were only an excuse for orgies and sacrificing human lives to evil demons, but as hard as they tried, they couldn't stop all from participating in these sacred rituals.

After many decades of fighting what seemed like a loosing battle, a small group of the elders decided to use these religions to their advantage by combining it with their beliefs and creating a new religion that would appeal to both those who were true believers as well as to the common people. One of the beliefs that was unique to the ancient Hebrew people was that of a coming messiah, a man born of a virgin, who would destroy all evil and unite the people of the world. Wasn't this messiah already being worshipped in one of the Mystery religions, they thought? By modifying one of the dying and resurrecting Gods that was already being worshipped, and turning him into their messiah who was expected to come to earth and unit all people, this small group of men were able to convert many of the followers of the old religion while giving this new religion a history that could be used to their advantage.

This messiah, who would become known throughout the ages as Jesus Christ, was a God that I have already introduced you to; he was known as Dionysus for centuries before receiving this new name. I'm sure that some who read this will think that what I say here is blasphemy, but before you turn your head to what I'm saying, look at some of the similarities between both Jesus and Dionysus. Jesus was believed to be born to a mortal woman named Mary, who as a virgin was impregnated by the word of the God of the Hebrew people alone, and as a virgin she gave birth to the messiah. Was not Dionysus also born to a mortal woman, a virgin named Semele who never saw the Greek God who loved her? Both mothers were taken up to the heavens when they died; it is believed that Mary never died, at least not physically, instead she was transported up to sit at her son's side, and even though Semele spent many years within the Underworld before becoming an immortal, she too was lifted to Mount Olympus to live with her son. Jesus is a Dying and Resurrecting God, and so is Dionysus. Jesus' death was at the hands of his enemies, and he was crucified only to rise after entering into the womb of the earth; Dionysus also died at the hands of his enemies, instead of the Romans, it was the Titans who killed him, and his soul was placed into the womb of a mortal to be reborn again to life. Is it a coincidence that Dionysus is the God of Wine, and when his followers drank the sacred wine during their festivals, they believed that they were actually consuming the blood of the God, thus uniting with his divine presence; during communion the Christians also believe the wine had miraculously been turned into the blood of their savior. Those who were initiated into the Mysteries of Dionysus were believed to be born again and were promised eternal life; those who converted to the Christian religion thought that the belief in Jesus Chris alone would ensure that their soul would join him and dwell within the heavens after death, and that after baptism their souls were born again in the faith of Christ.

Now during the first few centuries of this new religion, which was called the Jewish Christian movement, it grew and grew until it reached all corners of the world. Theoretical equality of all men and a promise of forgiveness for repented sins, beliefs that were similar to the Mystery Religions, made this religion attractive to the common people of all nations, and soon they embraced it. Had not Christianity began, I'm sure that one of the other Mystery Religions would have evolved into something very similar. For the first few hundred years this religion there was no organization of the Church, and doctrines varied from town to town. It was centuries later that the Emperor of Rome, Constantine united Christianity while making it the official religion of the Roman Empire and all Pagan religions were proclaimed to be demonic. Constantine wanted an authoritarian religion, encouraging his subjects to have blind faith in those who held power within his structure. It was during his life and by his laws that most of the damage to the old religions occurred, before he came into power religious tolerance was still practiced and the people were allowed to continue to worship in their local temples. But once the Emperor adopted this new religion this tolerance was no longer practiced. He ordered all the so-called Pagan temples to be destroyed, along with any who still worshipped the old Gods. Many innocent lives were ended during this period in history and forced to enter into the Underworld before their lives were complete, all this in the name of the one true god.

Constantine took Cyrus' belief in One God, One Religion and made it his own, knowing that this would consolidate his claim of One Empire, One Emperor. And even though he embraced this new religion publicly, he refused to be baptized until on his deathbed. He did this so he could continue to commit atrocities throughout his life and still be guaranteed a place in heaven after his death, believing that a Christian baptism would purify his soul of all his sins. In the last year of his life he killed his only son, Crispus; suffocated his wife, Fausta; then killed his sister's husband and their son. He didn't care how his message was spread, only that it reached all of the civilized lands. Because of this, Christianity's early history is rife with bloodshed, forgery and fraud. I pause here to add; Constantine's shade still resides within the Dungeon of the Damned, Tartartus.

Even though many were put to death if caught worshipping the Pagan Gods and Goddesses, there were still many who continued to do so. Since Christianity couldn't totally destroy these Gods, they like the Persians, converted these pagan deities into the saints of this new religion. Those who were having problems with their love lives would not beg Aphrodite to have pity on their soul, instead they would direct their prayers to Saint Valentine. Ares was the War God, but Christian soldiers would never call to him, instead they would send their prayers to Saint George to protect them in battle. Blacksmiths gave Saint Dunstan honors instead of Hephaestus, while hunters prayed to Saint Eustace to ensure a successful hunt, ignoring Artemis altogether. Asclepius, the God of Medicine was replaced with many different saints; Saint Cosmas and Damian were the patrons of Doctors; while healers called to Saint Bridget; Saint Geregon was the saint that was invoked to relieve migraines; for rheumatism, James the Great was called; and if one was bitten by a snake they would pray to Saint Paul. The Muses were also replaced by saints; Luke was the saint of painters; Columba of poets, Genesius of actors, John the Apostle of writers; Vitus of dancers; and Cecilia of musicians.

The festivals that were once dedicated to these Gods were also not forgotten; instead they too were Christianized, and soon became Christian holidays with little trace of their pagan origins. The two major festivals of the Elusinian Mysteries were no exceptions. The Lesser Mysteries were celebrated in the autumn when the harvest was complete, but the Christians gave thanks not to Demeter for giving her blessings to the land, but to their God instead, and this became a day when all would thank the Lord for the blessings they received for the previous year. The Greater Mysteries, which were held in the early spring and were associated with the Dying and Resurrecting God were tuned into what has become known in modern times as Easter, a time to celebrate the return of Jesus, or to the pagans, it was the return of their God Dionysus and the fertility of the land. By allowing the populace to celebrate the same holidays they were used to, the Christians were able to convert still more followers in these early years. Some of the Christian scholars attempt to explain the many similarities of the Christian faith with those of the pagan cults as a compromise that was necessary in order to gain converts. Worship rites, locations, dates and many of the attributes of the Gods were absorbed into early Christianity.

Goddess worship was something that the early Christian leaders didn't tolerate, nor did they allow it to be assimilated into their sacred rites. Since it was a woman who they believed was responsible for original sin, they felt that women could never be equal to man, and wanting to keep them subordinated tried to exterminate all worship of the Goddess, but they were unsuccessful. While pagans believed that it was the God who ruled the Heavens, it was the Goddess who controlled the land and all fertility, therefore she was thought of as more important to physical life. Since the Church leaders, who were all men, couldn't destroy Goddess worship entirely they were forced to give her honor as the mother of Jesus, and soon Mary, the Virgin Mother became the Mother Goddess that was worshipped since the beginning of human origins as my mother, Demeter once was. Not only women, but men also embraced the worship of the Virgin Mary, seeing in her worship a way of honoring the Goddess that was missing from their lives. Both Jesus and his Father were thought to be concerned with Heavenly matters, while Mary would be there to hear the prayers offered to her by the common people. She would then intercede on their behalf and deliver these prayers to her son, the savior Jesus. Being mortal herself, she understood the pains that humans felt and wouldn't hesitate in offering her assistance when called. Again, these believes were very similar to those of my brother Dionysus.

You might think that these qualities aren't what you would expect of Demeter. I have portrayed her here as being selfish and spiteful, and I admit that at times she is, but you must realize that no one, not even the Gods are perfect. Demeter had her motives for her actions so many years ago, and I truly believe that she has regretted some of these. As I had stated many times during my story the Fates control even the lives of the Gods, and she was only acting the role that she was destined to play. No matter how I feel about her she is not only my mother, but like Mary she is the Mother of all Life; weather spiritual or mortal.

All prayers directed to Demeter were answered. When Psyche called to her, she couldn't refuse; when I went to her, accusing her of tempting Hades with the mortal woman Minthe, she held me in her arms and comforted me. Even though I slapped her face, it was her love that forced me to return to my husband and allowed him to explain what had happened. It was also mother who stood by my side as both Hades and I were transformed from being Gods, who though not worshipped were given honors, into hideous demons and almost destroyed us.

XXIII
Demeter

WHILE CHRISTIANITY EMBRACED the image of Zeus as their Father God, the creator of all life; Dionysus as Jesus, the God who lived a mortal life and who yearly allowed himself to be ritually killed to save humanity; and I, Demeter as the Virgin Mary; it nearly destroyed my brother Hades and my daughter Kore. Hades and those who lived within the Underworld had no place within the hierarchy of the Christian saints even as a servant of the Father as he had once been; therefore it was believed that Hades was thrown out of Mount Olympus in a war that was modeled on the war between the Titans and the Olympians. The Christian version has Hades plotting a way to control his own destiny and persuading one-third of the other Gods, or Angels as they soon became known, to wage war on the one true god for supremacy. The two mighty armies fought for centuries, but since their god, like Zeus, could control the elements he was finally able to overthrow the rebels. With the war lost Hades, who was now known as Lucifer by the Christians, was thrown out of Heaven by God and for nine days and nights he tumbled down through the universe, spinning and spinning until the earth finally broke his fall. The impact didn't stop him though, for where he hit a giant fissure formed and once freed from the surface of the earth he continued to fall for nine more days and nine more nights until he reached the very heart of the earth. He had reached the fiery pit that was to become his kingdom Hell, where all unbelievers would be punished for eternity.

All of the other Gods and Goddesses who lived with my daughter in the Underworld were doomed to the same fate as Hades, now known as Satan, Lucifer, the Prince of Evil or the simply the Devil. They were no longer neither Gods nor the once beautiful Nymphs that they once were, but since they are immortals and couldn't be destroyed, they were transformed into the minions of Satan who would be allowed by their leader to leave the fiery pit, Hell, only to travel to earth to tempt those pure of heart and condemn them to the same fate as their pagan brothers and sisters.

My daughter explained earlier how that Judaism and early Christianity viewed Hades only as a servant of the Father God, used by him as a henchman who would carry out the creator's evil instructions. Through Satan, on the command of God, plagues and floods were sent to destroy the wicked. Two cities, Sodom and Gomorrah were completely destroyed not by the hand God himself, but by the Angel of the Lord, who acting only on his boss's orders sent fire and brimstone raining down on these cities, destroying all life that dwelt there. During the early years of this religion there was neither an all-good creator God nor an all-evil Devil, it was God who judged all and those who he wished to punish he would give over to Satan to do his dirty work. Like all beliefs, these views slowly changed and it was during the Middle Ages that Hades became the Devil, as he is known today, who was responsible for all evil throughout the universe, removing God's hand entirely from all that was not pure. He had become not only the enemy of humanity, but also of the creator, and the Church preached that humans should not only fear him, but do whatever was in their power to destroy him totally.

At first neither Hades nor my daughter noticed the mortals changing views of them, you see Hades never cared to involve himself with mortal life at all and very seldom left the Underworld, and since mortals had never made offering to him, it would have been several centuries before he even realized that his image had been distorted into that of a evil demon who wished only to destroy humans if it wasn't for my beloved daughter. Being born of a Fertility Goddess it was hard for her to adjust to life within the Underworld; it is not natural for one who gives life to be content surrounded by nothing but death and decay for so long during the year, so when she became Hades wife she did her best to greet each soul who crossed over into the land of phantoms and make their transition as pleasant as possible. Even thought she wasn't worshipped as the Goddess of the Underworld, she was given honors during the Mystery Religions in both her functions as Goddess of Death but more importantly as Goddess of Rebirth. When the Christians took over she too was transformed into a demon, a demon who they believed would attack sleeping men and suck their life away as she made love with them the entire night. She was transformed into the demon named Lilith. I found it ironic that she, one of the few Goddesses who still remains faithful to her husband through the many that centuries have passed since their marriage, and even though she ruled over the dead, she never brought any mortals to her world, that her image was mutated into this sex starved beast who would drag the souls of those she had made love with down to the Underworld for all eternity.

Kore tried to pretend that this new image didn't bothered her, but I could see the sorrow in her eyes every spring when she would greet me for our brief time together, and I shared her pain. You see, we Gods thought that since we were immortal that nothing could touch us; we were mistaken. The Gods created mortal life on earth, but throughout the centuries that this life has existed we became dependent on these mortals. We gained our strength through the offerings and prayers dedicated to us. When these stopped, our entire existence was threatened. We began to transform and to become what we were believed to be. After a few hundred years Kore greeted me one summer and the sight of her caused me to faint. Her once beautiful white skin had a blue-green tint to it and there were dark circles under her lifeless eyes. She was terribly thin, her cheekbones prominent and her beautiful dark brown hair was nothing but a matted mess that hung loosely over her tattered robe. She looked worn and weary, and all around her was the smell of death. My heart broke at this sight.

"My dear daughter, what has happened to you"?

"Mother, don't worry, I'm fine". Was all that she would say to me, but I'm her mother, and I knew that she wasn't all right.

She was no longer my daughter Kore, but had become the demon Lilith, and even though her image was mutated into this hideous demon, I think that it was her husband's transformation that nearly destroyed her. Hades' nose and chin became elongated, and his ears pointed while his face became as red as blood and two large horns started to protrude from his forehead and grew until they curved over his head. His beautiful green eyes became the yellow glowing eyes of a hungry beast. His lower body was entirely covered with thick gray fur and his legs were bent like those of a goat, while his toes atrophied and his feet slowly transformed into the hoofs of a wild beast. He also assimilated some of the characteristics of Thanatos, the God of Death, as large bat-like wings, associating him with the night and all that was considered evil, sprouted from his back. This image of him was one of the more benign; artists of the time portrayed him with fiery red glowing eyes, spewing mouths covering his entire body, spindly arms and legs with a bloated torso that was covered with oozing sores and breath that could melt steel.

The church had preached to the masses to fear the Devil, who it was believed would come to earth with his phallus hanging out only to tempt those he came across, both male and female, to give into their lust and allow him to satisfy their sexual desires. It was thought that when they gave into him, they were being pulled further away from God and dragged closer to Hell for eternity. As I had already said, this was the furthest from the truth; both Hades and my daughter were and still are faithful to each other. Yes Hades slept with Minthe, but as I had stated before, it isn't natural for the Gods to be faithful for eternity. No matter what my feelings for him are, I'm positive he would never have done anything to hurt my daughter.

It was natural for mortals to give these characteristics to Hades; during this period unprecedented catastrophes almost destroyed one-third the population of Europe. Famine due to climate change, economic collapse, social upheaval, war and plagues such as the Black Death had not only frightened mortals, but also changed their views on both God and the Devil. With nothing else, they viewed salvation of the soul as paramount. It was during this time that the devil was believed by all to have the ability to posses individuals, causing them to foam at the mouth and thrash around on the ground. Blindness, deformities and illness, both physical and mental were all thought to come not from God as punishment for some sin as earlier generations believed, instead it was the Devil who inflicted these evils on mortals. His only reason for causing such suffering was to gain pleasure from tormenting the poor mortal souls.

The church preached of the devil, a totally evil being who would consume the poor souls of sinners, scaring the common people into following their rules, and by keeping the masses ignorant they would ensure their success. They used this fear of the Devil to their advantage, stating that life on Earth is a battle between God and Satan, who had by now become humanities greatest enemy. It was the church's duty to reform the pagans, and if they couldn't do this, they must be destroyed. It was this thinking that sent tens of thousands of innocent victims to their new home, the Underworld, during the witch-hunts.

During these centuries when my daughter returned to me for the spring and summer months she didn't come with me as I traveled around the globe insuring fertility, instead she stayed on Mount Olympus and tried to assist those who were suffering almost as bad as those on earth. You must understand that the Gods of the Underworld weren't the only ones affected, those who remained on Mount Olympus also suffered by these changing beliefs. Before Christianity developed, and even during its early history, the Gods and Goddesses living in Zeus' palace didn't even notice any changes. Of course our names where changed, along with the rituals honoring us, but we were still worshipped, if only as saints. We existed like this for many centuries, but slowly the followers of the Old Religions died and were replaced by Christians who would no longer worship the older Gods, under any name. What happened next, no one on Mount Olympus expected; some of the Gods and Goddesses began to fade. At first no one noticed what was happening, their voices became softer, their skin a little paler, hardly noticeable at first, but over time, some of the lesser immortals faded completely from existence.

Now of course, I was still worshipped, if only as Mother Nature, and I suffer only a little. Zeus survived only because he is such a strong God, but he no longer was the youthful God he once was, his hair and beard became as gray as that of mortal men when they grow older and his body was bent over with weariness, causing him to have to use a cane to support him when he walked. The Christians envisioned their God as an elderly man dressed in long white robes who sat on this thrown while his son Jesus ruled the Heavens, and this is what the once youthful God Zeus had become. It was hard for me to see Zeus, the most powerful of the Gods slowly turn into this feeble old man.

You see the Gods and Goddesses are immortal, we cannot die, but what we didn't know at the time was that we obtained our strength and vigor through the rituals that were performed in our honor. Once these rituals stopped, our vitality slowly began to fade away. As I had mentioned earlier I was hardly affected at all, being a Fertility Goddess I was able to sustain on the folk traditions associated with the fertility of the land, and also prayers directed to the Virgin Mary. Dionysus became the Dying and Resurrecting God that the new religion created and continued to be worshipped as Jesus Christ and actually became stronger during this period. Aphrodite was also one of the lucky Goddesses, for no matter how many times they were warned, young men and women alike would pray to the Goddess of Love. The Goddesses of Fate along with Ares, the War God were also only affected a little, these concepts were kept alive with the War between Heaven and Hell and the belief in the predestination of the human soul.

But others weren't so lucky, Hera and Poseidon were both almost entirely destroyed. Poseidon took to his palace deep within the sea and dared not venture out for many centuries, even now he seldom leaves his palace. Hera, who had no place to hide, suffered tremendously; she, like her husband grew old frail. It was hard for her, the wife of the Great God Zeus to be turned into nothing more than an old hag. When I was in the palace I would hear her at night crying, and Zeus would try his best to comfort her, speaking gently,

"My love, don't worry, this too shall pass and we Gods will return to our former glory".

I wanted desperately to believe his words, but I didn't think we would survive.

After a few centuries Mount Olympus became deserted, the only residents were Zeus and Hera; Hestia, who would not leave her brother's side; Hermes, who traveled between the Underworld and the palace and Dionysus, who as Zeus' favorite son took over ruling the Heavens. The other Gods and Goddesses left and dwelt on earth disguised as mere mortals, hiding their true identity, hoping that they will once again be able to return to their home and sit next to the great

God Zeus. Now the palace, without servants to take care of, started to become rundown. Zeus, not able to control the skies as he once was able to, couldn't prevent harsh weather from entering into the palace. After a few years the rain and snow caused the marble to discolor and crack so Zeus called to the Cyclopes to build a roof over the Great Hall. There were only a few of the Cyclopes left and those who survived no longer had the strength or ability needed to complete such a tremendous task, so the Great Hall was deserted.

Zeus and Hera would stay in their private chamber, allowing only Hestia or myself to bring them their evening meals. Dionysus tried to take over running the palace, and it isn't that he was not able to do this, but without servants assisting him it was impossible to run such a place. He also wasn't there year-round, during the summer months it was his duty to assist me with the fertility on earth since Kore could not. At first I didn't wish for Kore to spend the short time we had together in the palace and so far away from me since I missed her dearly, but I knew that she wouldn't be able to endure her life much longer if she didn't allow herself the rest that she desperately needed. During these six months Hermes would attend to her, and while this bothered Hades greatly, I was glad that there was someone there for her who I knew would care for her as I would have. Hades couldn't stand the though of losing his beloved wife to Hermes and enduring eternity as this horrible beast that he had now become, tried desperately to keep Hermes in the Underworld during the spring and summer months.

I have to admit that at first I was surprised that Hermes didn't try to take advantage of the situation, knowing that he desired Kore, but now that I look back I realize that he didn't have enough strength to play his little games. Since he is associated with the Underworld in his role as Psychompompus, he didn't suffer the pain of slowly fading, but he wasn't able to escape the destruction of the Gods entirely. I think that Hermes was just a little afraid of incurring Hades wrath by seducing his wife. During these centuries Hades had increased his powers ten-fold and was now the most powerful of the Gods. He could have easily overthrown his brother and ruled in his place, but he became accustomed to being alone after millennium of living within the Underworld. That was not the only reason why Hades didn't try to take over the thrown, after seeing what had happened to his brother Zeus, he realized that he couldn't endured the torture of slowly withering away.

The Gods who dwelled within the Underworld didn't have to endure the fate of slowly fading away or growing old and weary that those who were on Mount Olympus did, you see fear is a strong emotion, much stronger than love, therefore once they were transferred into demons they actually started to become stronger. Kore also gained new powers and during this period she no longer had to ask permission from the Moirai to release a soul from death, she possessed this power herself. Even if she knew that she had this power I don't think she would have released any souls. She had become bitter to the mortals who had destroyed her husband and created a monster in his place. After watching those who I loved slowly fade as I sat by helpless, I thought that nothing could be worst. But I was mistaken; the sight of my daughter nearly broke my heart. I don't know which was worst, sitting by idly as you slowly fade from existence without being able to do anything about it, or being turned into a hideous monster but with tremendous strength.

XXIV
Persephone

I DON'T KNOW how we endured these long years within our prison, the Underworld, and even though I still loved my husband dearly we slowly grew apart. For several hundred years Hades and I didn't share a bed, instead he spent his nights alone in his private chamber and no matter how many times I would try to visit him there he would refuse me. I imagined that the sight of what I had become repelled him, and yes I became bitter. During those long years I, like Hades, grew in strength, and as mother had stated, I no longer needed to ask the Moirai to release the soul of one that I felt pity on, but I didn't once free any soul who entered our world. I felt no pity on these mortals, mortals who nearly destroyed my world. We endured like this for centuries and I watched as Gods who were much older than I faded completely from existence, and I waited patiently until this same fate would befall me.

It was during the Industrial Age that I thought that this time had finally come, and I welcomed it. The people of this age would not allow silly superstitions rule their lives; they no longer believed that the Gods alone held their fate. Science was slowly replacing religion as new discoveries were being made almost daily. It was during this period that Zeus suffered the most, and if he were not the strongest of the Gods I don't think he would have survived. During the part of the year that I was on Mount Olympus I would take him his meals and could hardly believe my eyes. Father, who I feared my entire life was nothing more than a feeble old man who only sat on his thrown drooling. My heart broke every time I saw him. As the God of the Christians faded from people's thoughts, so too did Zeus, and I knew that it wouldn't be long before he too would finally be destroyed. At that time I couldn't understand how mother survived these long years, she was not as strong as Zeus, and yet it was he who I was looking after not her. Much later I realized that Demeter survived by taking on a different role during these years, she was no longer the Goddess of Grain and Fertility but had become Mother Nature itself. No matter how hard science tried to explain nature, it could not, therefore Demeter not only survived, but grew in strength.

It was near the end of the summer at the turn of the century that mother requested Hermes to deliver a message to Hades inviting him to Mount Olympus where they could discuss the future of the Gods. I was surprised that he came, knowing that he didn't like leaving the Underworld, especially during this period. The sight of him caused mother to gasp. She hadn't seen her brother in hundreds of years and even though I tried to prepare her for the sight, it still shocked her. It took mother a few moments to gather herself before finally speaking to him, trying to convince him to return to Mount Olympus and rule in Zeus' place, for of all the Gods left he was the strongest. He couldn't consent to her wish. For thousands of years the Underworld was his home and he wouldn't leave it now.

"You must return to Mount Olympus and rule in your brother's place, if you don't I fear that our home will be destroyed". She begged him.

He didn't respond.

"Once Mount Olympus had been destroyed and the Gods are all gone, who will look after the mortals on earth"? She asked.

"Why should I care what happens to these mortals, were they not the ones who turned me into this hideous monster", He said, adding after a few seconds, "I care not what happens to them".

"It isn't for their sake that I ask you to take over Zeus' rule, but for our sake. We will all fade from existence if nothing is done".

"Don't you think I know that, every day when I look at your daughter I see that she is slowly becoming transparent. I know that she doesn't have much more time left before she too fades from existence". He shouted at Demeter. I don't believe that he would have said those words if I was present in the room with them. I waited outside with Hermes and when I heard his words I looked down at my hands and gasped. He was right, my skin was becoming translucent. I knew than that it wouldn't be long before I would fade completely away like so many of the Gods already had.

"Let them die, I would gladly welcome their shades in the Underworld". I heard him say and these words brought me back to the moment. Hermes tried to pull me away, so I wouldn't hear any more,

"Come on Persephone, let's go to your father, it is time for our daily visit".

I wouldn't leave until I had a chance to speak with my husband. I had to know what was happening to me. I couldn't understand how I could be fading, I was no longer a Goddess, but was now a demon. For the last few centuries I had been growing stronger and stronger.

"You must do something to stop this". I heard mother saying through her sobs.

"Can you not see that Persephone is slowly fading? It won't be long before she too is taken from me. I refuse to lift a hand to help these mortals". He barked at her.

"If you decline to help then I am afraid that all of the Gods will soon be destroyed".

"Nothing you say can change my mind". He said, then all was quiet. I heard his footsteps and knew that he was about to leave. I rushed into the room hoping to get some answers from him, but he was already gone. He had disappeared back to the Underworld. With nowhere else to go, I went to Hermes crying.

"Hermes, what is happening to me"? I begged him for an explanation.

He didn't answer.

"I am a demon now, how could I be fading"?

He finally answered me, "Persephone, you are fading because you have given up on life".

"I don't understand what you mean". I asked, hoping that he would explain what was happening.

"You have no love left in your life, and I fear that you have simply given up on life."

I thought that this was another one of his little tricks to get me into his bed. Without saying a word I turned to leave, but he grabbed me by the arm and forced me to look at him.

"It is not my love you need, but your husbands".

As he said this he held out his arms and I fell into his embrace.

"How long has it been since you and Hades made love"? He asked me.

"It was so long ago that I don't even remember". I answered. I would have cried, but there were no tears left in me.

"Come, I'll prepare you and tonight I'll take you back to your home to be with your husband".

Hermes took me and led me to his private chamber and I must admit I was still a little skeptical when he loosened my robe and guided me to his bath, but he continued to assure me that he wouldn't try anything. Slowly, I allowed the warm water of the bath surround my body and I closed my eyes. I allowed myself to totally relax as Hermes patiently brushed all the tangles from my matted hair and plaited it. When he was finished he led me from the bath and slowly dried me before dressing me in the finest robes he could find and when I looked in the mirror I was surprised that I looked almost human agian. My skin was still a sickly blue-green color and there were still dark circles under my eyes, but with the new hope that Hermes gave me I was able to see my eyes sparkle as they once did. Hermes stood behind and me and when he saw my smile he placed one kiss on my forehead.

"Come, it is time for you to return home".

Hermes led me back to the Underworld and when we reached the front of the palace I kissed him and thanked him for everything. I didn't want him to leave, I was so nervous, but I was glad that he did. I knew that Hades still felt some jealousy toward him, especially now, and I didn't want anything to go wrong. I walked into the palace and called out to Hades, but he didn't answer. I went to the main hall where I found him sitting on his thrown while two of his servants knelt at his feet. I stood there silent, fearing that I had come in vain. Hades finally saw me and said,

"Persephone, why have you come home? It is not time for you to return yet".

The two servants looked up at their master wanting to know if they should stay or leave.

"Leave us alone! I will call when we are through". He said as he waived his hand.

Instantly the servants got up and scurried out of the room. I was alone with my husband.

"What do you want"? he asked as if I didn't really belong here. I waited a few moments before speaking,

"I've missed your touch for too long my Lord, and I fear that without it I too will fade away". I said as I walked up to him, my eyes lowered, and to my surprise Hades stood up and embraced me. His claw-like nails dug into my back and I pull back slightly and as I did this Hades pushed me away.

"I see how much you have missed my touch". He said. "I'm no longer your husband, but only this monster you see".

"You will always be my husband, and I will never stop loving you". I begged him.

He slowly opened his robes and the sight almost made me vomit. Huge sores, leaking a green puss covered his chest and arms, the fur on his legs was matted with this same puss, and I could see that there were patches of bare skin where the fur had fallen out completely. The smell made me gag.

"Don't you see what I have become; do you still want this horrible creature to make love to you"? He yelled at me.

I too dropped my robe and the sight of my naked body made him pounce on me as an animal would attack it's prey. His kisses were neither gentle nor filled with passion, but hard and his sharp teeth bit into my lips causing blood to drip down my chin. I tried to pull away and when I was finally able to get away from his grip I watched in disgust as he licked my blood as it ran down from his mouth. As he did this he smiled at me. I should have run then, but I didn't. Before I knew what was happening he grabbed me by the hair and threw me to the stone floor. Slowly he lowered on top me and I felt his mouth touch my breast. I was so stupid, I expected his kissed to fill my body with pleasure, but instead I felt the sharp pain of his teeth biting into my breast. Blood poured out and I screamed with pain. He didn't stop. I continued to scream out, but I think these only caused him to become more excited. He lifted his head and I could see that his face was covered with blood, my blood.

"No! Please don't". I begged him, but he was deaf to my pleas. He thrust himself into me. I again screamed out in pain,

"Stop! Stop!"

But he didn't, he continued to thrust into me. The two servants who were attending him when I entered came back into the room to see why I was screaming. Hades lifted his head and shouted at them,

"Get out!"

At first they didn't move, not knowing if they should obey him or try to assist me and Hades once more yelled at them,

"I said GET OUT!" As he shouted this at them they flew from where they were standing as if there was an invisible rope tied to their waist pulling from the chamber where they crashed hard into the wall. Hades waved his hand and the massive doors instantly shut with a loud bang. I heard the bolt slide into place and knew that none would come to my aid now. He lowered back on me and continued to thrust inside me until I thought I could take no more. Finally he held up his head and howled as he climaxed. After he finished he didn't hesitate, but pulled himself out picked up his robe and left me lying on the floor covered in blood, crying.

After a few minuets I stood up and wiped the blood that still ran down my chest. I put on my robe and went to Hades private chamber. I knocked at the door. There was no answer. I knocked again harder this time. Still no answer. I did not knock a third time, instead I focused all of the fear and all of the pain that I was feeling into a mass of glowing energy which I threw at the door and instantly it blew apart, shards of wood flying in every direction. Hades was sitting in the corner. He didn't look up as I entered his room.

"Leave me!" he shouted at me.

"I won't". Was all that I said in response.

"Don't you see that I am no longer a man, but have become this beast? I no longer can control my myself, leave now before I hurt you again". As he said this he lowered his head into his hands and allowed the tears to fall. This was the first time in all the centuries that we were together that I had seen him so freely cry. I sat down on the bed next to him and took his hands in mine.

"We can't live like this much longer. It is time that we fight back. We must claim what was once ours".

"What can we do"? He said as he lowered his head in defeat.

"They have turned us into monsters, so as monsters we must go to these mortals and destroy them, before they destroy us".

"I would gladly drag their souls to Tartarus if I thought it would help".

Even though the church preached to fear the Devil, there were always some foolish enough to risk eternal punishment for the riches that only the Devil could give them. These would-be magicians would draw a five-pointed star enclosed in a circle around their body and at each point would place a single black candle, thinking that this would prevent the Devil from being able to harm them. Using incantations, they believed they could force Satan to appear to them and do their bidding. At first Hades didn't appear, but once we decided that we would no longer sit by and watch as the mortals tried to destroy our lives, he came when he was called. Most of the magicians who called him didn't expect the horrid creature that towered in front of them, and they gasped as they held their chest and died from fright. Others who were bolder didn't flinch from the sight of Hades and with these he would play cat and mouse games with. He gave them a few trinkets, wetting their appetite for further riches. He would play with some of these magicians for a few weeks, sometimes longer, but when he would tire, he would return to the Underworld dragging their screaming shade behind him. We had gained much strength during the previous centuries and neither of us needed to follow the laws of destiny. We took thousands of these magicians' souls back to our world, where they still dwell. Our goal was to destroy those who had tried to destroy us.

I stopped fading now that I had my husband back and I assisted him willingly. Both of us, along with those in the Underworld grew in strength until we thought that we would succeed in destroying all mortal life, but then something I didn't expect happened. No longer were magicians were calling us to give them rewards, instead the new generations of mortals were calling the old Gods once again, not for fame or wealth, but for knowledge. It started with mother being called. The Christian faith never really include the Goddess and many felt her presence missing from their lives, and with the beginnings of the new century some started to call to her in a variety of her older names. She came when called and soon I too was being worshipped again in rituals similar to the old Eleusis Mysteries. I would appear to those few who called to us and once again explained the mysteries of both life and death to them as I had done so many centuries ago. As the years passed more and more were calling to us for knowledge and they began passing this on to others. Hades and I stopped destroying life, a new hope had entered and we decided to wait and see what would happen next.

Slowly, very slowly at first, the Gods on Mount Olympus began to regain their former strength. Zeus was the first, and soon he was back on his thrown. Once his strength came back to him, he started to repair the palace, and now it is almost back to its former glory and most of the Gods and Goddesses that survived have returned. Hera and my mother have forgotten their hatred for each other and have finally become friends. Hestia didn't survive, but her memory has, for she still is honored above all the Gods and even though she is no longer with us I am assured that her memory will live forever, within each flame. Zeus still has gray hair and beard, but al least he has regained his youthful appearance. I hear that he has started seducing both Goddesses and mortals once again. I don't think he will ever change, and it won't be long before his children began to fill the world again.

It has been over a hundred years since we decided to fight back and now when I look into the mirror I no longer see the ugly demon that I once was, I now see the Goddess of Death and Rebirth that I was destine to become. Hades too has started to return to the God that I had fallen in love with so many centuries ago. His skin is no longer blood red, it is back to its normal color, and his horns have started to atrophy. All that is left are two small horns about two inches long that protrude from his forehead. Actually I think they are kind of cute, but he hates them. He legs are still covered with dark fur, but it is much thinner then it was and his hoofs have been replaced with feet. I am happy that I have been able to reclaim my life back.

Once everything was back to normal, mother insisted that I returned to splitting my year between living in the Underworld with my husband during the dark half of the year when I am Queen of the Dead, and traveling with her during the light half as Goddess of Rebirth. I can't complain thought. When I look back at all that has happened to me I realize that this was not a painful as I though it would be. I remember when Rhea had told me that I would only be allowed to stay half the year with Hades, I though my heart would break. I remember her words to me,

"You must realize that your mother is not doing this to hurt you, but because she loves you".

I have realized that, but it took me centuries. I'm glad that mother was there for me when I needed her.

Epilogue
Zeus

LET ME INTRODUCE myself to you, I am the God Zeus; I have sat here and patiently listened to my daughter, Persephone, tell you the story of her life, while her mother and my sister, Demeter tried to explain the reasons for her behavior. Some who have read this story don't know which Goddess to believe and they have called to me to revel the truth.

Believe both Goddesses, for they both have spoken the truth.

My dear sister Demeter feels that I had deceived her, and she is correct in this belief, I did deceive her, but I had my reasons just as she had reasons for her behavior. To truly understand the story I will have to explain events that neither Persephone nor Demeter knew about, events that have affected both of their lives.

Demeter was not my first love, that honor belongs to the Titan Metis. It was Metis who first came to me with the magical potion that would force my father Cronus to regurgitate my brothers and sisters, and the sight of her beauty caused me to fall in love with her instantly. It was my intention to marry her, but when she told me that she was pregnant with my child, my first child, I decided to visit the Oracle. I knew what the Oracle would say, but I had to hear it for myself:

> *Metis has conceived a Goddess who will rival her father in strength and wisdom, but who will love him dearly. It will be the second child born to Metis, a son that you should fear. This child will grow into a powerful God who will one day rebel against his father and destroy him. If this child is allowed to be born, he will not only destroy his father's kingdom, but the entire Universe.*

I don't need to tell you that I couldn't let this happen, I was young at the time and didn't believe that I could be destroyed, but as ruler of the Universe, and the Giver of all Life, I couldn't let my unborn child destroy everything that I just created. I behaved just as my father had, but instead of trying to destroy the child, I tried to destroy my love Metis. When she asked what the Oracle said, I didn't tell her the entire truth, instead I told her that our child would be a beautiful Goddess and that night as she slept peacefully, I swallowed her whole.

Nine months later as I sat on my throne I felt a sharp pain in my temple. Soon I had a splitting headache, the pain so great that I called to Thanatos, the God of Death begging him to come and claim my soul, but he didn't answer, he couldn't, for you see I am immortal and he has no power over the immortals. I slumped to the floor, the pain so intense that I blacked out. Unconscious, I could still feel the pain, and in a stupor I called to any of the Gods to assist. None appeared. I called out for anyone to help me... but still no one came. I was falling in and out of consciousness, the pain overwhelming. Several hours passed before one of the Gods finally came to my aid. It was my son Hephaestus, the God of Fire, who came to me and lifted me back on my thrown, and once seated he held his golden axe up, and for a moment I was sure he meant to kill me. I tried to move, but the pain in my head paralyzed me. I watches as if the centuries were passing slowly by as I saw the glistening axe come toward my head. When the axe finally reached my skull I expected to feel pain, but instead I felt a slight relief. Once split open my daughter, the Goddess Athena, sprang forth fully armored from my still throbbing head. Of all the children I have, and I have many, Athena still remains my favorite. She looks so much like her mother, and when I see her I still think of my first love Metis.

I could tell you that Demeter was my second love, that after Athena was born I gave myself to her totally, but that would be a lie. I have had many lovers before her and many more since her. Demeter was proud, and couldn't stand the thought of sharing me with the other Goddesses, so she devised a plan, a plan that is still used by mortal women to this day. Her plan was simple, she was going to make me jealous by turning her affections to my dear brother Hades. She was destined to fail, as you probably know by now that both Hades and I have the ability to read other's thoughts and he knew what she was up to instantly. Hades tried to tell her that while he was attracted to her he couldn't give her his heart; it belonged to another.

She swore that she would get revenge. You have to understand that Demeter is an Olympian Goddess, just as I am an Olympian God; we don't like being told no. Her revenge on Hades was complete, she striped both him and his lover of the ability to procreate, but she failed in making me jealous. She didn't give up. I came to her one night, wanting to make love to her and her alone, but she wouldn't admit me into her chamber. This went on for many months, but finally she couldn't deny the feelings that we held for each other and finally gave in to passion. We continued to be lovers and even though I wasn't faithful to her, I was very discreet and I was sure she was ignorant of my infidelity.

It wasn't until I announced to all that I would marry Hera, did Demeter stopped allowing me into her bed. I loved my dear sister, Demeter, and would have continued to love her even after I married, but she wouldn't allow that. Now I could tell you that I married Hera because it was our destiny and that wouldn't be a lie, but I must stress the fact that I married Hera because I fell totally in love with her the first time our eyes met. It is for this reason alone that I sent her away during the long years of the war between the Titans and the Olympians, for I feared that if she stayed, I would loose her and I couldn't bear life without her love. Even though many centuries have passed since I married, I must admit that I still feel my heart skip a beat when our eyes meet. Don't think I was being selfish when I was with the other Goddesses or mortal women who have given birth to my many children. You see I am a God who loves life, and I can't deny my feelings for all life, whether mortal or immortal and when a beautiful woman gives her heart to me, I can't refuse her. But I'm going on about things that you mortals cannot possibly understand.

I lost Demeter's love and when it was announced that it would be our daughter that would be given to Hades to rule with him in the Underworld I became concerned. I knew that Demeter was with child, but I also knew that this child would be a God, and that she would never allow me to father another child with her. After all left I called to Hades, hoping to make a compromise with him. At the time he was in love with a Nymph named Leuce, and I assured him that I would arrange for her to spend the rest of her life within the Underworld to relieve his loneliness, if he would allow me some time to come up with a plan to trick Demeter. It would have been easy for me to enchant the Nymph, but I allowed the Goddess Aphrodite that privilege. I wouldn't allow Leuce to enter into that horrid place until Hades made it somewhat livable, and after many years Leuce was begging him to make her his companion. I knew that this would buy me some time, and so I relaxed. I didn't think of the matter until many centuries later when Hades came to me asking that I make Leuce immortal. She was dying and he knew that she had only a few days left, he pleaded with me, but I couldn't grant his request.

"I was assured that I would not spend eternity in the Underworld alone. I was promised a bride who would be immortal, but here I am forced to watch as my love dies". He shouted at me.

"I cannot make her immortal, it is beyond my powers". I told him. Yes, I have made many others immortal since then, but at the time I was still young and foolish enough to believe that destiny could not be changed.

Hades, in a fury, swore that he wouldn't continue his rule of the Underworld unless I give him my daughter. Since Demeter still wouldn't even speak to me I had no other choice but to devise a plan to deceive her. Being an Earth Goddess she was used to staying on earth and at that time she was having an affair with one of my sons, a mortal named Iasion. It was a beautiful night and Demeter was in Iasion's bed, they had just finished making love. I came into his house, invisible, and while Demeter slept in her lover's arms, I silently called to him forcing him to leave his warm bed and go out into the night. Once out of the house, I caused a deep sleep to overcome my son and as he lay in the soft grass unconscious, I used my powers to change my form into his likeness. Once convinced that Demeter wouldn't be able to tell that it was not her lover Iasion, I walked into the room.

"My dear, where did you go"? She asked tenderly

"I though I heard a noise, but it was nothing". Her lover's voice reassured her.

As I climbed into the bed and touched her soft skin the centuries that had passed since the last time I held her faded and I felt as if I was transferred back to the past. She no longer hated me, but became the beautiful Goddess that once loved me and who I loved back. It felt as if we were alone in the Universe, that there was nothing by our bodies, and our love. She gave herself to me in passion that night, and even though we made love for hours she didn't suspect that it wasn't her lover who was holding her. When she finally fell asleep I looked into her soul and was assured that she had conceived a daughter. I left my son's house and once back on Mount Olympus I called to my faithful servant, Hermes to deliver a message to my brother Hades, telling him that my plan was a success, Demeter would soon give birth to a Goddess, a Goddess that was destined to one day be his wife.

When Demeter finally figured out that it was I instead of her lover Iasion who fathered her unborn child she left Mount Olympus and traveled deep into the sea to the palace of our brother Poseidon. It was here that she gave birth to a beautiful daughter who she named Kore, and for many years Poseidon protected both of them. Hades was furious. Again he came to Mount Olympus threatening me, stating that he will leave the Underworld unless I give him my daughter. I went to Poseidon's palace when Demeter was on earth, fulfilling her duties as Goddess of Fertility and knowing that he loved Demeter I convinced him to make advances toward her.

"Poseidon, I can't believe that during these years that Demeter has stayed with you, you haven't figured out that she has fallen in love with you". I said to my brother, knowing all too well that he loved our sister dearly.

"I have told her many times how I feel, but she has only refused me". He replied coldly.

"Dear brother, I can see her thoughts, and I know that she cares deeply for you", I said, and instantly I knew that he believed me.

He pursued her until she turned herself into a mare hoping to deceive him. It didn't work, Poseidon only transformed himself into a magnificent stallion and the two of them finally made love. After Demeter gave birth to her son Arion, who was born in the form of a winged horse, and her beautiful daughter

Despoena, she returned to Mount Olympus with Kore. Both Arion and Despoena stayed on earth.

Now that both were back home I made arrangements for our daughter to meet and fall in love with Hades. I sent Hermes to the Underworld with the message that I wished for my dear brother to come to Mount Olympus to make the wedding arrangements. I found Kore in the garden that same morning and I was easily able to convince her to go down to earth and pick some flowers for her mother's bedside table. I told her about these beautiful flowers that only grew in this certain place, telling her that her mother would love those flowers. Next I sent Eros, instructing him to hid among the trees, and when my daughter saw Hades chariot breaking free of the Underworld, he was to shoot her with one of his arrows, causing her to fall madly in love with him.

That evening when she returned to Mount Olympus, I knew that my plan worked, Kore had indeed fallen madly in love with Hades. Everything was complete; all I had left to do was wait. For the next year I waited, a little impatiently though. After several months of her sitting in that field waiting for Hades to appear again, and him being stubborn and locked within the dungeon of the Underworld I had to take matters into my own hands, once again. I knew that Kore would spend her days in the meadow where she first laid eyes on Hades, so I again sent Hermes with another message to Hades.

Meet me on the island of Crete, I wish to finalize our plan.

My deception worked. Hades, excited that soon he would have his bride, left immediately and as soon as his chariot broke free from the Underworld he saw Kore there waiting for him. He was able to detect her thoughts and knew that it wouldn't be long before they married. She came with him to Crete and there she stayed with my son Minos for the next year while I did my best to conceal my actions from Demeter. I assured her that Kore was in safe hands; that I wanted her to learn the ways of mortals, hoping that the experience would assist her when she one day would become a Fertility Goddess like her mother, this pleased my sister. A couple of times during the year Demeter became suspicious, so I caused a few droughts to occur on earth. This kept her occupied and all thoughts of deception were gone. It wasn't until the night of Kore's wedding that her mother found out about our plan. I guess I was confident that night and when I ran into our sister Hestia I didn't conceal my thoughts as I had been for the previous year and instantly she saw through the deception and understood everything.

When Demeter finally found out about my trickery, she left Mount Olympus once again and searched for days for her daughter. When she couldn't find her she went back to the one God she knew would assist her, Poseidon. I would have destroyed him if I could have for assisting with her revenge on my son Minos and his wife Pasiphae. But again, Destiny would rule. I couldn't stop my beloved son Minos' death, I watched helpless as the events that were already told to you enfolded. Demeter though didn't feel satisfied with the death of Minos and the destruction of his kingdom so she left Mount Olympus and wandered the world alone. During this time she withheld her gifts and soon the land and all mortal life became barren.

After many months and the loss of almost one-third of all mortal life I decided that I must once again take action. I couldn't let Demeter's wrath destroy all that I had work so hard to create. I sent a message with the Goddess Iris for Demeter to return home. She refused and you can imagine my anger when Iris returned the next day alone. I told Hermes that he should use his gift of communication and return immediately with my dear sister. Hermes promised her that he would reunite her with her beloved daughter. The next morning I sensed trouble when I saw that Hades accompanied Persephone to Mount Olympus, for I knew that Demeter had not wished to speak with him. Hades only came because his wife begged him, hoping that once her mother had seen how happy she was she would forget her hatred for him. My brother knew better, but no matter how hard he tried he couldn't convince his young wife.

I knew that Demeter would never forgive Hades, so I told Persephone to meet her mother in the garden, hoping that when Demeter saw her daughter she would at once remove her curse from the land. She didn't though, and after several hours of arguing I called for our mother, Rhea. I knew that it was my daughter's destiny to spend one-half the year with Hades in the Underworld, and the other half with her mother, but no matter what I said, Demeter wouldn't listen. She couldn't disobey our mother. Finally, just before sunset it was agreed that Persephone would split the year between her husband in the Underworld and her mother. Demeter lifted her curse on the land, but only for that part of the year when her daughter would be united with her. Thus the seasons were created. There was nothing I could do to change it; you see the Gods cannot take back their pledges.

Many centuries have passed since my daughter's marriage and I thought that the universe would continue as is, but during these centuries many changes have occurred. Yes, as new religions evolved the old Gods, the Gods who had existed since the beginning of creation, were forgotten. As my daughter had told you in her story we, the Gods, began to become dependant on the prayers and rituals dedicated to us, and as these stopped, we slowly became weak. Most of the Gods on Mount Olympus were affected, and I won't go into detail here; Persephone and Demeter had explained this exactly as it happened. It would be impossible for you to imagine how I, once the most powerful God in the Universe felt. I, who had created the world as it is known, had become a frail old man.

As this was happening to me, I saw that my dear brother and all those who still dwelled within the Underworld were becoming stronger. I didn't know how this was possible; I was the stronger brother. For years I was in denial, not believing that I was fading, as so many of the other Gods had already. I knew that I would once again have to take action to save the universe. I spoke with Hermes, whispering to him that I wished to speak with Hades, that I wanted him to take my place as the ruler of the Heavens. I knew that he would refuse. After so many centuries he had become accustomed to a life alone in the Underworld. He cared nothing for mortal life, and since he knew that it wouldn't be long before his dear wife would fade, as so many before had, he felt no pity for these creatures. I knew that he would not assist them, but still I feared that if he didn't soon all would be destroyed.

I was not strong enough to change the world, and while Hades was, he would not, so I devised a plan where I could use his strength.

"My dear brother, it won't be long before my daughter fades and you will be alone once again". I said to him, grabbing his arm and bringing him closer to me so he could hear my feeble whispers.

"What do you want me to do"? he asked, and I saw the pain he felt.

"You must take over for me, I won't be able to rule much longer". I said as I feigned a cough.

"Zeus, you know I can't do that. Why not ask Dionysus or Hermes"?

"Dionysus is too busy with his duties on earth. As for Hermes well, you know as well as I do that that would be a mistake".

It's not that Hermes wasn't capable of ruling the Heavens, but being a Trickster God, I could only imagine what havoc he would create if he were left in charge.

All the while I was speaking with Hades, Hermes was using his way with words, convincing Persephone to return to the Underworld and unite with her husband to destroy the mortals. It was not my intention to destroy all mortal life, but only to scare them a little. Persephone returned and after a minor confrontation she was able to convince Hades that it was time for them to take their lives back. Hades appeared to those who were foolish enough to try and control him and took great pleasure in dragging their souls with him to the Underworld. Even my dear daughter, Persephone, the Goddess of Rebirth, took pleasure in seeing these mortals joining the phantoms that wander through the Underworld.

It was my intention to scare these poor mortals only, and then I would send Hermes or one of the other Gods who was still strong enough to appear to the world and tell them that the old Gods were no longer going to hide, that we have returned. But this never happened. What did happen next I never expected. The mortals began to tire of their beliefs and seeking something new and exciting, they turned to the old Gods. I remember when this happened. I was laying in bed with my dear wife at my side, too weak to get up when suddenly I felt a surging through my body, causing me to jump from the bed. I didn't think that only a few prayers dedicated to me would give me so much energy, but it has given me the strength to tell you these truths.